RYAN K. HOWARD

BLACK MACHETES

For Brian,

Thanks for entering the Goodreads giveaway and congratulations for winning. I hope you enjoy reading the book as much as I enjoyed writing it.

All my best,

Ryan K. Howard

6-22-2014

http://www.ryankhoward.com
https://www.facebook.com/ryankhoward
https://twitter.com/RyanKHoward

This book is dedicated to a very special Squirrel & to my boys: Zachary, Justus, Jacob, & Joshua.

Squirrel, without you there would be no Maddie—just one of the many reasons I love you.

Jacob, thank you for expecting a new chapter from me every week & for hanging on the edge of your seat during the readings.

BLACK MACHETES

PART I

- 1 -

SHINER

GILMER, TEXAS – JANUARY 1983

IT WAS A NUMBINGLY COLD MORNING and one that would turn out to be a record-setter for East Texas that year. But it wouldn't be the freezing temperatures that Benjamin Wilder would remember. Nor would it be the fact that weather records had been set. He wouldn't even remember it for being the day he first noticed real facial hair above his upper lip. But that day—the next two in fact—would be days he'd never be able to forget even though he'd spend the rest of his life trying to.

There were only two space heaters in Ben's house, both of which were the toasty open-gas variety, but neither of which were in his room. Sitting on a milk-crate nightstand next to his bed was a cheap, digital alarm clock that glowed '7:09 AM'. The clock was a salvaged throwaway, with the minute's '9' looking more like an 'S' because of a burned-out digit-segment. But the buzzer worked fine and was cycling again for the second time since daybreak.

Ben stirred just long enough to push the snooze-button and think to himself: *Just one more time.*

He re-covered his head and quickly fell back to sleep while cocooning himself under a blue-flannel blanket that had been his one-and-only Christmas present from the previous year. Spread on top of the new blanket was Ben's ancient patch-quilt that he'd had since the first grade. It was his only possession that pre-dated his mom's marriage to Jessup James Boone. And even though the old comforter had started hemorrhaging its wool innards a year prior, it was still his only reminder of a time in his life when he felt safe, which is why he refused to let the tattered quilt give up the ghost.

Eight minutes later, Ben stirred once again, but not to the alarm this time. The latest sound that woke him was much more effective than a million buzzers, but unfortunately it was one that didn't have a snooze feature.

If only.

The ruckus that bolted Ben from his slumber was Jessup, barking like the rabid dog that he was. The man's voluminous cursing pierced Ben's conscious and caused him to shoot straight out of bed after realizing that the Rabid Dog hadn't left for work yet. Ben's azure blue eyes watered at the thought of having to tip-toe around Jessup without committing a foul, which could entail the most inconsequential of things—say for instance, breathing the wrong

2

way. And fouls always preceded some form of harm in the Rabid Dog's presence.

No harm no foul—yeah, right.

Ben gently felt the swelling of his right eye and thought about the "foul" he'd committed the night before: eating the last leftover piece of take-out fried chicken from the fridge. Apparently, he'd known "damned well" that Jessup was going to bring the drumstick to work the next day. He knew this because he was a mind-reader.

Not.

Ben frantically reached down to grab his jeans lying on the floor, pumped both legs in and stood with a jump to his feet. He paused to listen and then shivered, but more because of the Rabid Dog's tone than because of the cold. He quickly rummaged through a pile of clean laundry not yet put away and found a pair of white tube socks, the kind with different colored stripes that hugged the calf. He found two that matched and sat back down on his bed to put them on while thinking: *A blue day it is.*

"Godammit, who didn't turn off the back porch light last night?"

The Rabid Dog's latest bark came through loud and clear and even though Ben wasn't the culprit, he knew he'd still be blamed. The springy slam of the old house's back-porch screen-door gave him hope for a possible reprieve. He held his breath until he heard the four hundred twenty-six cubic-inches of Hemi roar to life. The loud engine powered the Rabid Dog's pride and joy: a mint 1966 Dodge Charger.

First-year production owned by a first-rate bastard. Match made in hell.

Ben pulled back a small section of tinfoil that covered the panes of glass in his room. He watched as the Charger turned onto the street and he smiled in relief when the muscle-car disappeared from sight. He stood there in sweet silence until his alarm clock's buzzer began applauding his rare moment of luck. Ben turned and raised his arm, pointing at the clock with his index finger and concentrated hard, holding the pose for a few seconds until his determination finally gave way to a frown.

And then with a spot-on Yoda impression he croaked, "Ah, Father. Powerful Jedi was he. Powerful Jedi."

TOMMY BOONE WAS STRETCHED backwards in front of the living room's space heater with his close-cropped blond cranium resting on the cheap-paneled wall behind him. Ben looked at Tommy leaning back and thought about how much he hated him. It was the same scene every cold morning: Tommy, with nothing but his skivvies on, standing with his bare legs only a foot away from the furnace's glowing ceramic blocks, hogging all the heat.

"Faggot," Tommy said as Ben walked past.

Ben didn't respond—he knew better. Tommy was the Rabid Dog's sixteen-year-old son from a previous marriage-gone-wrong, and that meant Ben wasn't even a half-blood in Tommy's eyes, which was fine by him. The truth of the matter was that Ben was thankful to not share the same gene pool with the biggest asshole this side of the Milky Way.

"That's right, you little faggot, keep walking," Tommy said as he flexed his beefy pectoral muscles. He noticed Ben's eye and added with a laugh, "Want another shiner to match?"

Ben gave Tommy no satisfaction of seeing an emotional response. Instead, he made his way to the kitchen corridor and shuffled across the cold linoleum floor to the pantry. He opened the small door and stretched to reach up for a box of cereal on the top shelf. He momentarily frowned from having to still tiptoe to accomplish the small feat, which was just one of his daily check-ins on his growth progress, or the lack thereof.

Maybe tomorrow.

Ben removed some dirty plates from the sink to expose the blue, thin plastic bowl he'd used the morning before. He dumped out the milky pool of water from the cheap dish and washed it with an icy stream that sputtered to life from the faucet. He wiped the bowl clean with a quicker-picker-upper knock-off and poured some likewise knock-off snap-crackle-pops, but hesitated before pouring the milk.

Almost forgot.

He took a spoon and methodically sifted through the small puffs of grain, picking out the dead weevils he found until he was satisfied he'd gotten them all. He found three of the black specs and lined them up on the counter in a way which made them resemble a tight formation of miniature mouse turds.

Only three today, I think that's a record.

Ben finished his breakfast, checked the time and decided to look in on his mom. He walked down the hallway to a small master bedroom that reeked of spilled booze and stale cigarettes. Its wall color was supposed to be white but looked more like the color of smoke rising from an old burning tire. Ben was about to knock on the bedroom door when he heard a noise coming from the hall bathroom behind him. The repetitious noise sounded like a quarterback sounding off a snap count in eerie slow motion.

"Hut, hut, hut, huuuut."

Ben had heard the sound many times and knew damn well it had nothing to do with football. Kneeling on the floor, hugging the only toilet the 1940's-era house afforded, was Angie Boone, Ben's mom. Her bleach-blonde hair had declared civil war against its own dark roots, and the roots had started to gain the upper hand in the battle. She looked much older than her actual age, having a hardness to her complexion that came from years of self-neglect and substance abuse. Angie no longer used drugs though—Jessup just wouldn't have it. Yep, Jessup Boone turned out to be the most effective drug rehab counselor on earth with a real "do-or-die" interventional approach. Needless to say, Angie had long since been motivated to graduate and become a chain-smoking alcoholic. Smoking and drinking were both vices that Jessup not only tolerated, but ones he enjoyed to partake in himself. In fact, condoning those bad habits was the only thing in this world that Ben could think of that Jessup wasn't a hypocrite about.

Angie was vomiting her last bit of mucus-lined stomach acid and by the time Ben reached her, the regurgitations had transformed into gasping dry-heaves. The caustic smell of gin and tonic-gone-bad forced Ben to grimace and give pause.

Ugh, it's a bad one today.

He leaned his head back into the nasal safety of the doorway while still standing next to the lavatory. He reached in and turned on the cold water and breathed in slowly to adjust to the rancid smell. He grabbed a terrycloth washrag and as he wet it he caught a glance of himself in the mirror. He took a moment to slightly grin at the dark facial fuzz that had appeared above his lip that morning. But his attention was quickly distracted by his mom's movement in the mirror's reflection. He then turned and held the cold washcloth to her forehead as if it were a daily routine like brushing his teeth.

Angie took the rag from Ben's hand and looked up at him with a smile that faded as fast as it had appeared. The momentary exchange made Ben think about her smiles and how they were just apparitions—not of this world and gone in the blink of an eye.

"Thanks, Benjamin. I'm fine." She noticed his shiner and said, "Oh, baby. What happened to your eye?"

"Jessup from last night. You don't remember?"

The slow, shameful close of her eyes was his answer.

"You run on to school. You can't be late, baby."

Ben understood what she meant by not being late and it wasn't remotely close to what other moms intended when they said such things. Angie was really warning him to not give Jessup any excuse to fly off the handle at him. Ben heeded the warning with a nod and left her alone, as she leaned forward on her knees in front of the porcelain altar, making ready to recite another verse of the drunkard's daily prayer.

LATER AT SCHOOL, Ben waited in the cafeteria line behind a girl he didn't really know—only that she was one grade behind him and also a good foot taller.

How inspiring.

He looked up at her hair in pigtails and thought that they looked like two spouts spitting out frozen sprays of brown water on each side of her head. She reached to pay for her lunch, causing her pronounced shoulder blades to move and draw Ben's attention. Ben leveled his eyes and marveled at the bony bumps poking out from her lime green cotton shirt. They reminded him of alien eyeballs rolling around in desperation as if trying to see what's going on from behind but unable to because of the irritating earthling cover blocking the view. Ben woke from his moment of imagination and slid his tray along the satin nickel rails as the alien walked away. He stopped once he was in front of the cash register and noted how it was *also* annoyingly eye-level.

"Hi, sugar-baby," said the cafeteria lady whose turn it had been to be cashier that day. "Got your card for me?"

The cafeteria ladies cycled shifts at the register, but all of them always seemed to remember that Ben was on the reduced-cost food program. It embarrassed him to no end—being remembered for that was about as bad as being pointed out as the shortest kid in a room.

"Yes ma'am."

He handed her the faded blue index card, which was curling on the edges and creased from folds made by a seventh grade boy who had no proper wallet to keep it in.

"This one sure has seen better days," she said while using a chrome puncher to pierce that day's lunch slot.

The cafeteria lady smiled at Ben as he watched the blue chad fall into the cash register's open drawer. She handed the lunch-voucher back to him and he stared at the little blue circle that had found its new home on top of a five dollar bill in the till. Lost in thought, he recalled a memory of him asking his mom for a wallet to keep the card and other things in. Jessup had been in the room and quickly took it upon himself to nip the budding question before his mom ever had a chance to respond.

"You don't need no goddamn wallet, boy. What you gonna put in it, anyway? Dirt? It sure the fuck won't be money, you little shit," the Rabid Dog had snarled.

As usual there had been nobody there to counter or defend on Ben's behalf. Instead, his mom had given him her habitual response: "Sorry, baby."

Once finally climbing back up to earth from the bowels of the bad memory, Ben took the card from the cafeteria lady's hand and politely said, "Thank you, ma'am." He lifted his lunch-tray and turned to walk away. That's when she noticed his black eye.

"Ooooooh, baby child. Are you okay?"

He stopped in his tracks and closed his eyes at her question of concern, hoping that nobody else heard her making a big deal of his black eye.

"Yes ma'am, thank you for asking."

Ben resumed his walk with his head held a little lower, but he recovered little-by-little with each step that got him closer to the table where the other Machetes were already sitting and scarfing down their lunches.

- 2 -

HORA-LE

BEN SAT DOWN next to Demarcus Snow, his best friend out of the group. Also at the table were Octavio Muñoz and Scott "Scooter" Henderson. Collectively, they called themselves the Black Machetes, named after the black-handled blades that they used to cut trails and to build forts. Regarding the ethnicities of the boys, Demarcus was black, Octavio was Mexican, and both Ben and Scooter were white. They were a diverse group of outcasts, with their differences being the common thread that stitched them all together.

Demarcus was a minority but that wasn't sufficient to qualify him as being different enough, as there were a lot of black kids that went to their school. Demarcus had three older siblings, two of which were twin brothers off attending college. The giant twins were still football legends at Gilmer High School, remembered for putting the fear of God in all of the opposing teams that had been unlucky enough to face them. Demarcus's other sibling closest in age to him was his sister who had just made the high school varsity cheer leading team. She was, without a doubt, the prettiest girl on the squad and as such was also very popular. But Demarcus wasn't athletic, overly handsome, or even remotely popular. He had a toothpick frame, with height being the only thing he shared in common with his older brothers. And he had absolutely no interest in sports. Instead, he loved computers and technology, which was the catalyst that bonded him and Ben together as best friends.

Conversely, Octavio's Mexican nationality had been enough of an outlier to qualify him for the club. Gilmer had a very small Hispanic population overall and even less of a presence in school. Octavio had been held back in the second grade from missing too many school days due to chronic ear infections, so being a year older than everyone else also helped boost him as an official outcast. He was the part-time clown of the Machetes, although *he* thought of himself as more of the charmer. But he was serious about one thing and that was boxing. His hero was the great Mexican fighter, Julio César Chávez. Octavio's dad had first put Octavio in the ring when he was just eight years old. Octavio had won the match with a unanimous decision and had become hooked ever since. He no longer trained or competed since moving to Gilmer five years ago, because there were no gyms for Mexican kids. But he could still kick some ass, and that made him the full-time muscle of the group.

Regarding Scooter, he was the chubbiest kid in the seventh grade plus he wore glasses. Those two handicaps were more than enough to qualify him for membership as a fellow Machete. His dad owned

11

the local Western Auto store and that made Scooter the financier of sorts to any adventures that would require things of value. In fact, it was Scooter that talked his dad into donating the actual black-handled machetes for the club. Scooter also happened to be the source of quenching Ben's passion for technology. It wouldn't have ever been possible for Ben to see hide or hair of anything electronic if it weren't for Scooter, and that included Ben's favorite periodical: *Byte*. Jessup would never condone the purchase of a non-pornographic magazine—not ever. And as silly as it was, Ben had to hide all of his loaners else the Rabid Dog would trash them just for spite.

As for Ben, he had three strikes that qualified him for membership: he was dirt poor, he was fatherless, and last but not least, he was the shortest kid in all of junior high, including girls. In terms of contributions, Ben added value to the group with his leadership skills. He'd not only envisioned most of the Black Machete adventures, but he'd also driven them through to fruition. But if you asked him, he would say that his role in the group wasn't being a leader at all, rather it was being the club's black-market smuggler. On the occasions when the other Machetes wanted to try a vice, Ben would be the supplier: porno magazines, cigarettes, and of course booze. The Rabid Dog had plenty of all those things and for the most part wasn't the type to keep track of them. So, on the occasions when Demarcus, Octavio, or Scooter would bug him enough, Ben would carefully sneak items out to satisfy their curiosities. He did this even though he lived a painful life that was framed by those same taboo goods, which in turn caused him to personally despise the vices altogether.

"Ouch. Where did you get that shiner?" Demarcus asked Ben

after noticing the black eye.

"Somebody's ass I need to kick?" Octavio asked as he reached under his shirt, pulled out his sterling silver Saint Michael medallion and kissed it.

"It's nothing. No ass kicking required," Ben said. "What time are we meeting tomorrow?"

"First thing after we wake up," Demarcus said. "Your dad going to let you spend the night for once?"

"He's not my dad. And no, not a chance in hell."

"Sorry man, that sucks."

Twelve years old and Ben had never spent the night over at a friend's house—and not because he had overprotective parents that loved him either.

Yeah, right.

It was instead because of that hateful Rabid Dog. Ben recalled the one and only time he'd ever asked Jessup if he could spend the night over at Demarcus's house. In retrospect, it had been a stupid thing to do and of course Jessup's response had been *painfully* clear.

"You ain't sleeping over at no nigger's house. Not while you live under my roof, boy. Damn nigger lovin' bastard."

Jessup had followed the verbal bark with one of his infamous backhands that sent Ben flying into a wall.

Good times.

"Yoo-hoo. You in there?" Demarcus said while waiving his hand in front of Ben's eyes.

Ben snapped back to the present after a few moments of being lost in yet another bad memory.

"Yeah, I'm in here."

"So why don't you just meet us at the fort? We should get there

13

around eight."

"We got to eat first," Scooter said.

"Better make it tomorrow night then," Octavio grinned.

"Very funny."

"Gracias."

Demarcus settled the volley, "Let's say nine so you're not out there waiting on us."

Ben didn't hear their discussion because he was too busy mulling over the risk he was now contemplating.

Screw it. "No, I'm coming tonight. I'll sneak out."

"You sure?"

"Yeah, I'm sure."

"What time will you be over?"

"I'll try to get there around nine." *Hopefully the Rabid Dog will be lost in a bottle by then.*

"Cool."

"Hora-le!" Octavio said and then realizing he hadn't used English corrected, "I mean awesome!"

"Yeah, totally orda-lay!" Scooter said.

They all laughed, but Ben's chuckle was artificial. The others had no idea that painful gutterflies, as Ben called them, were fluttering inside his abdomen at that moment. He was deathly terrified at the thought of getting caught, to the point of becoming nauseous.

No matter, I'm doing it.

- 3 -

COON TAIL

JESSUP'S CHOSEN TRADE, when he decided to get off his lazy ass to do it, was cutting and hauling pulpwood. He owned an old eyesore of a logging truck: a dark green Ford plagued with numerous rusted holes that made it look as if sulfuric tree rosin had oozed and burned holes through its body. Jessup was infamous for hiring young day workers, whom he'd always short on pay by claiming that they hadn't worked hard enough to earn recognition, much less a full wage. As such, he cycled through a lot of helpers except for one: Wade Strickland. Wade was Jessup's only constant help and the only to ever get equal shares—partly because they were business partners, but mainly because they had been best friends since grade school.

Over the years Jessup and Wade had earned a reputation as the two biggest men in town, but only in the metaphorical sense. Jessup was only a tad taller than average and Wade went the other direction by being a good bit shorter than average. Regardless of their appearance, most folks knew of them as a bar-brawling duo not to be reckoned with. It was safe to say that Wade was just as salty as Jessup, if not more so, but in a different kind of way—in a more reserved and internal fashion, if you will.

The day's entire crew, six in all including Jessup and Wade, were taking a break and trying to keep warm by standing around a small pile of brush they were burning. Jessup nipped on some whiskey from an old WWII Army canteen and then glanced around at the fresh young faces of his temporary employees.

One of the young hands asked, "Can I have a sip of that there water, Jessup?"

Jessup returned the young man a look that didn't require words, but he decided to share anyway—words that is.

"It's not water, you dipshit. Flasks are for pussies, if you catch my drift. And no, you can't have none, dumbass."

Jessup abruptly decided that the damn trees could wait.

They ain't fucking goin' nowhere.

He then commenced to holding service, which he loved to do for a new crew.

"You boys know my last name, don't ya? 'Course you do. Everyone knows me and ole Wade here's last names. But what you may not know is that my Great Grand Pappy was none other than Daniel Boone."

The revelation caused a couple of the young men's eyes to widen in awe. One of them made the mistake of saying, "No fucking way!"

Jessup cut the lad a glance that let the overzealous kid know he wasn't to speak again for the remainder of the day.

"As I was sayin', old Daniel liked more than just coon tail, if you know what I mean. He stuck it good to my Great Grand Mammy and planted the seed of hope for generations of loggers to come. Yessireee, my grandpappy was a son-of-a-bitch from his diapered beginning let me tell ya, and Daniel used to give him lashings that would make a grown man cry. And now you'd better believe that that was a trait passed down to ever Boone since. Except for me of course. I'm an angel."

The group recognized Jessup's desire for them to laugh and did so, even though they knew damn well he was no angel and certainly was no comic either. Wade laughed the hardest though and his larks were the only ones genuine. He always enjoyed the Daniel Boone story, even though it was one he'd heard a legion of times and also one he knew was complete and utter bullshit. In truth, Jessup's dad was adopted by a German man who'd decided on a whim to change his name to Boone later in life. Not to mention it was extremely bad math. Daniel Boone would've had to been as old as the biblical Noah's age during the great flood for the years to come close to even adding up.

Jessup had just begun to resume his story when the owner of the land that they were clearing walked up from behind and interrupted the service by asking, "You boys just going to sit around all day?"

The landowner's idiotic question pissed Jessup off to no end and it embarrassed him too, which was a far worse infraction. The old man's blatant disregard for a good story also angered Wade, but as far as the others were concerned, they weren't really interested in

Jessup's tale anyway. Truth be told, the young workers were ready to get back to work; the sooner they got it over, the better. Unfortunately for the proprietor, that wasn't going to happen just yet.

Jessup slowly turned around to face the man with a demeanor that can best be described as demonic in nature. The landowner quickly realized his mistake but it was far too late to undo the damage. Jessup James Boone, the great-great-grand-logger of Daniel Boone, didn't accept take-backs of any nature, especially the disrespectful variety. Before the poor man's brain even had a chance to process what was happening, he had been driven backwards by the force of Jessup's powerful hand wrapped around his neck. Jessup, half pushing and half dragging the landowner, finally pinned him against an old oak tree that was a good twenty feet from where they were standing just moments before. The violent act forced the old man's gold wire-framed glasses to cock diagonally until they barely held onto his face by one stubborn ear.

Six or so inches above the landowner's head, a Day-Glo pink plastic-tape tree-marker flapped in the cold wind as if to desperately flag someone down for help, but sadly no one was coming to the man's rescue. Even the man's wife, who was watching from a kitchen window, was too afraid to confront Jessup. Instead, she did the smart thing and immediately called the sheriff's office.

Jessup stared into the man's eyes and decided that he hadn't seen enough fear or pain to satisfy him, so he proceeded to lift the proprietor up off of the ground while clenching the man's neck even tighter. The old man's eyes bulged and rolled back into his head until only white orbs could be seen, but Jessup didn't stop.

The Rabid Dog kept lifting the landowner up until the man's balding scalp was level to the tree marker, and only then did Wade finally pull Jessup's arm, along with the man, down.

"Jessup, let the fucker go. You gonna kill'em."

Jessup finally released the man once Wade's words penetrated the rage in his head. The landowner fell to the ground and started coughing and gasping for breath while curling up into a fetal position. Jessup looked down at the weakling with an evil grin, taking in with great satisfaction the damage that he'd inflicted. But the moment of gloating was short-lived as Jessup slowly closed his eyes in disgust once he heard the crunching gravel sound of a vehicle pulling up the driveway. He didn't have to look to know it was an Upshur County Sherriff's Department patrol car, because it was an approaching sound that he was no stranger to.

Motherfucker, he thought while gritting his teeth.

WADE WAS THERE WAITING at the end of the day when the heavy steel-door buzzed open. Jessup led the way as a young, imposing county jailor trailed close behind. The deputy was just a tad shy of six foot eight inches tall and weighed well over three hundred pounds. Jessup walked straight to the outside exit door, passing Wade without even a glance at his best friend as Wade gawked at the large peace officer.

Wade eye-balled the jailor in the brown deputy's uniform up-and-down and thought: *Damn, that boy's arms are the size of my thighs.*

The giant jailor waved at Jessup and said, "We'll keep the lights on there for ya, Jessup."

Jessup didn't look back and didn't even pause, instead he just lifted his right arm with hand closed in a fist and thumped up his middle finger to flip-off the young man. The jailor mocked a look of non-surprise and blew a kiss in return that Jessup would've only seen with eyes in the back of his head. Wade saw it though—there wasn't much in life that Wade didn't see. He locked eye contact with the guard and made sure his cobalt-blue-eyed expression of disdain was clearly received. And then in an equally disdain tone, Wade simply said, "Yup," and just stared coldly at the uniformed deputy.

The young man was the first to break eye contact when he noticed the huge sheathed Bowie knife attached to Wade's belt on his left side. The jailor made a downward nod with his likewise huge head, aiming for the knife.

"What's that for?" the young man asked.

Wade used his tongue to move a big wad of chewing tobacco from one cheek to the other before replying.

"Ahhh, nuttin' too intrastin'. Good for castratin' my hogs. Ya know, evry' once in a while I'll come across one that's got a purdy big set on 'em."

Wade's eyes never left the jailor's, whose complexion transitioned to a red hue that made his head look like a big tomato that would've taken blue ribbon at the county fair. The young man's voice turned to a not-so-cool tone and his ensuing stare matched the sentiment.

"Just get the fuck outta here before I scratch an itch I just got."

Wade held his glare for a few moments more and then finally, as slow as he could, formed a big grin that looked like a Venus flytrap opening after successfully digesting its prey.

"Yessir, will do there ociffer."

Wade slowly turned and opened the exit door that Jessup had clamored shut a good minute beforehand. He briskly, but coolly caught up to Jessup who was already half way to where the green pulpwood truck was double-parked on the uncrowded side of the county square. Wade took big strides to make sure he passed Jessup to reach the truck before him. He quickly opened the driver's side door and climbed in behind the wheel. Jessup stopped in his tracks and stared at his best friend with an absolutely expressionless face until Wade rolled down the window to offer up his explanatory advice.

"Pro'lly best I drive so you can cool off, don't ya think?"

Jessup didn't respond—he just walked around to the passenger's side and got in. Once seated, Wade handed him a small fold of money.

"From today's haul. I already took out the bail."

Jessup accepted the cash from Wade, again without a word, and slid it behind the Marlboros in the front pocket of his blue-flannel button-down. After sitting in silence for a couple minutes, Wade tried to break up the tension by laughing and shaking his head while talking.

"Shit, you sure did make that old man piss his pants good. Was so scared he paid a little extra at the end of the day. And I gotta feelin' he's smart enough to drop those boool-shit charges. If not, I'll go pay him a visit and have a little parlay with 'em."

Wade knew the volcano was going to erupt sooner rather than later, which is why he'd made the strategic decision to drive the old pulpwood truck to the courthouse instead of using his own car. It's also why he was now stalling to ensure that it happened while they were stationary. After a few more moments of sitting in silence, Jessup finally exploded with a left hook to the passenger side window, smashing it to tiny bits and pieces. Afterwards, he stared out of where the glass used to be and muttered the only words needed, "Just fucking drive."

Wade threw the old Army canteen on the seat next to Jessup and then spit some tobacco juice out of his own window, now the only one intact. Jessup picked up the canteen and violently slammed back a big chug of the whiskey.

"Yup," Wade said as he nodded. Then he started the engine, grinded the truck's old black-ball-shifter in gear and then did exactly what Jessup told him to do—he drove.

- 4 -

PRAY

SCATTERED PUFFS OF GRAY WINTER CLOUDS painted the baby blue-sky as the afternoon sun began its western trek. Ben walked with his head tilted upwards at the rays and thought how peaceful the warmth felt as it performed its duty to offset the bitter cold. He wondered if the contrasting sensation was perhaps what it felt like to take a nice winter dip in an outside hot tub. He didn't think he'd ever find out firsthand and then as if to agree, a grouping of clouds drifted in front of the sun, tinting its warmth and making cold reality pore back into Ben's mind.

I'll try one more time. Last ditch effort. But I'll have to lie and say the sleepover is at Scooter's. Jessup will probably say no, just like a hundred times before, but he'll say no for sure if I say it's at Demarcus's house.

The contemplation woke up the gutterflies in Ben's stomach and a sudden chill made Ben think that even the sun was turning its back on him.

Just like God always does.

It was true that Ben had asked God *why* too many times for someone of his young age. So many times that the thought of Him caring enough to actually help was beyond Ben's belief, yet Ben still talked to Him nevertheless—always holding out hope for the chance of sooner-or-later divine intervention.

"Dear God. I know it seems like a small thing to you, but could you please help me just this one time?"

Pfft. Lot of good that'll do. Still, best to cover all bases though Ben.

With each step he took, the gutterflies became more irritated at his hard-headed persistence to go through with the sleepover plan. Ben's house was finally in sight which was a good thing because those nervous little fluttering insects in his stomach were begging to be released into the wild.

Ben walked past an old rusted mailbox whose weathered timber post was leaning forward as if to cower in fear from all passersby. Ben had thought on more than one occasion that the Rabid Dog probably scared the post into its current posture. Parked next to the mailbox, just close enough to irk the mailman, was Angie's light brown Ford conversion van. It was decked out with the TexSun package and came with full options, but of course none of them worked anymore. The van still looked decent, that is only if you cocked your head just a little to the right. Jessup had procured the vehicle by bartering with the owner of a local body shop in exchange for clearing a quarter acre of oak. It had been a win-win deal because Jessup got good cash from the lumberyard for the

24

hardwood and also got the van's pink-slip to boot. He didn't much care that it had been totaled a couple years prior. Nor did he care that the man had picked it up for next to nothing at auction and had his body shop employees clumsily put it all back together again. He didn't even care that the frame was bent, which caused the steering to pull hard to the right and the body to likewise cock. But the crooked van passed inspection and ran okay and that's all Jessup gave a damn about.

Ben's steps became hurried as his stomach made a gaseous groan. He stepped onto their ash colored aggregate driveway and looked for the Charger—thankfully, there was no sign of the Rabid Dog's pride and joy. A momentary relief came over Ben until a seismic cramp reminded him that his bowels were in dire need of relief of a different nature. He clenched tight, ran into the house, and made another fast prayer to God that the one and only bathroom was vacant.

BEN WAS IN THE SPARSE Boone family living room sitting in front of an equally sparse black-and-white TV. An episode of *Gilligan's Island* was on—a show which Ben usually loved—but today Ben wasn't paying any attention to it. The Professor had just traded bodies with Mary Ann when Ben's thoughts focused harder on how to approach the Rabid Dog, specifically on a strategy for making his case to spend the night. None of the scenarios that he came up with worked and so he concluded that it was pretty much hopeless. The only shot he had was enlisting the help of his mom, and he hadn't yet seen her since getting home. If he was lottery-lucky, she would be taking a *sober* afternoon nap, but he knew the odds of that were slim to none—at least on the *sober* part of the equation.

The telephone in the kitchen rang and startled Ben enough to make him slightly jump. Being in a superstitious mood, he got up and rushed to the kitchen, trying to beat the next ring, believing that answering on the third ring would doom him for sure. The yellowed white rotary hung vertically on the wall next to the fridge and had one of those super-duper-long curly-cords that always seem to be tangled. Ben picked up the phone off of its hook barely a second after the third ring had started.

Dang it. Now I'm a goner for sure.

"Hello?" Ben answered as he struggled to untangle the long cord.

"Hey, it's Scooter."

"Hey Scooter, what's up?"

"I was wondering...can you bring one of your dad's mags with you tonight?"

"For chrissakes, he's not my dad!"

"You know what I mean. Can you?"

"I don't know, man. He's moved his stash. Too risky."

"You sure? This month's *Byte* just came in the mail. I haven't even taken it out of the plastic bag, yet. It's yours if—"

"Okay, already. I'll bring one."

"Cool! Thanks man, see you tonight." Click.

Jesus, Ben thought as he hung up the phone. *Great, more crap to worry about.*

Then he heard the bathroom door down the hall shut.

She's finally up.

Ben waited until he heard his mom come out of the bathroom

and then he began to head her way until he realized that she was already walking towards the kitchen.

"Benjamin," she called out.

"In the kitchen, mom."

She stepped into the U-shaped galley and caressed Ben's face as she walked past him and made her way over to the far counter. She picked up her keys from the almond Formica surface and walked back to where Ben was still standing. He recognized the way she was floating and knew that she was already well passed the sloshy phase of inebriation.

There goes Plan 'A'. Typical.

She handed him the keys to her van, and began to ask him something until she noticed his black eye again, only it was the drunken Angie concerned this time.

"What happened to your eye, baby?"

"You already asked me this morning, mom."

"Oh, well you should be more careful, okay?"

"Sure, mom. I'll try."

"All right baby. Be good." She began to walk off and then stopped, turned back, and drunkenly laughed. "I almost forgot. Be a good boy and take the van to the liquor store and pick up some gin and cigarettes for me. Should probably grab some whiskey for Jessup, too. You know what to get. And tell mister...what's his name, again?"

"Mr. Norton."

"Right. Norton. You tell him to put it on our tab."

"Mom, last time Mr. Norton said it was past due."

"Well you talk him into it. If he gives you any trouble, you just mention Jessup's name. That'll straighten him out. Okay, baby?"

Ben inhaled deep and slowly exhaled.

"Yes ma'am."

"Good boy."

She caressed his face one last time before floating away.

Ben started making booze runs almost a year ago. He'd been making cigarette runs since he was five, but of course he walked to the store back then. When he became barely tall enough to see over the wheel, he'd been promptly promoted to booze delivery boy, which was a nice pet for the *drunken* Angie to have. It was fine by Ben because he didn't mind driving and besides, he was actually good at it. And to that, what choice did he have? The thought of Jessup punishing him for getting into a wreck was all the motivation and driver's education Ben would ever need in the world.

AFTER RUNNING THE ERRAND for his mom, Ben parked the van back in the same spot as it was before. He made his way up the driveway and straight away noticed that the Rabid Dog was home.

Ugh. I hate this, he thought as he again contemplated his plan.

Then he imagined a little devil standing on his shoulder egging him on, "Ben, don't wuss out. It's very simple. Don't overcomplicate it. Just ask the man. The worse he can do is say no."

The last statement was so ridiculous that it made Ben laugh aloud. The frowning little devil flipped Ben off for being so cynical and then poof, it disappeared.

Suddenly, a crash came from inside the house followed by some Rabid Dog barking—major barking—and then more. Ben couldn't make out what Jessup was yelling about, but he knew for certain they were not happy words.

Tommy stormed out of the front door and mumbled, "I'm outta here." When he reached Ben, he bumped him so hard that the bag of bad-habits came loose from Ben's bear hug, causing him to almost drop them.

"Asshole", Ben muttered under his breath. He imagined dropping the bag and wasting the coveted liquids and tobacco and then shivered at the thought of how bad that would've been for him.

Ben didn't want to go inside, but he knew he had no choice. He thought—hoped—that maybe, just maybe showing up with booze and cigarettes would be his saving grace. One thing he knew for sure was that it now had to be Plan 'C'—he would have to sneak out tonight because for sure he wasn't going to go anywhere near the Rabid Dog with him being in such a pissy state. Ben took a deep breath and reached for the doorknob, pausing just long enough for one more quick prayer.

- 5 -

ELLA

THE BLACK MACHETES, sans Ben, were sitting Indian-style on the taupe carpeted floor in Demarcus's bedroom while the DAZZ BAND's breakout hit play_d on the radio in the background. They were all gathered around in a circle, focused on a cassette-tape recorder lying on the floor in front of them. Octavio pressed its play button and they listened as his thick-accented voice attempted to impersonate that of a news-reporter.

"And today, the Black Machetes were spotted downtown preparing for their upcoming concert. Their guapo leader, known only as Octavio, had to fight off the girls who were all crying because they loved him mucho."

The boys laughed, but of course Octavio's cackles were the

loudest of all.

"My turn," Scooter said as he picked up the recorder and pressed down simultaneously on the play and record buttons. He leaned forward on his knees and while holding the recorder to his rear, let out a loud, long fart.

"Ewwwwwww. Bueno!" Octavio said.

"Ahhh man, that's naaaaaasty!" Demarcus gasped as he pulled his white t-shirt up over his nose.

Scooter sat the recorder back down and held down rewind for a couple seconds before pressing the play button. The end of Octavio's skit finished and then a clicking noise was heard followed by the music of the DAZZ BAND being played back. The lyrics rang out, "So let it whip..." and then Scooter's fart blasted across the tape recorder's speaker, immediately followed by, "let's whip it baby."

All three of them flailed on the floor laughing uncontrollably. Demarcus's sister, Raina, opened the door to see what all the carrying-on was about. She saw the tape recorder sitting in front of them and reached down to pick it up. The lingering smell from Scooter's flatulence found its way to her nostrils and she pinched her nose in disgust.

"You guys are gross," she said before walking out with the recorder tucked under her right arm.

"Hey, bring that back," Demarcus said.

"I will in a few minutes. Don't get your Underoos all twisted," she said with fading words as she walked down the hallway.

Octavio laughed and said, "Hora-le."

"Whatever," Demarcus said.

"Your sister's hot. Prettiest black girl I've ever seen," Scooter said.

"Sí, estoy totalmente de acuerdo," Octavio mumbled and once he noticed Demarcus and Scooter frowning at him, he corrected, "Sorry. I mean, I agree." He then thought (in Spanish) how he and Raina would make beautiful babies together.

RAINA EJECTED THE MACHETES CASSETTE and put in her own. She sat the recorder on the end of her pink polka dot bed and knelt down as if she were about to say her nightly prayers. She pressed the buttons on the recorder, cleared her voice and said, "This is for T" and proceeded to sing her rendition of Diana Ross's MUSCLES. Raina had a voice that was a modern reincarnation of Ella Fitzgerald. It's safe to say that Diana Ross would've been flattered, if not dumbfoundedly jealous by Raina's version of her song. Raina had transformed it into a slow, sultry cup of jazz that had long since been absent from mainstream radio play. It was also safe to say that Raina had the talent to go places in life—a young, beautiful star that had the potential to illuminate the world.

BEN HAD ESCAPED INJURY earlier when he got home by quietly setting the bag of booze and cigarettes on the kitchen table without notice and then making a straight beeline to his room. It was 9:45 PM before Ben slowly opened his bedroom window. It had taken longer than he'd hoped for the Rabid Dog to settle down into a buzz and catch-up with his mom. Already late for the sleepover, Ben got one leg out of the window and then shook his head out of frustration.

"Dammit." *Scooter's friggin' magazine.*

He pulled his leg back in and hesitated, listening for the Rabid Dog. He heard his mom giggling and could tell that they were in their bedroom toasting it up. Ben tiptoed to the bathroom and found the Rabid Dog's porno stash under a plastic tub of cleaning supplies stored beneath the sink.

"Where you going? Get back here," Ben heard his mom say through the thin wall.

"What do you want, bitch?" Jessup replied. "I'm going to take a dump."

Shit fire and fall back in it, Ben thought.

He frantically grabbed the first magazine on top, closed the cabinet door and rushed back to his bedroom. Wasting no more time, he climbed out the window in such a hurry that he forgot to close it behind him. Once outside, he paused a moment to listen for the Rabid Dog.

Nothing. Good.

He looked up at the clear sky, surveyed the stars looking down on him and decided that just one more quick prayer couldn't hurt.

Okay God, please watch over me on this one.

Ben rolled up Scooter's magazine and stuffed it into the breast pocket of his winter jacket. He then began jogging until he reached the blacktop road, where he switched gears to a moderate run, keeping the pace for the full five miles to Demarcus's house.

JESSUP PLOPPED DOWN on the toilet, opened the sink cabinet, and reached under to pull out his brand new, untarnished New

Year's Special Edition of *Cherry* magazine. He sat the periodical down on his knees and just before opening the front page cover, he noticed it was last month's edition of *Playboy*. He pulled the blue tub of cleaners out with a flick of his strong wrist, causing it to slam against the wall so hard that spray bottles crashed along the baseboard. He impatiently fanned through the entire collection of pornography on the floor making the magazines look like oversized adult poker-cards.

"Motherfucker!" he said and then first thought, *Tommy. He goddamn knows better.*

The veins on the side of his forehead throbbed as his heartbeat pounded in his ears. It didn't take long for him to come to the conclusion that the culprit was undoubtedly Ben.

That little piece of shit.

Jessup shot up, causing the *Playboy* to dismount from his lap and nail a perfect landing that splayed out a tri-page spread of December's Playmate of the Month.

Jessup stormed to Ben's room with intent to cause severe harm but of course Ben wasn't there. Right way, Jessup noticed Ben's open window and hot-blood once again rushed to his head.

"Fuckin' motherfucker son-of-a-bitch!"

He processed the situation and began nodding his head like a madman.

Enjoy your one night of freedom, Benny-Boy. You will have earned it once I'm done with your ass. I shit you not.

- 6 -

BACON

THE BLACK MACHETES, with full posse in attendance, had stayed up most of the night. They made prank calls to random people until midnight and then played Atari until their eyes burned so bad that they could no longer focus on the choppy pixels flying around on the TV screen. Everyone except Ben fell fast asleep once their heads hit the floor. But without the laughter and antics of his best friends to help keep his mind distracted, Ben instead lay awake and worried. And as silly as he knew it was, he missed his patch-quilt even though Demarcus's house was so warm that covers weren't required. So many things were different and out-of-place for Ben. The house was too quiet. There was no yelling, no sex noises and no loud radio blasting. In fact, the only sound to focus on while he lay there awake was the low-volume static from the TV's off-air signal. He couldn't shake his bad feeling and his imagination began transforming the static-sound into the Rabid Dog's growl. Ben then watched the screen as the evil beast gradually appeared through the fuzzy snow until its mean face stared at Ben, viciously growling and foaming at the mouth, making ready for the kill.

EARLY THE FOLLOWING MORNING, the scrumptious smell of frying bacon woke the Black Machetes from their slumber. One-by-one they sat up from the living room floor like dominos falling in reverse. The sun was out and its light beamed through the living room windows, making the boys wince as they all yawned and stretched in varying sounds and forms.

Demarcus's mom had setup a folding-leg table in the den for them as a makeshift dining area. They each filed in, groggily swaying like zombies on the prowl.

"Any of you boys drop food on my carpet, and I'll ring your neck. Comprende?" warned Demarcus's mom.

"Si, no problemas, y gracias, Mrs. Nieve," Octavio said.

Octavio's silliness made her shake her head and chuckle before walking to leave them to consume her hard work.

Ben had never experienced such a feast, especially never at his own house. He could only remember his mom cooking a meal of any size a handful of times, but never of this quantity or quality. For the most part, he grew up on fried bologna sandwiches and mac-n-cheese. No doubt, the spread that was laid out before them was definitely a special treat for Ben, and he savored every moment of it.

Eggs—scrambled and fried, grits, bacon, sausage patties, pancakes, butter, maple syrup, fried potatoes, biscuits, apple jelly, sawmill gravy, ice cold milk, and pulp-free orange juice.

This is unbelievable! I must still be asleep. I'm dreaming. Gotta be a dream.

But it was no dream, and afterwards the Black Machetes were miserably stuffed—all falling to the floor while rubbing their stomachs. Demarcus slowly crawled towards the Atari console and stretched his arm to turn it on, but his mom spotted his attempt from the kitchen. She walked into the living room and stood looking at them with her hands on her waist.

"You boys aren't going to sit in my house all day. Mmm-mmm. No way. You all get up and go play outside. It's a nice day and you're not going to waste it."

With groans of protest, they all obeyed, grabbing their jackets before they followed the motherly orders and within moments the cold, fresh air perked them right up.

"We wanted to make good progress on the fort today anyway, so we might as well get started," Ben said.

"Yeah, let's do it," Demarcus agreed.

Scooter and Octavio likewise nodded in agreement and they all began walking towards the tree line of the woods. Raina opened the front door and called out to Ben. He turned to look at her standing in the doorway and she waved him over to her. He walked back and thought how beautiful she was with the sun hitting her face and highlighting her perfect smile.

"Will you please do me a huge favor, Ben?"

"Sure, I guesso."

Raina's smile widened and she handed him the cassette tape that she had made. Ben took the recording and thought that the impossible had just happened.

God, her smile just got even more perfect.

"Please give the tape to your brother."

"Sure, no problem," he replied after thinking: *he's not my brother, dang it...and what the heck is on this tape and why do you want that butthead to have it?*

"Thank you!" Raina grinned before leaning in to kiss Ben on the cheek. He felt his face blush hot red, so he quickly turned around and ran back to the others before anything else embarrassing happened to uncontrollably appear. In retrospect, it was a kiss—rather a moment—which Ben would remember and think often on for the rest of his life.

God she's so nice. Scratch that...she's amazing!

BEN LED THE OTHERS down a narrow trail with thick brush on both sides as a smile appeared on his face at the thought of where they were heading. He always loved making trails in the woods. With every path cut, it meant that in all probability, he was stepping where no man had before. He liked to imagine that it was maybe, at an atomic scale, just a hint of the feeling that the astronauts felt when they first stepped foot on the moon. Ben spent a lot of time outside in those woods thinking like that—it was his church of sorts. Out there, he was as close as he could be to God, if there was a god as he would sometimes question. But he didn't have to look far for proof, finding evidence by climbing the tall trees, wading in the winding creeks, hopping across large stones in the streams, and fishing the numerous naturally-stocked ponds. But not all of his time spent in the woods was filled with happiness. There were plenty of moments when he'd release his built-up anger by breaking big sticks over tree trunks that he pretended were the Rabid Dog's head. Then there were other occasions when he'd just sit on a log and cry like a little baby while thinking that if only those East Texas Piney Woods had been the moon, then maybe he could've been Neil Armstrong instead of Benjamin Wilder.

After a two mile trek, they finally reached it: Fort Black Machetes. Mother Nature had seen it fitting to open up a large red clay gully smack dab in the middle of the woods. The small canyon had no business there and was a freak of nature, which is precisely why Ben and the others thought it was so perfect. It was their below-ground clubhouse and even though it was wet and cold, it was unique and different, just like the Black Machetes.

Within the gully, they had created mini-cave storage areas by digging out large sections of clay. One of the dens contained an old burlap potato sack, which was right where Ben headed to. He dragged the bag out to the larger fort area, squatted down and dumped out the sack's contents. Ben looked down and took quick inventory of four black-handled machetes, one blue aluminum-frame bow-saw, and a single Army spade. The fat part of each of the machete blades was marked with names in white paint. He spotted the one tagged BEN and grabbed it by its black-plastic handle. He stood and held it out and smiled at how good it felt in his hand. The machete was one of his prized possessions, almost a companion you could say, and one he'd cleared a lot of brush and cut a lot of campfire kindling with. He'd also killed a few cotton-mouths and a couple copperheads with the long blade, so it was a symbol of protection for him as well. Ben believed that the machete was a part of him and rightly figured that it always would be.

The boys had also carved seats into the clay in various places and covered them with small pine boughs. Scooter sat on one of the makeshift chairs to rest his out-of-shape body from the stress of the long hike. He put his hands down and grabbed the ledge of the seat to rest his arms but quickly pulled one hand back and looked at the goop stuck to his palm. The still-attached pine-needles did a good job of keeping their jeans dry from the wet clay, but at the same time exposed them to its sticky pine-rosin. It wasn't the first pine rosin incident, but remedying the problem hadn't yet made it to the top of their to-do list, even though everyone but Ben had in the past gotten into trouble for ruining their pants. Ben always escaped repercussions because Angie felt no pain when she did laundry and thus would never notice, or she would never remember it later. If the others knew that Ben never got a scolding for destroying his jeans, they would've thought that he was so lucky. Ben believed just the opposite, because in truth he'd take a million punishments from his mom if she'd only be sober enough to administer them. Ben knew that they had no idea how lucky they were for getting into trouble for such things.

Ben immediately went into leader-mode and kicked the current project into gear, which entailed putting a roof over their earthy clubhouse. The blue bow-saw was a loaner that Ben had taken from the Rabid Dog's portable tool shed, but of course Ben never *actually* asked to borrow it. There had been three other saws in the shed that were in much better condition so Ben figured taking the rusty one from the back was safe enough. The saw's blade was dull but the Machetes didn't really know any better, and it didn't matter anyway because a determined boy will saw a tree all day long when he puts his mind to it, which was exactly what *one* of them was going to be doing while the remaining three searched the woods for fallen saplings.

Ben picked up four pine needles of varying lengths and waved for Demarcus and Octavio to join him where he was standing next to Scooter.

"Time to draw to see who's gotta saw today."

They each grabbed a needle from Ben's clenched hand and held it in front of their faces.

Scooter drew short straw and said, "Ahhh, man. I had to saw last time."

"No you didn't, I did." Octavio corrected.

"All right," Scooter surrendered while looking over at the dreaded bow-saw on the ground.

The others took their machetes and started their climb up a staircase carved out of the red clay. Ben was about to make his way upstairs when Scooter called him back over to where he was still sitting.

What now? Ben thought.

"Hey, you never did give me your pop's mag," Scooter said, whetting his lips.

"For the love of God, he's not my pop! And where's the *Byte*?"

"Errrr, I forgot it. Sorry. I laid it on my desk so I wouldn't, but I did. My bad. You didn't forget the porno, right?"

Typical!

Ben took the magazine from his chest pocket and held it out to Scooter without letting go.

"I still want this month's *Byte*, unopened—and, I want some time on your new Compaq."

"Man, my dad's not going to let you use the new computer. No way. You know how much that thing cost for chrissake?"

"Really, Scooter? Do you understand the bodily harm I've risked just so you can jack off?"

Ben started pulling the magazine back. Scooter noticed that the porno was a *Cherry*. His eyes widened with excitement.

"Okay, fine!"

"I mean it, Scooter."

Scooter's mouth was salivating at the hardcore porn that was just inches from his grasp.

"Deal already. I promise. Cross my heart. Swear on my mom and dad's souls. What other assurance do you want?"

"That'll do."

Ben handed the periodical to Scooter, whose eyes were bugging out in anticipation. Scooter took the magazine and walked over to another mini-cave, stooped down, and pulled out a plastic bag from inside.

"Now what are you doing?" Ben asked.

Scooter pulled out a roll of toilet paper. Ben shook his head in disbelief.

"Are you kidding me? Here? Now?"

"What? I need to take a dump."

"Yeah, right...dump, my ass," Ben concluded before making his way up the reddish gray staircase to catch up with Demarcus and Octavio.

- 7 -

DEFENDER

THE BLACK MACHETES WRAPPED UP at the fort and got back to Demarcus's house late afternoon, just in time to sneak in some Atari play before dinner. Out of the corner of his eyes, Ben caught glimpses of Gabe Snow, Demarcus's dad. The man was quite tall and had a very intimidating stature. Even so, Ben quickly decided that he was one of the nicest men he'd ever met. He'd been studying Gabe's interaction with his kids and wife ever since the Machetes had returned from the fort that day. Ben was intrigued, even in awe at how a grown man, so scary in size, could be so loving to his wife and so gentle-natured with his kids. He couldn't recall a single minute when Gabe wasn't laughing and smiling and flirting with his wife. He was a happy man and Ben could see that the happiness was infectious to his family. Ben fell into a daydream in which he had been adopted by the Snow family. It was a very nice reverie, but one that was quickly interrupted by a prodding, thick Spanish accent.

"Ben? Yoooo-Hoooo?," Octavio said while waiving his arm in front of Ben. "Holaaaaaa?"

Ben snapped out of the nice daydream and before answering Octavio, he first noticed the unbelievably good smell of food in the air. He wasn't sure what it was, only that it made his stomach growl and his palate whet.

"Sorry, what?" Ben said.

"Hora-le. We've been asking if you're leaving with us. Scooter and I have to go home."

Ben knew it was well past time for him to get home, too but he was genuinely afraid to face the Rabid Dog. So, he decided to try to put it out of his mind and stall for as long as he could and enjoy the hospitality at his friend's nice house. Maybe by the time he did go home, the Rabid Dog and his mom would be gone or locked in their bedroom.

Fat chance of that. "Ummm. Nah, think I'm going to hang out for a little while." Ben looked over at Demarcus who was busy on the Atari, and asked, "That okay, Demarcus?"

"Sure, no problem," Demarcus replied without taking his eyes off of the small Defender spaceship that he was focused on maneuvering.

"Bien," Octavio replied and then turned to Scooter and said, "Vámonos."

"Vomit what?" Scooter asked, looking confused.

"Just come on." *Pinche gringo.*

44

Octavio and Scooter left through the front door as the video game blurted out a synthesizer death-sound.

"Crud. Your turn," Demarcus said.

Ben picked up his joystick and imagined that he'd just climbed into the cockpit of his spaceship.

Time to defend the galaxy.

But before he could get started, Demarcus's mom approached the two of them. Demarcus, ever quick on the draw, thoughtfully pushed the console's pause button.

"Dinner will be done in five minutes, so you boys go and wash up."

"Thank you ma'am, but I've already eaten way too many of your groceries for one day. Even for a year," Ben politely said all the while hoping she would insist.

"Now you're not going to hurt my feelings by turning down my special pot roast are you?"

Ben smiled and said, "Well, I wouldn't want to hurt your feelings." *Score.*

"Wise decision, young man, especially considering I made extra. Now go and wash up. The both of you."

WADE PARKED ON THE ROAD'S SHOULDER directly behind Angie's van. He drove a 1976 Chevrolet Caprice that was camel beige and completely nondescript. The car had nothing of any merit to note except that it had started smoking profusely two weeks ago, and he hadn't yet put the car up on the racks to fix her. Other than the emission disease, the car was about as common and bland and unnoticeable as an automobile could get. Wade gave the accelerator a quick nudge before killing the engine to make the two-barrel 350 purr a little before going to sleep. A waft of the black smoke drifted into the interior, and as if annoyed by it, Wade spit a mouthful of tobacco out his window that cut through the oil-ridden smoke and chased it away.

Wade lowered his head to get a better view of the old house where his best friend of thirty-four years lived. The house's exterior was made of wood slats that were in a dilapidated state, having more exposed areas of weathered gray plank than those of faded white paint. What little coat had remained was cracked and looked like a bunch of busted eggshells that had been flattened out and glued to the boards. The yard hadn't been mowed since early summer, and from a distance the brooms-edge-bluestem and overgrown weeds had the appearance of a wild wheat field that one would expect to see in some health-food commercial. Only difference is that on TV there wouldn't be the gravesite of a rusted out 1936 Ford sedan sitting in the middle of the field. The ancient Ford had belonged to Jessup's dad. Its tires had been flat for decades, but the classic white walls were still intact. Wade thought of it as a cherished dinosaur fossil, and he always chose to walk through the overgrown field of gold just so he could touch her. He pressed his fingers against the rust and felt the cold steel underneath the red chalk. Each time he laid hands on the old car, he imagined being born a generation back—enjoying racing the old girl down a dirt road and stirring up dust for three counties while being chased by clumsy County Mounties.

Wade continued on and squashed a path through the overgrowth until he made his way to the front porch. The legs of his jeans had picked up scattered clusters of sticker burrs that reminded him of pictures of pollen spurs from the schoolbooks he'd studied when he was just a squirt. But he didn't have time to fool with picking sticker burrs off of his pants nor did he have time to dream of old rusted out cars for that matter. And he damn sure didn't have time to think about long-since-gone schoolbooks. No, Wade had more important matters to tend to.

Yup.

He gave two raps on the front door before opening it. Jessup and Angie were sitting at the kitchen table eating supper, which on that day consisted of Jessup's proud hodge-podge crockpot stew. The Rabid Dog bragged that it was a fine delicacy, especially since it had the variety of being different every time he cooked it—always depending on what cans of vegetables had been in the pantry beforehand.

Wade stood in the doorway and nodded in an upward motion at Jessup.

"Minute?"

Wade turned and went back outside to the front porch without closing the door and without waiting for a response. Jessup immediately joined him and shut the door so Angie couldn't hear what he knew she didn't need to.

"Water broke," Wade said.

"Hmmph. Guess we'd best go take care of it, then," Jessup replied. He motioned his head towards Wade's car. "She still burning oil?"

Wade nodded. Once Wade stopped nodding his head, Jessup started nodding his as if the nod had been handed off to him in a relay race.

"All right, guess we got to use the Charger this time 'round," Jessup said.

"Yup," Wade acknowledged.

DINNER HAD BEEN EVEN BETTER than breakfast, even though Ben didn't think that was even possible until he'd taken his first bite of the scrumptious meat dish. After everyone finished, Mrs. Snow began clearing the table and Ben stood up to help.

"Sit down, Ben. Gabe and I have this, but thank you for your good manners."

"Thank you ma'am for dinner. It was the best food I've ever had."

Ben's compliment put a huge smile on Mrs. Snow's face and he immediately saw where Raina got her beautiful looks from.

"Say, why do I have to help?" Gabe said, smiling just as wide, just not near as pretty as his wife.

"Because if you don't, I'll have to whip you in front of company. Now wouldn't that be embarrassing?"

"Whip me. Woman I will—"

With just the raise of one eyebrow and an index finger, she stopped his words cold in their tracks.

Gabe laughed again and said, "I'm coming, but only because I want to."

His wife gave him a look of you-are-not-so-tough and said, "Uhuh, that's what I thought."

Demarcus and Raina shook their heads, happily embarrassed at their parents' flirting. The three of them remained sitting at the table, and Ben couldn't stop thinking how great the Snow family was.

Maybe great isn't the right word. Perfect. They are the perfect family.

"Show Raina your double joints," Demarcus said to Ben.

"It will gross her out," Ben said.

"No it won't. I've heard Demarcus talk about it before. I want to see. Please," Raina pleaded.

"Okay, but I warned you."

Ben held up his right hand and then using his left hand, bent his right thumb back all the way flush against his forearm.

Raina made a face like she'd just swallowed a lemon and said, "Ewwww. That's gross!"

"See, I told you!"

Demarcus slapped his hand down on the table in laughter and said, "I think it is so cool!"

Gabe walked back into the dining room and said, "Ben, we're thinking about going to catch a movie tonight. You up for seeing *The Toy*?"

Ben wanted to say yes so bad, especially since he'd only been to the movies a couple of times in his entire life. He was allowed to tag along with Tommy a couple of times but always had to sit by himself as Tommy would never let Ben sit anywhere in his vicinity. Even still, one of Ben's most fond memories was watching *Star Wars* in a packed theater. The unfortunate reality was that Ben knew he'd already pushed his luck. If Jessup found out about him spending the night, much less staying for breakfast and then for dinner, it would surely be the end of Benjamin Wilder as the world knew him. There would be no take-backs accepted, no escape, and the Rabid Dog wouldn't pull any punches, either.

"No, sir. I should really be getting home."

"You sure, it's got Richard Pryor in it and he's funny as all get out."

"Thank you sir, but the Rab...my step-dad doesn't allow me to see movies."

Gabe's face held a genuine look of sympathy. Gabe knew full well Jessup's reputation and in truth had already known the answer to his question before even asking it, but he'd held out earnest hope, just in case. Gabe reached down and squeezed Ben's shoulder with his strong but kind hands.

"Well I'm sorry to hear that, Ben. We would've liked for you to join us, son," Gabe said.

Son.

Ben had never had a grown man call him son, and especially not while having a tender hand laid on him. He'd certainly been called a name that started the word *son* while having violent hands laid on him, but Gabe's kind affection's contrasted Ben's experience so much that it was astounding to him. A sentimental lump formed in his throat but it dissipated as quickly as it appeared when he heard Gabe's next words.

"We'll give you a ride home on our way to the theatre then."

"No sir, I can walk fine."

"I realize that you're able to walk Ben, but we'll drive you. It's cold outside and it'll be dark before long. So, that's the end of the discussion, you hear?"

"Yes sir," Ben said as his old friends, the gutterflies, returned.

THE RIDE HOME WAS CROWDED, with Ben sitting in the backseat behind Gabe, Raina in the middle, and then Demarcus on the other side. The body heat from Raina made Ben's mind wonder to places that shamed him. He didn't know what was recorded on the cassette tape that now rested safely in his jacket pocket, but he did know one thing for a fact: Tommy was one lucky asshole for having a girl like Raina make it for him. Ben had heard people use the word karma on TV and maybe even in passing, but he didn't know what it meant, really. If he had, at the time he would've thought, like prayer, karma was a bunch of hot air.

It was a quiet ride for the most part and that didn't help calm Ben's nerves from worrying about Jessup spotting him joy riding with a car full of black folk. He literally trembled at the thought and Raina, sitting next to him, felt the shudder.

"You okay?" she whispered.

All Ben could muster was a nod. She'd helped though, and her perfume smelled like a fresh bloom from the Tyler Rose Garden and Ben liked it—he liked it a lot. It got him to thinking that he wished he'd been wearing deodorant. He was sure he was nervously sweating and was also sure he didn't smell the least bit floral.

They were a quarter mile away from the turn off to Ben's house when he leaned forward and cleared his voice.

"You can just drop me off here, Mr. Snow. Thank you."

He didn't have to tell Gabe why he wanted to be dropped off a distance away, and even though it seemed as if they were in the middle of nowhere, Gabe understood completely and it really infuriated him—not just as a proud black man, but more as a father.

What kind of asshole dad, step or not, puts this kind of fear in a kid? Five minutes alone with that son-of-a-bitch. Five is all I would need.

Gabe pulled the car over to the shoulder of the farm-to-market road and put the car in park. Ben opened his door and just before getting out thanked them all one last time. He went to shut the door behind him but stopped when he heard a noise that echoed in the distance—it was a sound that made his heart drop in fear.

- 8 -

FAM'LY MATTERS

JESSUP WAS BEHIND THE WHEEL of the Charger with his left arm resting on the open window as a Marlboro pinched between his calloused fingers stoked hot-red from the rushing outside air flow. Between his legs rested a half-drank bottle of Jack Daniels and riding shotgun was Wade, who as usual had a big wad of Red Man chewing tobacco in his mouth. Jessup made a right hand turn off of his street onto FM-2685 and headed north. He pulled his arm inside to take a drag from the cigarette and then noticed a car pulled over just ahead on the opposite side of the road. He made out dark bodies sitting in the front seats and grinned in thought.

"What's funnier than seeing a bunch of niggers broken down on the side of the road?"

Wade knew the answer and replied, "See 'n a bunch of niggers dead on the side of the road."

Jessup's grin transformed into a smile at Wade's good guess, but the smile straightened into an all-out grit when he saw Ben get out of the car as they passed. Jessup popped the Charger into low gear and jerked the wheel hard to the left. The bootleg turn slammed Wade's head into his side window and caused him to almost lose his chewing tobacco in the process.

"The hell!" Wade growled.

Jessup didn't acknowledge Wade because the pounding rage burning inside his head was all he was able to focus on. He slammed on the brakes and steered the Charger to the right skidding to a stop directly in front of Gabe's car, causing gravel to kick-up and swirl around in the air like a dust devil. Before the disturbed soft shoulder had a chance to settle, Jessup was already to Ben. Ben backed up slowly out of self-preservation, but it was in vain. The first punch was swift and Ben never even saw it coming. Jessup's powerful right-hand fist landed deep in Ben's abdomen, causing him to double over and immediately puke up Mrs. Snow's special pot roast. There was no time for recovery before the second blow came. A left cross landed on Ben's right cheek, and even though it was a grazing blow, it still knocked his head into the rear fender of Gabe's car, causing him to fall to the ground. Ben was seventy-five percent dazed and twenty-five percent confused, but his body's reflexes took over and he curled up into a ball like a pill bug that was in the clutches of a wolf spider.

Jessup's heart raced with a fury as he reached down to pick Ben up. Just as his fingertips made contact with the light-blue material of Ben's jacket, Jessup's head was suddenly pulled back by Gabe's massive forearms. Gabe quickly maneuvered Jessup into a full-on sleeper hold, and he constricted tighter until he felt a small puff of air exit from Jessup's nostrils. Within seconds, Jessup's body started to become heavier and his desperate clutch on Gabe's forearms loosened until finally letting go.

But then Gabe held his breath and froze when he felt the cold metal press against his right-side temple. Pausing just half of a second for effect, Wade squeezed the trigger of the double-action .38 Special that he was now holding to Gabe's head.

Click.

Gabe shuttered and then closed his eyes as soon as he realized he was still alive.

"Next chamber ain't empty, guarooo'teeed. Turn 'em loose."

Gabe released the hold on Jessup and the Rabid Dog fell to the ground, still fast asleep. Wade used his steel-toed boot to kick the back of Gabe's knee and the big man went down to a half-up, half-down position that made him look like a lineman taking a knee on the sidelines of a football game. Wade backed up, holding the gun steady on Gabe, and looked inside the car. The brave-intentioned Demarcus had already opened his door to get out and help his dad.

"Boy, unless you like pain, you'd best get back in that car," Wade said.

The self-preserving Demarcus complied while both his mom and Raina held on to one another, doing their best to soothe their hysterical tears.

Wade walked around to the front of Gabe in a wide, safe radius and then crouched down so they were closer to eye-level with one other.

"What this here is, is a fam'ly matter. Ain't none of your bid'ness.

But if you wanna make it your bid'ness, well, I guess I could respect that. But then you'll have to respect me getting involved in your fam'ly matters."

Wade then looked at Gabe's beautiful family in the car. He smiled at them with half-rotten tobacco-stained teeth and then glanced back at Gabe.

"So, what's it gonna be, boy?"

Gabe realized that there was only one possible answer to Wade's question, even though he wanted to go for the gun and kill the son-of-a-bitch, but for the sake of his family he knew he couldn't risk it.

"Your business is your business, mister."

"Well now, you seem pretty smart for a nigger. You must be one of those eduuuu'cated porch monkeys. But an even smarter nigger would come down with a case of amnesia. Are you a smarter nigger, boy?"

"Yes."

"Say it then."

"I'm smarter."

"Say it right, boy."

"Yes, I'm a smarter nigger."

"That's better. Now get y'ur black ass up, limp to y'ur car, get in it and go home and forget 'bout Ben o'er there. He ain't none of yo' nigger concern." Wade motioned with his gun. "Go on. Get up. Get on with it."

Gabe slowly did what he was told, limp and all.

Once Gabe turned his car around and headed back towards town, Wade walked over to Ben who was still lying in a fetal position. Ben peeked up at Wade standing over him and Wade spat a wad of tobacco directly into Ben's eyes just before kicking him in the head with one of those god-forsaken steel-toed boots.

- 9 -

SQUIRREL CAGES

BEN AND DEMARCUS WERE BUCKLED TIGHT into the steel-grate enclosure and Demarcus had a look on his face like he was about to cry. It was close quarters and the ride would be very scary, but Ben also knew it would be so much fun. He pulled back hard on the metal loop welded to the white painted bar across their laps. The cage screeched like a metal chalkboard as it braked and held. Five seconds later after climbing counter-clockwise, they were at the apex of the six-story Ferris wheel structure, and as Ben held the brake they went from being right-side-up to being upside-down. Their cage started back to Earth and Ben took in the view as his eyes procured a snapshot of the black rubber cables that ran along the ground below.

Once a year, the red bricks that paved the Gilmer town square were covered with those thick black electric-cables. Ben had attended the fair a couple of years back and had finally satisfied his curiosity about those cables by figuring out that they snaked off to a diesel generator concealed close-by in a semi-truck trailer. Over half a dozen of the trailers were scattered at points along the square perimeter of the Upshur County Courthouse, and it was those noisy generators that would power the Yamboree Fair's rides. And Ben's favorite was a ride named 'Squirrel Cages'.

Ben let go of the brake and the cage spun around, slamming them back and forth as the ground below came at them fast. Even more fun than the ride, was watching the terrified look on Demarcus's face each time Ben pulled on the brake and held them upside down. On the next loop, Ben did the same hold, only this time when he let go, a rickety sound came from the large cotter pin that kept the cage on its axel. As the cage again reached the top of the tall wheel, the pin snapped and their cage slipped from its axel, throwing the round basket off-course and into a freefall. Ben again opened his eyes to look but the ground seemed different this time, and instead of being over the town square's pavers and the electrical cables, they were now above the corn dog stand. The concession building was getting bigger and bigger with each passing second as Demarcus screamed and Ben held tight onto the lap bar. They both clenched their eyes shut and just as they were about to plunge into the aluminum roof, Ben asthmatically gasped for breath as he surfaced from the dream that had been mostly good but had went horribly bad towards the end. He opened his eyes and was confused, but would soon realize that he'd just woken from one nightmare to yet another.

Ben's arms were tied behind his back, making him squirm and push hard with his legs to sit up. He was in the backseat of the Charger, but for a full minute was completely confused about where he was—even who he was. When his senses faded back in, his attention drew to the throbbing pain on the back of his head, and then he slowly remembered what had happened.

Why, God? Why?

No answer came to Ben's question, and that's when the decision welled up from his heart and then into his cerebral cortex. He'd had enough with his life, and who could argue? If he got out of this mess, he was going to run and never look back.

Ever.

It was pretty dark outside with only a little of dusk's light remaining, but Ben could tell where he was, because of the old pulpwood truck that was sitting in between the barn and the house. Ben had never been there before, but he'd heard it described enough to know that it was Wade's place. Back at Jessup's house, they didn't have a driveway big enough to park the big truck, so Wade had let Jessup park it on his family acreage. Only Wade no longer had any family left, which meant he had the remote spread of two hundred acres all to himself. It was the perfect place for the eyesore of the old green Ford to be stored.

Ben pulled hard with his arms but the hay rope securing them didn't budge. He leaned back, lifted his leg, and with the toe of his tennis shoe, he managed to pull the door's latch back, but the door didn't open. All of the door locks were down and there was no way Ben could pull any of them up with his foot or by using his mouth.

Think. Think. Think.

He sat back up and pulled harder at his wrists and then harder to the point of rope burn and ligament pain. That's when the memory flashed in his mind. It was the look on Raina's face when she'd become grossed out over his freakish double-joint. Ben worked his left thumb up under his right thumb and pushed as hard as he could. It wasn't the best angle and a searing pain shot through his right hand, but he kept pushing until he felt it pull free from the rope. Ben wasted no time freeing his other hand and then popping up the door lock. Before opening the door, he paused and with a sickening anticipation in his gut, reached back and felt the large lump on the back of his head. He swirled his fingers around the swollen knot until they reached his scalp. The lump was throbbing and it hurt, but he felt no blood. A temporary relief came over him before his sense of current urgency returned.

Ben quietly shut the Charger's car door and turned to run, and run hard. But then a sound stopped him cold in his tracks. It was the scream of a girl. His heart raced as he turned to where the sound came from and then another scream shot out from Wade's house.

Just go. Run and don't look back.

Another scream rang into the night and this one was laced with more pain. The little devil was back on Ben's shoulder again and this time it said, "Go ahead, Ben. Go in the house and see what that noise is all about. Go ahead. It will all be fine."

He heard the girl sobbing loudly and yelling, "No, no, no, no!"

Shit he thought, and then poof, the devil was gone again, but before it vanished, Ben swore he heard it emit an evil chuckle.

- 10 -

ADRENALINE

WADE STOOD WATCHING THE GIRL from one corner of the bed's footboard and Jessup likewise watched from the other corner. They both had their arms folded and looked like emotionless psychopaths who were curiously staring at one of their victims as she lay agonizing in pain before them. It was about as accurate a description as one could paint. Only this time they weren't observing the results of pain that they had inflicted as was usually the case. This time around they had the privilege of watching Mother Nature handle all of the torture without having to lift a single finger.

On the bed before them lay a young Asian girl in her late teens. Her arms were bound to the headboard above her, which made the pushing stage of labor that much worse. She had no name as far as anyone else in the room was concerned, because she was just another toy to be used and then to be thrown away once it wore out. Jessup and Wade had plucked this one from the east side of Dallas, not far from the Cotton Bowl. To them, she was just another runaway statistic, nothing more, nothing less. If anything, they would argue that they'd done her a huge favor. At least for the last eight months she'd had the comfort of a home, and she'd been waited on hand and foot by Wade. While it was true that she'd been fed, clothed, bathed, and triaged, it all came at the cost of suffering horrible things that would make any human with an atom of decency cringe. Jessup had come over for "visits" as often as he could. He hadn't helped with her care because he knew it was Wade's thing, and that was fine by him because his lazy ass only wanted to participate in the pleasure and pain side of the formula anyway.

"Suppose we should shut that racket up?" Jessup suggested.

"Yup, pro'lly," Wade agreed.

Wade walked over to the nightstand, opened the top drawer and pulled out a red-and-black ball-gag. He swiftly grabbed the wriggling girl by her neck and squeezed hard to steady her head. Her eyes bulged and her torso flailed while Wade pinned her skull still. Jessup laughed aloud thinking that she sort of looked like a channel-cat that keeps flapping its fins and tail when you hold it down to remove a hook. With Wade's free hand, he attached the ball-gag to her head and mouth with a precision that only came from practice—lots and lots of practice.

BEN STARED INTO THE BEDROOM WINDOW from outside of the house. The glass was dirty and the screen further distorted his view so that the only thing he could make out was Wade and the Rabid Dog standing over a bed. Ben quivered with goose-bumps in full bloom as he listened to the agonizing shrieks. He'd heard the conversation earlier between Gabe and Wade, and he'd also heard Gabe's family safely drive away, but the adrenaline pumping through Ben's system in conjunction with that throbbing lump on the back of his head had clouded his ability to assimilate sensible logic. Consequently, all he could think was that the girl being tortured must be none other than Raina Snow.

Ben went around to the front door, which by luck was the farthest entrance away from the bedroom. He slowly turned the knob and opened the door; it creaked like an alley-cat and made Ben freeze in a cringing pose. Fortunately for Ben, the girl's screams were a nightmarish white-noise that muffled out all other sounds in the house. He looked around the living room to get his bearings so he could figure out a path for a better view. The first thing he noticed was the hundreds of books resting on oak shelves that lined the walls.

Wade reads?

The second thing he noticed was how well furnished and spotless the house was. Everything was neat and tidy, especially the bookshelves. He could tell by looking that the books had been organized by volume because the different color bindings were all in line. The clustered bindings reminded Ben of the medals attached to the breast of an over-decorated army officer in formal uniform. And he also thought that the house made his mom's housekeeping skills look pig-pennish. Needless to say, his head was having real problems processing what he was taking in. He spotted a corridor and continued down the only hallway in the house, which was the direction from which the echoes of the girl's agony were coming from.

Ben hugged the bare walls and tried to blend into them like a chameleon does the jungle, as if the beige-painted drywall would somehow help conceal him. He saw a bedroom at the end of the hall on the left, which was the only room that was spilling light into the dark hallway. He walked to where the incandescent rays stretched to illuminate the hall's olive-green carpet. Ben looked down at the shag under his feet and thanked God for the soft padding in lieu of creaky wood planks, especially now that the girl had finally stopped screaming.

Ben came to an open door on his right that was catty-corner from the bedroom where he was sure the girl was. He jolted into the dark room and then after slowing his breathing, he poked his head out of the doorway to take a look. The angled perspective provided a clear view of a scene so horrific that it made Ben's head start spinning. Unable to fully comprehend what he was seeing, Ben held his gaze at the girl's legs as they kicked from under the rose patterned nightgown she wore. He noticed her pale complexion and a relief came over him that the girl wasn't Raina. He felt horribly guilty immediately afterwards and could feel himself about to get sick. He swallowed hard to keep the bile down just as the Rabid Dog began talking.

"Uhtt, there it comes. Would ya look at the head of hair on that thing!"

"You go o'er and grab 'er left leg and I'll get 'er right leg. We need to lift 'er and spread 'er legs," Wade instructed.

The baby had just started to crown when Wade and Jessup moved their positions so that Jessup was on the left side of the bed and Wade was on the right. They both reached down and hooked their arms up under the back of the girl's knees and then lifted her legs while spreading them apart to create quasi stirrups. Their new sickening places gave Ben a much better view and one that would be burned into his head forever. The girl gave one last hard push and the baby stubbornly slid out. Before the newborn's feet fully cleared the safe womb, its mother had already stopped struggling. Ben covered his mouth in horror at the site of the small, still baby on the blood-stained bed and the mom just lying there dead as the monsters held her limp legs.

Looking back, it was a miracle that Ben hadn't cried aloud and ran like the wind. Instead, he continued to watch as they let go of the girl's legs and as Wade bent over, picked up the quiet blue baby by its legs, and held it in the air like a rabbit by its ears. Ben grimaced and gritted his teeth hard when the Rabid Dog reached over and spanked the baby on its buttocks.

"Always wanted to do that," Jessup said as the little infant swung back and forth in Wade's hand.

Ben grimaced even harder when he saw Wade take his Bowie knife out of its sheath and cut the umbilical cord. The baby never did start crying, it just hung there in the air like that for what seemed like a lifetime to Ben.

"Still born. Good," Wade said.

He began to turn around and Ben took quick cover behind the interior wall. Ben heard Wade walk towards him and he closed his eyes and thought for sure that he would soon be the next human to stop breathing for good in that house of horrors. But Wade didn't step into the room where Ben was hiding, even though Ben could tell he was very close. Then he heard a click noise and could tell that a light had just been turned on. What soon followed was the sound of a strange water-plopping noise.

As soon as Ben heard Wade back in the bedroom with the Rabid Dog, he peeked through the door and saw an open bathroom directly across the hall with its light now on. What he witnessed next made his knees literally buckle. Head down in the toilet was the baby, with its bloody little legs hooked over the edge of the bowl. Ben was sure he let out a whimper before catching himself from falling. He grabbed the doorjamb to straighten back up but never took his eyes off of the baby. He couldn't. It was the most horrible thing he'd ever seen and something he'd never be able to forget, no matter how hard he tried.

Ben's vision faded to the focus of nothingness. The bathroom was still in his view, but its details were becoming blurry as his mind began to shut down on him. He was still sitting there frozen in a trance when his peripheral vision picked up on movement. His brain sent a current of electrical signals to unfreeze his senses enough to focus on the source. His heart panged when he saw the baby's legs moving. He didn't think about what to do. He didn't think about getting caught. He didn't make a list of any how's or why's. What he did next was driven by pure instinct—an adrenaline-fueled auto-pilot; although there may be some who would argue that it was actually the will of God that took over for that dirt-poor, fatherless, twelve year old boy from the Piney Woods of East Texas.

ONCE AGAIN USING THE BOWIE KNIFE, Wade cut through the rope that still bound the dead girl's arms to the bed and then motioned with his head towards her feet.

"Grab 'er feet and I'll get 'er arms."

Jessup grabbed her by the bottom of her feet while Wade sat her up so he could pull her over towards him. In the process, her night gown slipped off of her shoulder exposing one of her small breasts. Wade used his right hand to gently pull the gown back up over her shoulder. He'd driven all the way to the Dollar General in Winnsboro to buy that night gown, along with some other necessities for his new toy. A Walmart was in Gilmer and was a lot closer, but Wade Strickland, a textbook psychopath and serial rapist, was way too smart to use a local store to shop for his hobby supplies.

Wade hooked his elbows under her armpits and lifted. Jessup lifted his end and they carried her over and sat her down on a large moving-blanket that they had already spread out on the floor. They began rolling her small, lifeless body side-over-side. Once she was wrapped with the last yard of blanket, Wade reached under the bed and grabbed a roll of duct tape. He pulled off about six inches of the adhesive and pressed it firmly on the blanket at the point where the girl's ankles rested within. He lifted the blanket off of the floor and continued wrapping the silver-gray tape around and around.

"Where you thinkin' this time?" Jessup asked.

"Lake Bob Sandlin," Wade replied.

"Pro'lly be the first chink to ever get dumped in those waters."

"Yup, I reckon so."

BEN RAN INTO THE BATHROOM and grabbed a towel hanging on a bar, and as gently and quickly as he could, he picked up the baby by its legs and lifted it away from the mouth of the toilet. He wrapped the baby with the cotton cloth, and in the process he'd noticed two things. One was that it was a baby girl, and two that she had a unique birthmark on the left side of her head. The reddish brown discoloration started in the corner of the baby's forehead and traveled down just a little in the direction of her tiny nose and then hooked back towards her likewise tiny ear. A millisecond thought flashed through Ben's mind that the blemish looked like a small tattoo of a boomerang.

The baby was still moving but wasn't crying. Divine intervention, maybe, but whatever the reason, it kept Ben from detection as he retraced his path back to exit through the front of the house. On the way, his peripherals caught a glimpse of something familiar lying on an unfamiliar surface. He paused to look down and saw the Rabid Dog's keys lying on Wade's counter. Jessup had the habit of throwing his keys onto the kitchen table every time he walked through the door back at their house, and it turned out that the routine wasn't location-specific. Ben had a glancing thought of how it was the only habit of the Rabid Dog's that had actually helped, rather than hurt him. He swiftly picked up the keys, making them jangle in the process. He cringed in fear of thinking that they made too much noise, but he could hear Jessup and Wade's muffled voices in the far bedroom.

Ben wasted no more time as he gently hugged the baby close to his chest and ran as fast as he could to the Charger. He opened the passenger's side door and sat the baby in the seat. Before closing the door, he noticed an Igloo Ice chest lying on the floorboard. The

Rabid Dog used it almost daily to carry his lunch or a six pack of beer and oftentimes both. Ben opened the ice chest, checked to make sure it was dry, and then gently laid the baby in it. He quietly shut the door and ran to the other side of the Charger, opened the driver's side door, quickly climbed in, and sat behind the wheel. He took just a second to catch his breath before putting the keys in the ignition and turning the switch one notch forward to unlock the steering column. He pulled the console shifter down into neutral and disengaged the parking brake. He got back out and began pushing the Charger backwards down the long, flat graveled road that led to Wade's house.

Ben, unknowingly, in a span of just twelve minutes pushed that car for over a quarter mile until he finally reached the connecting black-top road. As if on cue, the baby started wailing as soon as the car's tires touched the asphalt. Ben hopped into the car, started it, and coasted at idle using the light of the full moon to see the road. The lunar glare barely made the asphalt's edge visible but Ben managed. When he was no longer afraid that the Charger's loud horses could be heard from the house, he switched on the lights and pushed down harder on the gas and then drove faster than he ever had before.

The baby was still crying, but the purr of the Charger seemed to calm her a bit. Ben prayed that he turned in the right direction and his prayer was answered in grace when he passed a 'Highway-155 Junction' sign. He sighed with a breath of relief and turned in the direction of Gilmer. Within fifteen minutes he reached the hospital, parked the Charger to the far right of the ER's doors, and left the engine running. He surveyed the drive-thru that ambulances use to unload their needy cargo. Ben studied the portico that had an overhang which was supported by three brick columns. He carried the Igloo chest with the baby still inside, and sat the newborn down against the outward facing side of the overhang's middle column. He quickly ran over to where some shrubs hugged the brick building and picked up the largest iron-ore rock he could find. He looked at the baby, who was still crying in the chest, and double-checked to make sure she was a safe distance away from the entrance. He then threw the rock as hard as he could at the glass doors of the ER. The impact didn't shatter the glass, but it did its intended job just the same.

Ben hid around the corner of the building until he saw people walk outside through the automatic sliding doors to investigate the loud thud that they just heard. Once he was sure that their attention had been drawn to the baby, he sprinted as fast as he could to the Charger and hopped back in. He caught his breath and sat there for a moment while trying to steady his spinning head. He rolled down the driver's side window and let the cold night air hit his face. He took in a deep breath of the fresh breeze, put the Charger in gear and drove north, never looking back.

Ever.

- 11 -

HOPE

BEN PUT THIRTY MILES between him and Gilmer before his adrenaline auto-pilot finally wore off. When he entered the Mt. Pleasant city limits, his gut told him that he needed to stop and figure out a plan—at the very least figure out where to go next. When he saw the sign that read 'I-30 AHEAD', he became nervously uncertain.

Should I go East or West?

He noticed a gas station coming up on the right and he suddenly realized that it had never occurred to him to check the Charger's gas level. The car could've been running on nothing but fumes for all he would've known. The sight of the station made his stomach pang at the thought of getting stranded so close to Wade's house. He said a quick prayer and then glanced down at the gauge and breathed a sigh of relief when he saw that it was all the way past the full marker. Apparently, the sick and twisted Jessup James Boone had filled up the Charger in anticipation of having to do a little driving that night.

What a surprise the Rabid Dog's in for when he notices his pride and joy is gone.

At that thought, Ben couldn't help but laugh aloud. He continued to laugh as he pulled the Charger into one of the gas station's empty spaces. Once he came to his senses, he looked around the lot and over at the pumps and momentarily felt safe because the gas station was busy.

Busy is good, he initially thought, and then rethought, *but the Charger sticks out like a sore thumb.*

He was sure that the Rabid Dog and Jessup were hot on his trail in the old pulpwood truck. He imagined them pulling up from behind and blocking his way at any second, so with survival foresight, he pulled the Charger around the gas station and parked in the back. He was out of sight from the highway but he was still cautious to the point of being paranoid.

Best keep the engine running just in case.

Ben's little laughing fit had been a good thing, just what he needed. Unfortunately, he wasn't strong enough to completely get his mind off of what had happened. He tried hard to think about what to do next and where to go, but his thoughts kept reeling back and forth replaying the traumatic events. His memory repeated the vivid details, jumping from the girl to the baby to the wickedness and back again. The recollection caused the emotions inside his heart to boil up and spill over until the sobs came. The first hard cry was for the girl and for her baby. The second was out of fear for his life. And then the third and final was out of rage for all the evil things that Wade and the Rabid Dog had done. When he finally stopped weeping, he began wondering about the newborn baby.

Did she survive?

He thought for sure that she hadn't.

How could she?

Then he wondered if there was something more he could've done. After wondering and wondering more, he finally regained his composure, which was more than most men twice his age would've been able to do in the same situation. He blotted his eyes with the palms of his hands and used the sleeve of his jacket to wipe the snot from his nose and gave a final big sniff.

One and done, no more of that crap.

Ben reached over to the glove box and opened it. His hand searched inside for the map that he knew Jessup kept inside. When his fingers felt the folds of paper, he clenched his hand around the map and picked it up. In doing so, he noticed that it was bulky and heavy, and when he pulled it out and opened one fold, he saw Wade's .38 Special. He picked up the pistol in his hand and thought about its weight and how it wasn't as heavy as he'd imagined a gun would be. He fiddled with the firearm, careful to keep his fingers away from its trigger, and eventually figured out how to work the latch. He pushed the cylinder out from the gun's body and immediately noticed that all chambers were loaded, save one.

It's friggin' loaded, he thought and then in a self-deprecating follow-up: *it's Wade's, of course it's loaded, you idiot!*

He flicked the pistol to the right and the cylinder swung into its locked position. He'd seen it done before on TV and he remembered how cool it had looked, and now that he'd had firsthand experience, he concluded that it was indeed pretty darn cool. He put the pistol back in the glove box, fully unfolded the map, found Texas and then found Gilmer. With his finger, he traced HWY-271 up to Mt. Pleasant and then to I-30. He then traced I-30 to the west and saw that the first major city it went to was Dallas. Next he traced the interstate to the east and saw that it went all the way to Little Rock, Arkansas. He'd remembered hearing the Rabid Dog badmouth people from Arkansas and talk down on them. He'd also remembered the evil man talking on several occasions about honky-tonkin in Dallas and having a good ole time. That made it a no-brainer decision.

Little Rock, or bust.

Ben got back on the road and took the onramp for I-30 East. As he drove, he thanked God for the inconspicuous nature of night. He was sure that the Texas Highway Patrol wouldn't look the other way if they spotted an almost-teen kid driving on the interstate. He knew that there was a chance that even at night he could still get pulled over—but no matter, if it happened it happened. Truth be told, a part of Ben even wanted to get stopped by the police. He was smart enough to understand the reality of being a runaway kid with no means. The word "runaway" sunk in and the situation suddenly felt very lonely to him. He'd surely miss the Machetes, both his friends and the bladed kind. He'd miss the fort and the piney woods of East Texas. He'd miss his old multi-colored patch-quilt, and he'd even miss his alcoholic sorry-excuse-of-a-mom, Angie.

BEN WASN'T SURE WHY, but the eighteen wheelers sharing the nighttime interstate made him feel safe. He supposed it was because the big rigs gave him cover, or maybe because they stayed the course with him, in a way keeping him company. In any case, he was thankful for them, and he did his best to keep their pace, even though the Charger's horses didn't like being held back. At one point he realized he was leaving a convoy behind and approaching another, looking down to see that the speedometer was just beyond the ninety miles-per-hour marker. Ben really enjoyed the feeling of going fast, but his survival instincts immediately overruled his boyish temptations and from then on he adamantly refrained from speeding again all the way to his destination.

After about an hour, Ben passed the Texas state line and entered the 'Natural State' of Arkansas. Something changed in him when he crossed the line, although he didn't know it at the time. All he knew was that being out of Texas meant that he was away from Jessup and away from Wade, which felt like a ton of bricks being removed from his shoulders. He concluded that even if he froze to death or died from starvation, at least it wouldn't be at their hands. And there would be no more beatings and no more mental abuse, either. Ben smiled at the thought of the Rabid Dog never again hurting him—it was a happy thought, indeed.

Ben looked down at the gas gauge and for the first time noticed that there was less than a quarter tank of gas left in the car. A lump formed in his throat when he realized that he wouldn't make it to Little Rock. And then a feeling of hopelessness welled up inside him, almost to the point of tears again. Before the sadness could take hold, he saw a road-sign that read 'HOPE 20 MILES AHEAD.'

"Hope?" he said aloud to himself, unable to recall seeing the city on the map.

It actually sounds better than Little Rock.

Ben didn't have a clue how big of a city it was, or if it was even a safe place. But he reasoned that if he couldn't find hope in a placed called Hope, then he'd probably never be able to find it anywhere.

Once Ben saw the sign that let him know his new home was just four miles away, he began looking for exits. At about three miles away, he finally came to one that didn't have a name, just a number. He took the exit and then turned right onto the road it accessed. It reminded him of the farm-to-markets in East Texas and that was a good thing because it meant countryside, and that meant country roads with plenty of places to pull over and hide for the night. Ben had done a lot of thinking while driving and had decided that it probably wasn't a good idea to go into a strange town at nighttime. He knew things at night took on a different look and feel and he really didn't want to get the wrong first impression. Instead, he decided to let the following morning's daylight help in giving Hope the benefit of the doubt—not to mention that he wanted the security of daylight. Likewise, he felt better having the familiarity of the countryside, which in truth he was more comfortable with as opposed to a busy metropolis. Miles of woods he could deal with, but miles of city blocks he wasn't so sure about. He'd been to Dallas once in his life and it had scared the piss out of him. Vagrants, beggars, dirty streets, and bar after bar. That was Ben's memory of Dallas and therefore any unknown town he would come upon would naturally assume the big city's seedy characteristics until proven otherwise.

Another decision Ben had made was to part ways with the Charger. Besides the fact that it was useless to him without gas, it would only be a matter of time before it was traced back to Jessup and that meant a breadcrumb trail straight to Ben. No way around it, he was on foot after that night—but until then, the plan was to find a remote place and camp until morning. Then he'd figure out what to do with the car before heading off to go see what Hope was all about.

EVEN THOUGH BEN WAS DRIVING SLOWLY, he still didn't notice the old dirt road until he caught a glimpse of its reddish brown dirt as he passed it. He backed the Charger up, turned in and then proceeded extra slow while looking for signs of life within the dense trees. He kept scanning left-to-right in the direction the dirt road was taking him, but he saw no houselights or signs of human habitation. The road was lined on both sides with large oaks that made it seem as if he were driving down a spooky, dark tunnel. He actually got a little frightened when he imagined the boogie-man pulling him from the car and using its hooked hand to disembowel him. His fear went from that to other scary threats, like devil worshippers who would sacrifice him over a bonfire, or maybe two country hillbillies like Jessup and Wade who would torture him for months and then finally kill him once he begged them enough for it. Deep down he knew the thoughts were silly, but he was still just a kid alone in a strange dark place. The probable truth is that most any man would have similar thoughts and fears if he found himself alone in those woods at night. Eventually, the thought of the gun in the glove box made Ben feel better, reassuring him of protection against any bumps that may try to get him in the middle of the night.

After about a mile, the road dead-ended into a large circular open-area that was completely surrounded by the thick woods. Ben drove around the perimeter to figure out if it was a good place to hole up for the night. As he drove around, he began noticing shadows of things with various shapes and sizes and colors. He became confused at what he was seeing, or rather at what he was trying to see. The confusion and uncertainty caused him to become scared, and then the fright skipped to pure terror once he saw a man standing in the middle area of the circular path.

Ben stopped the car and squinted hard, only able to make out the man's outline. All he knew for sure was that the man was extremely big around and very tall. Ben's adrenaline surged and he almost wet himself as he continued to stare at the gigantic man who was just standing there straight as a post and not moving a muscle. The goose-bumps up and down Ben's arms doubled in quantity and his body began shivering uncontrollably from the terror. Finally finding the courage to move, he reached into the glove box and pulled out the gun and held it tight in his right hand. He took his foot off of the brake and came back around the open area for a second pass, cutting the wheel more to the left so he could get a better view. He stopped the car and let the Charger's headlights settle on the eerie boogie-man. Ben tilted his head in confusion, trying to figure out what the man was doing.

What the hell?

After his brain figured out what his eyes were adjusting to, he began laughing aloud. What his imagination had thought was a big man was really just an old almond-colored refrigerator that somebody had abandoned. It, along with many other items, had been dumped in the perimeter's middle area—the same area that Ben was fearlessly patrolling just two minutes ago. After Ben stopped laughing at himself, he reached up with the gun still in his hand and wiped the sweat from his forehead. He felt the cold metal touch his temple and it immediately brought back the image of Wade pressing the gun against Gabe's head. Ben shivered and quickly put the gun away. He looked up and around at the old junk that the Charger's headlights now illuminated and nodded his head in approval, thinking he'd done a good job of finding the perfect spot to rest for the night.

- 12 -

EVERCLEAR

AS LUCK WOULD HAVE IT, that night would turn out to be the coldest of the year for that region of Arkansas, with temperatures dropping down to twenty-one degrees before dawn. Ben's jacket wasn't enough protection to keep him from freezing, so he went outside to rummage through the trunk to look for something— anything to warm him up. Thick cloud's had rolled in and snuffed out any illumination that the moon afforded and the trunk's old light was very dim, making it hard for Ben to see much of anything inside the trunk. He resorted to feeling around with his hands until he felt a cold cylindrical shape. He said a quick prayer that it was a flashlight before picking up the object and holding it in front of his face. When the long-handled lamp was visible enough for confirmation, he smiled and pushed its grooved switch forward. The light didn't come on and then he looked up at the sky and said, "Please God!"

Ben banged the flashlight against the spare tire in the trunk and breathed a sigh of relief when the bulb lazily came to life. He began searching the trunk and scratched his head at the items he took inventory of. He found a bundle of big yard-leaf black trash bags, two cinderblocks, a length of rope, a shovel, a 40-lb bag of lime, a package of bright red mechanic's rags, a jack stand, a bottle of Everclear-190, and two polyester-fiber furniture-blankets.

"Yes!" he said and grabbed the blankets, squeezing them against his chest. "Maybe there is a God after all!"

BEN RECLINED THE BUCKET SEAT BACK as far as it would go and stared up at the Charger's white perforated headliner. He closed his eyes while snuggling under the rough blanket and began itching—only a little here and there at first, but soon the irritations became profusely nerve-racking. Even though most of his skin was covered by his clothing, the cheap blankets still seemed to find ways to make contact with Ben's flesh. He pulled his hands up inside the arms of his jacket but as soon as he would almost doze off, either his hands would come out or the blanket would sneak up and nuzzle with his face. The itching became unbearable to the point of driving him crazy. He sat there scratching for several minutes in frustration, all the while thinking about his comfortable old patch-quilt blanket at home. He suddenly shot up out of the seat when it finally occurred to him that the old Charger had come equipped with an excellent heater that was just *itching* to be turned on.

"What a dumbass I am!"

He started the engine of the Charger, switched the fan to full speed and pushed the temperature control all the way over to the red mark. He shivered at the initial gust of cold air coming from the vents, but within a few minutes they warmed into toasty blasts of goodness. It wasn't long before Ben could shed the itchy blankets. In fact, the Charger's heater core did such an exemplary job of transferring its hooded horses into scorching heat that Ben had to turn the blower to its lowest setting to keep from sweating. He leaned over and cracked the passenger's side window to allow a little cool air in. He then cradled into a fetal position, facing the cracked window, and smiled at how refreshing the night air felt against the heater's contrasting output. Ben closed his eyes, and just before falling asleep, he thanked God for the heater and then closed the prayer with a prodding joke that He could've given Ben the idea a little sooner.

The remaining gas in the Charger's tank only kept the engine idling for two hours, but it had been long enough for Ben to fall into a deep sleep. Once the cold set back in, he reflexively reached for the itchy blankets again, but his body quickly acclimated to the uncomfortable material without interrupting his slumber any further.

BEN WAS FAST ASLEEP curled into a fetal position in the reclined seat when the sun's bright orb began to peek over the eastern tree line. A ray of the sun's warmth made its way through the front windshield and painted a false sense of security onto Ben. It wasn't the driver side door opening that woke Ben; rather it was the hand reaching in to grab his feet that did. Ben turned around with wide eyes to see Jessup smiling as the evil man pulled Ben from the car by his legs. Ben struggled against the Rabid Dog's grasp as best he could and then heard the gut-wrenching sound of Wade chuckling in the background. Ben kicked hard and he bear-hugged the driver's seatback, holding on for literal dear life. On Ben's last mule-kick, his foot got stuck in the steering wheel and pressed down on the car's horn. The blasting sound scared a nearby nestle of white-crowned sparrows that flew off to safety. The horn also graciously saved Ben from the clutches of the Rabid Dog by waking him from the horrible dream just in the nick of time.

Ben had actually kicked in his sleep and his leg did in fact get twisted and stuck against the steering column. But he happily welcomed his ankle's throbbing pain because it was a million times better than what the Rabid Dog would have inflicted on Ben had it not been just a bad dream.

After groggily realizing that he was still safe-and-sound, Ben smiled wide and proclaimed himself the merriest creature in those Arkansas woods that morning—even merrier than the group of sparrows that had decided it was safe to return and forage.

Ben got out of the car, stretched, and hopped around until his ankle started feeling better. He took a look at the dump site in the daylight and smiled at the memory of the junk monsters from the night before. He leaned up against the Charger and patted her on the hood.

"Well girl, it's time we say goodbye."

He went and gathered the things from the car that he thought he would need and then started walking towards the road. He stopped and turned back for one last look and thought about the Rabid Dog getting his pride-and-joy back safe and sound. The thought simmered in Ben's head to the point of mental disgust.

"No way in hell that's going to happen."

He walked back to the car and re-opened its trunk. He pulled out a mechanic's rag along with the Everclear bottle of 190-proof grain alcohol. He stuffed the cloth down into the neck of the bottle and sat it on the hood of the Charger. He reached inside the car and pushed in the cigarette lighter. He stood back up and waited for the lighter to heat up. He glanced at the bottle with the rag protruding from its top and thought it looked like a glass volcano spewing lava. When he heard the lighter finally click ready, he reached back in and reappeared with the lighter in his hand, its end glowing orange-red. He grabbed the bottle and held the lighter's hot coils against the outside corner of the rag. A bit of smoke formed as the material frayed but it didn't catch fire.

Dang it.

Ben put the lighter back into its receptacle and pushed it in again. Then he grabbed the bottle and tipped it until the clear alcohol made contact with the rag from the inside. He pulled the cloth out and reversed it so that the wet, darkened-red end was now hanging over the outside neck of the bottle. This time when he touched the lighter to the rag it made a low poof noise and caught fire just as he had imagined it would. He held the bottle away from his body and walked as far away from the car as he thought he could while still being able to make an accurate throw.

"Sorry old girl," Ben said before hurling the Molotov cocktail at the Charger, which had also been something he'd seen done on TV.

Upon impact, the bottle splashed its burning alcohol all over the rear panel of the car. The flames scurried to feed on the booze and began consuming everything else it could in the process.

Ben watched for a couple of minutes and then made a washing-hands-of-it gesture before walking away. He got about fifty yards down the road when the fiery flames finally made their way to the fumes of the car's empty gas tank. The resulting explosion wasn't as big as those in the Hollywood movies, but it was enough to make Ben shudder and look back. He smiled at the rising pillar of black smoke and nodded his head in satisfaction.

"Hope you enjoy what I did to your pride-and-joy you son-of-a-bitch."

Ben continued his trek until the main road was within sight, which is when he noticed a large power-line clearing to his right. He'd followed lines just like it many times during his exploration hikes in the East Texas Piney Woods, so he had a good idea that the trail would eventually come to a populated area. He figured it would be better taking the path less traveled rather than walking along a busy road. So, he turned towards the big buzzing electrical lines and began his hike towards what he *hoped* was a safe town where he could begin the rest of his life.

- 13 -

MORGAN RIVER

CLOUDS HAD MOVED IN and snuffed out the sunny morning that Ben had awoke to. He traveled a couple miles along the power-line trail and looked up at the changing clouds and held out hope that they wouldn't bring anything more than a light sprinkle. A small drop of rain soon landed on his cheek and after he wiped it away, a few more fell to take its place.

Typical, he thought.

Within a few more minutes, larger drops started pouring down on his unprotected head. He glanced up at the pummeling water-darts and one hit him square in the eye.

"Oh come on!"

Ben's jacket had a snap-on hood but of course it was buried in his old bedroom closet back in Gilmer. He stopped walking in the open clearing and instead tried to stay beneath the tall pines that bordered the trail. The trees provided some cover but navigating them slowed him down from finding real shelter. He contemplated just stopping under the largest pine he could find to ride it out, but he figured with his luck it would rain all day. He decided to press-on at the slower pace to keep as dry as he could. Regardless, after walking another mile in the rain, his body became so cold that it started trembling uncontrollably. He knew he needed to warm up somehow and the only way he could think of was to get his blood pumping faster. So, he moved back out into the open trail and picked up his pace to a light jog. Once his body adjusted to the trot, he resolved to just let the downpour do its worst and began running at a faster pace. He went as far as he could until his body became so hot that he felt like he would explode from the inside-out. He slowed back down to a jog and eventually to a slow crawl as his physical condition continued to worsen.

Ben finally spotted a clearing through the tree-line to his left. He was relieved at the thought of shelter and navigated through the greenbelt where he spotted a small cluster of buildings. By the time he finally reached them, the rain had mockingly stopped.

Unbelievable.

He'd been coughing intermittently over the last half-hour and after clearing the greenbelt, he'd started feeling even more feverish, but he'd marched on—dripping and sloshing all the way to the first storefront he came to. The place of business was a pawnshop that sat away from the other buildings, having its own front lot along with a razor fenced back lot. Ben looked up at the store's sign, which read 'RIVER PAWN', and his countenance momentarily perked-up at the thought of stumbling upon a pawn shop. His head got a little woozy as he approached the entrance but he managed to shake it off. He opened the barred-glass door, looked inside and didn't notice any other customers in sight.

Good.

He walked up to the counter but didn't see anyone. He noticed a little ding-bell on top of the main display case, but thought twice about ringing it as he assumed it was rude to do so without first calling out.

"Hello?" Ben called out.

He heard a clanking noise that came from a backroom, followed by an aged voice.

"Be right there."

A short, elderly man appeared from a door behind the counter and swiftly made his way to see who the young-sounding patron was. The old man smiled at Ben and immediately noticed that his jacket and hair were completely soaked.

"Well ain't you worse for wear. You resemble a deckhand who just pulled a storm-shift in the Bering Sea. And that's also a nasty shiner you have there, son. Got caught in that tempest of a rainstorm, did ya?"

"Yes sir," Ben replied.

"Happens to the best of us. What can I do you for there, young man?"

Ben was nervous about the cockamamie story the he'd just come up with in his head, so he began trying to stall so he could quickly reassess how he was going to approach the man.

"Hello, sir. How are you doing today?"

"Well, if I was any better, I'd have to get a haircut."

Ben was at first confused with the man's friendly reply, but then Ben looked up at his balding head and laughed when the joke finally became clear. The old man saw an opening and took it.

"Say, did you hear the one about the cat that ate half a ball of black yarn, half a ball of orange yarn, and a full ball of white yarn?"

"No sir, haven't heard that one."

"She had calico mittens!"

The man laughed at his own joke and Ben thought that his cheerfulness was just as entertaining as the joke, if not more so.

"Good one, sir," and after a moment's hesitation, "I'm curious sir, which river is close around here?"

"River?"

"Yes, sir. Since this is River Pawn, I figured a river must be close by. I don't remember seeing one on my map."

The old man chuckled and began nodding his head.

"Oh yes, Morgan River's pretty close by, indeed."

He waited for Ben to volley, but Ben just stood there. The man had been around long enough to know when someone was in some sort of predicament, so he set aside the jokes.

"Son, are you in some kind of a fix?"

Ben paused and then replied, "Yes sir, I suppose I am."

Ben took a moment to study the man and attempted to size him up. He detected a kindness in the man's dark eyes but also sensed something else, an underlying sadness of sorts. And it was that hint of placid pain that made Ben believe in his heart that the old man staring back at him was good and trustworthy. He decided to ditch his plan of telling a tall story and instead took a gamble and went with the truth.

"Sir, to be honest, I'm on my own and need money. So I was

90

hoping, even praying, I could sell you this."

Ben opened the Velcro pocket on the right side of his jacket, pulled out one of the grease rags that he'd taken from the Charger and sat it down on the counter.

It was the man's turn to look at Ben and perform his own evaluation. In doing so, he noticed the light brown bruise on Ben's cheek from where Jessup had grazed him the day before. He looked up at Ben's shiner and then glanced back down at the bulky rag on the counter. He unfolded the bright-red material to expose the .38 Special, and then after a moment folded the rag back just as Ben had laid it.

"Is that there pistol loaded, son?"

Ben pulled out another mechanic's rag, only this one from his jacket's matching left pocket. That time Ben did the honors and unfolded the rag to expose the bullets he'd already taken from the gun.

"No sir. I may not know much, but I do know better than to walk into a pawn shop with a loaded gun."

The man chuckled and said, "I have a sneaky suspicion that you always know more than you let on to, son. I might be interested in making you an offer, but before I do, I need to know—I ain't gonna find out later that someone's been killed with that there snub nose now am I?"

"I...I don't think...I'm not really sure, sir. I can't guarantee my step-dad or his best-friend haven't used it on somebody. They're both bad men, so it's possible."

"You didn't kill *them* now did ya, son?"

"Many times, sir—but only in my dreams."

Ben looked up at the overhead light as it seemed to sway and emit a strange glare. His knees suddenly became weak and he stumbled backwards a few steps before passing out on the pawn shop's slab floor.

THE DOORWAY BEHIND THE PAWNSHOP COUNTER led to a room full of various goods that were stored on steel bookshelves along one wall. Some items were pawns that the old man hadn't yet tagged and put out for display, while other items were projects he had intentions of tinkering with. In the middle of the room were two desks butted-up to one another with papers on them neatly organized in bins. In one corner of the room was a card table with a small black-and-white TV sitting on it. In another corner was a wood table that held a small fridge and a hot-plate along with a few grocery items. Next to the table was another doorway that led to a bathroom, which is where the old man was, wetting a washcloth for Ben. Right next to the back door was the final corner of the room that contained an old green army-cot on which Ben was sleeping in snore.

The sound of the running faucet woke Ben and he opened his eyes to see a water-stained ceiling staring back down at him. He was confused and had absolutely no idea where he was, only vaguely remembering the old man and the shop. While still lying down, he looked around the room and spotted his wet jacket hanging on a chair and his socks and shoes on the floor underneath. He sat up to see where the faucet sound was coming from but moved too quickly and caused blood to rush to his head. The resulting vertigo forced him to lie back down, and then after taking a few deep breaths he tried to slowly sit up again.

The old man walked into the room holding a wet rag in his hand. He gently smiled at Ben before handing the washcloth to him.

"You should put that on your head and just take it nice and easy, son. You blacked out on me once, don't want you doing it again."

Ben followed the wise instructions and welcomed the cold cloth against his feverish brow. The man picked up a plastic cup of water from a table and pulled up a chair close to Ben's side.

"Here, drink some water."

He placed the cup to Ben's lips and Ben sipped the water.

"When's the last time you ate, son?"

Ben took another healthy drink of the water and thought how good it felt and tasted. He had to think back on the question and then remembered it was Mrs. Snow's special pot roast.

"Yesterday evening, but it all came up when..." and then Ben just sat there in a daze without finishing his answer.

The old man didn't press Ben to complete the sentence. By the looks of the young lad, the pawn shop's proprietor had a pretty good idea of how to fill in the blanks.

"Well, I apologize for eating the last bit of soup just before you came in. Runnin' kinda low on supplies here at the shop. But you need to eat something. I do have a little cereal. How about some Rice Krispies?"

Ben nodded and slowly swiveled around to the edge of the cot so he could face the old man.

"Thank you, sir. You're very kind."

"You just wait there and I'll fix you a bowl."

The old man came back and handed Ben a full bowl of cereal that was popping happy to be covered in ice cold milk. Ben picked up the spoon and started sifting through the cereal looking for weevils. The man watched with curiosity and finally interrupted Ben's routine.

"What in the tarnation are you doing, son?"

"Looking for bugs. I usually find at least four or five."

"Well there's no bugs in that cereal. And for your information, there's not supposed to be. It's not a normal thing."

Ben gave the man a "Really?" look before scarfing down the cereal and washing it down with two more cups of water.

"Thank you, again," Ben finally said before covering his mouth and burping louder than he intended. "Oops. Excuse me."

"Good one," laughed the old man, "and you're welcome."

"My name is Ben, by the way."

The old man turned white as a ghost and just stared at nothing, frozen in time it seemed to Ben.

"You okay, sir?" Ben asked.

The old mans snapped out of his trance and said, "Yes, son. I'm fine. My name is Morgan River and I own this here shop."

"Pleasure to meet you, sir," and then Ben realized that the shop was named after the man and that there was probably no river at all. "And I'm glad I got to see that river I was asking about earlier."

Morgan chuckled and said, "Likewise, it's a pleasure to meet you, Ben."

They shook hands before Ben quickly withdrew from the grip to cover his mouth as he started coughing. The deep, hard hacks made him grab his left side and grimace in pain.

Morgan pointed to Ben's side and said, "Lift up your shirt."

Ben did as he was told and exposed two swollen red ribs. Morgan motioned for Ben to put his shirt back down and got up to wash out the dirty cereal bowl. Morgan then began taking to Ben from the bathroom.

"Let's see here, you've got two bruised—maybe broken ribs, a busted face, a black eye, you're running a fever and you've got a nasty cough to boot. Anything I miss?"

Ben thought, *Yes, the lump on the back of my head* but shook his head. When he realized Morgan wasn't looking at him, he replied aloud, "No sir."

"Well, that all spells hospital to me, Ben."

"No!" Ben's heart raced fast at the mention of it. "I mean no thank you, sir. I'm fine. I just need to get that money and be on my way." Ben's head started spinning fast and he laid back down involuntarily without realizing it.

"Yeah, I don't much like hospitals either. Suppose I could take you to the house and get you patched-up."

By the time Morgan walked back out from the bathroom, Ben had fallen back to sleep. Morgan stared at Ben and felt an overwhelming compassion for the boy. He wasn't sure where exactly Ben had come from or what he'd been through, but Morgan was certain that both must be pretty bad.

PART II

- 14 -

GHOST

HOPE, ARKANSAS – AUGUST 1984

MORGAN HAD ENROLLED BEN *River* into the eighth grade during the spring of 1983. That was a full year ahead of where Ben *Wilder* was supposed to be, not to mention that it was smack dab during mid-term to boot. Making a new identity for Ben was fraudulent and certainly illegal, no question, but Morgan viewed the act as more of a white-lie than a true crime. And considering Ben's abusive past, Morgan believed it was an imperative step to ensure that Ben had a safe, fair-shake in life.

Morgan River never did have a son, but he did have a daughter who had grown up to have a child of her own—a baby boy who she just happened to name Benjamin. Tragically, both Morgan's daughter and grandson were killed in a car accident a little over ten years before Ben had dripped and sloshed into the pawn shop.

It didn't take Morgan long to figure out that fate had come calling on that rainy day in January and had subsequently passed right out on his doorstep. And so he'd taken Ben in and helped him establish the ghost identity of his long lost grandson. Morgan's daughter had never married and her pregnancy had been the result of a one night stand, so the child's father was never really known. Morgan had never contacted the social security office or any other government agency to file the deaths of his grandson and at the time the county's recordkeeping had been behind the times, so as far as the world was concerned, Benjamin Wilder was now Benjamin River and always had been. And for all matters practical and of the heart, Ben had actually become his grandson and the feeling was mutual as Ben even affectionately referred to Morgan as his 'Gramps'.

Ben had struggled to keep his head above water in terms of the school studies when he first started in the eighth grade, but once he'd planted his feet and dug in (along with having some help from Morgan) he was able to catch up and even scholastically surpass his fellow elder students. As a result, Ben not only finished eighth grade with an 'A' average, he also amazingly finished his following freshman year as an honors student with a *perfect* grade-point-average. And now Ben was just beginning his sophomore year at Hope High School and it seemed to Morgan that not even the sky was the limit for his newfound grandson.

Ben's stature was still smallish, but he'd actually had a growth spurt, and believe it or not wasn't the shortest boy in his grade anymore, just a very close second. He never did make best friends like he had with the Black Machetes, but he did socialize and had school friends—and was even liked by his peers. But Ben chose to dedicate all of his time outside school to his studies and to spending as much time as he could with his Gramps. He did miss the Machetes but resolved to never see them again, and of course he often wondered how his mom was doing, even though sometimes he cursed her for not protecting him as a child. Then there were other times when he would wish he could go back and whisk her away so she could come live with him and Gramps. He was pretty sure that if anyone could help get her cleaned up to the point of being happy again, Gramps could. Deep down Ben knew it was nothing more than a pipe dream, but he still day-dreamed about it regularly just the same.

In terms of the Piney Woods of East Texas, Ben had come to find out that the forests around Hope were just as fulfilling, if not more so. More importantly, he'd found something in Morgan he'd never had before. For once in his life, Ben had a loving parent figure in his life someone who cared for him and who made sacrifices. Thinking about where he came from and where he was now, he had become thankful for that gas-guzzling Charger and scary dumpsite. And for the first time in his life, he was happy and was no longer afraid and even though he did miss a handful of the people from his past, he was grateful for his new life and resolved to never look back.

- 15 -

HERCULES

AFTER HAVING ENLISTED in the Army to fight the Germans at the sprite young age of nineteen, Private Morgan River had been recruited into the US Army's 23rd Headquarters Special Troops unit, otherwise known as the Ghost Army. It was a very unique unit with very unique requirements. The thing that made Morgan exceptional enough to qualify as a member of the special outfit was his God-given talent to sketch and paint. He was an artist and had been ever since he could remember, and it was that talent which landed him in the 603rd Camouflage Engineers sub-unit. The Ghost Army's primary job was to visually deceive the Nazis into believing that Allied Forces were amassing in areas where in fact they were not. Or, as Morgan put it, they were master conmen who utilized the stage of war as just that, a stage on which to mesmerize the enemy with grand illusions.

Grand indeed Ben would always think as he listened to Morgan's stories.

Ben had just finished breakfast and still had thirty minutes before he needed to leave for school. He looked across the kitchen table at Morgan who was lost in his morning cup.

"Gramps, tell me a story."

"Naah, you got to get to school."

"I have half an hour before I need to leave. That's plenty of time. Please, Gramps. If you tell me a good one, I promise to clean up the weeds behind the shop after school."

"Well, since you put it like that, how could I say no? Okay, let's see here. Something that is short enough to get you on your way but good enough so you won't renege on your offer. Hmmm."

Ben leaned forward, eager for what was about to be told. Morgan adjusted in his seat, took another sip of coffee, and then began his story.

"What I'm about to tell you is classified, Ben. I've never told this story to anyone and as far as I know, I'm not supposed to, even after all this time. So you can never repeat it, but I know you won't because I asked you not to. Well, I've told you a story or two before about Smitty, my pal from the 406th Combat Engineers group. You know part of his job was to patrol our work perimeters and keeps us safe, something he was very good at. You also know Smitty was a very big man, over six feet five inches tall, weighing in at around two-fifty. All muscle, too. No fat on that man. He was a corn fed Nebraska boy and strong as an ox. Smart, too but nobody ever would think that at first glance. And boy let me tell you, he always played that to his advantage.

"Smitty and I were hanging out one day during a break. I remember it well because I had just finished one of my most proud works of art. My unit had built an inflatable, full-size M4 Sherman tank, and I was in charge of making it look real. And not to brag, but I did a good job, if I do say so myself. The camo paint was perfect, but that was the easy part. What was hard was the realistic touches I put on her. Like the mud. I had built it up so thick that everyone swore it was real sludge from the countryside. The grooves I painted on the tracks had dimension and the powder burns on the cannon's muzzle brake made her look as if she'd fired her fair share of shells. Of course the only thing she could really fire was a bunch of air. Boy howdy, if you sat her next to a real M4, you wouldn't be able to tell the difference. Honest injun.

"Anyway, like I said, Smitty and I were on a break and we watched as a company from the British Second Army marched into our camp. I remember that the Brits looked all rested and jovial, joking and in good spirits considering the hell that they had been through up to that point. Well, a few of them had been drinking and decided to make fun of none other than yours truly. I didn't mind because I was used to it, always being the smallest soldier and all. So, I didn't pay much mind to the teasing. To tell you the truth, I looked at as doing my part in boosting their spirits. But Smitty didn't see it that way at all. Something about the Brits having fun at my expense really rubbed him the wrong way. Now he could've whipped them easy, but he was smarter than that. Instead, he called the jokesters over and said, 'You see my friend here? His name is Morgan River. You need to remember that.'

"One of the Brits replied, 'Why is that, because the chap is so short that we would miss him, otherwise?'

"'Nope, because he has the strength of Hercules.'

"Of course the Brits laughed and then the one said, 'Is that so?'

"'Yep,' Smitty replied and then, 'but I can see you don't believe it. So how about a little wager. I bet you a case of that cognac I smell on your breath that Morgan here can lift that M4 over there clear off the ground. Not much, maybe only six inches, but off the ground just the same.'

"This made the Brits roll on the ground in hysteria. The one Smitty was talking to said, 'All right Yank, you've got a bet.'

"Smitty looked over at me and winked and said, 'Okay, but Morgan gets three tries. Agreed?'

"'Sure. Three tries or a baker's dozen—no man can lift a tank, old chap.'

"Smitty nodded over at me and I was scared out of my wits. Not that I couldn't do it, of course I could, it was just a rubber inflatable. I was scared because I knew it was against regulations and could land me in the brig. Still, I couldn't let Smitty down and of course he already had his mind set on getting us that fine cognac. So, I went over to that beautiful piece of work I had created, and I squatted down and gave my first attempt. I strained so hard that my head looked like a ripe tomato but I didn't budge the rubber tank. Of course the Brits thought it was hilarious me even trying. I stood up to catch my breath and then squatted for try number two. Again, I strained to the point that beads of sweat formed on my forehead, but no go. I stood and turned to them so they could see how exhausted it had made me. That's when Smitty raised his hand and said, 'It looks like Morgan may be having an off day. I still believe in him though. How about we double that bet. If he can lift it, then we get two cases of that cognac. If he can't, we'll give you a case of our finest Tennessee whiskey?'

"The Brit agreed and so I went back over to the tank, crouched down and strained to lift it six inches off the ground. I held it there for a good ten seconds just so there was no arguing and then I laid her back down as gentle as a baby. I'll never forget the look on those Brits' faces when I turned around. All of them were just staring with their mouths gaping wide open. None of them were laughing, I can tell you that. Anyway, being gentlemen that they were, they gave us the two cases and each and every one of them lined up to shake the hand of yours truly. Never again did I get made fun of from that company. Word traveled fast and I became sort of an urban legend with those Brits. I wonder to this day if any of them still believed what they had seen or maybe even if any of them had passed the story down to their families."

Ben was smiling the entire time. He couldn't help it. His Gramps told the best war stories, and he could sit and listen to them for hours on end. He loved getting lost in Morgan's words and imagining being right there with him, doing his part to defeat the Third Reich. Conversely, Morgan finally found someone whom he wanted to share his experiences with. That made Ben special because it's something that Morgan had never done before in all his life after the war. Maybe it was because he'd come to love Ben like his own grandson, or maybe even more like the son he always wanted but never had, or maybe it was because he saw that, like him, Ben was different from most other people in the world. But Morgan was sure that it was more than that, because when he looked at Ben, he saw a special young man standing on the frays of humankind. And of course it didn't hurt that Ben loved to listen to his stories. Ben made Morgan feel alive again for the first time since losing his daughter and grandson—and for that, he was just as indebted to Ben as Ben was to him.

Ben looked at Morgan's grinning face and asked, "You and Smitty were pretty close weren't you, Gramps?"

Morgan's grin turned a little sad and he replied, "Yes, I guess we were."

"You never did tell me how you and Smitty met."

"Well, that is another story for another time. You had better get to school now before you're late."

"Yes sir, I know, but do you promise to tell me that story someday?"

"We'll see. Maybe we can work out another deal. Tit-for-tat."

Ben got up to leave, but before walking out of the kitchen door, he turned around and said, "Gramps, that was an awesome story." Morgan's eyes welled up a little and replied not with words, rather with one of his trademark-gentle smiles.

- 16 -

SMITTY

BEN WAS HARD AT WORK pulling up the weeds from the back lot, just as he'd promised to do. Morgan had been watching him through the shop's back screen-door while thinking how proud he was of Ben. He couldn't have asked for a better grandson or a better son for that matter. Morgan had saved Ben, but Morgan knew that the inverse was just as true because he truly had something to live for now. Just to see the man that this young, respectful, smart, eager boy would soon grow up to be—well, the thought excited Morgan because he knew Ben had the potential to do great things in life, and Morgan would do everything in his power to help Ben get there.

Morgan opened the screen door and called to Ben, "Come on in. You've fulfilled your end of the bargain."

"Yes sir."

Ben took a quick look at his handy work and smiled before heading into the shop.

"Follow me. I want to show you something," Morgan said.

Ben followed his Gramps into the back office where Morgan had already taped three paper bulls-eye targets on one of the far walls. Ben noticed them immediately and asked, "What are those for, Gramps?"

"Well, you wanted me to tell you the story about how I met Smitty, and this is a good way to help tell that story. Fetch me three steak knives from the tray over there and set them down on the table here in front of me."

Ben did as he was told and Morgan organized the knives in a neat row on the table, spaced about four inches apart from one another.

"One day a bunch of us in my unit were sitting around waiting for our orders like we often had to do, which always made us a little antsy. If I recall, it wasn't too long after we'd landed in Normandy but well after the D-Day invasion. Anyway, to settle our nerves with nothing but time on our hands, we would often venture out and start sketching different landscapes of the countryside, buildings, wild life—whatever we came across that piqued our interest. On this one particular day, I was perched on a large piece of rubble sketching up an old artillery bunker. I was a good way into the drawing when I heard this voice behind me say, 'Gosh, you sure are lucky.' I turned around and was surprised to see this huge man standing behind me.

"'How long you been standing there for?' I asked.

"'Oh, since before you started I guess,' Smitty replied.

"'You're pretty sneaky for a big man.'

"'Yeah, I guess I am at that.'

"'So, what did you mean when you said I'm lucky?'

"'Because you can draw those pretty pictures. I always wished that I could draw.'

"'Well, have you ever tried to?'

"'What? Draw? Heck no. Not really. My pa would never allow me to sit around and do anything like that. Too much work on the farm to tend to.'

"'Well, I wish I was as tall as you. You're lucky for that, and I'm sure you have a slew of other things I wish I had.'

"'I dunno. Maybe. Say, there's one thing I could show you.'

"'One what?'"

"'A talent, I guess.'

"'I'd like to see. Please show me.'

"'Okay. Do you mind drawing me a bulls-eye on one of those pieces of paper you have?'

"So I drew a big bulls-eye as he asked me to. Then he walked over to a bare tree that stood a good thirty feet away and pinned that bulls-eye to the tree using a couple of the pins from his uniform. He walked back to where I was still perched and pulled out his Army-issue knife. He told me to watch closely, which I did. With a lightning fast underhanded throw, he made that blade pierce the bulls-eye dead center and damn near split that little tree in two. I had never seen anything like that before in my life.

"And that's how Smitty and I met. After that display of skill, I felt obliged to offer to teach him to sketch. I had never seen a grown man's face light up like a Christmas tree, but his did. He couldn't wait to learn. He did learn, too and a pretty quick study at that. I'm not exaggerating when I say that he was actually good, too. I guess you could say he was a giant with a gentle stroke. He was definitely one of a kind for sure. And do you know what I got in return for teaching him how to sketch, aside from his friendship?"

"No sir."

Before Ben realized it Morgan had already reached down for the first steak knife and with an agile flick of his wrist he hurled it and it hit dead center on the first bulls-eye. He did the same with the remaining two knives in such a fast succession that the whole exposition was complete before Ben had time to blink. Ben stood in awe, just as he imagined those Brits had done when his Gramps lifted that inflatable Sherman tank up off of the ground. After staring at the knives stuck in the wall, he finally found his tongue.

"Gramps, that was amazing!"

"Thank you, my boy. Looks like I haven't forgotten what Smitty taught me."

"Will you teach me?"

"Teach you to sketch? Of course I will."

"No. I mean yes, I want to learn to sketch, but also to throw knives."

"Sketching for sure. Knives...well, if you're serious enough about art, then maybe I'll consider the knives out of respect for Smitty."

"So what ever happened to Smitty anyway? Did you two just lose track of each other after the war?"

Morgan found a chair and took a seat and Ben noticed the deflated look on his face.

"No, Ben. Smitty never made it back from the war. It's a memory I sometimes wish I could forget, but one I've never been able to."

Ben took a seat across from Morgan and had his own deflated

look.

"I know all about those kinds of memories, Gramps. I'm sorry."

"I'm sorry too, Ben. For Smitty, it was war and those things are to be expected. But for you, well there's no excuse for kids to have memories like that. No excuse."

Morgan stared off into the background for a few moments and Ben noticed that his eyes had watered.

"You okay, Gramps?"

"Yep, I'm fine. Just haven't thought about that memory in a while. It was a long time ago. Enough time for me to talk about it I guess. Maybe it's what I need after all these years. If you want to hear what happened, I'll tell it. But Ben, it's not a happy story."

"I'd still like to hear it if you want to tell it. But only if you want to, Gramps."

Morgan took a deep breath and began.

"It was late December in 1944 and a handful of us from the 23rd had been ordered to stay behind in Bastogne while the rest of our unit convoyed on to the east. Why we were ordered to stay behind is a mystery to me even to this day. As usual, we waited for orders, only they never came because a fierce battle broke out. You may know of it from your studies as the Battle of the Bulge. Bastogne was a small town caught up in a part of that offensive as were Smitty and I. Also in town was this high profile medical officer. From what I've learned since, he was a captain who'd been brought in to perform surgery on a wounded, immobile full-bird colonel.

"Well, as you probably have learned, things in Bastogne got pretty ugly and that medical officer, Smitty, and I somehow found ourselves in a foxhole together. Heck, I wouldn't even really call it a foxhole. Mud hole was more like it. We were taking heavy artillery from all around us. It was a maddening state of confusion. That's the best way I can describe it. All we could do was duck and pray. One of the mortar shells hit too close to our hole and Smitty took a piece of shrapnel in his leg. It wasn't life threatening but was bad enough that he couldn't walk. The medical officer tied off the wound as best he could. That's when we heard the Germans advancing on our position. They kept getting closer and closer and as they approached we could hear the other Americans hunkered down out ahead of us screaming. Later, I pieced together that it was the sound of them being stabbed by bayonets because the Krauts didn't want to waste their bullets.

"I suppose it was that horrible sound that caused the medical officer to snap and just run off without even a word. He just left me and Smitty there and Smitty was way too big for me to carry by myself. I cursed God for making me so small at that moment, let me tell you. And that bastard medical officer, he had just signed Smitty's death warrant. Smitty looked at me and told me to go. I didn't budge and that's when he punched me hard, square in the mouth. Busted my lip up good. He told me that if I didn't go then the next one was going to knock me out cold. I could tell he meant it, too. I took one last look at my friend lying there helpless and then I ran in the same direction that the medical officer had. I found him fifty yards away rolling on the ground with a Kraut he'd run smack dab into. The Kraut had got the best of him by the time I got there and had pinned him down, making ready for a bayonet to the medical officer's heart. I'm not sure how far away I was, but I guess my instincts kicked in and realized that I couldn't wait any longer. Without thinking, I drew my knife and hurled it as hard and as true as I could, just like Smitty had taught me. I struck that Kraut in the back of the neck right as he raised his bayonet. He froze in that position for what seemed like a lifetime to me, with his arms raised and my knife sticking out from the back of his head. I guess for me, he's been frozen like that for a lifetime and I suppose he always will be. It's a horrible thing to take another man's life, Ben. Horrible thing.

"Anyway, my knife had hit that German with such force that part of the handle actually penetrated his skin. Needless to say, he fell over dead on top of the medical officer. The blade protruding from the enemy's Adam's apple barely missed stabbing the officer's own neck. I'd be lying if I didn't admit that for a while I wished that it had.

Later that day when our boys finally took back control of the area, they found Smitty in that same foxhole. The way it was told to me, good ole Smitty had taken out at least three of the Krauts before he was finally killed."

A couple lines of tears ran down Morgan's cheeks. He wiped them away and somehow found a smile for Ben when he saw that Ben also had tears in his eyes.

"Gramps, I'm very sorry about Smitty and I'm sorry you had to leave him. I'm sorry about it all."

"Thank you, Ben. And thanks for listening to an old man tell his war stories. I guess you're my shrink in a way. Maybe I should be paying you."

"You've been paying me ever since the first day I met you, Gramps."

Ben stood up to let Morgan mourn the memory in peace, but hesitated first to ask a question.

"Gramps, what happened to that medical officer?"

"Dr. James Reeves. That's his name. He went on to become an important surgeon who helped pioneer heart transplants. He lives up in New England somewhere and still has connections high up the chain in the military."

"You stayed in touch?"

"He did more than I. I suppose it was his way of appeasing his own conscious. I guess that's probably not fair, I know. He's actually shown a lot of gratitude to me over the years for having saved his life."

"Did you ever forgive him, Gramps?"

"Yep Ben, I did. It was a long time ago, but I never could bring myself to like the man. But I reckon Smitty's up in heaven, proud as a peacock at having made me run after Captain Reeves. Lord knows, the doctor has probably already saved more lives in his lifetime than I can even imagine. Yeah, I'm pretty sure Smitty's up there right now smiling down at us just talking about it."

- 17 -

THIEVES

NOVEMBER 1984

BEN WALKED THROUGH the pawn shop's front door just as he did most days after school. He headed for the office where Morgan usually was and on his way noticed that the glass counter had been shattered.

"Gramps! Are you okay?" he frantically yelled.

"Yes, Ben. I'm fine. I'm in the back."

Ben quickly found Morgan in the office where he was trying to fix the back door that had been taken off of its hinges.

"What happened, Gramps?"

"It's the darnedest thing I've ever seen. I can't figure out how they were able to pull this steel door off of its hinges. Must've used a wench. Had to have."

"Who, Gramps?"

"Damn thieves, that's who."

Ben looked around and noticed that most everything had been cleared from the shelves in the office.

"When did they do it?"

"Early, early this morning. I got a call from the police. Didn't want to wake you. The alarm went off right away so they only took things from the shelves here in the office and the items from the front counter, but that's it. Could've been a lot worse, that's for sure."

"Did the police catch them?"

"Lord no and likely never will. Most of the things stolen I hadn't even catalogued yet. They'll probably wind up hocked at one of my competitors across town. Now how's that for irony?"

"What can I do to help, Gramps?"

"I about cleaned up everything except the front counter. Do you mind starting in on it?"

"No sir, not at all."

"Thanks, Ben. But be careful of the sharp glass. I've got to start making a list of the items that were stolen for the police and also for the insurance company. That will take me a while, so you taking care of the front will surely help. I've spent all day dealing with the useless police and nosy-nellies and never got around to it. You sure you don't mind?"

"Of course not, Gramps. I'll go get the big trashcan from out back and get started."

- 18 -

SAPLINGS

GILMER, TEXAS – JANUARY 1985

"TWO YEARS. Man. I can't believe it's been two years," Demarcus said.

"Me either," Scooter replied.

"Are we meeting tomorrow?" Octavio asked.

"Yes. We agreed. Once every year. For Ben, we'll keep building," Demarcus answered.

"Maybe one of these days he'll meet us there," Scooter said.

"Hora-le," Octavio thought aloud.

After the short dialogue, the remaining members of the Black

Machetes daydreamed in silence while sitting at a cafeteria table, not touching the breakfasts in front of them. The school bell finally woke them from their dazes as if to officially kick off yet another year of them missing their friend.

THERE WERE PLENTY OF 'POSTED - KEEP OUT' and 'NO TRESPASSING' signs nailed-up throughout the woods in which Jessup and Wade prospected. They ignored the proprietary warnings even though the warnings applied to them like everyone else—perhaps, even more so. Not to mention that they knew full well that one of the richest families in the county owned the land that they now trespassed on. Jessup and Wade actually went to school with the eldest son of the landowner and the classmate never cared for Jessup or Wade and the bad feelings had always been reciprocal. Needless to say, permission would've never been given for them to poach lumber from the posted property, which was precisely why Jessup and Wade had never asked for permission in the first place. That and they couldn't give two shits what the proprietors thought about anything, including matters involving their own damned land.

Jessup snapped off a long piece of tree marker tape from the roll attached to his belt and wrapped it around the trunk of an oak and said, "She's a good one. Over a cord."

"Mmhhmmm," mumbled Wade as he found another tree and started marking it using his own tape.

"Let's take a break and head back towards that gully we saw earlier so we can find a good spot for a blind. I'd bet a case of that fine whiskey of yours that there'll be a good buck to trophy from that dried-up creek-bed."

"Yup."

They backtracked as agreed but stopped when they heard young voices up ahead. They crept forward and followed the sounds until they came to the large gully to find the fellow trespassers. Nearby, Demarcus was sawing on a young sapling and the sight of his labor made Jessup's ears turn red with anger. Wade nudged him with his elbow and pointed to a spot close to the fort where Scooter was sitting on a log reading a magazine.

"Little fuckers are stealing money from our pockets," whispered Jessup.

He looked at Wade and motioned for him to go one direction while he went the other, and Wade nodded back in acknowledgement. Jessup proceeded to sneak up on Scooter while Wade exercised his stealth on Demarcus. Like partners in crime who'd been together for decades and who instinctually knew each other's actions, they simultaneously took the boys by surprise.

Wade spun Demarcus around, pinned him against the sapling that he was sawing, and then grinned wide with his dirty teeth.

"Good to see ya again, boy."

Jessup grabbed Scooter from behind by his long hair and pulled his head back hard.

"Is that my long lost Cherry in your hands, you little fucker?"

Both Demarcus and Scooter screamed. Octavio was down inside the fort with his machete in hand, hacking away to carve out another seat. When he heard the screams of his friends, he rushed up the clay staircase and ran in the direction of where he knew Demarcus was. He stopped cold in his tracks as he watched Wade throw Demarcus to the ground. Wade glanced at Octavio and then slowly moved his glare down to the machete that was still in Octavio's hands. Octavio gripped it so hard that his knuckles had turned whiter than the meat of the sapling Demarcus had been sawing on moments before. Wade nonchalantly removed his Bowie knife from its sheath and again grinned wide.

"Boy, I wish you would."

Octavio began trembling, half from fear and half out of anger. He finally stabbed his machete deep into the large mound of clay that he stood next to and stepped away from it. Wade spit a mouthful of tobacco in Octavio's direction and slowly shook his head.

"Not good 'nough. Pull it out and throw it down that there gully you just come up from."

Demarcus did as he was told and Wade responded to the act of obedience by disappointedly shaking his head in disgust.

"Pity. Pussy wetback."

Jessup and Wade rounded up the boys and made them all kneel down on the cold ground, lining them up like prisoners about to be executed. Jessup walked around until he was face-to-face with the culprits to properly address them with his eyes.

"Do you stupid little shits know how much money you've cost us by cutting down all those saplings? And I see you been using my own goddamn saw to do the deed. I take it Benny-Boy stole it from me so you could. And you, piggy, I bet you've jerked off to my Cherry so much that all the pages are glued shut from your little pecker's jizz. It's clear that you boys need a lesson and I just happen to be in the learnin' mood. Lean forward. All of you. Now. Onto your hands."

Wade kicked Demarcus when none of the boys complied, which

prompted them to then lean forward on all fours, as ordered. Jessup slowly took off his thick rawhide-belt, looped it in his hand and walked around to get the best position to access to their backsides. The ensuing cries and screams could be heard throughout the woods as Jessup proceeded to give each of the boys the whipping of their lifetimes. After he dealt out the punishment, he again faced their sobbing faces.

"Now, I ain't gonna say this but once. I don't wanna see, hear, smell, or even have a suspicion that any of you boys have ever come back to this here fort or these here woods. And if you wanna go tell your parents about this, that's your peeee-roggative. But I'm sure that nigger there can tell you just how serious Wade and I are. So, think twice boys. Now get the fuck outta here before I commence to swinging again. Go!"

The boys got to their feet and ran as fast as they could, still crying from the pain and fear. Scooter's adrenaline was pumping so hard that even he was able to keep pace. They stopped once they fully cleared the woods and then huddled to catch their breath.

"We've got. To tell. Our parents," Scooter said in between deep gasps.

"No! They will kill us and our parents!" Demarcus replied.

"They. Can't do. That."

"Easy for you to say, Scooter. You're white. Octavio and I...nobody will give a shit if a nigger and a spic family are killed. You know that they probably killed Ben. Hell, now I'm sure of it."

"Jesus. What are we going to do?"

"Nothing. Not a damn thing. We never go back. End of story."

Octavio never said a word. Instead, he just gritted his teeth in anger. All he could think about was finding a way to beat the shit out of Jessup and Wade. He knew he couldn't really do that, but he had a good idea of someone else he could take it out on. And that someone else just happened to be close enough to those madre chingados to suffice.

- 19 -

SAINT

JESSUP, ANGIE, AND TOMMY were sitting in their living room watching the post-game show after Marino had just led the Dolphins to defeat the Steelers for the AFC Championship. As usual, both Angie and Jessup were well on their way to feeling no pain.

"I bet you Duhe never came in second on anything in high school. Runner-up this. Runner-up that. Pffft. Kind of embarrassing to tell the truth," Jessup said to Tommy.

"Sorry, Pop," Tommy said, as if by habit.

"Don't you listen to your dad, Tommy. We're very proud of you," Angie said.

"Woman, you had better shut the fuck up before I help you to.

It's boooolshit anyway. That boy from Indiana ain't near as good as you. Fucking quarterback. Linebacker's ain't never given enough credit. Mr. Football USA, Mr. Fucking Lucky more like it."

"He's a great player, Pop. He deserved it."

"Fuck'em. Deserved it my ass."

Tommy stood up and walked over to grab keys off the counter and made one final measure of his dad to make sure of the timing, because with Jessup, it was all about timing.

"You mind if I borrow the Nova to go see Jeff? He and I wanna go over some college stuff."

"Suppose. One scratch on her and it's your ass though."

"Sure, Pop."

TOMMY PULLED THE OLD BLUE NOVA to the back alley of the Piggly Wiggly and parked behind a likewise old blue dumpster. Five minutes later, Raina Snow peeked out from the store's back door and looked both ways, smiling the second she saw Tommy. She ran to the car and quickly got in the front passenger seat. Tommy looked at her beaming eyes and then down at the little pig logo on the apron she wore and said, "Fashion statement comes to mind."

Raina looked down and realized she hadn't taken off her work apron. She flirtatiously slapped Tommy on the arm and said, "You had better love everything I wear, boy."

"Is that so?"

"Mhmm. If you know what's good for you."

"Hmm. I think I know what's good for me."

"Think?"

Tommy smiled and caressed Raina's face before leaning in and kissing her. "Love you, Ray."

"Love you, T."

"Close your eyes."

"What? Why?"

"Just do it, already."

"Okay, okay. Big football player thinks he can get all bossy," Raina closed her eyes and said, "Now what?"

Tommy took out a gold necklace with a heart locket from his jacket pocket and held it out in front of her.

"Open your eyes."

Raina gasped and shrieked from joy at the sight of the gift.

"Happy Anniversary, baby," Tommy said.

Raina took the necklace from him and put it on. She reached down and held the heart in her palm.

"It's perfect, T. I love it. I love you!"

"It opens."

"Really?"

She opened the small heart. Inscribed inside was T+R=4EVR. Raina resumed her shrieking and hugged and kissed Tommy all over his neck and face. And he soaked it all up with the biggest smile that any Boone had ever displayed since Great-Great-Great-Grandpappy Daniel.

"Listen, I want us to get away from this place. I know you're sick of us hiding it. I hate it, too. I can't keep doing it much longer. Hopefully, we won't have to. It looks like UCLA is going to offer me a full ride to play football for them. Since you already accepted with them, I'm going to as well."

"Are you sure, T? I know there's other school's you'd rather go to, and your dad won't let you, will he?"

"I'm definitely sure. And it's not his decision, Ray, it's mine. I want us to be together and away from this place and especially away from my pop. You know I hate him for what he did to your family. Truth is, I can't wait to get as far away from him as I can."

"Oh Tommy, you've just made me the happiest girl in the world!"

"It just gets better from here on, Ray. NFL for me and a recording contract for you. Out of this hell-hole and then sky's the limit, beautiful."

THE NEXT DAY, RAINA PASSED BY TOMMY in the high school courtyard with a smile and another beaming look in her eyes. Inside she wanted to jump into his arms and hug him for everyone in the world to see. *Soon*, she thought. Tommy knelt down as if he'd dropped something on the ground and then casually glanced back just to catch a glimpse of the girl he loved as she walked away. At the same time, Octavio jumped to his feet from his perch on a nearby picnic table and approached Raina.

"Hola Raina," Octavio said.

"Hi Octavio," Raina replied while walking past him.

Octavio turned around as if to follow but instead pinched her ass. Raina spun around and pointed her finger at Octavio in anger.

"Don't do that again, Octavio!"

Tommy saw the whole thing and just like his pop, his head turned red hot with rage. Without thinking, he rushed forward and got right in Octavio's face, but Octavio was already waiting for Tommy's reaction. Octavio jumped back and with a smile, reached down and pulled out his Saint Michael medallion and kissed it.

"Esto va a ser para Ben (This is going to be for Ben)," Octavio said.

Tommy charged Octavio and was met with a blinding overhand right. Octavio followed up with a left hook and then an upper-hand right. The last blow sent Tommy stumbling back with his head angled towards the sky. His face looked like something out of a B-Horror flick, but his anger allowed him to shake it off and charge Octavio. Once again, Octavio was ready and jumped back enough to evade Tommy's effort except for letting him grab hold of his shirt and necklace. Octavio pulled back hard and freed himself and then with another lightning fast overhand right ended the one-sided fight just as fast as it had begun. Tommy was splayed out on the ground, knocked-out cold. Various whistles emitted from the crowd that surrounded the scene. Raina ran to Tommy and knelt down to take care of him. She cried and whispered in his ear that she loved him as everybody continued to watch.

Octavio shrugged his shoulders while saying, "Hora-le," and then contentedly walked straight to the principal's office where he knew his presence would soon be requested.

TOMMY DECIDED TO TAKE the rest of the day off from school—once he came-to that is. But he didn't go home until well after school let out. Instead, he went into the woods and punched a few trees, pretending that they were Octavio. Then he cooled down and started thinking about Raina and how everyone probably figured out that they were a couple now. He didn't care though—he was glad that they knew. Except for his pop that is—Jessup knowing legitimately frightened him. He racked his brain trying to figure out how to defend his love for Raina to his dad, but nothing would work and he knew it. His only course of action was to adamantly deny everything whenever his pop broached the subject, and in doing so, pray to instill reasonable doubt in the mean man.

When Tommy finally got home, he cringed at the sight of the Nova parked beside the house. There was no putting it off and there was no way to hide the marks on his face. So, he decided to just go on in and tell the story as straight as he could—without making a big deal of coming to Raina's defense. But as often happens in a small town, the news had already spread around enough to get back to Jessup. Truth is, it was hot gossip that the son of the town's biggest bad-ass had been beat up by a younger, smaller Mexican kid. If only Tommy had known this, he probably would've crashed at a friend's house for a couple of days, because as soon as he walked in, Jessup was waiting.

"You'd better be glad that little fucking Mexican did a good number on you, you pussy, else I'd fuck you up, myself. How dare you let a little wetback piece of shit kick your ass. A freshman at that. Goddamn! If you weren't embarrassin' enough already. Do you know who the fuck I am, boy? Nobody kicks a Boone ass. Nobody but me, motherfucker! Jesus Mary Joseph, for fuck sake!"

Jessup worked himself into enough of a rage that he decided to go ahead and add insult to literal injury by giving Tommy his second beating of the day. All Tommy could do was cover and take it, like he'd done many times before. Once Jessup got it all out, he balled-up a hand towel and threw it hard at Tommy.

"Clean yourself up before you bleed on the goddamn couch."

Not long after that, Angie walked into the living room with Tommy's bloody shirt in one hand and Octavio's chain and medallion in the other.

"Tommy, I was about to get the blood out of your shirt when I found this Catholic necklace in your pocket. Baby, I didn't know you were interested in Catholicism. When I was a girl, I used to—"

"Woman, shut the fuck up and hand that to me," Jessup said as he took Octavio's medallion, stared at it and then looked over at Tommy. "Is this that spic's?"

"Yessir."

"Well, at least you got something besides an ass woopin' out of it."

Jessup put the medallion in his front pocket and headed towards the back door.

"Where you going? Dinner's almost done," Angie said.

Jessup hesitated half way out the door and flipped her off before replying, "Choke on it, bitch!"

He slammed the door behind him and then Angie shrugged, picked up her gin-and-tonic from the counter and floated back to her hideaway down the hall.

- 20 -

TWO BIRDS

JESSUP TAPPED TWICE on Wade's front door before opening it and walking in.

"Beer?" Wade asked from the kitchen.

"Yeah."

Wade walked into the living room and tossed a long neck to Jessup.

"Angie burn dinner again?"

"Of course the cunt did, but that's not why I'm here. I found our next catch, but it has to be a quick release on this one."

"Don't sound like all that much fun."

"It will be. You'll have a good ole time, I promise."

"Where?"

"Right in our own back yard."

"You on that funny weed again?"

"Nope, but I can fuckin' guarantee you I'm pissed off enough that it wouldn't phase me if I was. This one's going to be personal."

"A'ight. When?"

"Tonight. After the niggers go to bed. When do you think they go to bed?" Jessup asked aloud, really talking to himself.

"S'pose that depends on the niggers."

"After midnight we'll go and see."

"Clue me in on what we're doin' zactly."

"Killing two birds with one fucking stone. That's what."

LATER THAT NIGHT JUST AFTER MIDNIGHT, Wade opened Rayna's window without even so much as a squeak. Rayna never knew that Jessup and Wade were staring down at her as she lay fast asleep in her bed. Jessup dabbed a cloth with chloroform and handed it to Wade.

Wade leaned over Raina and thought *I wanna see them scared eyes first.*

He grabbed her thin cheeks with one hand and just before she could scream, but right after he got a glimpse of the fear in her eyes, he slammed the cloth over her mouth and nose. Within a few seconds of struggling Raina's body went limp and still and afterwards, Wade was neither limp nor still.

TWO HOURS LATER, Raina woke up freezing-cold and half

choking on one of Wade's ball-gags. She still had her white blue-bonnet patterned pajamas on, although they were no longer really white, rather more of a muddy red color from all of the clay she'd been laid down on. She struggled to free her arms that were stretched back above her head. They, along with her legs, had been tied to small saplings—the ones that Demarcus had previously cut down a week beforehand. Wade had decided to make good use of the wasted lumber by burying a few deep in the soft earth. Jessup shined a flashlight down on Raina from above the top of the gully and thought that she looked like a dirty letter X all sprawled out below.

"Our little birdy just woke up," Jessup said.

"You first. I wanna be the last thing that nigger girl 'members," Wade replied.

"Ain't no sense in arguing with that."

Jessup climbed down the fort stairs and Wade followed. They both had their shoes covered with trash bags that were fastened to the shins of their jeans with duct tape. Jessup went ahead and walked into the area under the sapling roof, knelt down in between Raina's legs and began to grope her all over. Tears streamed from her eyes, but the gag prevented her from making any noise. Looking at her was like watching a silent horror film. It wasn't long before Jessup got impatient and just ripped open her pajama top to expose her young breasts. He reached and squeezed them hard as if he was juicing two orange halves. A brief moment of pain replaced the look in her eyes before the fear returned to take back over. Impatient again, the Rabid Dog reached down and ripped apart her pajama bottoms at her crotch. He leaned forward low to the ground so that his nose was buried in her panties. He took in a deep inhale of her scent and moaned. That was all it took. He ripped off her panties and raped her as fast and as hard as he could. He kept at it until he was finished and no longer could hurt her with his genitals. That's when he switched to hurting her mentally. While remaining on top of her and still inside, he began whispering in her ear.

"I bet daddy is going to miss his little chocolate girl, isn't he? Well, he should've kept his fucking hands off of me. Oh baby girl, I wish I could be there when he gets the call. To see the look on his face. And then at that exact moment, I wish I could look him in his nigger eyes and tell him just how sweet his little angel's pussy was. Ummmmmm, yeah. Wish upon a lucky star, ain't that right? Only it's a wish that won't come true, because I had an idea earlier today that takes priority. It came to me after I beat Tommy's ass. You know why I beat his ass? Sure, it was partly because he let that Mexican rough him up. But more than that, he picked a nigger girl to love on. That's right. I know all about his little brown sugar. At first I let it slide because I thought it was just that, him dipping his stick in some hot chocolate. But him getting his ass kicked for you like he did. Well, now it's apparent that it's more than him gettin' a little, ain't it? And I can't allow any Boone with blood relations to me to be hooked up with a nigger. But that's nothing for you to worry about anymore. What you need to worry about, you dark cunt, is that it's now Wade's turn with ya, and let me tell you, if there's one thing that complicated man knows, it's how to treat a little girl like you."

Jessup laughed as he got off of her and stood up. While zipping up his jeans and staring down at her, he noticed the gold chain around her neck. He reached down and pulled it off of her and held it in front of his flashlight's beam.

"Ain't that sweet. I bet your big nigger daddy got you this didn't he? You don't mind if I keep it do you? Keepsake of sorts."

He reached back down to grab her face and then forcefully shook her head back and forth like a rag doll.

"No, you don't mind then? Awww, much obliged nigger girl. I promise to keep it safe and sound."

Jessup motioned with his flashlight that it was Wade's turn. Wade approached from the other side of the fort where he was waiting and watching in the dark. Jessup took the same position where Wade had been waiting and settled in to get ready and enjoy the show. Wade always put on a good one—the only thing missing was some popcorn and a beer.

For over an hour, Wade took his time and did unspeakable things to Raina. He tortured her in ways that made what Jessup had done to her look like a PG-rated family movie. Raina finally died ten minutes before Wade finished his bag of sadistic tricks, but her being dead didn't stop him nor did it bother him in the least. He actually planned it that way, truth be told. He enjoyed feeling her body go cold, and even more he enjoyed seeing the light disappear from her eyes. Wade Strickland—torture god of lost little girls—had made sure the light from Raina Snow's rising star would shine no more.

Just like a wrestling team, Wade tagged with Jessup to finish things off. Wearing rawhide work gloves, Jessup took the machete with Octavio's name painted on it and began hacking away at Raina's cadaver. By the time he was finished, her head was almost fully detached from her neck. After cocking his head to take a look, he decided to continue chopping away at one of her arms for the sake of posterity. On the third blow, the blade wedged deep into the

135

marrow of Raina's arm, just below her left shoulder. Jessup decided that it was a fitting place for the machete to rest and left the blade stuck like that deep in her arm. After one last satisfying glance, he figured the scene would do a good job of sickening the cops and implanting permanent nightmares into the surviving members of Raina's family—especially her daddy.

Jessup took out Octavio's Saint Michael necklace and thoroughly wiped it with a clean rag. He placed it in Raina's right hand so that the medallion lay on the clay ground while the chain rested in her palm. He pressed her fingers closed over the necklace and stood back to make sure it looked as if she'd yanked it off of Octavio. He made a couple adjustments until it was staged as it should be. He stood over her looking like someone standing over a grave about to say some words, but instead he snorted a nose full of snot and phlegm, coughed it down into his throat and into his mouth, and leaned forward and spit it onto Raina's mutilated body. Then while smiling contentedly, he walked back to where Wade was standing.

"Good enough?" he asked.

"Yup, good 'nough."

"Alright. Let's clean up our tracks and wait and see how long it takes the dogs to find her."

- 21 -

CONCERTINA

IT WAS HALF WAY into lunch period when the P.A. system echoed, "Octavio Muñoz, please come to the principal's office." After a few more moments it echoed the same again, but Octavio had his headphones on, blasting Miami Sound Machine. He sat at his usual spot, perched on the picnic table with his back to the parking lot. Scooter sat on the other side and was likewise listening to his own selection of music while playing an electronic game he held in his hands.

A crowd formed on the edge of the campus, but neither Octavio nor Scooter noticed the commotion. An army of policemen cleared away the kids and slowly approached the picnic table with guns drawn.

"Slowly raise your hands," one of the policemen yelled at Octavio.

Scooter just happened to look up and his mouth gaped open at the sight of over one dozen guns drawn, pointed right in his direction. He dropped the electronic blackjack game from his hands to hold them high in the air, and then proceeded to wet his pants. Octavio had Gloria Estefan cranked so loud that he again didn't hear the police officer's second order. Scooter didn't dare move to get Octavio's attention so Octavio never had a reason to look up. Three of the policemen continued their slow approach. When they got to within six feet of the table, they holstered their weapons and did a finger countdown from three. Once they reached one, they charged Octavio, knocking him off of the table and onto the ground. All of the oxygen left his body from the shock impact and he began hyperventilating. An officer planted his knee dead center into Octavio's back and aggressively cuffed him. Octavio couldn't find his breath and felt as if he was going to die from lack of oxygen. The police officer turned him over and began lifting Octavio's waist up and down by his belt loops. A few seconds later his breathing returned to normal, but his heart was still racing so fast that it felt like it would explode inside his chest. His eyes were all blurry and his hearing was muffled from the shock of the moment. His world had just been turned upside down and shaken hard like a snow globe filled with muddy water, causing one big confusing blur.

The officers picked Octavio up from the ground and aggressively helped him get stable on his feet. They tugged firmly on his biceps and led him to a line of police cars and in the process marched him past the entire high school, including faculty. All of the gawking spectators had a puzzled look on their faces, but none more than

Tommy Boone. He looked everywhere in the crowd for Raina and a sickening feeling came over him when he couldn't find her. He also started looking for Demarcus but likewise he was nowhere in sight. Tommy's head began spinning and then he stumbled to the closest tree he could find and began puking up that morning's breakfast. A man approached Tommy from the front and handed him a handkerchief—Tommy took it without saying a word.

"You're Tommy Boone aren't you?" the man asked.

All Tommy could muster was a nod.

"I'm Texas Ranger Maynard Jameson. I've got a couple questions for you, son."

Tommy fell to his knees and his head started spinning faster like an out of control merry-go-round. At that moment, he realized that his worst fear had come true. He began sobbing as his heart knew he'd just lost the one and only good thing he'd ever had in his life.

OCTAVIO'S PARENTS COULDN'T AFFORD an attorney so the assigned public defender was the best representation he was going to get. Raina and her older brothers were loved among the folk of Gilmer, and that love reached out from all skin colors, including white. Needless to say, there had been no helping-hands extended to a poor Mexican family who'd raised such a monster. Unfortunately for Octavio, the evidence, both physical and circumstantial, tipped the scales of justice overwhelmingly in the favor of the prosecution. Not to mention, he had no alibi. His mom had been working an all-night housekeeping shift at the hospital and his dad likewise was twenty-four miles away, pulling a graveyard at the Lone Star Steel Mill. Even though Octavio was fast asleep in his bed when Raina was brutally murdered, he had no one to swear to it.

That left Octavio with two choices. One, go to trial for first degree murder and be tried as an adult, which in Texas meant the death penalty, if found guilty. Two, plead guilty and take a life sentence. His defense team had explained to him that all things considered, there was really only one choice to make. And Octavio was smart enough to listen to their counsel, so the judge accepted his guilty plea and passed down sentencing of life in prison without the possibility of parole. Afterwards, Octavio was only allowed to briefly wave goodbye to his family before being pulled away with tears streaming down his face that matched those of his mother. The deputies escorted him, bound in chains, through the back door of the court room and out of sight. The next day, the good, hard-working Muñoz family packed-up everything they owned and moved back to their hometown in Mexico. There was no longer an American dream for them in the United States—it had been unjustly taken away from them along with their only son.

JESSUP AND WADE WATCHED the news coverage of Octavio's murder sentencing on Wade's fancy, color console-TV. One would think by looking at the two of them that it was game day and they were watching the Super Bowl. Jessup hooped and hollered while Wade grinned wide.

"How's Tommy takin' it?" Wade finally asked.

"He's still tore up, but he'll fuckin' get over it. And if he don't, well fuck'em. Pussy shouldn't't've picked a nigger to love on."

"Yup."

Wade got up and left the room and shortly came back with his prized bottle of Glenlivet twenty-one year old Scotch in one hand and two thick cut crystal tumblers pinched in his other hand. He sat the tumblers down on the coffee table and nodded towards his beautifully stained humidor on the end table. Jessup did the honors by removing two Cubans from the box and making them ready for light as Wade broke the seal on the expensive whiskey and poured. And Wade kept pouring on into the night as both of them kept sipping and smoking and celebrating until the fine whiskey was no more.

TOMMY SAT BEHIND THE WHEEL of Angie's van, which he'd parked close to the courthouse. Deep down he knew that there was no way he could get close enough to Octavio to shoot him, but he brought the gun, just in case a miracle from God happened to smile down upon him. Resting between his thighs was a large bottle of Jack Daniels, half of which Tommy had already drank. He pulled a little plastic bag from his jacket pocket that contained as many downers as fifty bucks could buy, which turned out to be plenty. He popped four pills in his mouth and washed them down with a swig of the booze. He picked up the old .22 pistol from the console and stared at it. After having sat and drank and popped pills for over an hour, he knew he'd already missed the Sheriff's Department transferring Octavio. The fucker was gone and out of reach—and Raina was gone and out of reach, too.

Forever.

Tommy raised the gun to the side of his head, pressing the barrel against his temple. His finger moved to the trigger and began to squeeze. That's when he heard Raina's voice scold him in his head.

"Don't do that!" was what he heard, just as she'd yelled at Octavio that day of the fight.

Hearing her voice in his head caused Tommy to put down the gun and reply, "Okay, baby. Okay."

He took another big drink of whiskey and then proceeded to bawl like a baby until he finally passed out.

Gainesville State School – Cooke County, Texas

THE LARGE BLACK SHERIFF'S DEPARTMENT BUS pulled through the concertina lined gates of the maximum security juvenile correctional facility, located about seventy-five miles north of Dallas. Octavio and five others exited the bus, his shackles so short that he struggled to walk with baby steps. A line of deputies watched him in particular as he was escorted up to the prison entrance. The steel door closed behind him, but the deputies continued to glare even after the no good Mexican in the orange jumpsuit disappeared. They then all spat out a mouthful of chewing tobacco juice in unison as if they were performing a synchronized expectorating contest in the Law Enforcement Olympics.

Good riddance, each and everyone one of them thought.

Octavio was immediately processed into the boys' prison and

then escorted once again, only this time to his new four-walled home where a large metal door with a small wire glass pane opened to a two-bunk cell. Leaning on the far wall in a frisk stance with his back to the door was Octavio's new cellmate. Octavio stepped in and the guard took the handcuffs off. As soon as the door clamored shut, Octavio's cellmate straightened from his frisk position and slowly turned around. The inmate, standing there staring at Octavio with devil eyes, was also a young Mexican but had nothing else in common with Octavio other than nationality. He was a street-tough Chicano from El Paso who looked more man than kid. His arms were covered with poorly-done tattoos along with three tear drops permanently inked on his face under his right eye. His hair was slicked back and kept in a tight net and he had a goatee that was too thick for his age. He looked at Octavio from head-to-toe, paused with a slight tilt of his head and then loudly sucked his teeth. He continued to eyeball Octavio hard like a wolf about to attack another wolf, smiled a sick smile that showed off his gold rimmed teeth, and then growled the words, "Hora-le, chingada."

Unfortunately, Octavio's first week at Gainesville wasn't spent in his cell—it was spent in the infirmary. He tried to put up a good fight, but his new cellmate had been too strong and too mentally damaged. At the hands of a career juvenile inmate, Octavio suffered a type of abuse that instead of leaving the psyche of a human being, becomes a permanent cancer that continues to grow and transform its host from the inside-out.

BEN WAS SITTING at the TV table when Morgan walked in to ask for help with something in the front of the shop. The old black and white small screen had the news on, which at that moment was running special coverage of the Raina Snow story. Morgan had no idea what was wrong with Ben, but he could tell that something was off just by the way he was sitting. Ben's face was a strong pink color and his entire body was tense. He watched the small television with his arms folded and his teeth clenched tight. Morgan finally clued in on Ben's focus when the news story resonated in his ears. Morgan had been following the trial for the last week and knew Ben was from that part of Texas, but he had no idea Ben was acquainted with her. He hadn't exactly felt it kosher to broach the subject before that moment—Ben had seen too much evil already in his young life, so discussing negative news over dinner like one would bad weather had seemed like poor form to Morgan.

He sat down next to Ben, reached over and then squeezed his shoulder. He tried to assess what Ben needed, but wasn't able to figure out if it was an ear to listen or a hand to comfort. For the first time, he couldn't read the young man whom he'd come to love as his own flesh and blood.

"Did you know the girl, Ben?"

Almost in a lethargic state, Ben responded, "Yeah, her brother was my best friend. She was the prettiest, sweetest girl I'd ever known. Always smiling. Always making everyone around her feel good."

Morgan had seen photos of her and had to agree that the girl was indeed beautiful. He thought now, as he had many times while following the trial, that it was all a pitiful shame—an unfortunate, real-life tragedy.

"I'm sorry, son."

Ben had been suppressing his emotions all afternoon since he'd first started watching the story, but Morgan's compassion and maybe even his presence caused the barrel to tip and so he started sobbing. With tears streaming down his face, he looked up at Morgan and shook his head.

"He didn't do it, Gramps. I know he didn't. He couldn't. Not Octavio. He was a Black Mache..."

And Ben resumed his weeping, unable to finish.

"Shhhhh," Morgan said as he hugged and comforted Ben as best he could. After a few more moments of heart-wrenching sobs, Morgan heard words that kick started his adrenal glands.

"It was that rotten son-of-a-bitch, I know it."

Morgan lifted Ben's head and asked, "What are you talking about, Ben?"

"The Rabid Dog. Jessup. My step-dad. I know he did it. I just know it. I know it as sure as I'm breathing, Gramps. He did it and made it look like Octavio did it."

"Shhhhh," Morgan comforted as he continued to hold Ben, but what he'd just heard genuinely scared him. He knew Ben believed it, and he also knew Ben was smart enough to know the truth on things. People who had hard lives, like he and Ben both had, over time develop a knack for weeding through the bullshit, even in the face of contradictory certainty.

Ben wiped away his own tears, swallowed down the invisible rock in his throat, and once again in his life thought: *I'm done with crying like a baby*.

Morgan hugged Ben again and said, "Ben, if you want...if you need to go to the service, then you should go. I'll take you, son."

Ben had already imagined being there for Demarcus and

showing support for the Snow family while standing next to Scooter. But he'd also imagined the Rabid Dog close by, sniffing out his prey.

"No Gramps, I can't. Jessup will kill us as sure as we're breathing now. I just want to forget about that place. Forget about him. Forget everything. I want to erase it all."

Morgan gave Ben's shoulder one final squeeze before reaching over and turning off the TV. The simple act of flipping that switch was his way to help Ben take that step forward in the direction of leaving it all behind. Looking back, Ben would believe that by silencing the news story, Morgan had symbolically helped mute all of the evil things from Ben's past while introducing hope that one day they would be gone for good.

- 22 -

THE POINT

HOPE, ARKANSAS – FEBRUARY 1986

JUST LIKE HIS FRESHMAN YEAR, Benjamin "Wilder" River had finished his sophomore year with a perfect average while also becoming a member of the National Honor Society. He'd enrolled in advanced classes and had also taken extra courses in summer school. Morgan had urged Ben to also participate in physical conditioning activities, and even though Ben preferred to steer clear of team-focused sports, he had obeyed his Gramps's wishes by joining the track team, on which he went all-district in long distance and cross-country running.

Ben had done just what he'd set out to do by leaving his past behind—he'd focused on becoming a happy person and for him that meant doing good things in the world while soaking up as much knowledge as he could in the process. And Morgan couldn't have been more proud. Seeing the young man before him seemed like a surreal dream, and to bear witness to it all was a great honor. And never did Morgan think that he had any right to take even the smallest credit. Ben had worked so hard, harder than Morgan had ever worked and harder than he could imagine anyone ever working.

As such, going into his junior year of high school, Ben had enough credits accumulated to graduate, so he decided to skip forward and become a senior. Considering his actual age, he was advancing two years ahead, which made Ben's accomplishments even more astonishing. And having perfect grades, Ben could've chosen to go to any school of his choice. Many of the top universities had shown keen interest in him, including a couple of Ivy League schools, but after spending the last four years listening to his Gramps's war stories, Ben had his heart set on attending West Point. He'd even gone as far as mapping out his future plans within the United States Army.

Many times Morgan had shared stories about his run-ins with the men from Easy Company of the 101st Airborne Division. The heroic tales Morgan shared always fascinated Ben and he'd since read everything that he could get his hands on regarding the history of the group, including the battles that they fought in WWII. His love for military history soon led him to research modern day outfits in the Army. One such group of individuals that likewise fascinated him was the 1st Battalion, 75th Infantry Regiment, otherwise known as the Ranger Regiment. Their values resonated with Ben, but even more so did their original charter that was penned by none other than General Creighton Abrams:

> *The battalion is to be elite, light, and the most proficient infantry in the world. A battalion that can do things with its hands and weapons better than anyone. The battalion will contain no "hoodlums or brigands" and if the battalion is formed from such persons, it will be disbanded. Wherever the battalion goes, it must be apparent that it is the best.*

Ben had since memorized the creed and especially liked the part about the unit not allowing in any hoodlums or brigands. After thoroughly researching the commando organization, he'd set his goals to first graduate from the Military Academy and then become a U.S. Army Ranger. Morgan had long since given up trying to talk him out of it. Not because Morgan thought Ben's aspirations were bad, but because Morgan felt that there was so much more he could offer the world that was above and beyond a career in the military. On the other hand, Morgan was proud and thankful that Ben had developed such a strong sense of duty and patriotism for his country—and that was something he could never argue with.

As such, and for the first time ever, Morgan reached out to Dr. James Reeves instead of the other way around. Indeed, the doctor was surprised to have received the call, but glad to hear Morgan's voice nonetheless. Morgan didn't beat around the bush and came straight out with asking Dr. Reeves to put in a good word with his Army connections regarding Ben's application to West Point. Morgan also explained that Ben was a perfect student and an upstanding young man and didn't need any special favors, just a shot at getting noticed. He finally topped-off the abrupt ask by expressing how much he felt an obligation to help his grandson in any way he could and that making the call had been the only thing he could think of. The doctor understood and let Morgan know that he'd be happy to formally and even personally endorse Ben in any endeavor, especially one regarding his alma mater, The Point. He also ensured Morgan that he'd reach out to Morgan's Congressman, whom Dr. Reeves just so happened to be close friends with.

A FEW WEEKS LATER, Ben walked into the shop's office and found Morgan snoring in front of the small TV. Ben smelled split-pea-soup, Morgan's favorite, and saw a pan of it simmering on the old hot-plate, which Ben then went and unplugged.

"Gramps, you're going to burn this place down one of these days cooking that soup of yours."

Morgan jolted awake and said, "I'm watching it."

"Yeah, I saw that. Right through the back of your eyelids."

"No, that's ridiculous. I was using my autoscopy, or was it my astral body? One or the other. It's certainly debatable."

Ben laughed and said, "I see you've been reading my books again. No wonder you were sleeping."

"I wouldn't consider it reading, more muddling."

"I've never seen you muddle anything, Gramps. Except for maybe a can of split-pea-soup every now and then."

"Watch it, kiddo. Nobody talks about my soup like that."

Ben raised his hands in surrender and said, "Sorry, your soup

150

majesty. I give."

Morgan chuckled and shook his head and then got serious. "Ben, come sit down."

"Uht-oh, you barked an order. Means it's something serious."

Morgan took an envelope from a file-tray and placed it on the table. Ben looked down and saw that it was from the Admissions Committee of West Point. He sat across from Morgan and just stared at the parcel.

Morgan motioned with his hands as if to say *"Well?"*, and then said, "Do you realize how hard it's been to have that sitting here all day without knowing what it says? Are you really going to make an old man wait any longer?"

"Old-smold," Ben said and picked up the letter. "Well, here goes nothing."

He carefully opened the sealed flap, pulled out the formal business letterhead, and thoroughly read it to himself without showing any emotion. Once finished, he frowned, stood up and let the letter fall to the table. He turned around with slumped shoulders and walked towards the back door and kept his back to Morgan, whose heart sank at Ben's deflated reaction.

Damned medical officer. Should've let that Kraut kill him. Selfish bastard didn't do squat!

Morgan picked up the letter and read it. A big smile seized the property of his face and he jumped to his feet and laughingly yelled at Ben.

"That is *not* funny! You could've given me a heart attack!"

Ben turned around with his eyes gleaming and his face smiling just as wide as Morgan's. He walked over to the old man and gave him a big hug. They held the embrace and then Ben pulled back to look Morgan in his eyes.

"Thanks, Gramps—I know how you helped—the doctor told me. He had to interview me before he could endorse me. I'm sorry I never told you that we spoke. I know how hard picking up that phone must've been for you to do. I promise not to let you down for calling in that favor, Gramps."

"Ben, you did this all on your own. There's nothing this old man or that old doctor did that made any difference. It was all you and I can't tell you how proud and happy I am."

HOPE HIGH SCHOOL – MAY 1986

BEN WAS IN FIRST PERIOD when the principal's secretary came to fetch him. She led the way to the school's administrative building, and once inside, she stopped at her desk and pointed to the principal's small office just around the corner. Ben walked in and noticed Mrs. Lattimore, his counselor, sitting across from Mr. Lynn, the principal. Immediately, he became curious as to what he'd done wrong to deserve the audience.

"Good morning, sir. I was told you wanted to see me," Ben said.

"Ben, please come in and have a seat," Mr. Lynn replied.

"Yes, sir." Ben sat next to his counselor and then smiled his greeting to her, "Good morning, Mrs. Lattimore."

"Good morning, Ben," she responded before the principal began addressing Ben.

"Ben, first of all, I never got to personally congratulate you on your acceptance into The Military Academy. We're very proud of you here at Hope High School for having achieved that great accomplishment."

"Thank you, sir."

"You're probably wondering why we've called you here. Well, to tell you the truth, we're in a bit of a pickle, Ben. You're the first student to ever graduate a year early with a perfect GPA. We've of course had other graduates in the past with a perfect average, but none that were a year ahead. Traditionally, the valedictorian honor goes to the student with the highest average, and of course that would be you this year."

Ben nodded, trying to understand where this was going. He looked at Mrs. Lattimore with a puzzled look.

"I think you deserve to be valedictorian," Mrs. Lattimore said. "You've worked very hard these last three years and have accomplished so much. There are others in the faculty who feel that Wendy Underwood should be named valedictorian instead of salutatorian, because she's what they consider a 'true senior' with the highest average, second to yours of course."

"Yes, and I tend to agree with them," Mr. Lynn said before shifting his eyes from her to Ben. "I'm sorry Ben, but there's something to be said for having one of your peers that you've grown up with for the past four years giving the valediction speech."

"But there's also something to be said for working hard to be your best and getting recognized for it. What a great role model Ben is for younger students coming into high school," Mrs. Lattimore rebutted.

"While that is true, I do not believe that—"

"Excuse me," Ben interrupted.

His principal and counselor stopped arguing with each other and finally looked at Ben.

"Can I please say something?"

"I'm sorry. Of course, please go ahead," Mr. Lynn replied.

"Mrs. Lattimore, while I really, sincerely appreciate you feeling so strongly about me being valedictorian, I'm afraid I'm going to have to side with Mr. Lynn and the others. I don't think it's fair that I get to skip my junior year and have that honor. Wendy is very smart—way smarter than me actually, and she's very nice and works really hard. I've had a couple of classes with her, and she's always respectful and never did she shun me because of my age like some of the others did. If anyone deserves it, she does. So again, thank you, but I must decline being named either valedictorian or salutatorian. To be perfecily honest with you, I'm happy just to be able to graduate and get an early start at West Point."

"Well, even as much as I'd like to see you as this year's valedictorian, I respect your willingness to step aside. It's yet another reason you've given me to admire you, young man," Mrs. Lattimore said.

"Likewise, I admire and appreciate you for being so humble and gracious in this matter. I wish all students shared those traits with you," Mr. Lynn concluded.

LATER THAT MONTH, Benjamin River walked across the stage and received his high school diploma along with the other 'real seniors' in the graduating class of 1985-86. Ben actually was quite content at not having to give any speech—in truth maybe even a tad relieved.

Phew, barely dodged that bullet, Ben thought while listening to Wendy wrap-up her speech to the graduating class.

WEST POINT, NEW YORK – JULY 1986

IT WAS RECEPTION DAY at West Point and Eisenhower Hall was packed full of prospective cadets and family members. The low hum of a thousand voices floated throughout the air, laced with the occasional waft of complimentary coffee and donuts. And underneath it all was the tinged smell of anxiety emanating from all of the young men and women who were waiting for their lives to be forever changed.

"I'm a little nervous, Gramps."

"I am too, Ben. Look around. I've never seen an entire auditorium full of jittery everyday folk. It's exciting and scary at the same time, isn't it? Even for an old bugger like me."

"Yeah, it feels like the first time I stood in line for the squirrel cages."

"Squirrel cages?"

"Never mind, Gramps." Ben took a deep breath and slowly exhaled. "I can do this."

"Well of course you can. Ben, you're going to be a great soldier and an even better leader. I know it. This here—all this hoopla—it's just one of the hills to climb to get there. Just remember, what you're about to experience these next six weeks is really a mental game. That's all. Yes, it's important and serious, but it's a game nonetheless. It may be a lot different than the basic training I went through when I was young soldier, but it still serves the same purpose. What they mean to do is to break you, along with all these other youngsters, down to your basics. And *that's* really why it's called basic training. And since you have the strongest fortitude of any person I've ever known, for you it will be a snap." Morgan snapped his fingers to punctuate the point.

"Thanks, Gramps. I'm really glad you're here to see me off."

"You kidding? I wouldn't miss it for the world!"

Ben had read everything he could get his hands on about life at West Point, including Reception Day. So, when an officer walked up to the stage's podium and welcomed everyone, Ben knew that the officer's speech would be quick and to the point. After attentively listening for just four minutes, Ben nodded as the officer wrapped-up and abruptly left the podium.

Yep, that was pretty quick.

A serious looking young man in white formal cadet uniform then approached the podium. He was a third-year "cow" cadet and began to talk about what to expect from the impending Cadet Basic Training (CBT), affectionately referred to by cadets as Beast Barracks. The cow finished his speech even faster than the officer had with words that Ben knew were coming, but words that still hit home for him just as it did every other new cadet in the room.

"You have ninety seconds to say your goodbyes."

Everyone in the hall stood and the buzzing in the room resumed as before, only louder. Ben turned to Morgan and hugged him, not wanting to let go. Morgan squeezed back hard and then released him to gently grab both of his shoulders.

"Now listen to me, Ben. You remember who you are and how far you've come. It's more than anyone else in this room has had to overcome. I have no doubt about that. You are strong. You are good. You are wise. And I'm proud of you. But most importantly, remember that this old geezer loves you, son."

Ben did all he could do to choke down his emotions and keep from crying. Morgan was having the same problem, but they both contained the tears and didn't allow their eyes to go any further than watering.

"I love you too, Gramps. I'm going to miss you. Please take care of yourself and don't forget to write."

"You don't worry about me. I'll be fine. I'll send you letters and visit every chance I get."

"You don't have to come up for visits, Gramps. I know it costs a lot. Letters and phone calls are fine."

"Never you mind cost or anything about me. You just focus on the training and studies. You hear?"

"Yes, sir."

Morgan held out his hand and Ben shook it firmly. Ben turned and made his way down to the exit where upperclassmen were herding all of the other first year "plebe" cadets. Morgan watched as Ben vanished through the doorway with a thousand other youngsters. He stood there for a moment and finally let one of his contained tears make its exit as well.

CAMP BUCKNER, NEW YORK – AUGUST 11, 1986

IT WAS PRE-DAWN and like the other eleven-hundred plebes, Ben was in full camouflage-fatigues with his rucksack loaded, strapped in place on his shoulder along with his M-16 rifle. He was standing in an area with his Company and waiting for their turn to lineup in tactical formation for the twelve-mile hike back to West Point. The hike was an annual USMA tradition that always marked the end of the basic training for that year's respective class of plebes.

One of the tactical officers, along with a fit-looking elderly man, walked up to Ben.

"Cadet River," the officer said.

"Yes, sir," Ben replied.

The officer turned to the elderly man and asked him, "Will that be all, sir?"

"Yes, Captain and thank you," the man replied.

The officer walked away and Ben took a closer look at the fit-looking senior, trying to recall if he'd met him before. It was dark and hard to see with the sparse perimeter lighting, but Ben was able to make out that the man was wearing beige shorts along with a beige polo shirt, and a likewise beige jungle hat. He'd seen a lot of other people wearing the same outfit and therefore knew that he was a former West Point graduate participating in the annual Marchback event.

"Ben, it's nice to finally meet you face-to-face."

The old graduate held out his hand and Ben shook it firmly.

"Thank you, sir. I apologize, but I'm afraid I don't know who you are, sir."

The man chuckled and said, "Of course not, I don't suppose you do. We spoke on the phone back in January when I interviewed you. I'm Dr. Reeves—I served with your grandpa in World War

Two."

"Oh! Yes, sir. It's likewise a pleasure to finally meet you, sir. And thank you for the recommendation, sir. I'm very grateful."

"Don't mention it, son. It was an easy recommendation given your scholastic credentials, not to mention you being Morgan's grandson. Glad to have had the opportunity."

"Thank you again, sir."

"Say, do you mind if I walk alongside you during the hike?"

"I'd be honored, sir."

"Fantastic. I'm a feeble old man, so you may have to carry me halfway, just to warn you."

"You don't look so feeble to me, sir. It may turn out to be the other way around."

"I doubt that very seriously, but humility is an admirable trait that it seems we both share. So tell me, how do you feel about having CBT all done and over with?"

"I feel good, sir. And I'm definitely ready to start the academics."

"Good. You know, this is the sixteenth Marchback I've participated in over the years. I really enjoy the chance to mingle with future Academy graduates, especially those I sponsored. Ah, I remember my CBT like it was yesterday, which is amazing because it was a millennium ago. I'm curious, Ben, what would you say the most challenging aspect of CBT was, for you personally that is?"

"That's a no-brainer, sir. The hardest part for me was having to learn to depend on the other cadets in my company."

"Is that so? Well now, that's a new one. I can honestly say I've never heard that response before. Care to elaborate?"

"Well, I suppose you could say I was always a lone wolf in high school, sir. I didn't play any team-sports like most of the cadets here, so the teamwork was a learning experience for me."

"So, the transition between garrison exercises and field movements didn't throw you for a loop? Or handling the weapons? Or the massive amounts of Knowledge you had to learn?"

"No, sir. Most things I had already researched and was prepared for. I guess I'm kind of a military-history nerd. I've been reading everything about the Army ever since Gramps started telling me war stories. And when I decided I wanted to go to West Point, I tried to learn as much as I could and even found some former graduates through my high school and spoke to them. Of course I had never handled military weapons before CBT, but that was totally cool."

"Totally cool, huh? I see. How about the physical training then? If you didn't play sports in high school, did all the running and hiking get to you?"

"No sir, I ran track in high school, so I guess you could say that is a team-sport, but I mainly competed in cross-country runs, so I was still pretty much on my own. I've been hiking and running since I was a little kid. Long hikes through woods have always been one of my favorite things to do."

"Well that settles it then, you are definitely carrying me. But seriously, I'm glad you learned to depend on your comrades."

"Me too, sir. I do realize how important it is and also how crucial it will be in the Army. My men will have to lean on me and I will have to lean on them."

"Yes, that is true. But it's also very important outside the military as well, Ben. If you want to be truly successful in life, you must lean on others around you. No way around it."

"I understand, sir. Thank you. Do you mind me asking you what the hardest part of CBT was for you?"

"Ah, it was definitely handling the weapons. I've never been much for violence."

"I understand, sir. Neither am I, but it was still fun. I guess I shouldn't take it so lightly."

"Well, I must say, Ben, I can definitely see how you are related to Morgan. He's a special breed and one I care about dearly, even though we don't get to speak to one another as much as I'd like. I can tell you have a lot of his qualities, and that's a very good thing. There should be more people like you and your grandpa in the world. I sincerely mean that."

"Thank you, sir. I definitely agree, but only with the part about my Gramps."

"There's that humbleness kicking in again. Don't ever stop that, but—do you mind if I give you a piece of advice that I've learned over the years?"

"Of course, sir."

"Self-deprecation is an admirable act, but do learn to keep it in check. While it does show humility, it can also be seen as a weakness. That's true especially when you have to lead. As a leader, you must always maintain a level of confidence in front of your men—always. That is a fact that I wish I had learned earlier in my military career, as short-lived as it was. But it's also a fact that I use in my business practices. People do not follow others who are uncertain. Do you understand what I'm saying, Ben?"

"Yes, sir. And that's very good advice, sir. Thank you, again."

"You're welcome. Now, let's get ready for the long journey—I see your company is beginning to gather for the march."

"I'm ready, sir!"

- 23 -

TEXAS SYNDICATE

NEW BOSTON, TEXAS – JANUARY 1987

JUST LIKE TWO YEARS AGO, a large black bus pulled through concertina-lined gates and parked. Only this time it was a transport from the Department of Corrections, and the destination was one of the most dangerous maximum security prisons in Texas. In total, thirteen jumpsuit-clad prisoners were escorted from the large vehicle to their new home at the Barry B. Telford Correctional Facility. Octavio was third in line and anyone who had known him prior to his incarceration would've never been able to pick him out of a lineup. His outward appearance wasn't even a shell of his former self, except for the brown tint of his skin. Octavio's handsome face had done a one-eighty, only not by choice. The choice was made for him by a junior member of the Aryan Brotherhood who decided to earn "creds" by taking a sharpened piece of steel and slicing Octavio's muy-guapo mug. Octavio's retaliation had been swift and thorough, beating the cabrón so bad that it was over a month before the Aryan pup was able to leave the infirmary.

The shiv Octavio had taken to the face, along with the subsequent beating he'd handed out to his assailant, had received attention from the Syndicato Tejano, otherwise known as the Texas Syndicate. From that point forward, like it or lump it, Octavio had been recruited into one of the most feared Mexican prison gangs in Texas. The Syndicate saw promise in young Octavio as an enforcer, so they made an investment in him by pumping him full of smuggled-in steroids. The maxi, short for maxibolin, served two purposes for the hardcore gang's "enforcer recruitment program." One, it helped the new recruit pump-up and get scary-looking strong, which was a proven intimidation tactic for the organization. Two, the steroid had a side effect of making a recruit as mean as a gunpowder-fed pit-bull. Respective to Octavio, the maxi had fully done its job by helping transform him into what was referred to as a "hard-guy", which translated to mean that he was someone you didn't want to tangle with. There was no doubt that Octavio had become walking proof that the Syndicate was getting a very good return on their investment in him.

As Octavio walked towards the prison entrance, he reached up with his shackled hands and smoothed out his thick-black Zappa facial hair that partially covered his five-inch battle scar. At over six feet three inches tall, Octavio towered above all of the other new prisoners in the line. His neck was thick as a tree stump, and his shoulders looked as if small bowling balls had been surgically implanted at his socket joints. His forearms were bulging versions of vascular plank and his chest permanently puffed out like a banty rooster. Surprisingly enough, Octavio had no visible tattoos. He had plenty of representation but it was all hidden on his upper arms and on his back. And he never let anyone touch him with ink on his face. He'd always say the same thing when a facial tat would be suggested.

"My face is perfect already, bitch. Hora-le."

Two guards escorted Octavio to his new grown-up digs. On the walk to the cell, Octavio had mused over the amazing power that the Syndicato had inside. Guards were rewarded in many ways for favors and conversely punished for refusals. The cell that Octavio now stood in had been one such favor. Once the door locked shut behind him, he stood there staring with devil eyes at the back of his new cellmate. The other man, standing at the end of the cell, straightened from leaning forward on the far wall and slowly turned around. Octavio smiled when the wide eyes of his old puta-madre of a cellmate from Gainesville finally recognized him. Octavio tilted his head slightly, sucked his teeth loudly, and growled familiar words just before issuing vengeance on the sodomizer, who as it turned out wasn't so tough anymore.

"Déjà vu, chingada."

- 24 -

SCORPIO

DEMARCUS AND SCOOTER nervously waited for the judges to give them the go-ahead. A large crowd, curious about the boys' exhibit, had gathered around their staging area. The crowd didn't help calm their nerves and the news cameras and reporters certainly didn't either. They nervously looked at each other with beads of sweat forming on their brows.

"Did you double-check the servo connection?" Demarcus asked.

"Yeah," Scooter replied. "Did you put the charged batteries into the controller?"

"Of course."

"There sure are a lot of people watching. And the news people are here."

"I know. It's crazy. I just want to get it over with."

"Me, too."

Mrs. Snow smiled at the boys and gave them the thumbs up sign. Demarcus and Scooter unconfidently smiled back and returned two thumbs up. Their exhibit was a large, roped-off area that was made to look like a typical teenager's messy bedroom. At one corner they had placed an old cot with a cardboard box on each side. Each box had been painted to look like a nightstand, complete with a small bedside lamp. Adjacent to the faux bed was a small folding-table and chair made to look like a study area with books, paper, pencils, and a reading lamp. Strewn on the floor, chair, and on the bed were socks, t-shirts, and jeans.

Sitting on the ground in between Demarcus and Scooter was a machine that they had built—affectionately referred to as Scorpio. It was a project that their physics teacher had insisted they enter into the school district's science fair. And since a good portion of their semester grade depended on going through with it, they had little choice in the matter. Without any expectations, Demarcus and Scooter had won top award at district with Scorpio. They enjoyed the first competition so much that they decided to advance to the regional fair where they again took top honors. Now, they were trying to keep their winning streak going at the big enchilada, more commonly known as the Texas State Science Fair.

Their project was a robotic scorpion made up of a Radio Flyer toy wagon retrofitted with a belt-driven rear axle, a battery powered motor, servos on the front axle to steer, and a robotic arm, aka the stinger, which replaced the wagon's handle. The stinger was terminated with two pinchers that could reach down to pick items up off of the floor. The stinger also curled backwards so that the items its pinchers picked up could be dropped into the wagon body. And finally, the body was lined with a clothes hamper bag that had pull strings on each end.

The project had been a partnered effort, which meant Demarcus designed everything and did most of the work while Scooter purchased the materials and read a lot of porno magazines.

When the judges finally gave them the go-ahead, Demarcus signaled to his mom to take her place. Demarcus and Scooter then sat on the floor with a Yahtzee cup filled with dice placed between them. On cue, Mrs. Snow pretended to walk into the makeshift bedroom and interrupt their game.

"Demarcus Gabriel, you need to clean up this room!" Mrs. Snow said.

"I will Mom," Demarcus replied.

"Now! And Scooter, you help too. I feed you enough, you should pitch in!"

"Yes ma'am," Scooter whined.

The crowd laughed at the little skit, which gave the boys a boost of confidence. Demarcus picked up the scorpion's hand-held controller, which was a modified version of the same kind used to navigate radio-controlled airplanes. He began pushing and pulling knobs and the scorpion came to life and started moving. It stopped in front of a dirty sock on the floor and its stinger reached down to pick up the piece of laundry and then placed it into the wagon's bed-liner. The audience laughed with a few people already clapping in approval. The scorpion continued to roam around the room, gathering all of the dirty clothes. Everything had worked without a hitch until the stinger got caught on the underside of the cot and actually lifted it up off of the ground. The crowd thought it was part of the show and just laughed along. Demarcus backed up the scorpion and picked up the remaining clothes from the bed. He then made the scorpion's stinger reach back, grab the bed-liner's pull strings, and lift them up while drawing the bag closed with all of the laundry tucked away inside. Finally, the wagon made its way to Mrs. Snow and the stinger swung around to hand her the bag. She took it from the robot and said, "Hmmmph."

People began cheering as Demarcus guided the wagon back to where they were still sitting. The stinger reached down and picked up the Yahtzee cup, shook it side to side, and then dumped out the dice. The result wasn't a Yahtzee, but from the cheers and applause of the crowd you would've never known the difference.

Later in the day, Demarcus was disappointed to find out that they only won runner-up. He was sulking as he broke-down the staging area and packed things up. Scooter's allergies towards labor had kicked in, as usual, and he was at the concessions area getting a snack, again as usual. While Demarcus was hard at work, a man approached him.

"Excuse me, son," the man said.

Demarcus turned to look at him and replied, "Yes, sir?"

"I was very impressed with your exhibit. My name is Professor Jakob Nielsen and I run the robotics department at M.I.T."

The man held out his hand and Demarcus firmly shook it.

"My name is Demarcus Snow. Pleased to meet you, sir. And just to let you know, I've always dreamed of going to M.I.T. someday."

"Well, I'm pleased to hear that, because it just so happens that I want to leave you my business card. I really hope you reach out to me when considering a university. I think you'd be able to make incredible contributions to my department. And by the way, that robot of yours is quite impressive."

"I call her Scorpio. And thank you, sir!"

"You're welcome, Demarcus. Don't forget to call me. I look forward to seeing you in a couple years."

"You can definitely count on it, sir!"

The professor walked away and left Demarcus there smiling ear-to-ear. His mom had watched the whole exchange and stood in the background with tears of pride running down her gaunt cheeks.

WEST POINT, NEW YORK – SEPTEMBER 1987

IN MAY, BEN OFFICIALLY GRADUATED from his first year at West Point and like all the other plebes, he was promoted to Private First Class in the United States Corp of Cadets and then finally released for a much needed, three-week leave. Morgan had purchased a round-trip airplane ticket so Ben could come home, and the resulting time that he was able to spend with his gramps was just what he needed to recharge his batteries and to get ready for his next training challenge. Immediately after his return to West Point, he had begun the Cadet Field Training (CFT), which was four weeks of combat-focused military drills that climaxed with three intense days of field exercises. He had completed the training and then resumed his academic studies, which he found challenging along with all of the other duties he had at The Point. He was definitely due for another break to help him recuperate and to keep him from getting burned out. As usual, his Gramps came to the rescue.

It was a beautiful Labor Day weekend and Morgan had flown up to spend it with Ben. They were taking advantage of the nice weather by having a picnic at a good spot they found at Round Pond, a large park not far from the campus.

"You sure you wouldn't rather go sit down and have a nice meal at a restaurant? My treat. We can chuck this fast food in the trash bin over there and go get you some real grub."

"I'm sure, Gramps. I get to sit down three times a day and eat in a big hall with four thousand other people, so believe me when I say that eating a cheeseburger with just you, me, and this peaceful landscape is nothing less than heaven to me."

"Well, since you put it that way, how could I argue? Has the food there gotten any better?"

"Eh, it averages out to okay. For the amount that they have to cook at one time, it's actually very impressive. But it gets old, let me tell you."

"I bet it does. I guess it's just part of the routine."

"Yes, sir. Routine and tradition. Lots and lots of tradition."

"So, how does it feel to not be a plebe anymore? And what do they call you now?"

"I'm now a yearling, which is much better but I'm still low man on the totem-pole. Next year when I become a cow is when the worm starts turning."

"Those names are something else. I don't know how you keep it all straight. Hey, it was good to hear that you enjoyed CBT and that you did so well."

"CFT, Gramps. CBT was the basic training I did when I first got here. CFT was the field training I took at the start of my second year back in July."

"See, I can't even keep those straight. I don't know how you do it."

"I'm sorry, Gramps. I didn't mean to correct you. I guess getting everything right is starting to take over for me. That's the Point, pun intended."

"Good pun and it's definitely okay. I can see the change in you, but it's not a bad one. Just different and one I understand that is necessary, son. So, let me try again. It was good to hear how well you did at CFT?"

"Yeah, I really enjoyed it, Gramps. Even the seven mile run back from Camp Buckner was fun to me, but there was so much to learn. I hope I can remember it all when I need to."

"I have no doubt that you will recall everything perfectly. I'm glad you enjoyed it. What was your favorite part?

"Definitely the field exercises, especially the recon training. It sucks that I didn't win a Recondo badge though. I placed okay in the exercises but not as well as those that won the badge, so I'm not complaining."

"Well, I'm proud of you. You were given that Superintendent Excellence award for being in the top 5% of your class, right? And what was the other?"

"Distinguished Cadet Award."

"Remind me again what that one was all about."

"It's given every year to cadets who maintain at least a 3.67 GPA. Mine was 3.69 and *not* perfect like I'm used to having."

"Well, I don't know how you manage to keep such a high average with all you have to do here. I'm lucky if I can remember to lock up the store at night."

"Or turn off that hot-plate."

"I remember to turn it off, smarty pants."

"How is everything at the shop, by the way?"

"Good. Business is a little slow, but it'll pick back up in a month or two. I'm enjoying the lull to tell you the truth. Speaking of peace and quiet, that damn doctor keeps pestering me about you."

"Dr. Reeves?"

"Yes, he's quite interested in your progress and how you're doing overall."

"Hmm. I think he's more interested in checking up on you."

"Nah, I don't think so."

"Well, he could just write or call *me* instead of calling *you*. He really cares about you, Gramps."

"Hogwash. He's the last person in the world I need worrying about me. Speaking of, I read an article the other day about a new service that the telephone company will be offering in the very near future. It will allow you to see who is calling you before you even answer. They call it Caller ID, and I'll be the first one in line to sign up for it so I can screen that fool's calls."

"Gramps, that's not very nice."

"When you get my age, you don't have to be nice. Especially to someone with history we have."

"Well, he's very kind to me and he seems like a good man. You should give him a break."

"Hmmmph. I'll probably die before that happens."

- 25 -

RED MAN

GILMER, TEXAS – AUGUST 1988

SCOOTER WAS BUSY working the register at his dad's Western Auto store, which meant he was really watching a re-run of the *Beverly Hillbillies* on the small TV that was sitting on a hidden shelf under the counter. His dad walked in through the front door and made a bee-line for Scooter, who in turn nonchalantly, but hastily, switched off the little television.

"Scott, I need to talk to you."

Oh great, now what did I do—or not do? "Sure, Dad. What is it?"

"It's about your idea, the Radio Shack franchise. I've been giving it a lot of thought and I ran some numbers by Ed and then by Joyce—you know them, my accountant and my bookkeeper. Well, it seems like it's actually a solid financial investment. I just got back from Radio Shack's corporate headquarters in Fort Worth and met with one of their executives. He admitted that they had been considering opening a store here and were happy that I approached them to learn about investing in a franchise."

"What! Really!"

"Yes, really. But this is a big deal, Scott. I want you to be Store Manager, but I'm worried that you're too young for the responsibility. Even though you have more knowledge about electronics than anyone I know, I'm not sure you're ready."

"Dad, I'm totally ready. I promise I will do a good job and not let you down."

"Scott, as manager you will have the bulk of the operational responsibility. That means you'll be the day-to-day boss. You think you can oversee people and treat them fairly but firmly?"

"Yes, for sure. And, I'll provide the best customer service."

"Okay, that's what I like to hear. It's not a done-deal, but it sounds like it will happen. We need to start finding a location around town. I'll expect you to play a big part in that."

"Of course, I want to!"

"And you will have to go to Fort Worth for corporate training. You okay with just being Assistant Manager for the first six months? They said they would lend us one of their experienced managers to get the store up and running and to make sure you are good to take over."

"I'm good with that. Totally."

"Alright. Well, I'll get the ball rolling then."

Scooter's dad held out his hand. Scooter shook it and then pulled his dad in for a hug.

"Thanks, Dad. This is awesome!"

"Don't thank me, yet. It's going to take a lot of hard work and long hours."

"Yes sir. I'm ready. Can't wait!"

Scooter reached over and picked up the store telephone.

"Who are you calling?"

"Demarcus, to tell him the great news."

"Right now? It can't wait?"

It was really his idea! "I guess it can, but he's my best friend, Dad."

"Okay, but make it snappy. Remember, we don't like employees to make personal calls on the business phones."

"Right-o, Dad. I'll make it super-fast. And thanks again."

"Alright. I've got to go run some more errands, so hold down the fort until closing time, okay?"

"Yes sir."

As soon as Scooter's dad walked away, Scooter continued dialing the number to Demarcus's dorm room at M.I.T.

"Come on, pick up. I've got to tell you, man. Pick up!"

M.I.T. CAMPUS – CAMBRIDGE, MASSACHUSETTS

DEMARCUS WAS MAKING-OUT with his new girlfriend on a new couch in his new dorm room when his new telephone rang. Instead of answering, he continued making his way down his girlfriend's neck with kisses. The phone rang again and she tapped him on his back.

"Uh, you going to answer that?" she asked.

"What? No, I am not."

"What if it's important?"

"*This* is important. Errr, I mean *you* are important."

"Yeah, too late to backpedal on that one. Answer the phone."

"Okay, okay. But we're picking this back up right where we left off."

"Maybe, if you're lucky."

"Did you just say I was going to get lucky?"

"Umm, no and come to think of it, I need to go anyway. I have a big test tomorrow and I should be studying."

"What? No! You can't just leave me here like this!"

"Watch me, Mr. *This*-Is-Important." She pushed Demarcus all the way off of her and picked up the telephone and answered for him.

"Hello?"

"Hi, this is Scooter. Is Demarcus there?"

"Yeah, he *is* here. Let me get him for you, Scooter."

She handed the phone to Demarcus before getting up and leaving.

"Argh! Scooter, what the hell is it? Do you know what you just—"

"My dad liked your idea! We're going to open a Radio Shack!"

"What? You're actually going to own a Radio Shack!"

"Well, my dad is, but I'm going to be Manager."

"Manager, whatever. That is awesome!"

"Yeah, thanks. And thanks for giving me the idea."

"It was purely selfish, man. Now I have a direct hookup for my electronic supplies so I can stock-up for free."

"Free? Umm, no. At-cost, maybe."

"I had to give it a shot, right? At-cost sounds good to me. I've got a lot of projects I want to get started on."

"Well, it's going to take a while to get it up and running, but not too long, I hope."

"I'm not going anywhere!"

"When are you coming back to town?"

"I'm not sure, man. I've got a lot going on with school and my girlfriend. It won't be for a while."

"Well, we need to go pop some tops when you do."

"Definitely, I'm down with that."

GILMER, TEXAS

WADE STRICKLAND WAS ENJOYING one of his favorite pastimes—that is other than raping and killing young girls. He slowly browsed the goods up and down every aisle in the local Walmart and had made steady progress up to mid-store where all species of home furnishings were on display. He picked up a crème-colored glass candle, removed its lid, and smelled the fragranced wax.

Mmmm. 'Nilla. They should come out with one in a Red Man scent. I'd buy me that one f'ur sure.

As Wade took in the aroma, two deputies slowly approached him, one from each end of the aisle, and another two more waited by the store's entrance. Wade saw them from the corner of his eyes and made an over-exaggerated grimace, put the candle back down on the shelf and spoke loudly.

"That there candle smells like pig shit!"

He turned around so he could face both of the deputies coming his way.

"Be damned. Guess it wasn't the candle after all."

Wade noticed that neither of them had their guns drawn, so he eased up on the itch to go for his blade and then smiled at them.

"What can I do ya f'ur, boys?"

"We need you to come with us down to the office, Strickland," one of the deputies said.

"Is 'atta fact? Ya mean the office down...stairs? What, does the manager of this here fine establishment wanna present me with some kind of shoppin' spree? I'd like that. It'd be nice. Real nice."

"Quit being a smart-ass and come with us."

"Am I under arrest?"

"Strickland, we can do this with or without handcuffs. Your choice."

"I'll take what's behind door number two. Lead the way, Albert."

"My name is Jonathan, asshole. But Deputy will do just fine."

"Okie-dokie, Deputy Einstein. Let's go then. Go on. Get to it."

WADE SAT ALONE WAITING in the interrogation room with his eyes closed and his body in peaceful meditation. Sitting on the table in front of him was a Styrofoam cup filled with black coffee, but Wade was smart enough not to touch it. The door opened and a middle-aged man wearing a Sears and Roebuck suit walked in, took a seat across from Wade, and placed a file folder on the table. Wade opened his eyes from his meditation and grinned at the man.

"Mornin'."

"Good morning. I'm Detective Kevin Bolton with the Little Rock Metro Police Department," the detective said.

He watched Wade's eyes and facial expression in order to read his reaction. *Nothing*, he thought.

Wade thought, *Little Rock?* and then said, "Pleasure. How can I help ya, Detective?"

The detective opened the folder, pulled out a photo and slid it over closer to Wade. Wade looked down at the photo of his old .38 Special and thought, *well now ain't that intrastin'*.

"Do you recognize this gun?"

"Well now, it looks like one I used to own. Just like it. Hard to know f'ur sure though."

"So the gun is no longer in your possession?"

"No sir, it is not."

"Mind telling me what you did with it?"

"Nah, I don't mind a'tall. It was stolen. Let's see here..."

Wade looked up at the ceiling and rubbed his chin in faux deep thought.

"Reckon it was about four years back."

"I see. And did you report it stolen?"

"Nah."

"May I ask why not?"

"S'pose I forgot. I got lots of guns. What'unt a big deal to me none."

"Well, suppose I told you that your gun was used to murder

someone. What would you say to that, Mr. Strickland? Would that be a big deal to you?"

"Feel free to call me Wade, and I'd have to say that I'm sorry to hear that, if that is what you're sayin'."

"It is what I'm sayin', Wade. You seem pretty calm for someone who just found out that his gun was used to kill another human being."

"Do ya think I've a reason to not be calm, Deee-tective?"

"Maybe. Where were you last Saturday night at around eleven PM?"

"Well let's see here..."

Once again, Wade performed his idiot thinking gesture before resuming.

"I believe I was at home watchin' me some TV."

"Was anyone with you who can corroborate that?"

Wade thought, *Yeah, but that girl had worn out long since then*, and said, "Nahwww, 'fraid not."

"What were you watching?"

"'Scuse me?"

"You said you were home watching TV. What were you watching?"

"Ohhh. It was a re-run of *M.A.S.H.* I 'member 'cause it was the one where hot lips is pranked in the shower by Hawkeye and B.J. That there is one fine lookin' woman."

"Then you won't mind if we take a look around your place?"

"S'pose that'd be fine," Wade said and then thought *everything's already been cleaned up nice and tidy*.

Deputy Einstein poked his head in the room and said, "Print results just came back and Strickland here ain't a match."

A mockingly big smile grew on Wade's face and a red anger came over the detective's.

"Get the fuck out of my interrogation room, you dumbass!" the detective said to the deputy. "All right Mr. Strickland, you're free to go."

"Yup. Curious though, where'd my gun get hocked?"

"Hocked? What makes you ask that, Strickland?"

"Just makes sense is all. Whoever stole it from me pro'lly needed some cash, not a gun."

The detective tried to get a better read on the complex man sitting in front of him. His gut told him something was definitely off with Wade—he just didn't know what. After a few moments, he decided to tell him anyway, because it *was his* gun after all.

"We traced it back to a Pawn Shop in Hope. It was reported stolen there four years ago. That's all I can tell you. And I'm afraid you won't be getting your gun back, state's evidence and all."

"'Course not. The fine state of Arkansas needs it more than I do. Hell, I wouldn't want it back now anyhow. Havin' a gun that someone else used to kill with just wouldn't set right with me. God's truth."

WADE TURNED ON HIS BIG SCREEN TV and popped the top off of a cold beer, took a big chug and then pressed the mute button on the remote control. He picked up his phone and dialed Jessup's number.

"Who the fuck is it?" Jessup answered.

"It's me. Got some good news f'ur ya. May even help that pissy mood sounds like y'ur in."

"I'm all ears."

"Just found Benny-Boy."

"You're shitting me?"

"Nope."

"Where?"

"Hope, Arkansas."

"Fucking Arkansas?"

"Yup."

"You know where in Hope?"

"Yup."

"When are we going?"

"My calendar is purdy open 'morrow, how about y'urs?"

"Tomorrow is perfect. That little fucker is going to pay for taking my car. And for everything else."

"Yup."

- 26 -

GREEDY FINGERS

HOPE, ARKANSAS – AUGUST 1988

WADE SLOWLY OPENED the front door to the pawnshop. Once it was cracked enough, Jessup reached up and grabbed hold of the small jingle bell attached to the top of the door and muffled it. Wade crouched and walked under Jessup and then Jessup stepped into the shop and closed the door before locking its dead-bolt. Wade flipped the small plastic open-sign over so that 'CLOSED' displayed outward. He reached up and tugged an old pull string hanging from a large red neon open-sign. The neon's electricity buzzed off, and then to the outside world the pawn shop was officially closed for business. But inside, there was still plenty of business yet to be taken care of.

Jessup and Wade walked up to the counter and then followed their noses to the backroom office. Morgan was fast asleep, snoring in his chair while his lunch simmered on the old hot-plate. Wade picked up a framed photograph and stared at Ben and Morgan together, locked at the shoulders and happily smiling. Jessup kicked Morgan's chair and almost made him tip over backwards. Morgan jolted up and by habit thought it was Ben waking him.

"I'm watching the soup, Ben! Jiminy Cricket!"

Morgan turned and saw Jessup staring down at him with a big, ugly smile. He then looked over at Wade still holding the picture frame in his hand.

"Who the hell are you two? If you've come to rob me, I don't have much in the cash register, but you're welcome to it if you have bad intentions."

"Bad intentions? Now *that* is a real possibility old man. Where's Ben?" Jessup said.

"Ben?" Morgan's eyes got wide. "I know who you are. You're Jessup. And I suspect your pal there is Wade."

"So, little Ben has told you about his long lost family, has he?"

"Oh he's told me plenty. I know the hell you put him through, and I know that you killed that poor g..."

Morgan tried to stop himself before making the mistake, but it was too late. He was still groggy from the deep sleep and made a lethal error in judgment because of it. Jessup looked over at Wade who returned the glance with a methodical nod.

"Go ahead and finish what you were going to say, old man."

"I was saying I know that you killed that poor boy's spirit and most of his childhood."

Jessup laughed and said, "I don't think that's what you were going to fucking say at all. What do you think, Wade?"

"I think we have us a preeeeee-dicament. Yup, that's what my noggin's a tellin' me."

"I think you hit the nail right on the fucking head, Wade. What do you think old man?"

"I think the police will be here any minute, so you two best leave. Now."

"Is that so? Well, I don't fucking believe you, but just to be safe, I guess we'd better make a quick job of it then."

Wade took out the bottle of chloroform from his hunting vest along with a rag and before Morgan realized it, Wade had his mouth covered with the death-sedative. In the meantime, Jessup grabbed a small can of paint thinner that he spotted on one of the backroom's shelves and sloshed the entire office with the strong-smelling flammable until the can caved empty in his hands.

Wade grabbed the photo of Ben and Morgan as he made his way back into the main shop area. Jessup started to follow him, but just before, he set fire to one of the wet walls. The both of them took their time walking to the front door and by the time they reached it they could already hear the hungry flames making progress. Wade yanked the string again, bringing the neon sign back to life and then he flipped the little plastic sign back over. Jessup unlocked the deadbolt, and they closed the door behind them just as the fire started to curl its greedy fingers through the back-office doorway into the main shop area.

They walked back to the Nova but before getting in Jessup shook his head and started bitching.

"Fuck! I really wish we'd found the Charger. Goddammit!"

"Yup, shame."

"Now, we just need to find that little fucker."

"Yup. Ya know we gotta kill'em now."

"Of fucking course. That was always the plan. That motherfucker-son-of-a-bitch has had it coming now for a long time."

A FEW DAYS LATER, dozens of people formally dressed in black were seated around Ben with Dr. Reeves sitting at his side. Ben was wearing his formal cadet uniform and was doing his best to keep his composure. Looking around at all of the mourners in attendance, Ben thought back on how he'd never realized how many people Gramps had known and just how admired he had been. More folks than Ben cared to count had come up to him and praised Morgan as having always been kind, funny, giving, hardworking, and numerous other accolades. Every condolence Ben heard reminded him of how much he loved the man, more than he'd loved anyone else in his entire life. And when Ben was finally left alone again with nothing but his thoughts, he pondered back to the last time he'd seen Gramps. It was on Labor Day weekend when Morgan had flown up and they'd gotten cheeseburgers and ate them in the park. Ben remembered how he'd prodded Gramps about that hot-plate. Ben had been joking, of course, but he couldn't help but think that the possibly of him saying that had somehow jinxed Gramps and caused the accident to happen. He thought that by just jokingly saying it in passing, that maybe he had unintentionally put it out there for the universe and that the universe had eventually responded.

Ben tried not to feel sorry for himself, but it was a hard battle to fight. Once again, he was alone and had nobody, although that wasn't entirely true. He had The Point and he had his squad. If there was one thing that the Academy had taught him, and there was tons of things, it was that there is no 'I' in 'TEAM'. He'd learned to lean on others just as they had him. It's how it worked. And now he was thankful to have The Point to lean on. Ben was also thankful for Dr. Reeves. As negative as Morgan sometimes talked about the man, the doctor was actually a very selfless human being. Ben imagined that he was just a scared young officer during the war, and he also imagined that there wasn't a day that didn't go by where the good doctor didn't regret that day when he ran off and left Smitty and Gramps like he did. Ben actually felt sorry for Dr. Reeves for having to live with that horrible memory.

Ben looked around the cemetery and thought how it had turned out to be a beautiful day and how Morgan would've really liked it. Then Ben tried to believe that Morgan was up in heaven right at that moment looking down upon him, standing right next to Smitty just like Ben was standing next to the doctor. Ben tried to imagine it. He really did. And he tried again, and again, but he just couldn't believe in God or Heaven. And that hurt more than anything.

JESSUP AND WADE KEPT THEIR DISTANCE from the crowd and watched the service from the Nova.

"Looks like Benny-Boy is trying to grow up to be a soldier,"

Jessup said. "Maybe he'll have a training accident and get his fucking head blown off. Do us a solid and all."

"Stranger things have happened," Wade said.

"Goddammit, it's too fuckin' crowded!"

"Yup. We just gonna have to deal with 'em later. Until Uncle Sam lets go of Ben's little nut-sack, there ain't much we can do. Too risky."

LATER AFTER THE SERVICE, Dr. Reeves and Ben sat across from an estate lawyer that Morgan had hired three years ago to handle his affairs. The man looked like the typical nondescript lawyer, with a nondescript suit, nondescript glasses, nondescript comb-over, and working from a nondescript office.

"Ben, first I'd like to extend my condolences," the lawyer said. "And to let you know if you should need help with any financial matters going forward, don't hesitate to reach out to my office."

Dr. Reeves looked at Ben and slightly rolled his eyes. Ben appreciated the comical gesture because it actually made him smile for once since hearing the news about Gramps.

The lawyer continued, "Mr. River had taken out a sizable life insurance policy—a term life policy—on which you are named as the sole beneficiary, Ben. In addition to the term life, he'd also added an accident policy. In total, the insurance payout will be 1.25 million dollars. In terms of the properties, he also left both the place of business and the home to you. Unfortunately, only the lot remains at the pawnshop because of the fire, so my advice would be to sell. Of course, it's all completely up to you."

The lawyer paused, looked at Ben, and then over at the doctor, and waited for a response.

"Thank you, sir," Ben finally said. "Will that be all?"

The lawyer had a confused look on his face and said, "Yes son, unless you have questions for me."

"No sir," and Ben stood up along with Dr. Reeves, "Thank you, sir. I appreciate your condolences and you helping with my Gramps's affairs."

Ben reached out to shake the lawyer's hand, the lawyer accepted the shake and said, "You're welcome, son."

- 27 -

SALUTE

WEST POINT, NEW YORK – DECEMBER 25, 1988

IT WAS WINTER LEAVE and West Point was a ghost-school. To Ben, it seemed that he was the only apparition that had stayed behind for the long break. For the third day, he was sulking alone in his room, sitting at his desk. He'd just finished writing a short poem that reflected his somber mood. He held up his prose and read the finished product to himself.

"Abjection"
by Benjamin W. River

This fog that persists to inhibit my mind
And to suppress my spirit it so diligently binds,
If it could be peeled away and discarded anew
To vanish this persistent woebegone-hue,
How might this world look to me then?
How might then would I look within?
Would the newborn clarity bring euphoria or pain?
Would the new possibilities present loss or gain?
Perhaps even new love would finally reveal,
Or more likely it would remain hopelessly still.

"Wow, if that's not depressing, I don't know what is."

Even more than being alone on Christmas. That poem turned out about as well as I think my finals did. I'm pretty sure I sucked big time on them, too.

Ben stood up, crumpled the piece of paper and threw it into a waste bin. He walked over to the window and looked down at the vacant courtyard below that usually had cadets scurrying around at that time of the morning. Outside it was gloomy, overcast and still. It all made for a miserable atmosphere, which was the last thing Ben needed during the first Christmas after Morgan's death.

At least there were a few cadets that stayed behind on Thanksgiving. It was also nice to have Dr. Reeves come down and have dinner with me the night before Turkey Day. He and his family should be in New Zealand right about now enjoying their winter vacation. Must be nice to have the warm weather and a—family. God, I really miss Gramps. That damned pea-soup. That goddamned hot-plate. I should've trashed it and bought him something safer. But I never actually thought…

Ben started weeping for the first time since Morgan's funeral. He'd buried the hurt and sadness deep inside and up to that point had been able to keep it all weighed down by focusing on studies and his fellow cadets. During the last few days, left with nothing but his thoughts, it had all begun to float to the surface and now it breached in the form of painful sobs. He finally cleared his eyes when something in the sky caught his attention. He got closer to the window's glass until he could feel the cold emanating from it. He looked up and saw a large skein of geese flying south. He watched the birds until they disappeared from sight.

Wish I was one of those geese, soaring high above it all and always having a family to count on.

"Enough, Ben. You need to get out of here. I need to—to be around a large group of people."

People, not geese—idiot. But where? The Big Apple, maybe. It's been on my visit-list since I got here. I've got money, so why not? I could even get a hotel and stay through the New Year. Times Square on New Year's Eve—now that should give me a few people to be around. Watch the ball drop live instead of on TV, for once. Yeah, that's what I'm doing.

NEW YORK CITY, NEW YORK

AN ATM MACHINE SPIT OUT a thin stack of crisp, new twenties that Ben took from the dispensary, peeled off two of the bills and stuffed the rest into his wallet. He secured the remaining forty dollars with a money-clip and put it into his shirt's front pocket. He then put his wallet into the front-right pocket of his jeans. It was an old trick that Morgan had taught him to do if he ever visited a big city. Supposedly, the advice would come in handy if he found himself being mugged. According to his Gramps, you just reach into your front shirt-pocket and hand the muggers the money-clip and then tell them that's all you carry on you. That way they get enough of a take to be satisfied, and you never have to replace your credit cards or identification. Ben hoped he'd never have to find out if it was good advice, but he figured it was better to be safe than sorry, especially in one of the largest cities in the world. Besides, Gramps had never steered him wrong before.

Ben climbed into the backseat of the taxicab that was waiting for him and said, "Thank you for finding my bank for me. I appreciate it."

"Naa problem, mi mon. Weh ah now, mi bredda?" asked the dread-locked cabbie.

"I'm not really sure. Do you know of a good, crowded place to go on Christmas?"

The man smiled wide and said, "I knwo jus di ends. Yu si back ahnjoy di ride, mi mon."

Ben wasn't sure what the cabbie said other than "enjoy" and "ride", but he put full trust in the happy-go-lucky man and hoped for the best. As long as there would be people, it didn't really matter. What mattered was that Ben had done exactly what he'd decided to do and had gotten away from West Point with nothing but the clothes on his back. He was determined to spend his winter break amidst other human beings and maybe even have some fun, by God.

Ben took in the sights and thought how the driver was one-hundred percent correct, because the ride into the city was absolutely amazing. Like everyone else in God's creation, Ben had seen a million shots of the Big Apple's skyline on TV, but he wasn't prepared for it in-person. He was dumbfounded at the number of tall buildings nested one after the other, too many to count he had thought. It was the most impressive sight he'd ever taken in.

The cabbie finally pulled the taxi over to the curb on 50th Street and stopped directly in front of Rockefeller Center.

"Welcome ah di Rock. Irie-on Christmas. You good wit this, bredda?" the cabbie said.

"Wow!"

"I take tha as yah-mon."

Ben paid the cabbie, allowing him to keep the change with an additional twenty-dollar tip added. In return, Ben got one last warm smile from the man along with a "Tenk yu, mi bredda and a Merry Christmas ah yu now." Ben climbed out of the car, closed the door, and stood in awe at the skyscrapers surrounding him. He watched the dozens of people ice skating and then stared at the huge Christmas tree in the plaza. He couldn't get the exclamation "Wow!" out of his head.

He explored all of Rockefeller Center until he was satisfied that he'd seen it all. He then went into a souvenir shop where he browsed postcards on a small carousel. He turned the display until his heart told him to pick one with the Statue of Liberty on it. He bought the postcard along with a pen and a book of stamps. He stopped and sat on a bench in the plaza and wrote out a message to his mom, letting her know he was healthy and happy and that he hoped she hadn't worried about him too much. He apologized for not writing sooner and explained that it hadn't been safe to. He closed by saying that he loved her, signed the card, and then placed a stamp on it without including a return address.

He started walking again and eventually made his way to 5th Ave where he found a mailbox. After mailing the card, he walked along the storefront-lined street, pausing at every opportunity to study landmarks of various subjects and sizes.

The first attraction that made him come to a complete halt was the New York Public Library. West Point certainly had bragging rights with its own library, which was full of history and tradition, but the library Ben now stood in front of was a whole different animal. *Literally different animal*, Ben thought as he stood in front of the massively-sculpted stone lion that, along with a sibling on the left-side, stood guard to the library's outermost entrance. He looked beyond the lion to a statue of a balding, bearded man sitting high on a pedestal with his left hand held out in a philosophical gesture. From where Ben stood, he thought the man looked like Socrates and wondered if it was the sculptor's intent. He looked above the man and read large words chiseled into the stone:

'BUT ABOVE ALL THINGS TRUTH BEARETH AWAY THE VICTORY'

The words likewise chiseled their way into Ben's mind as he thought on them for several moments until he finally came away with his own take on the phrase.

Truth. Justice. Victory. Someday.

Ben counted the twenty stone-steps leading up to the Renaissance-marbled architecture and noticed a small scattering of people sitting; some ate food while others socialized. He smiled, thinking how wonderful New York City was and how even on Christmas, he'd already seen more people in a few city blocks than he had in the last few days since school let out.

He continued past numerous businesses and noticed a young couple holding each other tight, browsing a window display of an expensive-looking jewelry store. Seeing the happy pair made Ben wonder if he'd ever meet someone and fall in love. He tried to imagine his goals of a career in the military along with a family, and it was hard for him to reconcile. He didn't want a family of his own unless he could be there for them at every needed moment. He couldn't picture the military being conducive to that personal requirement, especially as a combat leader in the Ranger Regiment. He'd had no father growing up and he'd decided a long time ago that he'd never put his own children in that situation. So, he resolved to the possibility, even likelihood, that he may never have a family of his own.

Ben kept walking amidst a modest count of pedestrians and wondered how busy the street was on a normal day. Up ahead he noticed people coming in and out of a building. Curiosity caused him to look up at the tall structure, and an instant recognition of the historic landmark brought a child-like smile to his face. Wasting no time, he pushed through the revolving glass-door marked as the observatory entrance and made his way into the lobby of the Empire State Building. He purchased his ticket and rode an elevator up eighty-six floors until the doors dinged open to the gusty main deck. When Ben finally stepped outside onto the platform, he discovered two things. One, he loved heights and had no fear of them, and two, he couldn't wait to jump.

Ben looked out over the city, beyond the Hudson and into New

Jersey and wondered how many miles he could see. He had to admit the view he was taking in beat the cab ride hands-down. And he was now sure that in order to count all of the buildings in the city you'd have to be a madman with an awful lot of time on your hands. He walked around the perimeter of the observation deck and got a sense of the entire city and its surrounding areas. He stopped at one section and began thinking about the history of the building and how crazy it must have been to build. Then his mind wondered to the old black-and-white *King Kong* movie that he and Gramps had watched together. He imagined the gigantic gorilla's face staring at him as it hung onto the outside of the skyscraper. He then imagined the airplanes flying around and the resulting pestered look on the misunderstood monster's face.

I'm sorry Kong, they know not what they do, buddy.

Ben's imagination switched to seeing himself jump off of the building, falling so fast that the wind contorted his face to look funny and made the ground below get bigger and bigger and bigger. And then at the last second Ben imagined himself swooping horizontally and thrusting back up into the air, navigating between all of the buildings at dizzying speeds, just like Superman.

You can have Metropolis, Superman. If I could fly, I'd definitely live here.

Ben pressed his legs tight against the low stone-wall and grabbed the metal safety barrier with his hands. He poked his head through one of the barrier's crisscross openings and looked straight down at the street below and thought how the cars and people looked like toys. He pulled his head back in and looked up at the ten-foot high spiked fence and thought for sure that he could easily scale it, even with the curved blades at the top. He wondered if anyone had ever tried and then pictured himself doing it until a voice from behind startled him.

"Hey kid, don't even think about it," a security guard said.

Ben turned to look at the guard dressed in a cop-like black uniform. The man was tall with an intimidating stature that reminded him of Gabe Snow, more so because of the man's build than anything else.

"Sir?" Ben replied.

"You look like you're about to climb that fence."

"I was just thinking about it, sir."

Ben couldn't have given a more ignorantly-laced innocent reply, even if he had consciously tried. The guard made an "I knew it" face and sternly gestured Ben over to him.

"Where are you from, kid?"

"Arkansas, sir."

"Now that doesn't surprise me."

"Sir?"

"Are you here alone or with your family?"

"I'm alone. No family, sir."

Ben's countenance turned puppy-doggish as he heard how pathetic the words coming from his own mouth sounded.

"No family, huh? And on Christmas day you just decided to take an elevator to the tallest lookout in the city, did you? And all by yourself?"

"Yes, sir. I guesso."

"And all the way from Arkansas?"

"No, sir. From West Point."

"I see. You're a cadet. I figured the haircut was an Arkansas thing, but now I get it."

"Sir?"

"Let me see if I've got it straight. You're alone on Christmas, with no family, in the military academy, things aren't going so well, and you just decide to do what? End it all by jumping?"

"Sir? What? No!"

"You said so yourself. Admitted it already. You were thinking about jumping."

"No, sir. I was imagining that I could climb that fence if I wanted to. I imagine stupid things like that all the time, but I don't want to. That would be crazy."

"The city is full of crazy people. Welcome to New York. So, you're telling me you're not depressed and don't want to kill yourself then?"

"Well, depressed maybe, sir. But no, I don't want to kill myself. Although I'd be a liar if I said the thought had never crossed my mind before."

"Is that so? Tough life, huh?"

"At times, but I'm not complaining. Just stating a fact, sir."

"Doesn't sound like complaining at all."

"Good. I'm glad, sir."

"Sounds more like you're having a pity-party to me."

"It does? No, I don't mean to—"

"What's your name?"

"Cadet First Sergeant River, sir."

"Kid, do I look like I'm in the military?"

"You are in uniform, sir. So, sort of, sir."

"First name. What's your first name, kid? Jesus H Christ."

"Benjamin. Ben for short."

"I can see you're a real pain in the ass, Ben."

"Sir? I don't try to be. I'm sorry. I just—"

"My name is Gus. Gus for short."

Ben reached to shake and Gus squeezed his hand firmly and kept talking without letting go.

"My shift was supposed to end five minutes ago. I'm running late, but I'd like to invite you to a Christmas dinner. That is, if you don't have any other plans, like going to another city landmark to feel sorry for yourself."

"Sir, I don't feel sorry—"

Gus squeezed Ben's hand harder causing a pain to shoot up his knuckles.

"Yes or no, Ben?"

"Yes, sir."

"Good. Keep up. I walk fast."

AFTER FIFTEEN MINUTES of keeping pace with Gus, Ben wondered if the man was a former speed-walking Olympian. Gus's natural stride was much wider than Ben's and at the pace they walked, it was even more exaggerated. Ben almost had to invoke a light jog to keep up, but keep up he did. The security guard never said a word to Ben as they traveled.

So much for small talk, Ben thought.

Gus finally turned to climb up the stairs to a building that looked like a thousand others in the city, with red brick and a stone façade entrance. Ben followed him inside and immediately noticed a large line of people of all walks of life from young to old and from black to white and every size and shade between. Their attire was also eclectic but the common theme seemed to be tattered-and-unmatched vogue. It only took a few moments for Ben to realize that Gus had brought him to a homeless shelter. He'd never been to one before but it didn't exactly take a genius to figure it out. Ben also realized that Gus was quite the celebrity there.

"Gus! My man!" said one elderly man.

"Merry Christmas, Lamar," Gus replied.

"Who's that sun-deprived little brother with you?"

"This is Cadet First Sergeant River of the USMA."

The elderly homeless man snapped to attention and saluted Ben. It was obvious he had legitimately saluted many times in his past life. Usually, only former military could do that out of the blue with a proper form that took plebe cadets days to learn. Ben returned the salute, half out of natural respect and half out of habit, because now as a non-commissioned officer at The Point, he was saluted by underclassmen every day and had grown accustomed to it.

Ben looked at the disheveled old man and began to wonder what his story was until he felt Gus's tug on his arm.

"Follow me," Gus said.

Ben followed him through a swinging door and into a large kitchen. He grabbed an apron from a hook on the wall and handed it to Ben.

"Put this on."

Gus grabbed another apron and wrapped it around himself as Ben tied his. Without saying another word, Gus used two rags to pick up a hot stainless pan of cornbread dressing and carried it out through the same door they entered from. Ben stood there looking at numerous other pans, each full of steaming-hot food. He didn't want to be scolded by Gus so he did what he thought he was supposed to by picking up a tub of mashed potatoes and then following Gus's steps. Gus set the dressing down behind a large serving station and Ben sat the potatoes close by. He waited for either scolding or praise, but got neither, not even an acknowledgement. Gus quickly went back to the kitchen and once again Ben followed. After five more trips, they had all of the food moved. They then began serving the two-hundred-some-odd people who had been waiting patiently in line.

"What happens when I run out of food?" Ben asked.

"You do the best you can and apologize," Gus replied.

They eventually did run out of food, but everyone in line got served, with many of the patrons coming back for seconds. Ben found it amazing how a simple, hot meal made such a difference in the people's lives. But then he remembered the breakfast that Mrs. Snow had cooked for the Black Machetes and his own reaction. The memory made him realize that the effect the meal had on the people wasn't amazing like he'd first thought. Anyone who'd gone hungry and then had a meal would know so. Ben remembered going hungry when he was a young child. No, what he was privileged to participate in that evening wasn't amazing at all. It was better than amazing. It was special—very, very special.

AFTER DINNER, Ben discovered that next to the kitchen was a large gym where homeless people were given shelter for the holidays. It seemed the city had surprises for him at every turn, because yet again the sight of the basketball court filled with rows and rows of cots was something he'd never expected to see. It stirred very conflicting emotions in his heart. On one hand he was happy that the people had a warm, safe place to stay. On the other hand, he felt sad that they normally had no home to lay their head at night. That's when it finally hit him how Gus was really right about everything he'd seen in Ben's behavior. Ben had indeed felt sorry for himself and Ben now realized he had no real reason to. With Gus's help, he'd come to understand that he was so blessed compared to most. He started feeling very guilty for the selfish mood he'd been in since winter break. The realization was sobering but at the same time rewarding, because it taught him that helping others to feel good also helped make him feel good inside—and that was something that Ben had always needed help with and always would.

Ben never did get around to visiting Times Square for New Year's Eve. Instead, he spent his remaining time in the city, volunteering to help the homeless. Before leaving, he was able to thank Gus for bringing him to the shelter and for the slap of much-needed reality. While doing so, Ben may have let one or two tears escape, and in return, Gus finally acknowledged him with a strong bear hug and a heartfelt wish of Peace and Joy.

- 28 -

SPIT

NEW BOSTON, TEXAS – APRIL 1989

OCTAVIO FOLLOWED THE CAPTAIN of the guards through the secure back hallway to the warden's office with two correctional officers in tow. The Captain motioned to a side wall where a steel bench was positioned. Octavio looked around the office that he'd just been led into for the first time since being incarcerated at Telford. There were dozens of books on shelves, an oak desk, a decent view of the free world outside a reinforced window, and finally two flags held up with cherry-stained poles—one representing the State of Texas and the other the good ole US-of-A.

Octavio immediately noticed the one extremely out-of-place living creature in the office: a middle-aged white woman sitting in one of the two guest chairs in front of the warden's desk. Also sitting next to her, was a white man in his late fifties, and of course sitting behind the desk was the square-jawed warden. Octavio had the previous honor of making his acquaintances on a few occasions, only in much less comfortable surroundings.

The guards marched Octavio over to the bench and 'helped' him sit. Then they shackled him to the bench by both his feet and his hands.

"Is that really necessary?" the woman sternly questioned.

She'd been watching Octavio the second he walked in and had never taken her eyes off of him.

"Yes ma'am, it is policy," the Warden replied before nodding at the guards. "You men can leave now."

The correctional officers left but the Captain remained and took a seat not far from Octavio. The man and woman both turned their chairs around to face Octavio, and he stared back at all three of them with piqued curiosity. It wasn't his birthday, so he wondered what the fuck he'd done that had deserved the audience he now had before him.

There's so many possibilities to choose from. Hora-le.

The man sitting across from the warden spoke up and introduced himself as the Attorney General for the State of Texas. He then introduced the woman as counsel for The Innocence Project. Octavio responded not with words, but with an expression and body language that said, "*So, and?*"

On cue, the lady spoke up and said, "Mr. Muñoz, you're here— we're here because there's a new form of forensic science that allows more accurate analysis of police evidence. Specifically, it's called DNA testing. It allows the DNA evidence gathered from a crime scene to be compared with DNA samples taken from suspects. I work for a non-profit organization whose mission it is to use this new science and right the wrongs that have been committed in the judicial system. Your case is a prime example."

The woman's words made the Attorney General nervously squirm and caused adrenaline to rush to Octavio's heart. Octavio was smart enough to understand where she was going, even though he didn't exactly understand the technical details. But he wanted clarity and although he was only twenty years old, the prison system had long since transformed him into a to-the-point kind of man.

"What are you saying exactly?" he asked.

"I'm saying that I—we know that you did *not* kill Raina Snow."

The declaration now ringing through Octavio's ears caused the tough gang member to revert back to the innocent teenager of years ago as he lowered his head into his lap and began weeping.

Octavio's DNA was of course found on *his* machete, but so was another sequence. And that other DNA sequence just so happened to perfectly match one of the two DNA semen samples taken from Raina's tattered clothes. And to everyone else's (but Octavio's) surprise, the other DNA semen sample taken was a negative match to his DNA.

As ironic as it was, Jessup's final gesture to Raina Snow turned out to be the corroborating evidence that proved Octavio's innocence. The mouthful of vile-spit that Jessup had projected onto Raina just so happened to land on the handle of the machete, and in doing so was the key that set Octavio free.

GILMER, TEXAS

ONCE AGAIN JESSUP AND WADE SAT in Wade's living room and watched the news on TV, but this time there was no celebrating; however, there was plenty of drinking again, just not the good stuff. They listened as the breaking news story detailed the wrongful conviction of the infamous Octavio Muñoz. Octavio was shown on the news hugging his mom and dad, who had driven up from Mexico's side of Laredo to once again be with their only son and maybe even to once again chase that great American dream.

"Motherfucker! Goddammit motherfucker!" Jessup yelled.

"We got to kill 'em," Wade said calmly and evenly.

"What? Who?"

"All of 'em. Includin' that fuckin' Mexican. They'll eventually talk and tell the p'lice we whipped 'em at the gully that day. And that's all it'll take."

"Fuck!"

MT. PLEASANT, TEXAS

OCTAVIO SAT ON THE END of a cheap bed in an even cheaper motel room. Two other men were standing in front of him, both covered in tattoos and both fellow members of the Syndicate. They were from a special branch of the gang that operated outside the prison walls, primarily for a ruthless drug cartel that hailed south of the border.

"Three days from now between siete y media de la tarde y midnight. That's Wednesday night, esé. Make sure she's dead. And by that, I mean make sure you unload the clip. Comprende, vato?" one of the men said.

The other man dry-spat on a photograph of a teenage Mexican girl and threw it down on the room's small desk. He took a Beretta 9MM from his leather jacket's breast pocket and placed it on top of the glossy portrait. The first man tossed a small fold of money down next to the gun, nodded to his partner and then they both left the motel room without uttering another word.

Octavio grabbed a bottle of Tequila that was sitting on the floor and chugged it. He walked over to the desk, picked up the handgun and slid it down the back of his pants. He flipped over the photograph and read the poorly written El Paso address on the back. He slid the print off of the desk and held it in front of his face. He stared at the pretty chiquita smiling in the photo and wondered what she'd done to bring the wrath of the Syndicato down on her poor head. He'd wanted to know, only one didn't ask "why" when given an order by the Syndicate—one just carried the orders out, or else.

He folded the photo, stuffed it along with the cash into his front pocket, grabbed the desk with his powerful hand and then squeezed hard before slinging it across the room with such force that the only thing in the room brave enough to stop it was the ill-decorated, adjacent wall.

"Fuck!" Octavio growled and then stormed out of the motel

room, violently slamming the door behind him.

EL PASO, TEXAS

IT ONLY TOOK TWO DAYS of watching and following the young girl for Octavio to know how and when he was going to *maybe* kill her. He sat in a car in the dark watching her apartment and began thinking hard on the killing part. In his relatively short tenure of incarceration, he'd killed three people inside on behalf of the Syndicato Tejano and had hurt many more. But all of them had been bad men and certainly none of them had been women. He wasn't sure what the girl had done, but as he looked at her smile in the photo, he knew that she wasn't even close to being in the same league as the others he'd harmed in the past. He was genuinely loyal to the Syndicate for having protected him the last four years, but the current situation was making him wonder just how deep that loyalty would run.

I don't like this. I don't like this at all.

He had no choice though. It was him or her and if there was one thing that Octavio had learned in the past four years, it was to survive at all costs. He began justifying it by convincing himself that she must be a bad person, maybe even a former drug-dealing gang-member gone-bad or worse.

Fuck! he thought, finally settling on actually going through with it.

A pedestrian passed by his car and he glanced up to inspect. It was her—right on time walking home from work. He gave her a good lead before getting out of the car to follow. He closed the gap as soon as she approached her first-floor apartment's entrance. Once she unlocked the door and began to open it, he rushed her, pushing her inside and closing the door behind. He held his hand over her mouth and used his other hand to pull the gun out from his jeans. He then waved it in front of her face so she could clearly see it. He slowly released his hand from her mouth, ready to muffle her if she screamed. She didn't scream, instead she turned around with tears flowing from her face and looked Octavio square in his eyes.

Octavio made a "keep quiet" gesture with his finger on his lips and motioned with the gun for her to sit down on a loveseat in the living room. She followed his silent instructions and he sat on the adjacent sofa. He looked at her as she cried and felt a pang in his stomach. He knew his own fear was welling up inside and part of it was due to the way she was staring at him.

"You know why I'm here?"

"Yes."

"Tell me."

"To kill me."

"That's all you have to say?"

"What else is there *to* say? Please don't kill me? I promise to stop? I won't go through with it? What do you want to hear?"

"Promise to stop what? Go through with what?"

"It doesn't matter now does it? You're a thug like the gang you belong to, so just get it over with. But make no mistake—you will burn in Hell for it."

"Hora-le," Octavio said as he let her words sink in. "Tell me what you did. I want to know. Why does the Syndicato want you dead?"

"Why? So you can feel better about pulling the trigger?"

"No, so I can feel better about *not* pulling the trigger."

"So you're not going to kill me?"

"Sí, I'm serious, y no, I'm not."

She studied him until she was sure he was sincere.

"They want me dead because I'm testifying against two of your fellow gang members. I witnessed them murder a friend of mine."

"Hora-le. Why aren't you in protective custody then?"

"I was for two months, but then the trial got delayed because of defense motions. I refused to spend the next six months being drooled over by a detail of guards twenty-four hours a day, so they put me up in this apartment. The cops are supposed to be watching me around the clock, but I suppose the Syndicate took care of that didn't they?"

"Fuck!" Octavio growled as he gritted his teeth.

"Please watch your language."

"Oh my apologies, chica—I'm sure if you spent the last four years of your life in prison, your manners would be so much better."

"Prison? Yeah, I thought I recognized you. You're Octavio Muñoz, aren't you? We never met, but I'm from Lone Star and your dad used to work with my dad at the steel mill. I remember my parents talking about you at the dinner table during your trial. You were in their prayers every day from the day you got arrested. And why in the world would you come here to kill me if you're innocent? Unless. So you really did kill that girl!"

"No! I had nothing to do with that. I'm in debt to the Syndicato, that's what I'm doing here. Fuck!" Octavio made a pleading motion with his hands and said, "Sorry for the language."

"It's okay. I suppose you're right—I'd probably curse, too if I were you."

"So your pop actually worked with my pop for reals?"

"Yes."

"Hora-le. Cómo te llamas?"

"Gloria. Gloria Morales"

"Morales. Yeah, I think I remember my pop talking about a Morales. Your pop's name was Roberto, no?"

"Robert, yes."

"Talk about coincidence."

"Or maybe not."

"¿Qué quieres decir? (What do you mean?)"

"What if they want you back in prison? This would be a good way for them to get you back, don't you think? I mean if they really wanted to."

"I never thought about it, but si, they would like that—I'm sure of it. Hora-le."

Octavio put down the gun on a sofa cushion and once again buried his hands in his face. He finally looked up at Gloria and their eyes locked again.

"Do you want to live, Gloria?"

"Yes, of course I do."

"Me too, but they're gonna kill us both now for sure."

"Then why don't you just testify, too?"

"Pfffh. Pigs. And I'm no rat. Wouldn't matter anyways. They'll get us, eventually. They don't forget."

"Then what do we do?"

"We've got to run, chica. Somewhere they can't find us. And there's only one man I know of who can help us do that."

"Who?"

"Tío Sam. Hora-le."

- 29 -

POPPING TOPS

GILMER, TEXAS – MAY 1989

SCOOTER WAS DRIVING his dad's old red Ford pickup as Demarcus rode shotgun. Riding in the middle of the two was a Styrofoam cooler filled with half-melted ice and aluminum cans full of beer. Demarcus and Scooter didn't get together much anymore, but once in a blue moon they'd hijack some Colorado Kool-Aid and hit the red-dirt back roads. The old thoroughfares snaked for miles through the heavily wooded countryside and were the perfect drinking routes. Put her in gear, let her coast at idle, and start popping tops. Plenty good folk of East Texas had their drinking roads, and this one had always been Scooter's dad's favorite. On many occasions, the Black Machetes had come along with him on his drinking runs. Only they would sit on the tailgate of the old truck as he sipped and drove slowly. From time to time, they would jump off and run to catch back up, grab the tailgate, and let the truck force their cycling legs to pump. They, meaning everyone but Scooter, because he was allergic to exercise and damn sure didn't see any fun in it.

"Is it the good stuff or the cheap crap this time?" Demarcus asked.

"The old store did good last week, so my dad sprung for the good stuff."

Demarcus took the top off the cooler and grabbed a cold one.

"Awesome. That stale crap last time gave me the worst headache."

Demarcus popped the top on the can and handed it to Scooter. He opened another and took a good drink of the ice cold beer.

"Ahhh. Hits the spot on a hot day like today," Demarcus said.

"No doubt. So your freshman year at M.I.T. went good, huh?"

"Yeah, it was totally awesome, but really, really hard. Everyone's so damn smart. I had to study constantly to keep up, but I learned a lot and it's only the first year. Not to mention the projects we're working on are totally cool. Yeah, things are good. How about you? The Radio Shack still raking in the big bucks?"

"I wouldn't say big bucks, but yeah we're doing pretty good. I'm finally running it by myself now. I've got six employees total. Two of them are real dumb-asses, but the others are okay."

"That's cool. You'll probably own a whole chain of stores by the time you're thirty."

"I doubt that."

"You never know, man."

"Maybe. Change of subject. Do you ever wonder what Ben would be doing now if...?"

"Yeah. And I've been wondering what Octavio is going to do now, too. I haven't had a chance to talk to him since he got out. Have you?"

"No. I can't believe he hasn't come see me yet."

"Yeah. Well I guess we can't blame him. I wanted to kill him for the last four years. Dreamed about it every day. I'd really like to see him, mainly so I can apologize."

"Dude, did you see how scary he looked on TV?"

"Yeah, I did. By the looks of him, he may never re-adjust. I wonder what all happened to him."

"Besides bending over to pick up the soap?"

"He didn't look like the bending over type to me. I just hope *he* didn't rape anyone."

"Orda-lay."

"Yeah, orda-lay is right."

Scooter noticed a car in his rear view. Demarcus saw the same in his side mirror.

"Just let whoever it is pass," Demarcus said.

Scooter tapped on the brakes once and steered the truck over as far as he could without going into the deep ditch. He stuck his arm out of the window and waved for the car to go on.

"LOOKS LIKE WE just hit the lottery, at least a good chunk of it,"

Jessup said.

"Yup," Wade agreed.

Jessup was driving the old Nova and Wade was sitting shotgun. Sitting between them was an actual shotgun, the sawed-off variety. Jessup pulled alongside the old red pickup and when he got just ahead of them, he slowly turned the wheel to the right. Just as he knew Piggy would, Scooter got scared and jerked his wheel to the right and crashed the truck right into the deep ditch.

"Dumbass," Jessup said.

Wade grabbed the shotgun and got out of the car. Before Jessup could even make it over, Wade had already managed to line both of the boys up against a rickety, rusted-barbed-wire fence.

"Turn y'ur asses 'round and face that there fence," Wade ordered.

Demarcus and Scooter turned around as they were told, and just like on the day Octavio was arrested, Scooter proceeded to piss his pants.

"We didn't do anything," Scooter said with a trembling voice.

"It was them," Demarcus said with a hard edge to his voice.

"Them who?" Scooter asked.

"You motherfuckers killed my sister."

Demarcus started choking down tears until his boiling blood blocked the saline streaks.

"You just now figured that out, fuck-face?" Jessup said just before slamming a shovel into the back of Demarcus's head.

The blow damned near flipped Demarcus over the barbed-wire fence head-first. Scooter looked down at his friend who was eerily bouncing up and down and swaying front-to-back on the slack wire. Scooter noticed the thick blood oozing from Demarcus's head and he started to run away, but Jessup was cocked and ready for his second swing. The shovel connected against Scooter's face and knocked him backwards off of his feet. His glasses went flying through the air and landed in a patch of young, red blackberries.

Wade walked over and picked up the spectacles and said, "No loose ends this time."

IT WAS OVER AN EIGHTY MILE round-trip ride to and fro Lake Bob Sandlin. Jessup and Wade had managed to murder half of the Black Machetes, drive to the lake, dispose of the bodies, and then drive all the way back home in just over two and a half hours. They both agreed that they had made pretty damned good timing, all things considered.

"Now we just need to find that fucking Mexican," Jessup said.

"I been watchin' that motel room where he was a stayin'. He ain't been there for the last week," Wade said.

"Maybe the motherfucker high-tailed it back to Mexico."

"Could be."

- 30 -

FLY

WEST POINT, NEW YORK – NOVEMBER 1989

SIMILAR TO BEN'S VERY FIRST USMA experience four years ago during Reception Day, Eisenhower Hall's seats were filled again, only this time there were no family members present, just anxiously hopeful fourth-year firsties who were waiting to learn which branch of the Army they would be assigned to after graduation. The branch would in turn determine their post, which was decided on another ceremonious night later in the school year. But Branch Night came first, and for every firstie in the room that evening, it would reveal the already-decided career path that each would have as a commissioned officer in the U.S. Army.

One of the tactical officers handed Ben an envelope with his name on it, but like everyone else, Ben wouldn't be allowed to open it until the Commandant spoke first and then gave the order. Ben looked around as other firsties held their envelopes up to the light, trying to sneak a peak of the branch insignia on the paper within. Ben thought about the simple little piece of paper inside and the importance that it represented. The dreams that he'd worked so hard for the last six years all pivoted on being assigned to Infantry. There was some comfort in knowing that he was in the top one-hundred of his class and that he'd excelled in many areas over the last four years, not to mention he was a company commander. But Ben knew that when it came to the Army, nothing was a given, so he worried about it to the point of a sweat, just like every other cadet in the auditorium. He nervously began fidgeting with his new USMA class ring, spinning it around and around on his left ring-finger. He looked down at the West Point crest on the gold band and remembered that the crest was traditionally supposed to be always kept close to his heart, so he stopped fidgeting and aligned the ring appropriately.

The Commandant finally took the podium and began his speech. Ben listened to every word but stored them away for later. The forefront of his mind was still thinking about that little piece of paper. He pressed the envelope between his fingers and tried to feel any hint of a raised insignia but felt none. He held it to his forehead to see if he could read it with his mind, but he still hadn't yet, in his twenty years of life, mastered those Jedi tricks he'd been practicing since childhood. And then it came. The Commandant finally gave the order for them to open their envelopes. A deafening noise of ripping paper erupted in the air and was soon followed by a variable array of emotional outbursts ranging from celebrations to laments. Ben's two company commander buddies, one on his left and the other on his right, were both cheering and high-fiving each other. He knew that meant they got Infantry, which lessened the odds for him—at least it did in Ben's mind.

"Ben, you going to open it or what?" one of his buddies asked.

"Yes, just waiting," Ben answered.

"Waiting for what?"

"For you two clowns to settle down. Congratulations, guys!"

"Thanks, now open your damn envelope!"

Ben slowly peeled back the fold from its adhesive and then pinched the piece of paper inside. He closed his eyes and pulled the card from the envelope and held it up for his buddies to see, not knowing what it was.

"Damn! That's bullshit!"

Ben's heart dropped at the dismay of his friend's reaction until he heard his other buddy start laughing.

"I guess that means we're going to have to keep putting up with your scrawny ass!"

Ben opened his eyes and looked at the crossed rifles and jumped up high in the air, right into the arms of his buddy. Safe to say that Branch Night was a good night for Benjamin Wilder River, soon to be 2nd Lieutenant River of the U.S. Army Infantry.

THREE MONTHS LATER, Ben was once again sitting between his buddies but in a much smaller setting than Eisenhower Hall. Two hundred Infantry firsties piled into a large briefing room that was at capacity. Ben had ranked fifty-third overall in the entire firsties class, so one would've thought that he would be sitting pretty well with only about eleven others ahead of him in Infantry. Unfortunately, it turned out that half of the top fifty graduates for the 1989-1990 year got assigned to Infantry, and that meant there were twenty-six others ahead of him that got priority in choosing their first unit-post assignments as newly commissioned Infantry officers. The ranking math emphasized just how elite and sought-after the Infantry was, and it made Ben become nervous thinking that he wouldn't get the best placement to help him reach his goal of eventually being assigned to the Ranger Regiment. But even if he did get the best post assignment, it still meant at least two years of exemplary duty before he could even be considered for the honor. And that fact made every edge he could get even more important.

"Ben, you're almost there. Only five more ahead of you," his buddy on the Left said.

"Lucky bastard," his other buddy on the Right said.

"I'm ranked too far back. My first choice is going to be gone by the time I'm up," Ben replied.

"I can't believe you're bitching. We're dozens behind you, man," Right said.

"Did you actually count how many of your first-choices are up there on the board?" Left asked.

"No, I got tied up with my company and couldn't get over here to count them," Ben replied.

"Then how the hell do you know?"

"I don't. I'm just nervously superstitious."

"The correct adjective is incredulous. Tell me again how you ranked higher than me?"

"Because you're lazy."

"Oh yeah, that's right. Forgot."

"And forgetful," Right finally chimed in.

"Nobody's asking you," Left said.

"Suck it."

"My turn," Ben said.

"Good luck, bitch," Right said.

Ben walked up to the board and grinned wide as soon as his first choice came into focus. Ben pulled off the card adhered to the wall, turned back towards his buddies and with a fist-pump shouted, "Eighty-Deuce Airborne, Fort Bragg here I come! Hooah!"

MAY 1990

ON THE MORNING OF GRADUATION DAY, Ben sat at his desk and wrote out words that came from his heart onto a small piece of paper. He folded the note with a twenty-dollar bill inside and secured it to the inner headband of his cadet hat. He put the hat on, looked in the mirror, adjusted it and then made his way to meet his buddies for the upcoming ceremony.

LATER THAT MORNING, Ben stood on the football field in Michie Stadium with the rest of the USMA graduating class of 1989-1990.

Just like all of his peers, he awaited for his last call to attention at The Point, and then for what would follow moments later: the final dismissal. Standing there, Ben thought back on his last four years. They had, no doubt, been the most difficult years of his life in terms of the hard work. He began to reflect on the many things he was thankful for. Things that helped him get through it all. Like his peers who pushed him to get through so many of the seemingly impossible challenges he had faced. He was oddly thankful for the depression, or whatever it was that motivated him to get off of his ass after Gramps had died and go to New York City. He was thankful for that cab driver who'd let him out exactly where he needed to be let out. He was thankful for stumbling upon the Empire State Building that in turn led him straight to Gus, whom he was thankful for having had led him right to a place that opened his eyes to the truly important things in life. He was thankful for Dr. Reeves who had supported him in many ways over the last four years. He was thankful for the good memories he now had and how they had finally begun to overshadow the bad memories in his life. But more than anything, more than it all added together, he was thankful for his Gramps.

Ben finally concluded his reflection on his time at The Point and sealed it with a silent prayer.

Thank you, God. Thank you for putting up with my doubts. And thank you for all of the blessings you've bestowed upon me. I ask that you please give me the strength to live up to my end of the bargain to become the best leader I can be. Please give me the strength to make The Point proud, to make Gramps proud, and to make You proud. Amen.

As if God himself personally controlled the timing, the call to attention came at the close of Ben's prayer. Ben's conditioned reflexes naturally obeyed the command, same as his peers did. As he heard the snap of his class's feet, he thought how he would miss that awesome sound of unity. And then finally the dismissal rang across the field and hundreds of cadet hats flew high into the air, Ben's included. All of his peers then made their way to celebrate with their families and friends. Ben was glad that Dr. Reeves was there waiting to congratulate and celebrate with him. But oh what he would've given for Gramps to be there, too. The thought made him look up at the clear blue sky and smile as he imagined his Gramps sitting next to Smitty in heaven, with both of them having watched and cheered the whole while, and having even snickered a time or two at all of the ceremonious hoopla.

Even as Ben celebrated with the good doctor, his mind turned towards what was in store for him next. He had three months before needing to report to Infantry Officer Basic Course at Fort Benning in Georgia. In the meantime, Dr. Reeves had been very generous by extending an invitation for him to stay at his home in the Hamptons. Ben had already accepted the offer and looked forward to soon experiencing just how the other point-one percent of the population lived.

AFTER THE GRADUATING CLASS cleared the field, a storming garrison of charging children came running to retrieve the cadet hats from the grounds. One of those children was a little black girl, dressed in a light gray dress decorated with yellow flower sequins. She kept pace with the others, even though most were bigger than she was. She eyed a hat to her right and ran as hard and as fast as she could to get to it before anyone else—and she succeeded. The little girl picked up the cadet hat and excitedly pulled out the note. A twenty dollar bill slipped out of the paper and she picked it up with a smile. She unfolded the paper and looked at the hand-written message:

> *Life sometimes hurts and perhaps even oftentimes— but know this: YOU CAN rise above it all and FLY!*
>
> *- Ben W. River, USMA Class of 1989-1990*

After reading the message, the little girl looked up to the same blue sky Ben had looked up at just minutes before and then she awarded the ceremony with the most beautiful of smiles. And if only Ben could've seen her, he would've thought that the little girl's beaming radiance reminded him of another special girl that he'd briefly known in a previous life.

- 31 -

HERO

THE HAMPTONS, NEW YORK – JUNE 1990

BEN'S JAW DROPPED when the taxi left him standing at the front entrance of the Reeves Estate, where he just stood in awe at the massive twelve-thousand square foot brick mansion.

Holy shit.

The good doctor's home sat on a sprawling ten acres, complete with tennis courts, Olympic pool, and beachfront bungalow. A full staff of personnel worked on the estate, from housekeepers to a chef to a gardener to a chauffeur to a mechanic and finally to a security detail that would make one presume that the home belonged to a

United States Senator. Someone drawing a paycheck was always at
the Reeves Estate, twenty-four-seven, and that just blew Ben's mind
away. It also made him awkwardly uncomfortable, having come
from poverty. Even though he truly believed in working hard to
achieve comfort and reward, all of the surroundings now before
him felt in excess, which made him feel somewhat guilty to be
partaking in thereof.

Needless to say, Ben finally chose to stay in the bungalow. It was
on par with a five-star hotel, but at least it wasn't gaudy in size. Not
to mention that it was located on the beach, a bonus that Ben would
take advantage of every day. He knew he had to get into the best
shape of his life for Ranger School. As such, he ran in the sand for
two hours every morning and then in the mid-afternoons he swam
up and down the coast for another two hours, and then once dinner
had a chance to settle, he rounded out each day with some core
strength training. He was a regular summertime party animal.

Hooah!

Except for his first night's stay, Ben rarely saw Dr. Reeves as the
man was always traveling to conferences, working at a hospital, or
taking care of business affairs. Dr. Reeves was a regular workaholic,
and Ben had no doubt that it was something that he'd learned from
his own jaunt at The Point many years ago.

On the first night of Ben's arrival, the doctor had organized a
special dinner with all of the Reeves family in attendance. Everyone
applauded Ben for his accomplishments over the last four years,
which of course completely embarrassed Ben. Afterwards, Dr.
Reeves took Ben into his private study and presented him with a
fine glass of brandy along with a WWII Colt M1911A1. The Colt .45
had been shined to a bright finish and perfectly fitted in a deep-

blue, velvet-lined box made of walnut.

The doctor put his hand on Ben's shoulder and squeezed just the way Gramps used to.

"General Patton gave this gun to me after I had patched up one of his top officers. I thought he was an ass, so I didn't ever prize it as a possession per se. With you being a military history buff, I thought you would appreciate it much more than I, so please accept it as a graduation present."

Ben stood there, mouth gaping wide and speechless, which Dr. Reeves took as a good sign.

OVER THE COURSE OF HIS STAY, Ben made sparse appearances at the main house to have dinner with the Reeves family and had only eaten breakfast with Dr. Reeves on a couple of occasions. For the most part, Ben fended for himself from the fully stocked kitchen in the bungalow, which was replenished daily. Ben always shook his head at that one.

As if I'm going to run out of food after just one meal.

From the beginning of Ben's stay, Dr. Reeves had let him know he could, anytime he liked, take any one of the automobiles from the motor pool for a drive. Ben had initially refused the offer, but after getting a little stir crazy, he finally decided to get out and see what the Hamptons were all about. That is, from a perspective other than the five mile stretch of beach he'd been wearing out for the past eight weeks.

There were plenty of cars in the Reeves auto collection to choose from, some crazy flashy and some crazy luxury. Ben chose what he thought was the least of both, driving away from the Reeves estate in an Aston Martin Lagonda Series 3. He had no idea the car originally came with a six figure price tag. Likewise, he had no idea where he was going. The latter was okay because it felt good just to get out and drive. The sun was shining, the air was refreshingly cool, and he had nowhere to be for another month. Ben drove until he came to a junction where he watched the flow of traffic and turned with it. He followed the cadre of cars until he came to a major road. When he read the sign pointing to the onramp, he smiled and nodded.

Definitely taking this one.

Ben turned right onto Highway 27, otherwise known as the 'POW/MIA Memorial Highway'. After driving on the highway for about two miles, he noticed something out of place on the road ahead. He slowed the car down, scanned the highway's shoulder and made out two cars that had just violently collided. He pulled up about ten meters from the wreck and quickly parked. He could tell that a compact truck had crossed lanes and hit an old Karmann Ghia head-on. Ben was first on the scene and when he got a close-up look of the small pickup truck, he had to bury his face in his bicep to keep from puking up his lunch. The driver of the truck was protruding halfway out of the front windshield, his head split-wide open into two halves like a partially cracked walnut. Pieces of his brain matter had splattered onto the hood of the truck and they reminded Ben of plump grub worms bathed in blood. He knew there was nothing he could do for that man so he ran to the second vehicle, which had been flipped upside-down from the crash.

Ben fell down to his hands just like he'd done over six hundred times in the last four years when he'd been ordered to count out pushups. He lowered himself so he could see into the door window and immediately spotted the driver still secured by her seatbelt, hanging upside down. Her entire face, along with her dangling long hair, was red with blood. Ben thought she looked like an inverted version of Carrie in the prom scene after the pig blood had been poured over her head. Ben noticed a lot of fresh blood streaming down the girl's face and he knew it wasn't a good thing. He also knew he didn't have much time to free her from the car and then to stop the bleeding. Ben reached in and found the seatbelt buckle and clicked its release button. He caught her with his right arm and kept her steady. Once he had both of his hands under each of her arms, he pulled as hard and as fast as he could, careful not to cut her on the shards of ancient window glass.

He continued to drag her away from the car until they were safely away. He then quickly knelt down and found the laceration on the side of her neck that was the source of the bleeding. He pressed the wound hard with the palm of his hand, but still felt blood coming out, so he ripped off his old USMA t-shirt that was already soaked in blood and used it as a compression. Ben saw more blood streaming from his hand that held his shirt to the girl's neck.

"Goddammit, stop bleeding you fucking neck!"

Ben felt something being wrapped around his arm. He looked to his left and saw a guy tying off a belt just below his shoulder.

"That's your blood, man!" the guy yelled.

The world went hazily surreal and then Ben fell forward, catching himself with his right arm. With each heartbeat, blood continued to squirt out from his left arm until he felt a constricting pain as the guy pulled the belt tight. Ben had done a good job of

231

fully protecting the girl from all of the broken glass as he pulled her out from the car, but in the process he'd unknowingly scraped his arm deep against a sharp piece of twisted metal. As fate would have it, that small piece of jagged German steel had protruded just enough into Ben's arm to sever his brachial artery.

WHEN BEN WOKE UP in a hospital bed, his entire left arm and shoulder wrapped with bandages and contained in some contraption that kept him from moving that area of his body. His heart rate increased and the monitor's incessant beeping kept pace. Ben would always be ashamed as he looked back, but the first thing he thought about after waking was losing his arm and by that, losing his chance to become a US Army Ranger.

A nurse walked into his room and noticed he'd finally come-to. She smiled at him and said, "Look who's awake. Let me go get the doctor for you."

Moments later, a short elderly man dressed in scrubs walked in and over to Ben's right side of the bed.

"Hi Ben, I'm Dr. Hahn. I'm the vascular surgeon who patched you up."

"How bad is it?" Ben asked.

"Well, it was very serious. You partially severed your brachial artery. Good news is that you didn't completely sever it and unbelievably, there doesn't appear to be any nerve damage. All in all, you are extremely lucky."

"So I'm going to be okay, sir? There won't be any permanent damage?"

"You're going to be fine. Regarding permanent damage, that's hard to say. You're young and strong, so there's a good chance your arm will fully recover, but there are no guarantees, son."

"How long will it take to heal, sir?"

"I'm afraid you'll have to stay with us for a while. I'd say about a month."

"I can't stay a month. I have to report to—"

"Do *not* get yourself worked up, son. Now, I understand you have plans. Dr. Reeves has filled me in on everything. What you've got to understand is that first and foremost, you need to heal. And to do that, you have to take it easy. Do you understand me?"

"Yes sir." Ben took a moment to calm down and collect himself. "How about the girl. Is she okay, doc?"

"It's too early to say. She's in critical condition. One thing's for sure, if you hadn't pulled her from that car when you did, she would've died there on the highway. You're her hero, son."

"No sir. I just did what anyone would've done."

The doctor gave an emphasized look towards Ben's left arm and then said, "I'm not sure I agree. Neither do others at the scene. You're quite the buzz around town."

"How about the guy who helped me? Do you happen to know who he is?"

"No, I don't. There's plenty of time to figure all of that out. For now, you need to rest."

"Sir, earlier you mentioned that Dr. Reeves is here?"

"He was. He had to leave for a patient emergency elsewhere." The doctor unclipped a vibrating beeper from his belt, looked at it, and said, "Speaking of, I'll be back to check in on you tomorrow. Okay?"

"Yes sir. Thank you, sir."

"You're welcome, Ben."

Ben watched the man in scrubs walk away and thought how the surgeon hand a strong likeness to his Gramps.

They could've been brothers.

WITH EACH DAY THAT PASSED, Ben stressed more and more about being cooped up in a hospital. He could feel his body getting weaker and it was driving him crazy. He'd bugged the doctor everyday about being able to exercise until the doctor finally caved and ordered physical therapy. And Ben lived for it every day. It wasn't much, but it was better than nothing, Ben had thought.

Ben had ventured up to the ICU to try and visit the girl a few times, but every attempt failed as only family was allowed. He hadn't even been able to get a good look at her yet. She would have to be covered in blood before he would recognize her again and even then it happened so fast that he wouldn't be sure. He made a point to pray for her every day and he kept his optimism high, although he didn't see any assurance in the eyes of the nurses that monitored and cared for the girl. He supposed that being ICU veterans had made them callous to such emotions. At least he hoped that was the reason for their seemingly cold indifference.

A man whom Ben didn't recognize had dropped by the hospital to check up on him. The guy's name was Carl Avery, aka Ben's hero, the guy who had put the tourniquet on his arm and no doubt saved his life in the process. As Ben went to shake his hand, he noticed that Carl was missing his left arm from the elbow down.

Trying not to stare, Ben thanked Carl as he thought how impressive the disabled man was to have acted as he'd done at the accident. Ben did all he could to show his gratitude, short of offering to give him money, which had crossed Ben's mind but he'd smartly decided it would've been poor form to do so. They talked for a long while and Ben wasn't surprised to find out that Carl had graduated from The Point back in 1984. The USMA certainly taught cadets to act fast on their feet, and that's precisely what both of them had done that day.

Ben asked Carl about his unit and assignments after graduating. Carl only told him that he'd chosen to leave the Army after his first tour of duty, during which he lost his left arm in battle. Ben had politely asked him how it happened, but Carl had let Ben know that it was classified—the only thing he could tell Ben was that it happened in the Persian Gulf. Carl quickly switched the subject to his current passions, leaving the subject of the Army quickly behind. To Ben's elation, Carl also had a passion for computers and software, which was a subject that they sat and talked about for several hours. Having traded in stories of battle for stories of circuitry, Ben wasn't the least bit disappointed. It had been a very long time since he'd had a good technology discussion and it reminded him of his chats with Demarcus from years back. Carl finally wrapped up his visit and they exchanged contact information, promising one another that each would stay in touch.

AFTER THREE WEEKS IN THE HOSPITAL, Ben was finally discharged. Before leaving, he went to the ICU one last time to try and see the girl whom he'd pulled from the car. He'd imagined being able to spend time with her just as Carl had been able to do with him.

Ben tiptoed around the circular path that surrounded the nurse's station until he found the girl's hospital room on the perimeter wall. He peeked through the window but as usual, all kinds of equipment obstructed his view of the girl. He braved the wrath of the ICU nurses by reaching to open the door until he heard a nurse sternly call out to him.

"You can't go in there. Family only."

Argh!

Ben froze in his tracks, took his hands off of the door handle, did an about-face and then walked over to the nurse's station.

"How's she doing?" he asked.

The nurse recognized Ben as the West Point hero who had saved the girl and subsequently lightened her tone.

"I'm sorry to say that she fell into a coma yesterday."

Ben's perky mood transitioned into one of complete and utter deflation.

"Oh. Well...thank you."

Ben knew that there was now one more stop he needed to make before leaving the hospital. He walked to the elevators and pressed the 'DOWN' button. He got off on the first floor and then found the hospital chapel—he knelt in front of the altar and began praying as hard as he could for the girl.

ONCE BEN FINALLY GOT OUT OF THE HOSPITAL, he didn't

have much time left before he had to report to duty. So, he decided it would be best if he went ahead and checked out of the Reeves 5-Diamond Hotel and leave early for Fort Benning. He thanked Dr. Reeves over and over again to the point where the good doctor finally told him to stop or he was going to suture his mouth shut. Of course the doctor's threat made Ben tease him by thanking him even more. The doctor had a good bedside manner so played the game by switching his threat to instead giving Ben a lobotomy. With that, Ben finally surrendered, not wanting to push his luck.

You just never know about doctors.

He also thanked the doctor's family for their hospitality and slipped nice tips to all of the staff who he'd gotten to know a little during his brief stay.

As the cab finally pulled away from the large estate, he couldn't help but wonder what Gramps would've thought about all the hoopla that rich-money buys. He imagined that Gramps would say that no matter how comfortable it was, it could never replace happiness. Ben nodded with the thought as he took one last glance back at the good doctor's home.

I definitely don't need things like that to make me happy.

In his head, he heard his Gramps respond to the thought by saying, "No Ben, I raised you better than that."

- 32 -

THE GODFATHER

FORT BENNING, GEORGIA – DECEMBER 1990

BEN COMPLETED HIS FIVE MONTHS of Infantry Officer Basic Course training and now had one week to mentally prepare for Ranger School. He knew the first phase of the training, called the Ranger Assessment Phase (RAP), was going to be the hardest mental and physical test that he'd ever faced in his life—but he welcomed the challenge. He'd dreamed for the last eight years about becoming a leader in the Ranger Regiment and now the first major milestone for realizing his dream was upon him. There would be no weekend breaks in this training, so Ben was taking advantage of the few days he had off to get things done. He'd just finished running errands, one of which had been sending his mom another postcard. It had been two years since he sent the first one, and he felt guilty about not writing her since. He hoped she'd received the Statue of Liberty card and now he was hoping that she would also receive the 'Georgia Peach' postcard he just mailed. His message on the latest had been the same as before—no details, just letting her know he was safe and sound and that he still thought about her a lot, which was true. He wished he could share the details of his life with her, but it was too risky on many levels. It was an easy choice for Ben to make not to share details with his mom versus taking the risk of the Rabid Dog finding out about Ben's new life. Ben would go with door number-one each and every time to keep the evil man away.

Before heading home, Ben stopped by the bakery at the commissary to pick up some of their delicious, fresh-baked bagels. He knew that he would soon be starving during the Ranger training, so he was going to enjoy some high-calorie food while he still could. As such, he was on his way out of the bakery with a bag of the doughy goodness in-hand as a private entered the store. The private saluted Ben and Ben returned the salute as usual but then the private said Ben's first name. Ben paused to run the voice through his internal recognition software, trying to find a match.

Vaguely familiar.

"Ben? Benjamin Wilder?" the man asked.

Did he just say Wilder?

Ben turned around to face the private and asked, "Do I know you, private?"

He looked at the soldier's nametag and saw O. MUNOZ.

"Octavio?" Ben asked.

"Holy shit! I can't believe it!" Octavio exclaimed.

They embraced each other, holding on tight to make sure each other was in fact real. And then for the first time in a long time, Ben felt a sense of having someone in the world again. Not since the last time he'd hugged his Gramps had he felt any such emotion.

OCTAVIO HAD INVITED BEN OVER to his place for dinner so he could introduce him to his wife and so they could catch up. Ben arrived at the small base house and the awesome smell of fresh tamales made him salivate before he even had a chance to knock on the door.

Once they sat for dinner, there wasn't much talking as the two hungry soldiers scarfed down the delicious meal. Only passing words and a few m-m-m's were exchanged until Ben finally pushed his plate away. He rubbed his full stomach as if to give his digestive system some moral support and then he stood up.

"Gloria, dinner was fantastic. Best grub I've had in a very long time. Sincerely. Thank you."

Ben began to help clear the table when Gloria shook her head and motioned for him to sit back down.

"You're welcome Ben, but please sit back down. You two visit and catch-up. Believe me, I'll make a faster job of it without yet *another* soldier getting in the way." She touched her pregnant tummy to emphasize the little soldier inside before making the point, "and that was an order, by the way."

"Yes ma'am."

Ben laughed and, as ordered, sat back down. He looked over at Octavio and thought how hard it was to believe that across the table from him was an original member of the Black Machetes—the muscle of the group no less, alive and in the flesh.

Muscle may now be an understatement.

"Look at you, Octavio. I honestly never would've recognized you. You've changed a lot," Ben said with wide eyes.

"I'm not that small town kid anymore, no? Doing hard time, especially for something like I was accused of—well let's just say I adapted to my environment. Sí, I'm a little rough around the edges. Just part of survival is all."

"Hey man, I didn't mean to insult you. The new look is good on you."

"I got thick skin, bro. It's okay. But look at you. You haven't changed one bit. Maybe a little taller, pero muy poquito."

"Hey, come on. Maybe a little more than a little."

"Keep dreaming. Until you grow up, come get me when you need anyone's ass kicked. That hasn't changed and never will."

"I'm not going to lie. It's damn good to know that you've got my back."

"Hora-le."

"So, tell me how you and Gloria met."

"You won't believe it if I told you."

"Try me."

"I was sent to go kill her by a gang I belonged to in prison called the Texas Syndicate. But instead of killing her, I fell in love. I re-invented the whole love-at-first-sight thing."

"You're joking, right? That's not how you really met."

"No, I'm not joking. It's how we met. Some crazy shit, huh?"

"So what happened? You got them to call off the hit?"

"Call off the hit? You been watching crime movies or what? Yeah, no. First off, you don't tell the Syndicato anything, they tell you. We had to get out of dodge and hide. And the only way I knew to hide so they couldn't reach us was by signing up to 'be all I could be'." Octavio then saluted for effect.

"Wow. That's one for the record books. A good story to tell the grandkids one day."

"Hora-le."

"Speaking of. When is Gloria due? She looks like she's ready to pop."

"Don't let her hear you say that, dude. She's sensitive about all the weight."

"Oh. Sorry."

"Hell, me? I don't care. I know it's all baby." With a very low voice he added, "At least I hope it's all baby. Gloria was perfecto when we first met, but damn, she's a lot to handle right now, let me tell you."

"Okay, I get the picture. When is she due already?"

"In four weeks minus two days, and I ain't gonna be here for it. Saddam needs his ass kicked. No choice. Orders aren't optional. Something the Army has in common with the Syndicato."

"Yeah, that sucks man. I'm sorry."

"Hey, comes with the territory, right?"

"Yep, that it does."

"West Point. Holy shit, I'm sure that's some story you've got."

"No way it can compare to yours. Speaking of. Octavio, seriously, regarding you being accused...well, I'm sorry I wasn't there for you, man. I never believed it when I heard it on the news. I knew then just as I know now who killed Raina."

"Yeah. I do, too. And one of these days, I'm going to take care of those fuckers."

"Watch that language," Gloria said from the kitchen.

"Hora-le," Octavio said, "I would've already put them in the ground, but like I said already, we had to get out of dodge."

"Hold on a second. Who do *you* think killed her?"

"I don't think, I *know*. It was your step-dad and his hillbilly friend."

"Yeah, Jessup and Wade. How in the hell did you figure it out?"

"Because those fuckers..." Octavio squeamishly looked towards the kitchen to make sure Gloria didn't hear his curse words again, and then he cowered when he saw that she was already walking back into the dining area. "Oops, I'm in trouble now."

Gloria leaned over to kiss Octavio and when he puckered up, she instead kissed him on his forehead.

"Potty lips don't get kisses, papi," she said.

"Sí, amor mío."

"I'm tired, so I'm going to turn in and leave you men to it. Ben, it was so nice to meet you."

"Likewise, Gloria. And thanks again for an awesome dinner."

"You are very welcome, again. Good night, boys. Be good."

"Horla-le baby. I love you," Octavio said.

"Love you, too," Gloria said just before giving Octavio one final kiss, this time on the lips.

Octavio watched his beautiful, pregnant wife disappear behind their bedroom door, and then he turned back to Ben who was eagerly waiting for him to resume the story.

"Where was I?"

"You were telling me how you figured it out."

"That's right. It wasn't hard, actually. If the pigs had any brains they would've too by now. Anyways. Those fuckers caught us at the fort one day. We were there the second anniversary after you left. When you went missing, we made a pact to go back to the fort every year and keep building it. We hoped that one day you would show up and meet us there. We knew you were probably dead though, but it was a nice dream to have. Anyways, on that day, two years after you left, Jessup and Wade snuck up on us at the fort. They made us get on our knees and your step-dad whipped us with a belt. God it made me so mad. I wanted to kill them. And I'm going to, too."

"I still don't see the connection. Why does that make you think they killed Raina?"

"Because, they threatened our lives to never go back to the woods and of course we never did after that. Demarcus told us what happened that day on the side of the road, the day you ran away. We knew they were serious. We knew they'd do it. You gotta understand, we thought that they killed you, Ben. And then they killed..." Octavio cleared his throat and swallowed down the lump that had formed in his Adam's apple. "They killed Raina using my machete and then put my St. Michael medallion in her hand. Jessup got my chain from Tommy. Tommy had ripped it off of me during a fight we had after I pinched Raina's ass at school."

"Fight? With Tommy? Raina's ass? Man, I'm confused."

"Yeah, forgot you didn't know. Hora-le. Tommy and Raina were a thing, dude. They tried to hide it, but everyone knew. They were head over heels for each other. So, after those fuckers whipped us in the woods, I go so pissed at Tommy's dad that I decided to take it out on Tommy. Not to mention that I was also pissed at Tommy on your behalf, too. I blamed him for all the shit that happened to you just as much as I did your step-dad. I was just pissed about everything, so I kicked his ass. That's how Jessup got my necklace and put it in Raina's hand after they killed her using my machete. The fight...well, it is a mistake I pay for every day. Raina would still be alive if it weren't for my stupid ass."

"No man, I really don't think that's true. You weren't the reason they killed her, I'm sure of it. I know Jessup all too well. There's no way he would've let Tommy date, much less fall in love with any black girl. They killed her because of Tommy, not you. Jessup just saw an opportunity to also get back at you for kicking his son's ass. That's how that evil son-of-a-bitch thinks. Both of them. If this is anyone's fault, it's mine for just running away without trying to do something about them."

"You were twelve. If you tried, you'd be dead and you know it."

"Yeah, probably. But I still could've tried. Maybe if I had—"

"Hora-le, if I don't get to take blame, then neither do you."

"Well, I think we both agree on one thing, they need to pay for what they did."

"Sí, I'm going to make sure they do. They're going to suffer for killing every friend I cared about. Every friend but you now that I know you're alive and well. Gracias a dios."

"What do you mean every friend?"

"Que? Oh shit, I thought you knew. Of course you don't. Oh man."

"Know what?"

"I only found out after we moved to Georgia. They've both been missing."

245

"Missing? Who are you talking about?"

"Demarcus and Scooter. They're missing."

"What! For how long?"

"I guess it's…yeah, eighteen months now."

"Both of them? How? Why? I'm confused all over again."

"They went for a drive in Scooter's pop's old red pickup, same one with the tailgate we used to ride on. The truck was found on one of the dirt back-roads, but Demarcus and Scooter were nowhere to be found."

"No! Mother-fu…can't be."

"I'm sorry, Ben."

"I can't believe this. Goddammit! What about the police? Didn't they find anything? Any evidence from the truck?"

"No. Not a fucking thread. No sign of anything. Just the truck. There was a big rain storm around that time which would've cleared any tracks. It took the pigs three days just to find the pinche truck."

"Why would they just disappear out of the blue? And why do you think they're dead? Maybe they just ran away."

"No, Ben. They're dead. Those fuckers killed them. Don't you see? Once I was proven innocent from DNA testing, Jessup and Wade knew it was only a matter of time before Demarcus and Scooter figured it out. Fuck, I figured it out two years ago. It would only take a DNA sample from those fuckers and then the pigs would catch up and figure it out. We didn't tell anyone about that day in the woods. After all this time, they must've thought that we'd spill our guts now that I was proven innocent. Me, I want them dead so I had no intentions of talking. Prison is too good for them. They'd join the fucking Aryans and probably enjoy themselves inside."

"Jesus. I can't believe…Demarcus…Scooter. Why goddamn it? Why?" Ben's eyes started to water, but his mounting anger kept the tears at bay. "Didn't you talk to Demarcus or Scooter to tell them that you figured it out?"

"While I was inside? Fuck no! Everybody thought I did it, Ben. Including Demarcus. He wanted to kill me, man. Scooter was there and pissed his pants when I got arrested and so he probably thought I was guilty right then and there. You see, those hillbilly fuckers were smart about it. I kicked Tommy's ass in front of the whole school after I flirted with Raina. Everyone thought I had motive. Hora-le, even I wondered if I could've sleep-walked and somehow done it. Fuck."

"Why didn't you warn them when you got out then, Octavio?"

"I wish I had, dude. Every day of my life since then I wish. I was out of town trying to save Gloria's life and my own from The Syndicate. I should've at least went to see Scooter first thing, but I was still freaked out about being released. Everyone believed I was a killer, Ben. Then all of a sudden I'm let out and thrown into the middle of them all. It was fucked up. I was fucked up. So yeah, they're dead because of me. I know it. Every day I live with it."

"No, Octavio. It's not your fault at all. I'm sorry. I shouldn't have gone there. I get it now. Jessup and Wade began planning to kill all of you the very second they heard the news of your release. If you would've gone to tell them, they would've killed you, too."

"That's where I disagree, bro. See, that's my regret. I wish I had gone and I wish they would've tried. If so, we'd be having a much different conversation right now. Motherfuckers would be dead. Trust me."

The moment was surreal for Ben, in such a bad way, worse than a horrible dream. He thought about Scooter and how Scooter helped him as a kid to escape his abusive world through all of the electronics and techie magazines. Then Ben thought about Raina and her kiss, just like he had a million times before. He thought about Demarcus's family and all of the tragedy they had to endure. His memories finally turned to Demarcus and all the fun they used to have together, and then it finally sank-in that his best friend was no longer living.

Ben's head started spinning and he could tell he was going to get sick.

"Can I use your restroom?"

"Of course, down the hall, first door on the right. You okay, bro?"

Ben excused himself and gave Octavio the okay sign. Then he headed to the bathroom where all of the dinner from his stomach was expelled into the toilet via a heart wrenching strain of regurgitations. He stayed in there with the door locked and cried as quietly as he could until there were no more tears. Then he stayed even longer until his anger grew to the point of rage as he thought about how many times the Rabid Dog had made him senselessly cry over the years.

A thousand? Ten thousand? It's got to stop! But when? And how?

The questions required no answers. Deep down Ben already knew what had to be done.

BEN AND OCTAVIO SPENT as much of the next week together as

they could. Soon, Ben had to start Ranger School and Octavio had orders to deploy to the Persian Gulf. For their last meet, they agreed to go on a hike through the wooded trails not far from the military base. It was a fitting way to say goodbye and the closest that they could come to their old Black Machetes adventures. As they walked along, they came upon five young boys working on a fort of their own. Ben and Octavio stopped to talk to them and share some pointers. As kids do, they ignored all advice and did everything their own way, which made Ben and Octavio laugh because it's exactly how they would've reacted at that age. They walked away but turned to take one last look at the fort and the boys who were hard at work. Emotions swelled up in Ben and he wondered if they did the same for Octavio. Looking back at the fort, Ben was thankful for the good memories that the Black Machetes had given him and he was sure Octavio felt the same.

The sun would soon start to set, so they headed back, marking the end of a great day. Once they got to their vehicles, Octavio turned to Ben and smiled with as charming a grin as his hard face could muster.

"Ben, I've got something important to ask you. Two things, actually. Uno, I want you to be the godfather of my baby; Dos, I want you to check in on Gloria whenever you can. I know you won't have much time and that you're not going to be here long, but at least until you leave."

"Consider it done. I'll check in on Gloria every chance I get. And I'll make sure she has my number wherever I am. Now regarding being your baby's godfather, of course, I'd be sincerely honored. That's totally cool."

"Good answer. I was afraid I'd have to kick your gringo ass if you didn't get a little excited."

"Ummm, no thanks."

"Hora-le."

They said their final goodbyes and ended the exchange with a strong hug and several pats on the back. The next day Octavio was deployed to the faraway desert, and three days later, Gloria Muñoz gave birth to an eight-pound-three-ounce healthy baby boy who, of course, had been named Julio César-Chavez Muñoz.

- 33 -

INTREPIDITY

BEN HAD JUST ENOUGH TIME to do some quick laundry, call Gloria to check up on her, and catch a little coverage of Desert Storm before having to ship out to Georgia for the Mountain phase of Ranger Training. He'd passed the grueling Ranger Assessment Phase (RAP), which at the start had two-hundred-ninety students, with only one-hundred-and-one soldiers making it through to completion, including Ben. He reflected on how that final number could've easily been an even one-hundred with him on the other side of the fence. Truth be told, there were a few times when he really didn't think he was going to make it. He'd tried hard to prepare himself, but after the second day he realized that there is no way to really prepare. Ben was able to get ready for the Military

Academy through research and mental awareness, but nothing Ben read or mediated-on helped with RAP. He supposed it was a little different for every soldier, even though everyone had to perform the same hellaciously rigorous training without sleep and without food. For him, he had to focus on his Gramps during the times when he wanted to give up and quit. He would hear Morgan's always-good advice flow with a slight Arkansas drawl, and it would give Ben just enough will to dig deep and push through the pain. Ben smiled as he reflected on drawing from his Gramps for inner strength, and he was sure Gramps was up in heaven smiling right along with him while refusing to take any credit.

On top of all of the skills Ben gained, RAP also taught him the difference between muscle-power and heart. He now fully understood that without the will, the muscle is useless, but with just a little muscle, the will can do amazing things, even sometimes miraculous things. He'd witnessed such feats during the assessment exercises, and he was shocked that some of the soldiers whom he picked to finish at the top, actually dropped out early. Conversely, he was surprised that many of those who finished top of the class were everyday-looking people whom he'd discounted as non-contenders from the get-go. He now understood that the old idiom 'brain versus brawn' was missing an important element. When it came to the challenges he had faced, it was more *heart* versus brawn.

The TV in the Laundromat caught Ben's attention when its screen lit up with green streamers that streaked through the night sky from the munition fire that pelted away at its enemy targets. There was a party going on in Kuwait and Ben hadn't been invited. He thought how lucky Octavio was at that moment, to be there making history.

But more than envious, Ben was proud. It was humbling to think about where Octavio had come from, with all that he'd been through, to where he was now—taking it to that tyrant Saddam for the good ole US of A.

Black Machetes, Hooah!

FORTY-ONE DAYS LATER, Ben had successfully graduated from Ranger school. He was so excited to have received the Ranger tab that he drove around to three different alteration shops until he found one that would sew the special patches onto all of his uniforms while he waited. The Ranger tab would be a symbol of respect and one that would always be immediately looked-for by his superiors in the Infantry. It was true that many combat commanders in the Army believed that no tab on the left shoulder meant you weren't worthy to lead the best Infantry soldiers. Ben was proud and honored to be included in company so highly regarded.

Once again, Ben found himself doing laundry to make ready for more training. This time it was in preparation for Airborne school, which he knew would be a breeze after earning his Ranger tab. He'd been the only soldier in RAP who hadn't already gone to Airborne and consequently had received a bit of grief from the Ranger instructors razzing him that he only had "legs". Ben knew in advance that the usual training order was Airborne first and then Ranger school, but after finishing officer training, he'd been so anxious to get RAP over with that he'd deferred Airborne to get a *jump* on RAP—no pun intended. And now he was very much looking forward to jumping out of a perfectly fine aircraft, which was something that he'd dreamed about since first listening to Gramps tell stories of the paratroopers from WWII.

Eat. Sleep. Jump. Repeat. Hell, yeah!

Before heading out to his favorite hangout, aka the Laundromat, Ben stopped by to see how Gloria and his godson were holding up. Little Julio was growing so fast and Ben thought that maybe he was looking a little more like Octavio each time he saw him, at least the younger Octavio from childhood. But in Ben's opinion, for the most part, Julio got all of his looks from his mom.

Thank God for that one, little Julio.

Gloria really missed Octavio and Ben could tell she was depressed. She mentioned that she had found some emotional support from other army wives in her same situation, and she'd even joined a Mom's club so that Julio could have some playmates—as if he were old enough for such a thing. Ben hunkered down and listened to all of the latest happenings from Gloria, taking it all in while trying to be the best proxy for Octavio that he could be. It was plain to see that Octavio being deployed was taking a toll on her, and oddly enough, seeing her sad made Ben yearn for someone to love him as she did Octavio. He shrugged off the thought, again playing the Army card to snuff out any familial desires that entered his heart and mind.

Julio began his cyclic cry for milk, which Ben voluntarily took as his timely cue to leave. And as usual, he covertly placed an envelope of money on Gloria's kitchen table before letting himself out. Ben couldn't imagine having to support a wife and a baby on his own meager officer-salary, much less with the lower pay grade where Octavio was at. So ever since Octavio's deployment, Ben tried to help them out financially by slipping a little spending money to Gloria, each time without letting her notice.

The Laundromat was quiet and as usual, Ben pretty much had the place to himself. Earlier in the day, he'd received a letter in the mail from Octavio, but he'd decided to wait until his clothes were drying so he'd have something good to read while waiting. He finished putting the wet garments into the large drum and then fed it some quarters. He was about to put the remaining quarter back into his pocket when his peripheral vision caught a glimpse of an old childhood itch that he'd never had the chance to scratch. In the corner over by the detergent vending machine sat a small, red cast-iron and glass candy machine. He'd always wanted to stuff coins into the small contraptions when he was a kid but was never allowed to. He walked over to the dispenser like an inquisitive little child, put in the quarter, and then turned the thumb-crank until he heard it spit out something solid. He lifted the chrome tongue and took out a blue jawbreaker from the chute's mouth and plopped it into his own and smiled. Life was good. Everything was in balance. And now it was time to enjoy words from one tough Mexican grunt who was probably busy eating sand sandwiches right about now.

This jawbreaker's for you, Octavio.

Ben eased into a chair and began reading the letter from his dear friend:

> *Hola Ben,*
>
> *Thanks for your letter, bro. It was real good to hear from you, so keep them coming. Everything here is pretty slow. Nothing but sand, wind, heat, and more sand. Hora-le. MREs are a crapshoot, and we're doing a lot of waiting,*

so it pretty much sucks all around. Rumor is the ground assault will be happening soon. I hope so, or I may go loco from boredom. It was awesome to hear that you got thru RAP. I've talked to a few guys that washed out and one badass that made it thru. It sounds like it's fucking crazy hard. I'm proud of you, mi hermano. Also thanks for the money you gave Gloria (she told me). Uncle Sam pays too shitty for us to be too proud to accept it. I consider it a loan though and I will pay it back to you someday. And you'd better take it too, or I'll kick your Ranger ass. How embarrassing would that be for a piss-ant grunt to open a can of kick-ass on you? So, you'd better use your head. Hora-le.

Much Love,
Octavio

P.S. Black Machetes Rule! (still)

Ben folded the letter and inserted it back into its envelope, put his feet up on the table, and then leaned back in his chair.

"Orda-lay."

Life is good, indeed.

OCTAVIO FINALLY GOT HIS WISH for action on February 24th when his Company was ordered to take part in Phase Four of the Allied Advance. Unfortunately, as luck would have it, his squad became pinned down on the edge of a small town near the 'Iraq – Kuwait' border. Their radio operator had been killed in the skirmish and the radio along with him, leaving no way to call for support.

There were two flanking high ground positions held by Republican Guard soldiers who were laying down a constant burst of 50-caliber suppressive fire that had already killed two men, including the radioman. The second soldier who perished just happened to be a close buddy of Octavio's and naturally it angered Octavio more than it made him sad. As such, he volunteered to run to the structure where the enemy was fortified, which meant a forty meter sprint under heavy fire with little-to-no cover. Octavio's Sergeant agreed to let him go and launched a smoke grenade to kick start the Octavio Muñoz party. Once the smoke blanketed enough of the area, Octavio ran faster than he ever had in his entire life. As he sprinted, he could feel the wakes from large caliber bullets piercing the air all around him. He said a quick prayer that one of them didn't have his name on it, but in truth he expected to be knocked off his feet at any second. About three-quarters of the way to the concrete structure, he luckily tripped over some rubble and in doing so dodged a barrage of bullets that would've killed him otherwise. Now on all fours, he crawled for a couple of meters before getting back up to resume his sprint and continued running until finally making it to the building, safe and sound.

Another burst of pure adrenaline kicked into overdrive for Octavio at that point as he turned the corner of the building, expecting to face a line of Iraqi soldiers—but none were there. He quickly spotted a doorway that led inside the building and wasted no time running through it and then up a flight of stairs. Without stopping and without even thinking about it, he climbed three floors until he finally reached the roof access. He paused just long enough to calm his breathing and then quickly peeked through the doorway. In doing so, he was able to see both machine gun operators, one at each corner of the rooftop. He thanked Mary and Jesus above that he didn't see any other enemy soldiers, and after hearing the 50-caliber reports resume, he thanked them again since it seemed that the Iraqi soldiers were preoccupied with trying to kill his buddies. And that meant that they had no idea that their position had been compromised — or so Octavio hoped, which is why he said another quick prayer, just in case. He then quickly assessed the situation and came up with a mental plan. He knew he could take a little more time to aim on his first target, but the second one would have to be quick and dirty.

Fuck, I wish I knew which one of the putos was faster.

He took out the new Saint Michael medallion attached next to his dog tags that Gloria had given him right before he deployed. He kissed the medallion, readied his M16 rifle, and then waited until he heard the 50-caliber bursts start again. Octavio had no idea if both of the gunners were laying down the fire or if only one of them was, and that meant he had no idea which one to take out first, just as he hadn't known which one was faster. He finally decided that there was no more time left for recon.

Eeny, meeny, miny, moe. La derecha.

He jolted through the access threshold, turning towards the Republican Guard on the right, and in doing so he noticed that the soldier on the left wasn't firing his weapon.

Shit! No time to change my mind.

He quickly took aim at the middle of the enemy's back and squeezed the trigger. A three-round burst found its mark and opened the man up, spraying his blood into the air and sprinkling the ledge of the roof. Without waiting to do a damage assessment, Octavio quickly switched the rifle to full automatic and pivoted towards the guard on the left, who had already started his own turn towards Octavio. Octavio squeezed the trigger and unloaded his entire clip in the direction of the roof's left corner. As a result, the second Republican Guard took two bullets to the neck and three more to his lower body. It turned out that the two neck shots had been enough. Another spray of red mist filled the air around the enemy's head as he fell forward to his knees, and then finally to his face.

"Pinche cabróns," Octavio said as he tried to calm the adrenaline filled muscle in his chest. He then walked towards where the two men now lay dead. He took out a smoke grenade, pulled the pin, and threw the canister to the edge of the roof. Green puffs started to waft their way into the sky, signaling the all clear to his squad. Octavio watched as the smoke rose and thought how it reminded him of the wicked-witch's broom-exhaust from the Wizard of Oz. He started to turn around and go back to help evacuate his team when his knees locked-up and froze on him. His ears began ringing and a slow-motion, numbing sensation overcame him. Only then did he hear the enemy rifle's report and a brief, sharp sting. While Octavio had been watching the signal rise into the air, another Republican Guard, who had seen Octavio run into the building, had come up from behind. Octavio's passing moment of childhood recollection had given the enemy time to take accurate aim before pulling the deadly trigger. As a result, the bullet precisely pierced Octavio's aorta, killing him quickly with only a fleeting sensation of pain, while giving him just enough time to have one final thought on this earth.

Hora-le.

BEN WAS EXHAUSTED, so he sat down on his couch and leaned back to take a much needed breather. He'd just gotten home from completing Airborne School and needed to catch up on his bills and mail, which he was attempting to build-up energy to do. He woke up fifteen minutes after having accidentally fallen asleep. He looked at his watch and was refreshingly satisfied with the short cat nap.

Good to go.

He straightened his posture and sorted through the mound of mail on his coffee table. He separated the bills from the junk and was happy to see that he needed a third pile for two personal letters, both addressed by feminine hands. The first letter had 'MADELINE LEWIS' listed on the return address, and the sight of it made Ben smile. Madeline was the girl whom he pulled out of the car during his summer in the Hamptons. Not only had she come out of the coma, but she'd adamantly tracked Ben down to thank him for saving her life and had corresponded to him a couple of times since then. He supposed it was her way of showing continued gratitude, much like Dr. Reeves had done over the years to Morgan. In any case, Ben was glad because reading her words was a nice treat. She was a very witty girl and he got a kick out of the things she said in her letters as well as the way she signed them, with a very fancy 'M' and nothing else. He thought about her often, so he decided to save that one to read after dinner. He picked up the second envelope and noticed it was from Gloria, but the return address was Lone Star, Texas.

That's strange.

He opened the envelope and read her words that explained

Octavio's death and how she and Julio had no choice but to move back to Texas to live with her mom and dad. Ben re-read the horrible news to make sure his eyes weren't making up the whole thing, and then he dropped the letter and buried his face in his hands. After taking a couple of minutes to process the words, he hurled the coffee table across the room and then dropped to his knees, where he began sobbing the same as he did when Octavio had told him about the disappearance of Demarcus and Scooter. And just like the last time, his sadness eventually turned to anger, but this time it transformed into a maddening rage. Thankfully for the living room's sake, Ben was able to maintain his wits long enough to move his rage to the bedroom. And that's where he fell face-first and commenced to punch his twin mattress as hard as he could, and as long as he could until his arms finally gave out. The mattress would never recover from the beating and neither would Ben.

THROUGH OCTAVIO MUÑOZ'S CONSPICUOUS GALLANTRY and intrepidity at the risk of life above and beyond the call of duty, he was posthumously awarded The Medal of Honor during a ceremony held at the White House. Considering Octavio's wronged past, his heroic death made a great story, so the event was covered by every major national-news organization. Gloria feared that the media attention would put her back into the crosshairs of the Syndicate, so she watched the ceremony from afar on TV as Octavio's parents accepted the award from the President.

Not long after the Washington ceremony, the city of Gilmer held a parade and recognition event of their own, during which Octavio was posthumously given a key to the city along with having a stretch of Highway-155 named after him. There was no family member of Octavio in attendance, so Gabe Snow—the most unlikely of people—acted as Octavio's proxy to accept the gift. Even though it was probably safe for Gloria to make an appearance, she had declined, having had enough with reminders of her loss. And of course Ben didn't attend, but he was able to watch the ceremony on TV. It turned out that even the small town of Gilmer had gained some notoriety because of Octavio, and as such the memorial was picked up by a major news television show.

Ben couldn't help but think how disgustingly ironic the whole event was, although he felt better about it when Gabe Snow went up to the podium and spoke to the gathered crowd. Gabe cried as he praised the young man whom he'd once thought so horribly of. He publicly apologized to Octavio's family for all that had happened and spoke with a heartfelt sincerity to let the world know that he was honored to have known Octavio.

Tommy Strickland was also in attendance, but he only watched in hiding from a distance. In between hits from a meth pipe he would look up with paranoid ticks and wonder which motherfucker in the gathered crowd had murdered the love of his life.

"I love you, T," Raina would occasionally say in Tommy's head.

"I love you too, baby," Tommy would respond.

PART III

- 34 -

JONESY

FT. BRAGG, NORTH CAROLINA – FEBUARY 1992

BEN'S FIRST COMMAND TOUR assignment was within the 82nd Airborne Division, which had been his first choice on Branch Night back at The Point. Specifically, he now served as a Platoon Leader for the 1st Battalion, 504th Parachute Infantry Regiment—aka The Red Devils. The purpose of his regiment was to *"deploy worldwide within hours of notification, execute a parachute assault, conduct combat operations, and win"*. Ben loved his job along with all of the brave people that he worked with. Sadly though, ever since Octavio had been KIA, Ben had decided to no longer develop friendships— instead he made it a rule to have no more personal attachments whatsoever. As a result, he was all work and no play—only he would argue that there was plenty of play in his work. But most importantly, he understood the severity of being a leader who was directly responsible for the lives of his men. As such, he was serious about training, discipline, and obtaining as much knowledge as possible. So much so that his peers often ribbed him about being a genuine hard-ass, but truth be told, Ben would be one of the first soldiers that they would choose to cover their asses in any FUBAR situation. As far as Ben's superiors, they appreciated his serious, hard-edged spirit and saw great potential in him—an opinion that was shared up through the ranks of command.

As such, in February of 1992, Ben's superiors promoted him to 1st Lieutenant. Once the promotion had officially went through, he'd wasted no time submitting his application to be transferred to the 75th Infantry Regiment. Advancing to the next rank had been the only item left for him to accomplish, and now that that was out of the way, he was officially qualified to be considered for a move into the 75th. He'd come to love the 504th, but his heart was still set on his becoming a leader within the elite Ranger Regiment. Since his promotion, he'd obtained a recommendation from his Brigade Commander and had already gone before the Ranger Board. Now, it was just a waiting game to hear back on the Board's decision. Ben focused hard on his men and exercises but he would be a liar to claim that he wasn't anxious about the forthcoming decision.

FOR THE LAST TWO WEEKS, Ben's Company had been training for a possible upcoming mission. He had no briefing details, only that it involved a low-altitude jump, which was just one of the many trademarks of the 504th. A team from the 20th Engineer Brigade had been brought in to create what most assumed was a small landing strip in the middle of a wooded training area. The black asphalt was narrow and short by any aircraft standards, thus Ben had figured out that it wasn't meant to mock an airstrip at all, rather a small stretch of road. The last week of training had transitioned from daytime to nighttime jumps, so Ben had also correctly deduced that the mission was to be executed under stealth conditions. Although he didn't know the where or the when, he thought he had a pretty good handle on the how—and being a soldier, that's all he needed to know.

A black jump into a potential hostile urban area with little or no cover? Hell yeah, follow me! Hooah!

Ben stood in line, hooked-up and ready, calmly waiting behind six of his men from one of the squads he commanded. The inside glow of the airplane's hull finally turned from red to green when the jump-light on the C-141 jet switched over, giving the visual go-signal for jumping.

Sphincter-time!

The jumpmaster yelled "Go! Go! Go!" at the first man and Ben watched as his paratrooper vanished from the plane's opening. The mission training had entailed a static-line jump from 600 feet, which was moderately low but especially-so considering the hard asphalt that they were targeting below. Ben often awed at the historical fact that the D-Day paratroopers had trained with 150-foot jumps. He'd made a couple jumps at that altitude and it was an adrenaline-filled eight seconds that made bull-riding seem like a pussy sport.

Ben stared at Jonesy, his radio operator, who was one man ahead and Ben began feeling sorry for the guy. He was short, even shorter

267

than Ben, and had to endure the extra 160-lbs above and beyond his own body weight. To get a sense of the load, the radio gear that Jonesy was jumping with weighed 17-lbs more than anything the M60 gunner had to worry about. Bottom line, it meant a bitch of a landing that could easily crush an ankle or break a leg if not nailed correctly. But the guy was gung-ho and took on the craziest challenges just to mute the naysayers. Ben had respected that and could certainly relate and thus had allowed the grunt to be his radio operator, even at the advisement against doing so from one of his First Sergeants who had bluntly told Ben it was a serious err in judgment to allow it.

It was Jonesy's turn and Ben was next. He thought how the silliest things entered his mind right before he had to jump out of an airplane. Most people probably thought about the parachute not properly opening, or getting snagged on the jet and being dragged, or even on the hard landing. But not Ben, because at that moment he was wishing that he could pick the damn wedgie out of his ass that his friggin' leg-strap saddle had caused.

Baby powder: check.

Ben watched as his radioman disappeared and then his own adrenaline finally kicked in.

God, I love this shit.

Ben held the bight of the yellow 15-foot static-line in his left hand. He heard the "Go!-Go!-Go!" from the jumpmaster and then felt the pat on the back of his thigh. Ben jumped out of the opening and as required, held a tight body position to cut through the airflow. His rucksack, low on his legs, caught air first and then his torso followed suit. Once his line paid-out and the d-bag from his pack was yanked out by the force, then all of the suspension lines and risers followed suit and dragged out from the d-bag.

It's turbo-adrenaline time, ladies and gentlemen.

Once the 50-lbs of slack weight tugged hard, Ben's canopy ties broke free and the canopy started sneaking out from the pack. The canopy kept drawing out until all of the remaining slack was gone, which caused a final pull that broke the apex ties and fully freed the chute from its d-bag. That was Ben's first instinctual-check of knowing that he was completely free of the big jet. She was now safely above him, flying away while dragging his no-longer-needed d-bag in tow.

The first time Ben had experienced a static-line jump, it unfortunately reminded him of one of the worst memories of his lifetime. He had unwillingly compared his first time to Wade cutting the little baby's umbilical cord and pulling the newborn away from her mother's body. Needless to say, the memory had made the first experience an unpleasant one, so Ben had promised himself to never allow past memories to interfere with his training again. It had been the only mulligan he would allow himself to have, and the older Ben got, the better he got at suppressing such memories. Lord knows he had more than his fair share, but he could no longer afford them—his men depended on his sharp focus and he knew that singular thoughts on the objectives at hand, whatever they may be, were imperative.

Once the airstream wake of the big jet threw Ben forward, it caused the drag to finally catch him and then he tea-cupped from being sideways into an upright position. Over the course of many jumps, he'd learned to enjoy that opening shock, and even now it reminded him of the squirrel cages back at the Yamboree Fair. And the resulting hard tug marked the start of another critical phase of the fall.

One. Two. Three. Four.

After the count, Ben looked up and saw a full canopy above his head, which meant he could now cross off the second instinctual-check of having his chute fully deployed. There was yet a third and final phase of the jump remaining, which was safely landing in the drop-zone. Unfortunately, he wouldn't be able to cross that one off of the "successful jump" list. A freakish side-wind gusted him off-course—how bad he couldn't yet determine. He anxiously looked all around and at first didn't see any of his men. For a moment he was thankful that he was the only one caught in the strong wind, but his celebration was cut short when he saw a full canopy to his lower left, and he knew it had to be Jonesy.

Goddammit!

Ben kept his eyes on his radio man's chute as they both drifted into the same pattern. Ten seconds and another 200-feet passed by before Ben finally made the outlines of what he knew were tree-tops.

Fuck!

Ben disengaged his equipment harness to release his ruck and rifle. Utilizing the benefits of years of constant PT, he employed his core strength to curl into a fetal position, making ready as best he could for the impending impact with the beautiful pines that he'd admired many times in the last two weeks. He'd even been tempted to sneak off a few days back and go climb a tree or two.

Not what I fucking had in mind.

Ben experienced all kinds of hurt as he crashed through the trees but he ignored his own pain and instead prayed for Jonesy.

Please God let him be okay.

Once Ben's chute followed him down into the tree, it almost instantly shredded and sent him into a full-gravity freefall. He crashed through mostly small limbs until a fat branch knocked him out cold, and that was even with his helmet securely fastened in place. Luckily, his canopy finally caught on some boughs to stop his freefall, but only after a small limb had jabbed him in the right eye and another had pierced his left thigh. Fortunately, the large branch had spared him from realizing either injury by rendering him completely unconscious throughout the remainder of the fall.

Unfortunately, Jonesy hadn't been so lucky. He wasn't able to release the heavy radio in time and therefore couldn't protect himself as well as Ben did during his fall. A branch, which was sharply splintered in-two from a hard snow the previous winter, punctured the young soldier's back. The force impaled the radioman's major organs, and the only good thing about that was that he'd been mercifully killed without any pain, but killed nonetheless.

- 35 -

DÉJÀ VU

IT WAS DÉJÀ VU ALL OVER AGAIN—Ben woke up in a place confused about where the hell he was and what the hell he was doing there. He reached up to feel the gauze over his right eye and tried to recall why it was bandaged. He then nervously lifted the sheet and checked to make sure that his below-the-belt vitals were intact. He breathed a sigh of relief once he verified that all equipment was right where it should be with no apparent damage.

Thank you Lord. At least now I can rule out stepping on a Bouncing Betty.

He noticed more bandages on his left thigh and began comforting himself that none of it was serious because he wasn't in any pain. Little did he know that the only reason he wasn't sweating from agony was because of the high dosage of drugs flowing into his veins from the I.V. drip.

Why am I so damn thirsty?

Ben was barely coherent enough to notice the plastic water-pitcher sitting on the tray-table next to his bed. He picked the container up, stuck his face down inside and then celebrated by shouting, "Bingo!" He started guzzling the cold goodness straight from the pitcher without even bothering to pour it into the accompanying cup that was also on the tray-table. The water tasted delicious to Ben, and it also had the unfortunate side-effect of helping him to somewhat come to his senses. He continued gulping until he drank the last swallow and then he let out a loud belch that strangely seemed to trigger his memory. The training jump began to slowly fade-in until the accident was clear enough in his mind to bring about an urgent feeling of despair.

Jonesy!

Ben found the nurse's call button and impatiently pressed it. After a few minutes passed, a doctor entered the room and approached Ben.

"Good to see you awake, Lieutenant," the doctor said.

"How is Jonesy doing? Is he in the next room?" Ben asked.

"I'm not sure, son. You're the only one that was brought in to me. Maybe he's elsewhere."

Ben pushed himself up and started to get out of the bed, but was quickly halted by the doctor.

"I need to get back to—"

"Stop, Lieutenant! You get back in bed. That's an order."

Ben quickly noticed the oak leaf on the doctor's lapel and then eased back to comply with the stern order that he was just given.

"I need to find out what happened, sir."

"I understand that. One of the officers from your unit will be by to see you soon. All I can do is fill you in on your condition and that will just have to do for now."

"Yes, sir. Sorry, sir."

"Now...you've suffered some very serious injuries, son."

"But I feel fine, doc—sir."

"Well, you won't feel so great if I take you off of the pain meds, Lieutenant. Now shut up and listen." The doctor paused to make sure the new order was well received before continuing, "Your right eye has been severely damaged. It was—"

Ben reached up again to feel the bandages covering his eye and interrupted the doctor once again.

"Is it gone! Am I blind!"

"Please let me finish, Lieutenant! As I was saying, your right eye was severely punctured during your fall. A top surgeon was flown in to perform the optical reconstruction surgery. I'm afraid now all we can do is wait and evaluate how the nerves heal. But until they heal, we won't be able to tell to what extent the permanent damage will be, if any. Unfortunately, it will take at least three weeks before we can make that determination. The surgeon will fly back down and evaluate the healing at that time. Now, regarding—"

"Am I going to lose the eye, sir? What's the probability?"

"I'm not going to sugar coat it for you, son. The surgeon said that, based on the amount of reconstruction he had to perform, you have a fifty-fifty chance of having permanent damage and a twenty percent chance of blindness. Those are tough odds to hear. I'm sorry, son."

Ben quickly mulled it over and optimistically concluded that he could beat those odds—his eye was going to be fine.

Power of positive thinking.

The doctor continued, "Now, regarding your rectus femoris—it was also punctured during the fall."

"My asshole!" Ben exclaimed as he lifted up, ready to check for himself.

"No, not your rectum you idiot—your left quadracep—your thigh muscle. But I promise you this, if you interrupt me one more time, I'm going to surgically rip you a new asshole, Lieutenant."

"Sorry, sir."

"You also suffered a moderate concussion. All in all, you are extremely lucky, son. But again, I need to stress to you that you have some very serious injuries that require plenty of healing. Which is why if you try to get out of bed again, I'm going to have you restrained and heavily sedated. In the grand scheme of things, you will be fine if you take it easy. Now, with your *leg*, I'm mainly concerned about infection at this point. Your brain, assuming that you actually have one, should heal, so the only short-term effects from the concussion may be headaches and slight nausea. Now then, what other questions do you have for me?"

"I'm not sure I have anymore, sir. Wait. The mission. Is it possible for me to get back to work by next week, considering I keep my eye bandaged?"

"Do I really need to dignify that stupid question with a response, Lieutenant?"

"No sir."

"Good answer. Maybe you do have a brain after all. Now get some rest. I'll let your unit know that you're awake and I'll go ahead and allow visits."

"Thank you, sir."

The doctor left the room and Ben tried to settle his nerves, which were officially shot. It was hopeless to even attempt to stop worrying though as he cycled from stressing about his eye to becoming nauseous from wondering what happened to Jonesy. The truth was that deep down he had a bad feeling about everything. But the fear of Jonesy being killed was the clincher, causing tears of sorrow to well up in one of Ben's eye for sure—apparently, the other eye was a crap shoot at that point.

Nobody came to visit until the following morning, so Ben spent all night tormenting over Jonesy's fate. His first visitor was his Captain but it was a short visit and not so sweet. The news regarding Jonesy was the worst, just as Ben had feared. Once the Captain left, Ben sat in silence and wept for Jonesy. The tears of sadness slowly gave way to gut-wrenching sobs of overwhelming guilt, holding himself completely responsible for the private's death.

THE NEXT DAY BEN'S MAIL included a letter from the Ranger Board. He nervously opened the envelope and read the letter, which turned out to be a congratulatory dispatch explaining to him how to enroll into the Ranger Orientation program to make it all official. He smiled and thanked God that he'd finally made it. But then the guilt of Jonesy's death seeped back in and he began kicking himself again. He knew that he had no right to celebrate and was ashamed of himself for the brief moment of disrespect and complete selfishness. He sat there and continued to mentally torture himself until the meds finally dripped back into his system and put him to sleep again.

Four days later Ben was of the opinion that he was doing much better, as was evident—he thought—by the fact that he could finally go use the bathroom on his own. His thigh hurt like a motherfucker when he walked, but he was able to push through the pain.

One of Ben's fellow lieutenants came to visit to let him know that they'd been given the order to report to a mission briefing and that all signs pointed to the team deploying soon. When his colleague left, Ben wasted no time getting up and getting dressed. Once he was back in uniform, he snuck out of the hospital and went to his apartment to pack for the mission. There was no way in hell he was going to allow his men to be in harm's way without him being there to cover their asses—or so the high-dosage of meds still in his system made him think.

WHEN BEN GOT HOME, he removed the bandage from his eye but was too afraid to open it just yet. His solution to the problem was to wear army issue sunglasses and hide it as much as he could.

Who says you can't look cool at a mission briefing?

Ben floated his way to the headquarters building, only remembering leaving his apartment and then magically showing up on base, but nothing in between. He snuck into the commander's large meeting room undetected where it looked like everyone else was already seated and waiting.

I'm a ghost. Nobody even notices me. Hell yeah.

Ben stood at the back wall, far away from the door to the strategy room where he assumed the Colonel would enter the briefing area from. Ben listened to the buzz of the room full of officers and he could feel everyone's anticipation. All were gung-ho and ready.

Hooah, motherfuckers, hooah!

The front door that Ben was standing next to opened and the Colonel walked past him but then stopped and froze. He then did an agile about face, walked right up to Ben and stood only inches from his face.

"River, what in the hell do you think you're doing here? No, don't answer that. Don't say one word. I know what you *think* you're doing here, but deep down you know it's a stupid brain fart of a stunt. Now, here are your orders, Lieutenant. You will immediately exit my conference, go say goodbye to your men, and then march your ass back to the hospital. I'm going to pretend that you're not AWOL and in doing so, I'm going to forget that you were ever here. Do I make myself clear, Lieutenant?"

"Yes sir," Ben replied.

"Good, now get the fuck out of here."

Ben reluctantly followed the orders. He spent a lot of time talking with his sergeants, reviewing the training over-and-over until they finally told him to just shut-the-fuck-up—with all due respect, of course. He visited all of his men and gave them motivational speeches, which came out more as slurs from being under the influence of the damn meds. And in retrospect, his medicated state had obviously clouded his judgment and his actions that day. In fact, he scarcely remembered what he'd even said or what he'd even done. But one thing was for sure: his men had a hell of a time laughing at him as he floated around their barracks, slushing incomprehensible orders at everyone in sight.

BEN CAUGHT HOLY HELL from the Major, or as Ben referred to him: Dr. Bedside-Manners. Ben wasn't hearing anything but "blah-blah-blah" until the doctor said something about going blind, which jolted a harsh pang in Ben's heart like a sharp elbow getting his attention.

"You have got to be the dumbest West Point graduate I've ever met. Hell, I'm so dumbfounded by your stupidity that I had to pull your service record to see for myself. I find it hard to believe that you ranked 53rd in your graduating class at The Point. You must've cheated—either that or I need to run more MRIs on you to check for brain damage. Oh, I forgot, you don't have a brain! I should've followed my instinct and had you restrained night and day. Apparently the meds aren't enough to sedate your gung-ho Ranger ass. Stupid! And now that you've taken it upon yourself to remove the bandage and the isolation cup along with it, we have to assess the damage you've done, when we shouldn't be doing anything for another two weeks. But you've pushed that timetable up, Lieutenant. If I were you, I'd start praying, bug fuck!"

Ben waited for the Major to finish the ass chewing and then he did just that—he started praying. The major excused himself without saying another word and Ben hoped that the doctor was leaving to go and calm down. Fifteen minutes later the doctor came back into Ben's hospital room and his face wasn't as red as before. He fiddled with some items in a cabinet and walked back over to Ben. He told Ben to hold still and then took a wet cotton swab and gently moistened Ben's eyelids. The doctor continued swabbing until he was satisfied that the lids were pliable enough to be freed.

Then he used both hands to slowly push open Ben's right eye. Ben felt the sting from the lids and knew they were open, but all he saw out of his right eye was blackness. Ben's heart sank to the bottom of his stomach as he heard the doctor let out a defeated breath before re-closing the ruined eye.

"I'm sorry, son."

"It just needs more time to heal. Right, doc?"

"No Lieutenant. Your right eye is gone. There's complete corneal opacity. Nothing can be done. I'm very sorry."

The doctor squeezed Ben's shoulder and Ben went completely numb, praying and pleading once again.

Please God, let it be just a bad dream. Wake the fuck up, Ben! Wake up you stupid son-of-a-bitch!

ANOTHER TWO WEEKS had passed and Ben finally got released from the hospital. He'd had plenty of time to heal his outside wounds, and he'd also had time to dig deep and think about everything in his life. He realized that he would no longer be admitted into the Ranger Regiment—that he knew with certainty. More than likely he would be transferred to a desk job assignment, and if he was lucky he would become an instructor, which is what he was going to fight for. In any case, one thing was for sure: he would never lead men into battle—and after what had happened to Jonesy, Ben honestly believed that it was truly for the best.

Later in the day, Ben's Captain came to see him at his house, and once again, it wasn't a "how are you doing" kind of visit. It seemed that the Captain had become the bearer of nothing but bad-fucking-news. He let Ben know that his team's mission had failed miserably and that things had gotten all FUBAR. As a result, half of Ben's platoon had been killed by enemy rocket fire. After the Captain let himself out, Ben went to go throw up in the toilet and then followed-up with going to his bedroom and beating the living shit out of his mattress—once again summoning some of that good ole déjà vu.

LATER THAT NIGHT and for the first time in his life, Benjamin Wilder River decided to get drunk off of his ass. He visited a local bar and when asked what he wanted, he answered by telling the bartender to give him a brain grenade. When the bartender returned a "you're a dumbass look", Ben figured that his drink order apparently hadn't been specific enough. But honestly, he had no earthly idea what he wanted or what he needed. He knew for damn sure what he *wasn't* going to drink and that was whiskey. He'd never willingly have anything in common with the Rabid Dog, or Wade for that matter—so, whiskey was definitcly off the table. He thought about a gin and tonic like his mom used to drink, but the smell of her puke came back to him and he gagged at the thought. Then he recalled Octavio's choice of spirit and ordered a shot of Tequila. Ten shots and two fights later, the police were finally called to come pick Ben up. And once again, he woke up in a cold, strange place with absolutely no idea what had happened. He'd blacked out after six shots, but his gung-ho Ranger wannabe dumb-ass kept pushing through. And by the look of his bruised face, he'd made a lot of *friends* in the process. When the jailors let Ben go, they did their best to keep as much distance from him as possible. Why, Ben had no idea until he got home and finally caught a good whiff of himself. He hit the shower so that he could get rid of the puked tequila stench and more importantly, to completely sober up so he could feel like an absolute rotten piece of shit all over again.

As soon as Ben got dressed, he sat down to eat some cereal. He'd regurgitated all of his nutrients the night before and even though he didn't really feel like consuming any food, he'd become jittery and knew he needed to get something in his stomach. He looked down at the bowl filled with Rice Krispy's and reminisced back on the disgusting dead weevils he used to pick out of the stale puffs of rice back in Gilmer. Then he remembered how Gramps poured him a bowl the first time they met, and how that also had been the first time he had ever had real Rice Krispy's. He thought about how Gramps had introduced so many real things in life to him. He sat there and thought a lot about his Gramps and the man's kindness and sense of humor. He wondered what Morgan would say to him about everything that had just happened. He tried his best to imagine the words from the man who always seemed to say exactly what Ben needed to hear. Ben listened hard for several minutes and when the words finally came, he nodded his head and thanked his Gramps for still being there for him, even in spirit. He continued thinking about the realization that just came from his heart, even though to Ben it had come straight from his dearly departed Gramps. In truth, who's to say that both weren't one in the same?

Ben flipped on his small TV and watched a Road Runner cartoon to keep him distracted as he ate the cereal. He was still agitated, hurt, and feeling very guilty—but, like he told Gramps about becoming a cow at The Point—the worm was turning. The doorbell rang and it interrupted Wylie Coyote getting blown up by a stick of ACME Dynamite. Ben had a sneaky suspicion who was behind the interruption and like Wylie, his blood pressure elevated a little in anticipation.

If it's the goddamn Captain again, I'm going to fucking kill him—I shit myself not!

He opened the door and let the Colonel *and* the Captain in. Ben decided he would spare the bearer-of-bad-newsman's life since the Colonel decided to tag along for the happy-happy-joy-joy visit. The Colonel wasted no time by getting to the point to explain that it had been decided by the chain of command that Ben would be given the option to choose an honorable discharge or desk reassignment. The inflection and tone that the Colonel used to deliver the message broke Ben's heart, but at the same time it provided clarity and affirmation of the earlier words he'd received from his Gramps. So, instead of feeling hurt or angry or resentful, he instead chose to feel relief. As such, he didn't have to ponder the decision. Right then and there, he told the Colonel that he would officially and formally request an honorable discharge. Ben was done with death, and it was clear to him now that the military was no longer the answer to his life.

And for the first time, Ben finally understood why Gramps had never really wanted him to join the military in the first place. Gramps had known all along that Ben wasn't cut out for it—not that he couldn't—he'd already proven to himself and to everyone else that he could—it was just that he *shouldn't*. All along it had been that simple—too simple for Ben to see. And now there was a freedom that Ben hadn't felt since the day he stole the old Charger and left his abusive childhood behind. Only this time he was running towards what he hoped was a righteous manhood. He felt a glimpse of newfound hope and even a smidgeon of excitement at the thought of searching and one day finding his true calling in life.

HOPE, ARKANSAS – APRIL 1992

BEN CROSSED TWO MINIATURE U.S. FLAGS as he stuck them into the green grass in front of the gravestone. He then picked up a few dead leaves from the base and crumpled them in his hand before tracing the engraved letters with his finger.

He looked up at the clear blue sky and said, "I sure do miss you, Gramps. I pray you're not disappointed in me. I don't think you are, and I hope I'm right about that. I promise to try to make the best use of everything you gave me and everything you taught me. I probably won't be back for a while. I hope you understand. I think you do."

LATER AT MORGAN'S OLD HOUSE, Ben took a map of the U.S. and spread it out onto the old kitchen table. He tied one end of a long piece of black thread to a map pin and wound the other end around a yellow No. 2 pencil. He pushed the pin into the small circle on the map that represented the city of Hope, Arkansas. He then pulled the string taught and unwound the pencil until he could make a large sweeping arc around the map, with Hope acting as the arc's center point. He started unwinding the pencil until he found the maximum radius that intersected a major US city. To his surprise, it wasn't any city in New England like he'd originally guessed. As it turned out, the farthest metropolis from Hope, Arkansas appeared to be Seattle, WA.

Seattle it is then.

A car honked its horn and Ben peeked out of the window at the cab. He walked out the front door of the old house and locked it up behind him. He walked past a 'FOR SALE' sign and then with nothing but the clothes on his back, he got in a taxi and told the driver to take him to the Little Rock National Airport. He smiled one last time at the house as the cab drove away. It was a happy smile for a happy place and was also Ben's final salute to Morgan River. And it just so happened that a smile from Ben was the only kind of salute that his Gramps had ever really wanted.

GILMER, TEXAS

THE PICTURE-PERFECT BOONE FAMILY was gathered around the television watching the late evening news. Angie was sitting next to Jessup on the couch and Tommy was watching from a worn-out recliner in the corner of the living room. Tommy happened to be the only one not drunk out of his mind. Instead, he'd just come down off of a meth-high and felt himself becoming agitated, which meant he would need another fix—sooner the better.

"I can't believe the State of Texas voted a cunt into the office as governor," Jessup said.

"Why? I like her," Angie sloshed.

"Woman, who gives a fuck who you like?"

"I'm just saying. I liked her enough that I voted for her."

"You fucking did what?"

Angie cowered as Jessup viciously released his arm and backhanded her hard, causing her head to crash into the couch's arm and bounce up to the back cushion, just like a human bank-shot.

"You could've been the one fucking vote that tipped it in the favor of that cunt, you stupid bitch!"

Jessup stood up so he could do more, proper damage. He reared his hand back again but this time Tommy was there to grab it.

"Enough, Pop."

Jessup staggered a little, half in surprise and half from his inebriated state.

"What the fuck! Did you just tell me 'enough', fucker? And did you just touch me? I'm going to fucking kill you now."

Jessup went to grab Tommy but Tommy pushed his dad's arm away and then hit him with a good right cross, which turned out to inflict more damage on Jessup than anyone else had ever done before. The impact caused a tooth to fly from the Rabid Dog's mouth and land right into his whiskey glass. Jessup caught himself on the end table and pushed his tongue through the new opening in his mouth. His sharp cheeks tinted hot red as he slowly straightened up to turn and face Tommy.

Just like the rest of the tri-county area, Tommy knew that there was one sure-fire way to sober-up Jessup James Boone and that was with a good fight. Tommy saw the look in his dad's eyes and knew he was a goner if he didn't act fast—so in self-preservation, Tommy ran out of the front door as fast as he could. He headed straight for the woods and didn't stop until he was sure that his dad hadn't followed.

- 36 -

MADDIE

CHICAGO, ILLINOIS – APRIL 1992

AFTER DISCOVERING HE HAD a seven hour layover, Ben started walking through O'Hare International Airport searching for a Ranger grave where he could dig in and wait it out. Walking along the terminals, two grunts in camo fatigues approached him and his right hand twitched a little in anticipation of returning their salutes, but of course no salutes came. Ben's exit from military life hadn't yet sunk in, even to the point of still thinking he was in uniform. He'd been conditioned for the last five, damned near six years to react to his environment with regulatory responses—having been taught to be habitual in everything he did from dressing to grooming to eating to sleeping and yes, to even how he shat. But now he was a civilian and as such, he needed to focus on how to start acting like one.

This is going to take some time.

He found a small airport café that looked dead and took a corner booth. An unenthusiastic waitress brought him water and took his order of coffee with cream. Ben began reading a *Byte* magazine that he'd bought earlier from one of the airport gift shops. He began with page one and started reading every leaf with an academic thoroughness that would put most sane people to sleep and pausing only when his coffee was delivered. After toning down the steaming sludge with some cream, he picked up the mug and finally looked up from the periodical and took a sip. At the same moment, his acute tracking skills noticed a beautiful woman sitting in another booth in the other corner. She looked up from her own reading material just as the boiling hot liquid made contact and burned the living hell out of Ben's upper lip and tongue.

"Holy sh—!"

Ben clumsily tumbled the coffee, spilling it on his magazine in the process. He quickly reached for the ice water and used it to soothe his caffeine wounds. He heard a cute snicker and noticed that the beautiful woman was laughing at his ham-fisted maneuver.

Great.

The woman then pitched her head and squinted her eyes as if focusing. Ben thought that she was maybe legally blind and that perhaps she hadn't seen his smooth move after all. The woman's eyes finally straightened and then she smiled at him.

Damn, no such luck.

He returned an embarrassing grin and could feel his cheeks turn red in the process. Ben Wilder River, hot-shot West Point graduate, former Red Devil officer, and almost-bad-ass-Ranger had just got beat up by a cup of Joe.

Fucking hot-lava is what that shit is.

The woman picked up her glass of red wine along with her own reading material and slid out from her booth. Ben thought that at least he could feel stupid with some privacy now that she was leaving. But instead of leaving, the woman walked over to his booth and slid in right next to him. The same adrenaline that pumped through his veins before insanely jumping out of a perfectly fine aircraft had just kicked in gear, only this time it was induced by the female creature now sitting so close to him that he could feel her body heat. The woman continued to scoot even closer, never taking her eyes off of him.

Okay—this is a little awkward, Ben thought.

"Lieutenant Benjamin W. River," the woman said with the most perfect smile Ben had ever seen—Raina's included.

"I'm sorry, miss. Do we know each other?" Ben asked.

"Not really. Although, I have been trying to change that for the last few months now."

"Okay, now I'm officially confused."

"It's me. Maddie," and the woman held out her hand.

Ben couldn't help but think how incredibly sexy she was. Even her hand, now extended and waiting, caused things to stir in him. He reached and gently squeezed it and then said, "Pleasure, Maddie."

"That's quite the pussy handshake you have there for a tough soldier."

Her response completely threw Ben off his game, which was already pretty weak, and he scrambled for a few moments before attempting to regain his composure.

"I—I—I'm not a soldier anymore. How exactly do we know each other again?"

"Wow, even my name doesn't ring a bell. Did you even open the letters I sent you?"

Ben racked his head. *Maddie. Maddie. Maddie.* "Oh shit! Madeline Lewis! Yes, of course I read your letters. I—I just thought..."

"Do all military elites stutter and form incomplete thoughts?"

"What? No, no, it's—it's just..."

"Wow. See what I mean?"

"I thought you were a lot younger is all."

"You're on a roll, Ben. Not only have you insulted me by not recognizing me, but now you're insinuating that I write letters like an elementary student. Again, wow."

"No, no, no. That's not what I meant."

"Oh, so you're saying I'm an old maid then."

"Let me explain, please."

"Can't wait."

"I didn't recognize you because when I pulled you from your car, you were soaked in blood. To me, you looked like a teeny-bopper. And it happened so fast. And then I tried to go see you in the hospital, but they wouldn't let me in because I wasn't family. And I've been meaning to respond to your letters. Honest. I've just had a lot happening lately."

"Hmmmm. Okay, I suppose you've redeemed yourself—for the time being."

"Phuwwwweee. I've never had a drill instructor or even a

commander who made me sweat so much."

Maddie smiled and said, "I'm sorry to bust your balls, Ben. I was just having a little fun."

"At my expense, you mean."

"Yeah, I suppose. You forgive me?"

"For the time being."

Maddie raised an eyebrow and said, "Touché. And I like the patch, by the way."

"Yeah, right."

"Oh, I'm not joking. *That* I *am* serious about. It's very sexy."

Something again stirred in Ben. Truth be told, the way she'd just said that moved him in all kinds of ways.

"I'm embarrassingly speechless."

"That's okay, talking is overrated anyway. There are *other* things more fun to do."

Ben swallowed so hard that he was sure he made a gulping noise.

Maddie laughed and said, "Calm down there soldier, I'm *teasing* you. What, you think I'm that easy?"

"I think it's time I surrender."

"Smart boy. Now, why don't you fill me in on what's been going on in the life of Benjamin W. River. How about starting by telling me about that patch over your eye?"

Ben's mood immediately changed and a dark cloud came over his countenance.

"Maybe some other time, Maddie."

"I'm sorry. I didn't mean to upset you. I'll shut up now."

"No, don't do that. You didn't do anything wrong. I like listening to you, Maddie. Tell me about *you*. Tell me everything. I mean what

I don't already know from your letters. Are you still living in Southern California?"

"Oh. So you *did* read them. Good boy." Maddie smiled, sat back, bit her lower lip and stared at him in a way that made him forget about everything.

After having finally met Madeline Lewis, the *girl* that he had saved, Ben thought that she was nothing short of amazing.

I'd crash land into a thousand trees for this woman.

- 37 -

HOOK, LINE, SINKER

SEATTLE, WASHINGTON – APRIL 1992

THE AFTERNOON AIR WAS COOL and the steady drizzle exaggerated the hazy day's actual temperature. Ben had already ducked into a department store and purchased his Seattle survival kit: a hoodie, that day's issue of the *Seattle Times*, and of course a tall cup of hot java. It was Ben's first time to experience the emerald city and so he spent the day walking around the storefronts of Pioneer Square. Afterwards, he pondered his first impression of the city and settled on thinking that it was 'groovy'.

After walking all morning, Ben came to an intersection and

noticed an old 'MERCHANTS CAFÉ' sign on a building across the thoroughfare. The advertisement reminded him that he hadn't eaten anything solid since having dinner with Maddie at the airport the day before. He smiled at the memory of her and thought once again that fate had thrown him a curve ball, only this one felt especially good.

Ben crossed the street and headed towards the groovy-looking restaurant. He walked in and was seated at a table covered with a red velvet cloth. He placed the folded newspaper on the table next to a small lamp and he glanced up at the upper section of the wall. Directly above the lamp, hung an oil painting of a beautiful young woman sitting nude in a brown wing-back chair. Her long brunette hair flowed beyond her soft shoulders and her legs and feet were pulled up onto the seat in an almost upright fetal position. One of her breasts was barely visible and a long pearl necklace dangled from her right hand to a red rug on the floor.

Maybe it was because Ben had a case of Maddie-on-the-brain, but he was entranced at how the young woman in the painting bore a striking resemblance to Maddie.

Sister maybe? Maybe Maddie models? God knows she's pretty enough. Damn, it really looks like her.

His mind began wondering if the other parts in the painting matched Maddie's other respective parts. He finally broke his own trance and then firmly reprimanded himself for the horn-dog thoughts. But he couldn't help it—he'd been thinking a lot about Maddie ever since they had officially met the day before. In fact, he was finding it difficult to *not* think about her. He laughed at how he'd always assumed that she was a younger girl, when in fact she was three years older than him. Thinking back, he wasn't sure why he'd made the assumption—maybe it was the blood, or maybe because it happened so fast, or more likely because he was in shock from his own injury. In Ben's defense, she did have a youthful look to her, but she was also very womanly at the same time.

Sexy. Seductive. Sizzling hot.

She'd mentioned to Ben that people usually assumed she was younger, and then she jabbed him, yet again, by letting him know that he was, however, the first to accuse her of being a teeny-bopper.

Teeny-bopper? What a dumb-ass I was yesterday. A complete stuttering idiot. She probably won't answer the phone if I ever do decide to call her. If? Yeah, right. First chance you get, you're calling her and you know it. Stop kidding yourself, dumbass.

A waitress had been standing at Ben's table as he silently conversed with himself, which to her and everyone else made it look like he was just gawking at the painting of the nude woman. When he finally noticed the waitress, he once again turned beet-red—and once again because of Maddie. At first, the older waitress didn't look like she was impressed with Ben's appreciation of *fine* art but then she surprised him with her greeting.

"Don't worry young man. You're not the first to stare. What can I get you today?"

"To be honest, I haven't even looked at the menu, ma'am."

She laughed aloud, "I noticed."

"Umm. Sorry. What do you recommend?"

"Personally, I think the grilled cheese is hard to beat."

"Sounds perfect. With a diet coke, please."

"Fries okay with that?"

"Sure."

"Okay young man, you got it."

"Oh, do you happen to have a pen I can borrow?"

The waitress pulled four different pens from her apron's front pocket and said, "Take your pick."

"The red one, please. Thank you."

She handed him the pen and you're-welcomed him before disappearing into the kitchen. Ben took his checkbook and his latest savings account statement from his back pocket and sat them on the red velvet tablecloth. He opened the checkbook's register and looked at the $12,238.28 balance. He then unfolded the savings statement and read the balance of $1,704,223.63 as of the last closing period.

"I guess that means I can afford to buy a car."

He opened the newspaper and found the classifieds section and began looking at the used cars for sale. After reading numerous ads, a big smile suddenly formed on his face. He took the red pen and circled the print that advertised a 1967 Pontiac GTO in mint condition for sale.

Car: Check.

He turned a few pages ahead to the housing rental ads and began studying them. Not long afterwards, he made a 'hmmm' face and circled an ad for a one bedroom house in Alki Beach. Ben had no idea where the hell that was, but if it was a real beach, well then that was all he really needed to know.

Shelter: Check.

A MIRROR-BLACK FINISH 1967 GTO pulled up to the curb of a

small beach house that had a 'FOR RENT' sign in its front yard. Ben youthfully hopped out of his newly acquired car and walked towards the house when he noticed an eagle fly overhead. He smiled at the regal bird and continued his approach to the small rambler. A middle-aged man answered the door and introduced himself as the owner, and then welcomed Ben into the home. Ben followed the man as he began giving a tour of the rooms.

The small house had an open floor plan with plenty of full-height windows and new maple hardwood floors throughout. The owner walked down a small hallway that led to the bedroom, but Ben diverted and went his own way towards the living room's windowed French doors. He opened the doors and walked out onto a large deck that framed a serene view of Puget Sound painted against the majestic backdrop of Mount Rainier. Ben looked to his right and noticed a white lighthouse with a red roof in the distance up the beach-line. His stare straightened back to the front as his eyes tracked movement. He focused in on the eagle that he saw earlier and noticed that it had landed on the beach at the water's edge where it was waiting for its dinner to make the mistake of showing itself in the shallow surf.

Wow!

Just like in New York City, Ben was mesmerized by the beauty of his surroundings. The homeowner eventually caught on to Ben's escape and joined him out on the deck.

"Oh, hey, there you are. I thought I lost you."

"I'll take it."

Ben already knew what he would call his new home. It would henceforth be known as *The Eagle's Nest*.

A HUSKY BEARDED MAN had one end of the plastic covered couch and Ben had the other. They made their way into the living room and sat the piece of furniture down.

"Man, I appreciate the help, but you don't have to," the delivery man said.

"Well I'm not going to just watch you unload the furniture without helping. What asshole would do that?"

The delivery man laughed and said, "Everyone but you, my friend. Besides, my helper is the one who's supposed to be helping, thus his glamorous title. But now he's just sitting his ass on your toilet."

"You think he's stalling in the stall do ya?"

"Good one. Yeah, probably."

"Tell you what. We'll switch out. He and I will get the next piece out of the truck."

"Dude, you're nuts. But I like the way you operate."

They did just that until Ben's new place had been filled with new furniture in every room. Afterwards he handed each of the delivery men a twenty dollar tip.

"You know, usually we're supposed to ask you to refer your friends to us for business. But in this case, we should refer you to everyone who needs furniture delivered so you can teach them manners. It's been a pleasure, Ben. And welcome to Seattle," the burly delivery man said.

"No, thank you. I needed the exercise and the furniture was a nice bonus," Ben replied.

After they left, Ben plopped down on his new leather sofa,

propped his legs on his new coffee table and picked up his new phone that was sitting on his new end table. He called the number that he'd already memorized after having only dialed it two times prior.

"Hello?" Maddie answered.

"Hi. It's Ben."

"I know who it is, sexy."

There she goes again, making me speechless, he thought.

As usual, he had to recover from the sound of her voice and then proceeded to tell her about his new place. When he shared with her the name he'd given his new residence, Maddie responded by calling him a big dork. But that was okay, because even her insults turned him on. In truth, he'd never shared personal things with the opposite sex before. He found himself wanting to share everything with her—even the most inconsequential of things. But he'd decided that telling her anything about his past was off-limits. He didn't want to lie, so his brilliant plan was to just avoid the subject altogether.

"Do you mind if I ask you a question?" Maddie asked.

"Maybe," Ben replied.

"What does that mean?"

"Just kidding, beautiful. Of course, ask away."

"What does the 'W' stand for?"

"The 'W'?"

"Your middle initial."

"Oh. It doesn't stand for anything. My mom just gave it to me because she thought it looked good on paper."

"Ahhh, like Harry S. Truman."

"Yes, precisely."

"Another question."

"Okay, shoot."

"Why Seattle? Why not California where it's sunny and warm every day and where yours truly just happens to be?"

"Because Seattle is the farthest place from Hope."

"What? That's the dumbest thing I've ever heard."

Ben laughed and said, "Yeah, probably is," and then he thought, *if you only knew.*

"So what are you going to do in Seattle? Is there a job there for you?"

"I'm not sure, yet. I just needed to start anew, you know."

"Yeah, I can relate. Well, Seattle has a good university. Maybe you can go back to school."

"No, I've had enough schooling to last a lifetime."

"So, you're just going to be a bum?"

"Sounds like a good plan to me."

"Deal breaker. I don't date bums."

"So, we're dating?"

"If you're lucky."

"I hope I am."

"Well, this would be my first long distance relationship. So, I'm not sure how it will work."

"Well, this will be my first relationship *period*."

"What? Get out of here. Are you serious? You're serious aren't you?"

"Yep. Go ahead. Make fun of me."

"Awwwwww. That's so sweet. I wouldn't make fun of that, Ben. I'm flattered that I'm your first girlfriend. But you've..."

"I've what?"

"You've *been* with another woman before, right?"

"Hanging up now."

"Oh my God. That's so sweet. Well, we're going to have to alleviate that problem soon."

"Holy shit, you are something else, Maddie."

"Oh baby, you have no idea. Just you wait."

"Okay, we need to change the subject because it's getting way too hot in my new place."

Maddie laughed and said, "I'm sorry, sexy. I'll stop. So back to the subject of what you're going to do, which is *not* become a bum. Serious. That is a deal breaker. Is there any particular line of work that you're good at?"

"What, besides blowing shit up and jumping out of perfectly fine aircraft?"

"Ummm. Yeah, besides that."

"I don't know. I really have no damn idea."

"Well, is there something that you've always liked to do that you can somehow fit into a career? Besides killing people I mean."

"Computers. Particularly computer programs. I've always loved computer programs."

"Awwww. You're a nerd deep down inside."

"Funny."

"Sorry. You really should check into that computer stuff, though. I happen to know they can bank some serious greenbacks."

"Where did you learn to speak? Greenbacks? You're something else, Maddie."

"Just you stay tuned big boy. But seriously, if you like computers, maybe that's what you should do."

"Yeah, I think you're right."

"You will find that I am always right."

"I have a feeling that not only are you right again, but that you know you're right again."

"That was deep, Ben."

"Thank you."

"It wasn't a compliment. But you do really make me want you."

"Oh no. We're back on *that* subject again. Going to go start the cold shower now."

They talked for several more hours until Ben was certain his ear would fall off. It wouldn't have mattered though because he could no longer feel it anymore as it had gone numb two hours before they finally hung up—but that didn't matter either because he was smitten.

Hook. Line. Sinker.

THE FOLLOWING DAY, Ben drove to a large bookstore in which an entire wall was dedicated to computer software books. Ben scanned each and every one of them from top to bottom as the assistant store manager approached.

"Sir, is there something I can help you find," the manager asked.

"Do you have a book cart? Better make it a very large book cart." Ben replied.

Ben bought every computer software book they had. The assistant store manager helped him load the books into the GTO, and even did so with a smile. Ben thought that his purchase of sixty-five books probably made for a good day's commission, so he accepted the help but wasn't smiling. He'd already contracted a headache just thinking about all of the reading that was in store for him.

WHEN BEN GOT HOME, it took him several trips back and forth from the car to the house, but he finally finished unloading all of the books that he'd just bought.

That was a pretty damn good workout. Damn books are heavy.

He stood back and looked at the six stacks of knowledge just waiting for him to dive into. He shook his head at the thought and went into the kitchen to make himself a glass of ice water. With water in hand, he walked out to the deck and sat on his new patio furniture. He stared out at Mount Rainier and unknowingly held the gaze for over an hour. The glass of water sat sweating on the arm of the Adirondack chair without ever being touched. Ben's mind never thought about the mountain in his view. His eye never even registered it. He was elsewhere, visiting a very dark, lonely place. But not by choice, because he had no control over what held him in its clutches. All he could do was just sit there staring at a beautiful snowcapped volcano that he didn't even see, all the while crying silent sad tears.

- 38 -

MISSING PARTS

SEATTLE, WASHINGTON – JULY 1993

THE LONG DISTANCE RELATIONSHIP between Ben and Maddie had proven too difficult to maintain, so one year after them trading monthly in-person visits, Maddie decided to hold her breath and dive head first from her sunny warmth into Ben's overcast gloominess. After having settled in, she'd come to find that the Pacific Northwest wasn't all that bad, in fact she likewise found that it was kind of 'groovy'.

Ben once again was sitting in his favorite spot on the deck and also once again not taking in the view because he was in his elsewhere-state. Over the last year, he'd spent more and more time at that dark place, deep inside himself. Maddie had been watching him from the French doors in the living room. She'd watched him get lost like that many times over the months and it frustrated her that she didn't understand what was going on with the man she loved. Quite frankly, it bugged the living hell out of her because she wasn't the type to let misunderstandings go unchecked. If Maddie didn't know something, she would always figure it out by whatever means she could, only Ben had proven to be her very first nemesis in destroying that perfect record. And that pissed her off to no end, especially since her chosen profession was investigative services. On more than one occasion, Ben had joked that he'd never imagined being hooked up with a private dick. She loved him and therefore had let his manly stupidity slide—for the time being.

Maddie opened the French doors, which caused Ben to snap out of his trance and turn to her and smile.

"Hi beautiful," he said.

"What ya thinking about?" she asked.

"Nothing. Just meditating."

"I've been watching you *meditate* for the last fifteen minutes. You never moved one muscle the entire time. I don't think you even blinked. What's going on with you?"

"It's called meditation. You should consult a private investigator who can maybe check into the concept for you."

"Don't be a smartass, smartass. You're in one of your funks and they've been happening a lot more frequently lately. When are you going to talk to me about it?"

Ben stood up and walked over to the beautiful creature that was staring at him with worried concern. He eased into Maddie's space until their bodies were meshed together. Reaching down with his index finger, he gently traced the scar on her neck where he'd applied frantic pressure only three years ago. He slowly and lightly moved his fingers up her neck and onto her face. He cupped her jaw and neck in his hand and caressed her soft, beautiful complexion with his thumb. He looked into her eyes with the most real look of love and softly spoke to her.

"I'm fine, beautiful. Please don't worry about me."

He leaned in and kissed her strawberry lips and then Maddie Lewis got lost in his true affection, a collision averted once again—for the time being.

IT WAS TRUE that Ben was pondering his work a lot. He'd been employed as a programmer consultant for the last two and a half years, and while he enjoyed that, he craved more freedom in his artistic creativity and technical ambitions. It was a left brain, right brain dilemma, and Ben thought that creating his own software company would solve the predicament. As such, his new personal phrase had become: "Start-up or Shut-up", which he henceforth proclaimed as the motivational mission-blurb for his soon-to-be new company. He thought the phrase was catchy and clever, but Maddie of course thought that it was just like him: dorky.

After figuring out that he would need a little help to get his business off the ground, he decided to reach out to his hero, Carl Avery, whom he'd stayed in contact with over the years. Carl had listened to Ben's pitch for the new company and decided that he was in with a "Why not?" reply. So likened to Maddie, Carl moved away from his home to begin an adventure with Ben in Seattle. Unlike Maddie's initial reaction to the Pacific Northwest, Carl had immediately found it refreshing in contrast to New England's harsh seasons.

Ben got the idea for the business by replaying his time in the Army and even his time at The Point. He'd remembered how disorganized the tracking of materials and goods seemed to be as well as how a lot of things just plain sucked in terms of quality control. After thinking about how to solve those problems with technology, he came up with a concept for an inventory/quality-control software product. And not just for the military, as his research had proven that there were indeed other industries that had similar issues. Ben and Carl brainstormed on a name for the software product, both agreeing that they wanted it to reflect their partnership somehow, but without directly using their names. They finally settled with a play on words, considering Carl's amputated left arm and Ben's destroyed right eye. The software was called *Missing Parts v1.0* and likewise their company was named *Missing Parts, LLP*, which they officially started during the tail end of 1993.

NOT LONG AFTER SETTLING IN SEATTLE, Ben had started visiting a homeless shelter downtown. He'd taken the important life-lesson from his time at the shelter in New York City and had applied it by volunteering at least one day a week in Seattle. Like Gus back in Manhattan, Ben had become popular with the good, Seattle people-in-need and was on a first-name basis with all of the regulars, even though Ben did his best to make sure there were no regulars. It was one of his more idealistic goals to completely eliminate homelessness by helping to facilitate housing and job programs so that the folks who were down on their luck had a boost to get back up on the horse of life and ride off into the happy sunset. That, of course, was one of the many cheesy metaphors that Ben evangelized to prospective volunteers and donors—and surprisingly, it worked most of the time.

Maddie joined Ben to volunteer almost immediately after she moved to Seattle. The eclectic work hours of her growing investigation-services business inhibited her from a regular schedule like Ben, but she enjoyed spending time with the man she loved while helping others as much as she could. She would often watch Ben from afar as he interacted with the people. His face would light up with any chance of being able to help put a smile on someone else's face, which was often. Each time she witnessed him in that gentle zone, his outward compassion would cause her heart to pang with love without fail. Seeing him like that was something she was sure she could never get tired of.

Ben had been pestering Carl to come down to the shelter for the longest time, but Carl was more of an introverted homebody and thus shied away from social interaction. It wasn't until Ben asked him for a special favor that he finally agreed to go.

Carl had already started serving hot soup to the people in line when Ben walked in with a sheet of fresh baked sourdough. One of the new patrons, an elderly woman with straggly hair and no teeth, looked at Ben standing next to Carl and started emitting a strange chuckle that would've made most people a little nervous, but not Ben.

"I love funny. I want funny. So, tell me what's so funny,

sweetheart," Ben said in a cute, monster-like voice.

"You two are funny. Him no arm and you no eye. You're quite a pair standing next to each other," the elderly woman said.

"Yes, we are. We're definitely missing parts alright." Ben laughed and turned to Carl, nudged him with his elbow and said, "I love it when I get to say that."

"Well I'm glad you don't get the opportunity too often, Mr. Cheese," Carl replied.

"Hey, I thought you loved our company name?"

"I do. It's not cheesy, *you* are."

"Wise arse."

"Wise, yes. Arse, no. So when is this thing going down?"

"Maddie is due in twenty minutes, so I should have plenty of time to coordinate the plan of action. Speaking of, you've got this right? I need to get started."

"Yep, go."

"Thanks."

Ben went into the kitchen to put away his apron and then came back out and started browsing with all of the people while they ate their meals. Pockets of laughter could be heard as he made his rounds talking to folks. He couldn't get enough of their smiles, so the social time was always a perpetual cycle of him doing his best to keep the grins coming in waves.

Maddie showed up twenty minutes late, but that was good because it gave Ben more time to prepare. He and Carl had already put away the empty food pans and were standing next to the food line, discussing work. Maddie walked up to them and gave Ben a big kiss. A few comedic 'oohs', 'aahs' and whistles emitted from the patrons, which made Maddie shake her head in embarrassment.

Carl said hi to her before politely excusing himself.

"How was work, beautiful?" Ben asked.

"Long. Boring. Uneventful," Maddie replied.

"Nothing juicy, huh?"

"Nope. The woman I'm surveilling appears to be the model wife."

"Well, it is possible that such a creature exists, isn't it?"

"Not many that I've witnessed. But I suppose it *is* possible."

Ben pulled Maddie in close so that she was fully facing him with her back to the people who were still busy eating. That was the trigger for Carl to give the signal to that evening's customers. He held up and waved back-and-forth a large poster-board that said 'GET READY TO SAY IT!' The sign-waving caused a crescendo of murmurs and giggles to fill the dining hall. Ben was afraid that Maddie would be distracted by the sudden off-kilter noise, but she was too busy looking into his eyes and waiting for a kiss. Carl held up another sign that said 'DO IT NOW!' and then in staggered unison, the people called out.

"Maddie!" they all said loudly.

Maddie shuttered in surprise and turned around to look. Ben backed up two steps, dropped to one knee and opened a small velvet box to expose a shiny diamond ring. Carl gave the final signal, but it wasn't really necessary. The good people were well experienced in life and knew full-well what they needed to say next.

"Will you please marry Ben for us?" the crowd exclaimed again.

Maddie had a confused look on her face and then she quickly turned around and saw Ben on his knee with the ring held out. She covered her mouth and trembled as tears of happiness began to escape. She slightly turned her head back to the crowd and nodded her head and then looked at Ben and said, "Yes!"

BEN AND MADDIE SNUCK AWAY the next weekend and eloped. Maddie had no family to speak of and as far as she knew, neither did Ben, other than Carl and Dr. Reeves. So, they mutually agreed to just have a quick, private wedding without any ceremonial hoopla. Regardless of the lack of pomp and circumstance, it was still the best moment of Ben's life and likewise it was the same for Maddie.

A FEW MONTHS HAD PASSED since Ben and Maddie returned from their honeymoon in the Bahamas. They'd since settled into happily spending the rest of their lives together. And Ben was doing his part by getting in a nap on the living room couch, which meant that he had his predator-detection Ranger skills switched to their 'OFF' position. As such, Maddie was able to easily sneak up on him without discovery. She held a stack of thick library books out from her waist and hovered them above his splayed torso. Wearing nothing but a bathrobe and an evil grin, Maddie dropped the volumes onto his groin area and then quickly covered her mouth to make an "I just didn't do that" gesture. The impact of the dropped books caused Ben to shoot straight up with an attractive "ugg" noise.

"What the fu...dge! What the fudge-cicle are you doing, Maddie?" Ben looked at the source of his rude awakening and scowled.

"Fudge-cicle? Is that Army slang? Wow, you...are a dork."

"What are these for?"

"They're called books. You read them."

"Duh, I know that." Ben sifted through them and read their titles aloud. *"Modern Depression and its Cycles...Get the Funk Out...Blue Is the New Red.* Okay, I'm not one-hundred percent sure, but there seems to be a recurring theme here."

"Yes, those super-human powers of observation you have are really what won me over, baby."

"That and my ability to leave you speechless."

"Oh yes, that too. Again. Dork."

"Ugh! Do you know how many books I've read since high school? I cleared out an entire bookstore just to learn my current career. I'm done with reading books. No more. I've had my fill."

"Hmmm. You've probably read about one percent of the books I have in the same time-frame." Maddie made a pout-face and the resorted to baby talk. "You are just a poor little mistreated soldier boy, aren't you?"

"Not everyone is a book freak like you, Maddie."

"Tough. Deal with it."

"How about a compromise? What if I get these same exact books on audio? Will you get off my back then?"

"A, I'm not *on* your back *yet*, mister. B, I don't care as long as you *listen* to what they have to say."

"Fine. And by the way, dropping two-tons of depressing books on my jewels isn't a way to *lift* my spirits, if you know what I mean. And...just because you're older than me doesn't mean you have to act like you're my mother."

"Oh really? Well, would your mother do this?" Maddie opened

her robe and then let it fall off of her shoulders and onto the ground. She turned and walked away while saying, "How did *that* lift your spirits, baby?"

Ben wet his lips and swallowed hard. Wasting no more time, he haphazardly threw the books onto the floor and then with Ranger mad-skill agility, he chased after his beautifully naked wife.

- 39 -

WONDER

ON THE OUTSIDE, life was good. Missing Parts had taken off and sales were increasing with each passing month. Ben and Carl had started the journey as only two guys writing code around the clock until finally having a product that they could beta test ten months later. Then, after another two months, they had their first customer. Harnessing the power of their contacts along with a little lobbying by Dr. Reeves, Missing Parts had officially sold their first license contract to the U.S. Army. In just over a year, they had taken their company from an employee count of two to upwards of forty warm bodies. Their annual sales were looking to reach the single-digit millions, but it wasn't about that—not for Ben at least. It was all about the accomplishments that resulted from honest, hard work.

In terms of Ben and Maddie's marriage, there had been some contention that was primarily due to Ben's regular bouts of funk. He hadn't yet made any headway on controlling the depression, even though he did listen to the audio versions of the books that Maddie had given him. To mask the random feelings of despair and in the process adding insult to injury, Ben took it upon himself to try and mitigate his issues by burying himself in his work. As a result, Maddie had come to understand that there were few things in the world more fun than a clinically depressed workaholic. That is with the operative word "fun" having a completely facetious and cynical tone, which happened to be Maddie's favorite type of passive-aggressive punch to land.

The long hours and Ben's issues had built up to the point that Maddie couldn't take it anymore. She'd exhausted all efforts and was frankly tired as hell. She'd tried being supportive, loving, pampering, concerned, mother-hennish, and everything in between, but nothing got through to Ben. It had slowly escalated into more and more fights that Maddie, admittedly, instigated because of all the long hours her husband was putting in. Yet deep down she knew that Ben's detached bouts of depression were at the core of the problem. She wasn't a psychologist, but she was a damn good study of people and their traits and as such she knew that they, as a married couple, couldn't stay the course for much longer. Something was going to break, and she started to believe it would be their marriage. She'd thought a lot about that and had come to the conclusion that it was time to give him an ultimatum.

316

"Ben, we've been married for a year and you still won't talk to me about what's wrong with you. I'm beginning to believe that you never will and that really scares me."

"Beautiful, everything's okay. I'm fine. I really wish you would stop worrying about me."

"Everything is *not* fine. *We* are not fine. You know what I see now when I look into the eyes of my husband? I see all kinds of pain, and it's getting worse every week. *Pain* and I have no idea *why* or *where* it comes from."

"I'm just tired is all, baby. I promise to get more rest."

His avoidance of the subject was starting to really piss her off. He could see the change in her eyes and all he could think was *oh fuck, here it comes.*

"Rest is not the damn problem, Ben. Me not knowing a goddamn thing is the problem. How do you think that makes someone in my line of work feel? I don't even know what happened to your fucking eye for chrissakes. Your own wife, and I have no idea!"

"Yes, you do!"

"Training accident? Is that your idea of me knowing? I'm your best friend, Ben!"

"That's all I can tell you, baby."

"Lies. You're lying. And I know it. You're a shitty poker player, Ben. When are you going to stop lying to me?"

"I'm not!"

"Just stop! I don't care about the fucking accident. Let's talk about your goddamn bouts of funk. You need to talk to someone, Ben. I know you said you would never go to a shrink because you don't "believe" in them. Well, if you won't talk to me, then at least talk to *someone*! I can't count the number of times I've watched you sit alone staring out into nothingness without moving a muscle like a goddamn mannequin. You're the strongest man I know. The strongest man I've ever known. But you sit and cry fucking-weird, emotionless tears without making a sound. And all I can do is sit back like a good, little wife and wonder! Wonder what in the hell can make such a strong man hurt so much."

Maddie felt herself get to the point of giving up on everything and her anger turned to hurtful tears that worked their way up to involuntary sobs.

"I won't live like that, Ben. I can't anymore. I'm young enough to start over. I love you more than anything, but I'm not going to get trapped in that kind of pain with you, especially without understanding why."

"Don't talk like that, Maddie. Please, baby."

"I can't anymore, Ben. I just can't."

Ben fell to his knees and held her hips tight and locked his arm to let her know he would never let go. Her words had cut him deep, to the point of making him sob with her.

"I'll do whatever you want, Maddie. I'll go talk to whomever you want. Just don't leave me. You're everything to me. Please don't leave me. I can't. I can't live without...without you, baby. Please."

Maddie felt his quakes and then the resulting wetness on her stomach from his tears. She reached down and began to gently stroke his hair as they wept together. And with each of his sobs she got weaker and weaker until finally surrendering to what she had always known in her heart—that she couldn't live without him despite his frustrating complexities. He was the man she chose to be with forever, even though she knew that sometimes he wasn't a man at all, rather more a frightened child. She wouldn't give up and at the same time she couldn't stop wondering why he was the way he was. It was at that moment that she decided to make it her life's mission to find the answer—and come hell or high water she would discover the truth about Benjamin W. River.

MADELINE LEWIS RIVER was a highly skilled private investigator, especially considering her young age of twenty-seven years. She really believed that it was skip-generation genetics that gave her an inquisitive, observational nature. Her paternal grandpa was a Pinkerton and she liked to believe that she inherited her natural talents from him. So, in honor of his surname she'd decided to continue to use her maiden name in her practice, thus all of her clients knew her as just Madeline Lewis, and never by Ben's surname. Likewise, she never used her nickname in her P.I. business, either. She had a strict imperative to keep a clear delineation between work and personal life, but for the first time she had to break her own rule by performing a background check on Ben. She realized that it was a huge breach of trust and it was a decision that she didn't take lightly. She'd always promised herself that she'd never investigate someone she fell in love with, because she knew better than anyone that people always have skeletons in their closet.

You have your demons too, Maddie. Yes, but I keep them in check. I've dealt with them. I've gotten help in the past. It's different. This doesn't make me a hypocrite, dammit.

Maddie concluded that the current situation was well beyond the point of adhering to any self-registered moral sense of privacy. Her marriage was at stake and it didn't matter what she had to do or who she had to upset. She was determined to figure out the source of her husband's misery one way or the other. As such, she approached the subject like a real case and went through the habitual motions of getting a new banker's box and writing 'BWR' on top. She thought it best to be vague so she just used Ben's initials, just in case he happened to show up at her office, which was a rarity. She pulled out a small stack of brand new manila file folders from a drawer and sat them on her desk. She then flipped through her datebook and blocked-out time to work on the new 'BWR' case over the next week. She decided that dedicating at a minimum two hours a day to the new "project" would suffice without impacting her other cases.

If there's one thing Ben certainly is, it's a project.

Okay Maddie, it's go-time. Start with what you know for sure and work your way backwards. Well, you don't know squat about his military service, so you can't start there. Ben's connection with Dr. Reeves was through his grandpa and the doctor is high-profile, so that's more than likely a waste of time. You can always come back to him if needed. Gramps is a different story though. Ben loved the man like a father, that much is plain to see, but there's something there I can't put my finger on. Something's off with old Gramps.

Maddie took a folder off of the stack and wrote 'MORGAN RIVER' on it.

And Ben's mom is another good starting point. He said she was killed in a car accident when he was four years old, so that should be an easy one to track down.

Maddie wrote 'ANGELA RIVER' on another folder and opened

it. She took out a legal pad and sat it on the opened folder and wrote the woman's name again with a date and time. Maddie picked up her desk phone and called information to get the first number she knew she would need. She wrote the number down and then had the operator automatically connect her. The phone rang on the other end until a mature woman answered with a thick, Southern accent.

"Hope Public Library, how may I help you?"

"Hello, this is Madeline Lewis calling from Seattle. May I ask to whom I'm speaking with?"

"This is Evelyn Rogers."

"Evelyn, I'm an investigator doing a top-secret clearance background check on a person of interest that is from Hope, and I was hoping you could help me with something."

"Top-secret? My goodness, it sounds important. I'll help if I can. Who are you investigating? Or is that a secret?"

"No, Evelyn it's not a secret and I'm glad you asked. The man's name is Benjamin River. It's my job to interview people who know him. Do *you* by chance know a man by that name?"

"No, I can't say I do. Doesn't ring a bell either, but to tell you the truth, my husband and I just moved here last year to retire, so I don't really know many locals by name, yet."

"That's okay, Evelyn. You can still help me, if you don't mind."

"I'll do my best. What is it you need, dear?"

"The information I have in my file states that Benjamin's mother died in a car accident several years ago. Unfortunately, I don't have the exact year, but the accident is recalled to have happened in the 1973 to 1974 timeframe. With that being said, is there any way I can talk you into searching newspaper articles for any car-crash fatalities during that timeframe that involved a woman by the name of Angela River?"

"I should be able to help you with that, but it may take a while. How soon do you need it?"

"My timeline is pretty aggressive. When would you say is the soonest you can get to it?"

"Would tomorrow work?"

"Tomorrow would be lovely, Evelyn. I really appreciate your help in this very important matter. Let me give you my contact information."

"Of course. Give me a second to grab a pen and notepad so I can write everything down."

Maddie gave the librarian her contact information, repeated the research information, and then hung up. She took detailed notes of the conversation and then put them in the 'ANGELA RIVER' file. She sat back in her executive chair and stared out of her office window at the gloomy drizzle.

I think that was as good a start as any. From here I'll keep working back until I find it. I don't know what "it" is, but I know it's there somewhere. At least I hope it is. And if I'm lucky, the military won't be at the root of the mystery, because if this all points to some secret covert government crap, then it's definitely going to be a much tougher nut to crack. Something tells me it goes much deeper than his short military experience. My gut says it has to do with his childhood, and my gut is usually right.

THE FOLLOWING AFTERNOON, Maddie was just about to walk out her office door when the phone rang. She almost ignored the call but then thought twice, so she walked back in and answered.

"Inquisitive By Nature, Madeline speaking."

"Hi Madeline, this is Evelyn from the library."

"Oh yes, hello Evelyn. How are you doing today?"

"I'm fine thank you and yourself?"

"I'm doing very well, thank you. How's the search coming along?"

"Oh it's done. I finished going through all of the microfiche for both 1973 and 1974 like you asked. I also went through 1972 and 1975, just in case. As it turned out, there were no accidents, fatal or otherwise, involving the name you gave me. I did find an accident involving a woman with the same last name, but I'm afraid it was in 1972 and she had a different first name."

"It sounds like you did a very thorough job of researching this, Evelyn. I really appreciate that. Can you tell me the full name of the woman who died in 1972?"

"Yes, her name was Samantha River. There was no middle name given."

"Is there anything else you can tell me from the article?"

"Let's see. She was just twenty-three years old. And...oh dear."

"What is it, Evelyn? What did you read?"

"It looks like her four year old son was also killed in the accident as well. That's just horrible."

"Yes, that is horrible. Did it list the child's name, by chance?"

"Yes, and...goodness, that's strange."

"What is Evelyn?"

"It says here that the woman's son's name was Benjamin. Isn't that the same name of the man you're investigating?"

"Yes, it is."

"Well isn't that just a hoot of a coincidence?"

"Evelyn, in my line of work there *are* no coincidences."

"I'm sure, Madeline. Would you like me to pull up Samantha River's obituary while I have the film loaded?"

"Evelyn, I'd love for you to."

"Okie-dokie, let's see here. Samantha River, again no middle name. Not much here. Just that the only surviving member of her family was her father, Morgan River."

"Morgan River. Got it. Evelyn, I can't tell you how much of a huge help you've been. I also can't thank you enough. If I ever find myself in Hope, I'd love to buy you a cup of tea or coffee, your choice and maybe even lunch. And likewise, if you're ever in Seattle, please call me so I can thank you in person."

"You're welcome, Madeline. I may just do that someday. And do look me up if you're ever in Hope."

After Maddie hung up the phone, her mind began racing a million miles per hour. She found her chair and fell back in it and stared once again out at the rain. She turned her gaze to the 'BWR' banker's box that was sitting under the window.

You are in so much trouble, mister. Dammit! I can't believe I married a man with an assumed identity. I'm a private investigator for God's sake. I'm so fucking mad right now!"

Maddie took a deep breath and closed her eyes.

Calm down, Maddie. I'm sure he has a good reason. You know the man. You love him. He's a good person. There has to be a good reason. But what? C.I.A., maybe? No, they don't use ghost identities anymore. They make new people up out of thin air and manipulate records so they seem real. Besides, Ben a spy? Please. Then what? And why? Just ask him, Maddie. No, not yet. Keep going with the case. Don't give him the chance to lie anymore.

Where next then? He really lived with Morgan River. That much I do know. And he's not a figment of my imagination. He's a real man, which means he was a real child. But whose child? A friend of the River family maybe? No, doesn't fit. Is it possible he's really a family member and the names are just coincidence? No chance in hell. Samantha River was Morgan's daughter—the obituary said so. Morgan gave Ben the ghost identity. And supported him all the way through school. And with the Military Academy—up until his death, at least. Even had Dr. Reeves vouch for him. It doesn't make any sense! Unless.

Maddie reached behind her and pulled a road atlas from her bookshelf and fanned to a page that had a small-scale map of the Southern United States. She found Hope and then studied the surrounding regions.

When? Could be any time between 1972 and his freshman year of high school. Wait a minute, why did I just skip to his freshmen year? Because Maddie, he never talks about anything before high school. He never has. Even the times you asked about his childhood, he never went there. He'd always been vague, talking about Piney Woods or something like that. And he never mentioned his Gramps those few times he mentioned his childhood. So, it had to be around the time he started high school. That would be 1984, so start with 1983.

Maddie flipped through her rolodex to a number she hadn't dialed in a long, long time. It was one she didn't want to dial, but at this point she had no choice. There was no getting off of the rollercoaster now, so she punched the number into her phone and waited for a familiar voice to answer.

"National Center for Missing & Exploited Children. This is Micah Gallegos."

"Micah, it's Maddie."

"Maddie? My ex-fiancé, Maddie? The one who left me standing at the altar two years ago with one-hundred and twenty-seven guests, Maddie? The one who found love at first sight during a layover on her way to our wedding, Maddie?"

"Yes, yes, yes. The one and only."

"Hanging up now."

"Wait. I need your help."

"Why should I care? You didn't."

"Because, you do care about abused and missing children. That's what I need help with."

"Even I have limits, Maddie."

"Please. I'm sorry for being a bitch to you. For hurting you. For everything. You're better off, believe me. How many times do I have to apologize?"

"You're not even close to being there. Fine. Give me the DASL, dammit."

"Thanks, Micah. The date range is 1983 to 1984. Age between twelve and thirteen. Male. Location is the Ark-La-Tex region."

"That's an awful big area, Mad. You got anything to help narrow it down?"

"Try first name Benjamin or Ben."

"Okay. Computers are running slow today, so it may take a minute or two."

"I'll wait."

"So, does he make you happy?"

"Yes, Micah, he does. We got married last year."

"And you actually went through with it?"

"Funny."

"Well, congratulations. I'm glad you're happy. I think."

"Thank you, Micah. How about you? Anybody special in your life?"

"Yes, believe it or not I'm engaged again."

"That's fantastic! I'm happy for you."

"Thanks. Okay, report came back and it looks like you may have gotten lucky, or not. There was only one result. Let's see, a 'Benjamin Wilder' was reported missing on January 15, 1983 from Gilmer, Texas, wherever the hell that is. Date of birth is May 5, 1970. Parents are, let's see...only one parent listed. His mother. Her name is Angela Wilder Boone from the same location of Gilmer, Texas. Do you want the full address?"

"Yes, please."

MADDIE WROTE EVERYTHING DOWN on the legal pad and then re-read it a hundred times over. It was all too surreal for her to grasp. So, she kept going over it again and again. It all validated what she suspected all along. Her husband had demons and now that she knew that for sure, it scared her even more.

God, maybe I should've never started this.

Maddie heard her father's voice ring in her ears. Words he'd told her just months before he died: "Some things are better left alone, Maddie."

But I didn't leave it alone did I Dad? Because I finally started remembering. Remembering the visits. Your vodka breath on my face late at night. The horrible things you did to me. No, goddamit, things are NOT better left alone. I of all people know that.

But I'm not sure I can handle this kind of thing again. I'm afraid to know what happened in Texas to the man I love. Ben's pain. I think maybe I now understand it all too well. And what now? Do I keep digging until I unearth the demon? Like I unearthed my own?

Maddie kept mulling it all over-and-over in her head. Her gut had turned out to be right about his depression having to do with his childhood, and now her gut told her that the proverbial rabbit hole would go to very dark places.

No more digging. I'm too afraid of what I'll find. I have enough to confront him. He'll have no choice but to tell me the truth now. I'll leave it to him regarding how far down the rabbit hole he takes me. Only he can decide that.

MADDIE SAT IN HER CAR still thinking things over. The shock had worn off and now she was in logic mode. She knew she couldn't go inside and look into his eyes without him knowing something was wrong with her. She could never look at him the same again until this was all out in the open. She began to think over her strategy of how to approach Ben. Then she tried to think objectively about her own feelings.

I married a Texan for chrissakes. A Texan who's a year younger than I thought. So, now I'm three years older than my husband. Somehow that makes me feel even worse. Well, at least I know him by his actual first name. For that, I'm thankful. It's sweet that he called his ghost mom by his real mom's first name. And now I finally know that the "W." actually stands for his mother's maiden name. I suppose Ben wanted to keep something of hers with him after he ran away.

Alright, Maddie. Enough stalling. Just go in and get it over with.

Maddie finally went inside and searched for Ben, finding him sitting outside wearing his favorite Huskies hoodie in the drizzle. She could tell from his pose that he was in one of his deep funks.

Great.

She opened one of the French doors as loudly as she could, but he didn't budge. She walked outside and gently grabbed his shoulders from behind. He finally stirred and put his hand on one of hers and looked back up at her.

"Oh hi, beautiful. You just get home?"

"Hi, sexy man. Yep, just walked in the door. You have time to talk?"

"Ut-oh. That doesn't sound good. Baby, I'm fine. Really."

"Don't worry—I'm not going to bitch at you, but there is something very important we need to talk about."

"Alright. Is everything okay?"

"Not really. Come inside."

Maddie went back inside, sat on the couch and nervously waited. Ben followed behind only moments later and sat next to her.

"What is it, Maddie? Are you pregnant? Because you don't look happy about it if you are."

"What? No, I'm not pregnant. Jesus."

"Then what?"

"What I'm about to admit to you may hurt you—even make you angry at me. It wasn't something I did easily. It was hard, but I had to do it."

"What in the hell are you talking about, Maddie?"

"I investigated your background, Ben. And I figured out that you are really Ben Wilder and that you ran away from a place called

Gilmer, Texas. There, I said it."

Ben didn't reply, instead his head lowered and he stared at the ground. The tears tried to come but he choked them back down and gritted his teeth.

"I'm sorry, Ben. Are you mad at me?" Maddie asked.

"Tell me what you know?"

Maddie was taken aback at the seriousness of Ben's voice and how stern he sounded.

"That's about it, I promise. I only know when you were reported missing and who your mom is. I stopped after finding that much out. I want to hear the rest from you, but before you tell me anything, I need to tell you something important about my past, too. Actually, two things. I've kept them from you and it's been eating at me, but I was afraid to tell you before. But now...now I'm even more scared—but we need to tell each other everything."

"You first."

Again, she was frightened by the coldness of his voice.

Is he mad? Is he in military mode? No, it's something else. And it scares me.

"Okay. This is hard. I never wanted anyone in the world to know this, especially you. I don't want you to look at me any differently. Or touch me any differently. But I was abused by my father growing up. More specifically, I was molested."

Ben's face turned beet-red and he gritted his teeth even harder. Maddie had never seen him look that way. She'd never known Ben to be angry or violent, but that was the vibe she was getting from him. She was getting second thoughts again, but Pandora's Box had just been opened—there was no stopping it now.

"I suppressed the memories after he stopped, which was once I got too old for him. When he was diagnosed with cancer and given three months to live...well that's when the memories came pouring back in. I had a breakdown and had to be hospitalized. In short, I had to get help. And that's why I was always so concerned about you, baby. Don't you see? I recognized that look in your eyes. I recognized the pain."

Ben slowly started nodding his head. She could see the hate and anger start to leave his body and she thanked God for it. Tears finally escaped and ran down his face. He reached over and held her face in his hands, and the way he lovingly looked into her eyes opened the spillway for her tears, too.

"I'm sorry, Maddie. I'm so sorry that happened to you. And I'm sorry it had to come out like this. I'm not mad at you, beautiful. Regarding my past, I'm actually relieved you know. I've wanted to tell you so many times, but I also was afraid to."

He got control of his emotions and covered up the anger that resulted from hearing that the woman he loved had a cowardly dad who hurt her like that. Inside, he wanted to climb down into the depths of hell just to beat the shit out of the son-of-a-bitch. But he was able to smooth out his demeanor to an even keel. She always ribbed him about being a bad poker player, which was true most of the time, but when it came to the safety of the woman he loved more than anything, whom he'd die for...well, he could hold his own with the best poker players in the world. And now it was time for him to do his best at exercising that ability with some white lies. That is, if one considers omission a form of lying. Most do and he knew Maddie would, but he couldn't tell her everything about his past. He couldn't tell *anyone* everything, especially Maddie. Not until after.

"I'll tell you everything, Maddie. But there were two things you said you kept from me. What was the other?"

Jesus. Why did I even mention the other thing. That was a bonehead move, Maddie. Now is definitely not the time to tell him that I'm a runaway bride and that my ex helped me track him down. Yeah, let's defer that one, shall we?

"Later, Ben. It's not important. I want to hear your story. However you need to tell it, but I need to hear it."

Ben took a deep breath and exaggerated the exhale.

Easy, Ben. Don't overdo this. She's too damn smart. She'll smell the bullshit a mile away. Just tell the truth to a point and then cut it off.

"Okay. It is true I ran away when I was twelve. From Gilmer. I ran to get away from an abusive step-dad. I called him the Rabid Dog, because that's what he was. He was a mean drunk of the worst kind. And my mom, Angie, she was an alcoholic. Still is, I suppose. She never came to my aid. I know she loved me, but she was too caught up in her own pain to be able to protect me. So one day after the last beating I swore I would ever take, I stole the Rabid Dog's car and ran away. I've never looked back since.

"I had no idea where to go or what to do. I just ran. My plan was Little Rock, but the gas in the tank only got me to Hope. I walked into the first place I came to, which happened to be my Gramps's pawn shop. And make no mistake, he is my gramps. Nobody and I mean *nobody* ever protected me and loved me like he did, until you came along. Before he passed away, he was everything to me. He was my savior and if it weren't for him, I'm sure I'd be dead now. And I certainly never would've met you. Everything good in my life is because of that man. He saw my arrival at his doorstep as fate. You can piece it all together from there. I'm sure you already have anyway. My whole life from high school to now has been a big lie to everyone else but Gramps and me. To us, it was real. I was his grandson, even his son to a strong degree. And he was my dad I never had and my grandpa as well. The best of both worlds. And I couldn't tell you about this—you or anyone else for that matter. There would be serious consequences if the military ever found out that I'd duped them. I would lose everything and be sent to prison. Worse, I'd lose you."

"You will never lose me, Ben. I love you and always will. And I understand everything now. I'm sorry, baby. But I'm so thankful for Morgan River. I only wish I could've met him."

"Me too, beautiful. Me, too."

- 40 -

W.P.P.

SEATTLE, WASHINGTON – FEBRUARY 1995

IF THE HARDWOOD PLANKS in the hallway could've talked, they would've yelled, "Stop!" to Ben because he'd been nervously pacing outside the bathroom and wearing them out.

"Well?" Ben shouted through the door.

"Hold your horses!" Maddie shouted back.

Ben kept pacing and thought to himself, *this is driving me nuts* and then said, "You're driving me crazy and you're doing it on purpose!"

Maddie giggled from the other side, "Wow. Is this how you acted back in school when you waited to see what you had scored on a test?"

"Maybe."

"W.P.P."

"What the hell does that stand for?"

"West Point Pussy!"

"Yeah, and proud of it!"

Maddie opened the door with one hand behind her back. She looked up at Ben with a straight face.

"Well!?" Ben anxiously asked.

She brought the pregnancy test-stick out from behind her back and held it up for Ben to see. She smiled wide and said, "We're going to have a baby girl!"

Ben once again fell to his knees and hugged his wife at her hips— only this time he cheered. After a moment, all of her words were finally processed by his old-technology processor and he said, "What do you mean *girl*? How do you know it's a *girl*?"

"Because you're a West Point Pussy, that's how."

MADDIE WAS IN THE KITCHEN cooking dinner when Ben got home. The spicy smell of her famous Cajun Linis Alfredo drew him straight in like the Death Star's tractor beam did the Millennium Falcon, only the impending tortellini was a good thing.

"Is it ready, yet?"

"Ummm, that's not how this works, buster. You better get over here and acknowledge your pregnant wife with a kiss and a hug. Is it ready, yet—I should dump this whole batch down the garbage disposal."

"Don't do that! I mean, I love you beautiful. But you know what your linis do to me."

Ben walked over and pulled his wife in close like he's done a thousand times before, kissed her softly on the lips, hugged her and then silly-nibbled on her neck. She pushed him off of her and laughed.

"You love my linis more than you do me. I'm actually jealous."

"Don't be. I'd pick you over them any day. But a package deal, well hey, I am a man after all."

Maddie held up a chef's knife and waved it in the air.

"I can fix that you know."

"Eeek! Throw them down the damn garbage disposal. I'd rather keep you and my manhood."

"That's better. Now, are you going to tell me what's in the bag you've been holding in your hand this entire time?"

"Oh! Right-o!"

"God, you are a dork. Who says 'right-o' anyway?"

"I do, which makes it instantly cool."

"Too easy. Next."

"Dismiss me all you want my PIA, but you're going to want what I have in this bag."

"PIA? Did you just call me a pain in the ass?"

"No, I called you *my* pain in the ass."

"Wow. Lots and lots of brownie points. You are knocking them out of the park, soldier boy."

"Thank you. Now, for my next trick." Ben pulled two new cell phones out of a plastic bag and held them up for her to see. "Ta-da!"

"How anti-climactic. You bought ugly, little phones."

"They're cell phones."

"I know what they are, genius. Have you forgotten what I do for a living?"

"No, I have not. And that's precisely why you're going to take this thing and use it. I don't want you off on some stakeout and going into labor without being able to call me. And I can call you whenever I'm on the road without having to stop at a nasty payphone or get dinged by hotel phone charges."

"Speaking of charges, these things are too expensive. We don't need them, Ben."

"We can afford it. Besides, they are business write-offs. And, we *do* need them, Maddie."

"Fine, but if you start bugging me all the time when I'm out in the field, I'm going to kick your ass."

"I'd never. Well, maybe just call and say I love you every once in a while."

"You get one a day. That's it."

"Damn. Ball-buster."

"Do you really want to find out?"

"Nope. Message received loud-and-clear, over-and-out."

LATER THAT WEEK, Maddie was surveilling the home of her newest client. A woman, who'd been miserably married to the same man for twenty years, had hired Maddie to spy on the man. As it was told, the woman's husband had fallen from a ladder a couple of years back and had since stayed home drawing disability while the dutiful wife worked her ass off to make ends meet. She was a mid-level executive with a large insurance company and wanted Maddie to find out the truth behind two things. One, was her husband faking his injury? Two, was he having an affair?

The woman presumed that he was having an affair, but not with another woman, rather with a man—specifically, a good looking young man that the wife had seen a couple of times around the neighborhood. Maddie thought it was hilarious that the woman seemed angrier about the possibility of her husband faking his injuries more so than the purported homosexual love affair. Maddie supposed it was the industry-executive in the woman who couldn't get past the suspected insurance fraud.

Maddie sat and took in the huge house with its perfect yard.

Insurance execs must bank some serious greenbacks.

It had been an hour and nobody had come or gone. Then she noticed people walking back and forth in front of a window inside the house. She focused in with her high powered binoculars but the clothed bodies were partly hidden from view by window blinds, so all she could see were two torsos from the shoulders down.

Damn. Come on. Show me something.

She could tell by the body types that they were both men. She could also tell that one was old and one was very fit and young. She had to admit that the old man had done pretty well for himself, if in fact there was an actual affair going on.

She kept watching and finally saw the front door open.

Game time.

She raised her 35MM camera equipped with a telephoto lens and started taking shots. The young man was backing out of the door while embracing the old man. It was definitely Maddie's client's husband. She'd been given a photo of the philanderer, so there was no doubt about that part. She waited for the young man to turn around. The old man smiled wide and then the young man leaned in and kissed the geezer on the lips.

"Awwwww. That's so sweet! You don't need that old hag anyway. This young one's a keeper. Good for you!"

The young man backed down the steps, never taking his eye off of his old lover.

"Wow, what passion!"

And finally the young lover turned around and then Maddie dialed in tight, making ready for a perfectly focused head shot. She started snapping away when his face finally appeared.

"What the fuck!"

Maddie jumped out of her car and stormed to the house's front yard. The old man came out and stood next to Ben to greet her, while disgustingly wiping the kiss from his lips. Ben couldn't help it any longer and started laughing his ass off. There was no way he could keep the show going, so he fell to the green grass and started rolling around in laughter. Maddie approached him and kicked him hard in the ass as he was squirming around on the yard's turf.

"What the hell?" Maddie yelled.

Ben, still on the ground, was laughing too hard to speak. Maddie then focused her attention on the old man. The man actually got a little frightened by the look on her face and slowly backed up.

"It was his idea!" The man pointed down to Ben, "I'm just a real estate agent. I should've never gone along with it. I'm sorry. Don't hit me. Here. Here are the keys to your new house."

And he held out a pair of keys with his arm fully extended to keep his distance from the raging, young pregnant-woman.

"What? House? You mean...this is...house...really!"

It was the second time Ben had ever witnessed his wife in a stuttered state without words to articulate what was on her mind. The first being when he proposed to her. But this time was different in that he had completely hoodwinked her, which was no small feat. He was so thrilled at the success of his prank that he wanted to go buy her a first-time-fooled cake to celebrate, although he supposed that the shock of the house was enough of a score—for the time being.

The five hundred bucks he'd paid the actress to pretend to hire Maddie had been the strangest thing he'd ever spent money on. And then there was the additional two hundred dollars that was required to coax the real estate agent into going along. The kiss on the lips was a bonus that Ben spontaneously decided to throw in gratis. In the end, it had all been so worth it. Finally, Ben was able to pull one over on the sharp-eyed Maddie Lewis River: the unshakable queen of uber-perception.

Well worth it, indeed.

- 41 -

LOST FOREVER

SEATTLE, WASHINGTON – JUNE 1995

CARL WALKED INTO BEN'S OFFICE carrying a large parcel wrapped in plain brown paper. He sat it down in front of Ben on the top of his desk and gave him an inquisitive look.

"It's Monday, otherwise known as Package Day. And like clockwork, you're in the office extra early. Curious minds," Carl said.

"They're just newspapers from a small town in Texas."

"Cool, because that's normal."

"I served with someone from the town, and I promised to keep an eye on things if something were to ever happen to him. And something did. Not a big deal. You're welcome to read them after I'm done. Very exciting East Texas events...guaranteed to entertain."

"No thanks. I'll pass. We still on for lunch later?"

"Darn-tootin'. I want to try out that new Mexican joint."

"Good thing there's no afternoon meetings then."

"True, but I may come hang out in your office later so I can share the aftereffects."

"Nice, but be careful who you declare war on though. You may not like the defensive position I take."

Ben reached under his desk and pulled out a gas mask.

"Bring it."

"Why does you having that under your desk not surprise me?"

"What?"

Carl walked away shaking his head. Ben laughed and then opened the package to reveal a twine-bound stack of seven newspapers. He took the first one off the top, unfolded it and immediately turned to the obituaries in the back. His eyes quickly scanned the small black-and-white photos of the newly departed. When his scan reached the bottom of the page, his heart dropped. Not only did he recognize his mom, he knew exactly which photo had been given to the newspaper for publishing. He'd stared at the same pretty photo of her a hundred times before when he was a young boy. He remembered as a kid being so proud of how beautiful his mom looked in the photo. Now the grown-up Ben sat there staring at a woman he'd never met before. He became sad at how her beauty had diminished before he was old enough to remember. He couldn't recall her ever looking as pretty as she did in that photo, with clean brown hair instead of a streaky bleach-blonde, and smooth flawless skin instead of cigarette-and-God-knows-what-else-etched wrinkles, and very little makeup instead of caked-on foundation used to cover up her abuse-bruises. And he bet she never floated away at the time of the photo like he'd always known her to do in her majority-of-the-time drunken-state.

Ben snapped out of the depressing memories, looked at the obituary to note the date and time of her service, folded the newspaper back up, and then leaned forward on his desk with his forehead resting on its edge. He clasped his hands around the back of his neck while a million thoughts and emotions ran through his mind and heart. He finally raised his head and with a nod picked up his phone and called his travel agent. Once he finished the call, he stood and walked from his office to Carl's and let him know he'd be gone for a few days and that he'd call to check in every day.

There were only two required stops before the airport, and he knew he'd better practice on perfecting his convincing-tone the whole way to the first stop. He could just call Maddie, but no way would she let that fly. Not to mention, Ben wouldn't ever want her pulling a stunt like that on him.

Let's just hope the twenty minute drive is enough time for me to polish my story. But first things first.

Ben opened a file cabinet and took out a small cardboard box that was already sealed and ready for shipment. Inside was the Colt .45 that Dr. Reeves had given him, along with two fully loaded clips—wrapped separately from the gun, of course. His second stop was to have the gun overnighted to Mt. Pleasant, Texas. The errand would be a damned inconvenience, but he was pretty sure that airport security *would* care if he attempted to board a plane with a loaded weapon.

AFTER SIX YEARS OF A STRICT, early morning routine, Ben had now become accustomed to the software coder's schedule, which was a polar opposite routine of late-to-bed and late-to-rise. As such, 'Package Mondays' were especially challenging, which in retrospect made Ben laugh at himself thinking how his seemingly-meager four hours of sleep paled in comparison to the sleep deprivation he'd endured during RAP. He guessed he was just getting old—in any case, not getting his forty winks the night before, paired with the stuffiness of his car, caused him to begin to nod off at the wheel. He quickly caught himself, shook his head back to life and rolled down his window so the brisk, damp flow hit his face. Still feeling drowsy, he pulled out the big guns by sticking his entire head out the window and filling his lungs with the fresh air, thus finally defying the pesky sandman—hooah!

As luck would have it, he hit rush-hour traffic, which he also wasn't accustomed to, so the twenty-minute drive turned into forty-five. It gave him extra time to practice his pitch (read: lie) to Maddie, but it was time he didn't have considering his flight was scheduled to depart in just ninety minutes.

He finally arrived at Maddie's office, pulling in so fast next to Maddie's car that he ran over the parking block. Ignoring his reckless parking job, he ran up the outside stairs taking three steps at a time and quickly reached the second story balcony. The office of 'Inquisitive by Nature Investigations' was located in a small strip mall that had been converted several years ago into a cluster of business suites. Ben took a moment to steady his breathing before walking into the small reception area of Maddie's office. She hadn't yet employed an assistant, but it was on her to-do list as soon as she built up her clientele. Ben had told her that she could hire someone anytime and he would help cover the expense, but Maddie was too independent and as Ben knew she would, she'd rejected the offer by saying that she didn't need the help. Ben was glad at the moment because he didn't have time to play Mr. NiceHusbandOfTheBoss to any of her would-be employees.

THE SMALL SET OF WIND CHIMES that Maddie had attached to the inside of the external door jingled, which prompted her to get up from her desk and go see who the early morning caller was. She was surprised that it turned out to be her husband as he rarely came to her workplace and never that early. Her dorky husband usually slept-in well past nine every morning, which he claimed was the coder's mantra, *whatever the hell that meant* Maddie had thought. She was an early riser and always got to work before eight, and had only been in the office for half an hour when Ben walked in.

"Look at what the cat drug in: a bed-head dork," Maddie said.

Ben straightened out his wind-blown hair and gave Maddie a kiss. He followed up with a quick hug and then he gently rubbed the small bump on her tummy. She'd barely started showing and it was only noticeable if pointed out, which was all fine-and-good and even cute, but Maddie did *not* look forward to the day when she could no longer conceal being pregnant. Nobody in their right mind would hire a bloated private investigator—or so Maddie claimed.

Ben had countered that they didn't need the money, and that she should just take the time off. She'd rebutted that is wasn't about the money, rather it was about the *accomplishment*. At that point Ben surrendered with a, "touché", because if there was one thing Benjamin River wasn't, it was a hypocrite. Not to mention, he knew he was no match for Maddie in any kind of argument or debate.

"So, what's going on?" Maddie asked.

"Why would something be going on?"

"Really? Playing dumb is cute on you, but it really doesn't suit."

"You sure are paranoid for an investigator."

"Inquisitive—it's in the name. Now quit stalling. What's the matter?"

"My mom died."

"Oh baby, I'm sorry."

Maddie hugged Ben to comfort him and after a quick squeeze, he pulled back so he could look at her.

"I'm okay, beautiful. I've decided to go to the funeral. It's something I need to do."

"Of course, baby. Let me lock up and then I'll go get packed. I can be ready in an hour, tops."

"No time. My flight leaves in just over an hour, so I'm heading straight to the airport from here." *Lie. I hope that doesn't come back to bite me in the ass.*

"Just get a later flight. I'm sure there's plenty available. It won't take me long to—"

"No, Maddie. I need to do this alone. Please understand, beautiful. I'm only going to be gone for a couple days, I promise."

"If that's really what you want, Ben. But I think you should let me go with you. I want to be there for you."

"Thank you—that means a lot to me. I'm okay though. Really. I'll be back before you know it. Trust me, Gilmer isn't a place I want to hang around for long."

"Fine. But for the record, I don't like it."

"I know you don't. You just take care of yourself and the baby until I get back."

"We'll be fine. You take care of *you*."

One final, embracing kiss and then Ben told her he loved her before running back to his car, all the while racing against the clock.

DALLAS, TEXAS

IT WAS THE FIRST TIME Ben had set foot in Texas since the horrible day when he ran away twelve years ago. The long lost gutterflies began welcoming him home the second he deplaned, making him remember how the damned fluttering omens in his stomach always seemed to preempt horrible events. The last time he felt them was waiting to hear news about his eye. He hoped his damned nerves would finally be proven wrong for once. At that moment, the pesky pangs kicked him hard in his gut as if to say "keep dreaming, sucker—we have a perfect record and we're going to keep it that way."

Next to the car rental counter was a small kiosk selling books on audio. Ben thought that maybe having words to listen to during the two hour car-ride would take his mind off of things, better than the radio could. He started to browse the numerous titles and became impatient with all the options and finally just grabbed one in front. He quickly glanced at the cover's artwork and was reminded of a Robert Frost poem, and that was good enough of a product endorsement for Ben, so he paid for the content without even reading the title or author. Next up was the car, so he walked right up to the rental counter without having to take more than ten steps.

"Good afternoon. Do you have a reservation?" asked the rental agent.

"No, I don't. Any cars available by chance?"

"Yes, but I'm afraid only economy."

"Perfect. Give me the plainest car you have?"

"Excuse me?"

Ben read the man's nametag.

"I'd like your honest opinion, Jeff. Out of the cars you have available, which one would you pay attention to the least if you saw it on the road?"

"Hmmm, interesting question. Let me check the computer real quick. Let's see. Nope. Nope. Maybe. Oh, here we go. Definitely. I'd have to say a Chevrolet Cavalier—it's very common—in my opinion, of course."

"And I appreciate your opinion. Cavalier sounds exactly like what I need. Do you happen to have one available in blue?"

"Let's see here. Uhuh. As a matter of fact, yes. I have one in a cadet blue and another in a midnight blue."

"Cadet, huh? Very tempting." Ben chuckled to himself and said, "I'll take the midnight blue. Oh, wait. Does it have a CD player?"

"I'll check, give me a sec. Yes sir, you're in luck. It has a combination AM/FM radio, cassette and CD player."

"Sold."

Ben scanned the radio stations as he drove, looking for something, *anything* that suited his mood, finally settling on a classic rock station. He kept the volume low while he focused on navigating out of the Dallas metro area. After forty-five minutes of much-interrupted music, Ben got sick of the commercials with their amateurish advertisings, so he decided to give the book-on-audio that he'd bought at the airport a shot. He inserted the first of three discs into the player and after some introductory marketing, the narrator finally started the first chapter. Ben had absolutely no idea what the book was about or what to expect—he didn't even know the book's title, so his interest was actually piqued at the mystery of it. The distraction was a good thing, so he turned up the volume and began listening attentively.

"January Jaded, by Cornelius Baranowski" the narrator introduced.

"Naaant. Strike one on the title. Okay Baron, you only get two more. Don't let me down," Ben smirked.

"Chapter one. Edward Crane breathed in the surrounding nature and attempted to absorb any vigor she afforded, but the somberness of the day had already snuffed-out any chance of hope. He leaned against an ancient oak and straddled his feet over its massive roots that pierced the earth like aged veins. Edward's wool cloak blended in with the elder's darkened bark, and if it weren't for his fair complexion Edward could've been mistaken as being part of the tree. He embraced the freezing rain and shook hands with its cousin, the northern drifter, inhaling its salient breath as it whistled an appropriate, eerie tune. Edward never flinched and he never contemplated cover, because he was a ghost and ghosts need no shelter, especially on days such as this.

"He looked to the east at the snowy incline peppered with gravestones. He wondered how years had passed since the hillside had begun its watch over the plots and how many newcomers it had welcomed into its stoic community. He glanced to the west and scanned the even older grounds that were bound by white wizards of pine looking down upon its own descending acreage, acting as guardians to the antediluvian markers below. And then on the horizon, he watched as a parade of gray apparitions began their own billowy haunt to forecast the possibility of more snow to come.

"Edward stepped away from the tree to kneel below its icicled branches, watching as fat robins gave animation to patches of grass where the white ground had unbuttoned its shirt to reveal glimpses of hope to the songbirds. The procession and the stage on which it now played became a sobering affirmation to the realism emitted by the eventual day. He thought of the grief that masked the beautiful scenery and then pondered the evil man who was likely lurking in the shadows even now as he attempted his mourn. Edward prayed that the transgressions, which so easily dampened such gifts from God, would be dealt with in a manner befitting the devil and his due.

"Edward reached into his—"

Ben pushed the eject button to put an end to the narration and the player slowly spit out the shiny disc.

"That was way more than three strikes, Baron my friend. Talk about *not* helping my mood in the least, but that's what I get, isn't it? Not sure if it's because of your dreary prose, or because of my own 'procession', but I'm now nauseous. Haven't eaten since yesterday and I can tell. Maybe I need some food. What do you think, Baron?"

Why am I talking to someone who's not there? Okay, that settles it. Definitely stopping for sustenance before my blood sugar drops me into further delirium.

Ben took the next exit off of Highway-80 near the town of Mesquite—from there he didn't have to drive far to find a roadside diner. He parked and headed into the small restaurant and was glad it wasn't too busy. There was a 'SEAT YOURSELF' sign and so that's what Ben did, sitting down at a corner booth. The temperature inside was too warm for his taste, so he contorted his arms to remove his long-sleeve hoodie, looking like a struggling escape artist in the process.

Should've taken the damn thing off in the car. Now, I'll probably forget it. And then what would I do without my hoodie when I got back home? Hoodieless in Seattle—not a good thing to be. Bring me a menu for chrissakes...I'm getting more delirious by the second. Oh, duh. They're on the table. Another display of those powers of observation that Maddie loves about me. Maddie, I miss her already. Like I always do. Okay. Enough already! Food!

A pretty waitress in her early thirties walked up to Ben's table and sat a glass of ice water down.

"Hi there. Can I get you something to drink besides water?"

Ben looked up at her and his heart dropped a little. The waitress could've been his mother's younger sister, and Ben imagined Angie would've looked like this woman when he was a kid if his mom had only taken better care of herself. The waitress gave him a "stop staring at me and order" look that made Ben blush.

"I'm sorry, miss. I didn't mean to stare—it's just that you remind me of someone I used to know. I'll take a diet coke, please and I'm ready to order now if you're ready."

"Thanks for the apology. I don't hear those too often around here. So, what'll you have?"

"Cheeseburger and fries. Everything on the burger with mayo and mustard, please."

"Got it. I'll be right back with your diet."

"Thanks."

The waitress's resemblance to his mom got Ben to thinking about Angie. He wondered what the last twelve years of her life had been like. He also wondered if she ever got the postcard he'd sent from New York City or the one he'd sent from Fort Benning. He hoped so. Then the thought of the Rabid Dog intercepting them pissed Ben off to no end. Once he finally calmed down, he began to wonder if his mom's heart had ached for him as his used to ache for her. He'd prayed many times over the years that his running away hadn't caused her to drink more. When he was younger, he'd felt guilty about the possibility of her spiraling, but those days had long since passed. With Ben's crossover into manhood came his understanding that adults are responsible for their own actions, which is why a large part of him began hating Angie after his childhood naivetés had faded. He thought about that hate as he sat and sipped on his diet coke. It made him sad that he'd come to loathe her so much. So much so that, even to this day, it blocked him from being able to fully mourn for her—and that *did* make him feel guilty.

The waitress served him a delicious-smelling cheeseburger, saving him from his guilt-ridden conscious. He dug in, savoring the greasy goodness, and then started going over the tasks at hand. He'd reviewed his plan time-and-time again during the flight and now he resumed the repetitious process. The meticulous planning was something that the military had taught and subsequently had demanded him to do with precision. As a result, he'd uncovered a too many unknown variables in his own plan that he didn't care for. Regardless, he was committed to the plan's *execution*, so he'd just have to improvise and overcome. He'd waited a long time to put a stop to the evil that had destroyed so many lives—an evil that should've been taken care of a long time ago. Needless to say, the lack of an airtight plan wasn't going to stop him from meeting his objectives.

Nothing is going to stop me. Hooah, goddamit.

A man's raucous laugh and loud talking distracted Ben from his mission briefing. He glanced over at one of the waitress's other patrons who was busy giving the waitress a hard time. Ben was preparing to slide out from his booth after witnessing the sorry excuse for a man slap her rear. Ben stopped his move of gallantry once he noticed her own move to stand-up for herself: pointing her finger at the man and telling him to keep his hands to himself or else he'd have to leave. She turned to walk away when the man grabbed her wrist and told her to come back. With cat-like agility, the waitress spun around, slightly squatted at her knees, bent her arm back so that her elbow pointed towards the man and then leaned into him. The move skillfully released her wrist from his grip, which she followed up by rolling her hand under and around her assailant's wrist and then with just a gentle twist she put him into a mercy-hold. The idiotic man pressed his head hard on the table and began to quickly beg for her to *please* let go.

Ben began to laugh his ass off and nodded at the waitress's ability to clearly take care of herself. It made his thoughts go back to his mom and wondered how things in life might have been different if she'd only learned self-defense skills. But then reality set in and he knew it wouldn't have mattered—not with the Rabid Dog. Any success in defending herself would've only been temporary and would've made Jessup angrier to the point of causing even more damage. The realization pulled Ben back down to the real world where he resumed hating her for ever getting involved with the son-of-a-bitch in the first place.

What the hell could she have ever seen in that rotten, evil man?

Ben took one last sip of his soda and then put down money to cover the check along with a twenty-dollar tip for the waitress. He figured the awesome show was worth at least that. He only got two steps away from the booth before he froze and then slowly nodded.

Almost forgot...just like I said I would.

He reached over and grabbed his hoodie from the booth and left the restaurant. A few minutes later the waitress came to retrieve the check and noticed the big tip. It made her day and her smile showed it, but the smile faded when she saw Ben's cellphone wedged in the booth-seat's crevice. The phone had slipped out of his hoodie without him ever noticing. The waitress quickly picked up the phone and ran after the good tipper.

Ben pulled out of the restaurant's parking lot and back onto Highway-80, heading east. He thought about calling Maddie and felt bad that he hadn't already. He should've called first thing when he landed but had been so preoccupied with getting on with the damn road trip that he'd completely forgotten. He started to reach into his hoodie for the phone, but then decided to just wait until the next stop so he wouldn't be talking and driving at the same time. If only he'd checked his rearview mirror at that moment, he would've seen his mom's look-a-like frantically running behind him, trying to flag him down. The good woman stopped when she'd exhausted twenty dollars' worth of effort, which to her defense was a lot more than most would have.

After putting a few miles between him and the diner, the silence started getting to Ben again. So much so that he almost pushed the CD back in to see what Edward was going to do about that evil man lurking in the shadows, but then he remembered something he would much rather listen to. He took an old cassette tape from his pocket and pushed it into the player. Within a few seconds, Raina's voice said, "This is for T." Ben smiled at the sound of her voice, and then smiled even wider once the singing began.

"Now *this* is the inspiration I needed. Hey Baron, listen up and take notes."

SEATTLE, WASHINGTON

MADDIE CHECKED HER CELLPHONE again for messages and then tried calling Ben once more. She'd been doing it every twenty minutes since the time when Ben should've arrived in Dallas. She'd called the airlines and confirmed that his flight had safely landed.

You are in so much trouble, mister. You'd better have a damn good reason or else.

When two hours passed, her gut kicked in and told her that something was wrong. That was all it took to prompt her to get on the phone and procure her own airfare. When the agent told her that the next plane didn't leave for another two hours, she thought that at least it would give her enough time to go home and pack. When the agent explained that there were no more direct flights for the day and that she would have a two hour layover in Salt Lake City, Maddie agitatedly told the woman to go ahead and book the flight. She then hung up the phone by slamming it down and screamed, "Fudgesicle!"

GILMER, TEXAS

THE DAMNED GUTTERFLIES were really scurrying around inside Ben when he entered the Gilmer city limits. He thought he was going to have to pull over and throw up but told himself to man up and then managed to hold it down. Within minutes, he pulled into the cemetery where he knew Angie had been buried earlier that morning. Before parking, he first drove the entire site to survey who, if anyone, was there, finding only one car but no people in sight. Satisfied, he found a place to park, deciding it was time to go ahead and get the impending ass-chewing out of the way. Maddie was going to be madder than hell—that, he had no doubt about. He reached into the right pocket of his hoodie for his cellphone but of course it wasn't there. He checked the other pocket with no luck. He searched the entire car, and then he checked his pockets again, and then the car again. After fifteen minutes of diligent searching, he finally gave up with a resounding, "Son of a bitch!" He would call first thing when he got to the motel room, which would be soon just not soon enough.

Hell, two hours ago wouldn't have been soon enough. I'm in deep doo-doo and there's no getting out of it.

After the phone search debacle, Ben started walking on foot to find Angie's grave. He wasn't sure how long it would take him, but he looked for the section of the cemetery where the more modest markers were. He knew Jessup would've never buried her near any of the expensive plots, so he walked to the cheap rows and searched for the green AstroTurf that always covers a fresh grave. As if on cue, rain clouds moved in and cast shadows over the grounds, and Ben knew he'd have to put a rush on it or go back to the car and get his damn hoodie.

Screw walking back now. It's not like I haven't been stuck out in a rainstorm before without cover. Good times.

As Ben continued on, the Baron's words came back to him and he looked around the property and thought that the author's gravesite description could've worked for the cemetery that Ben was now haunting, if only it had been winter with snow on the ground. A gloomy afternoon with chance of showers would have to suffice, he supposed. He then recalled the story's lurking evil man again and wondered where Jessup was. Ben figured he was either out drinking to celebrate or with Wade stalking their next victim. In any case, Ben was pretty damn sure that he wouldn't be at the cemetery sobbing over Angie's grave. But make no mistake, wherever he was, Ben would soon find the son-of-a-bitch.

The Rabid Dog and I have an appointment tomorrow—only he doesn't know it, yet.

He finally spotted a fresh grave up a ways and in his gut he knew it was his mom's. He walked up to the newly constructed resting place and read the gravestone.

ANGELA W. BOONE
1951 – 1995

Ben stared at the nondescript tablet and choked down a sob, thinking that if ever sorrow could be framed, it would look like the view of his mom's exiguous headstone. He thought that whomever made the grave marker must have charged by the letter since the fucking Rabid Dog hadn't even included at least her date of birth, much less an epitaph. The whole memorial was more pathetic than sad, but then Ben supposed it accurately represented the life that could've been but never was. Even worse, it represented a life that to him had done more harm than good. Ben finally squatted down in front of Angie's grave and wept for her. Again as if on cue, sprinkles started falling from the sky. Soon the drops mixed with his tears until they, like all hope for his mom, were indiscernibly lost forever.

Once he had no more tears to give, Ben started to head back to his car. He was relieved to have gotten the final goodbye out of the way. And now with each step, his countenance morphed into that of a man with an acute purpose. There were a few matters he needed to take care—but first up, *a promise to keep.*

Ben heard a voice that was muffled and behind him, but he knew it was Tommy. Ben had seen him hiding behind a group of trees not long after he began the search for his mom's grave. His senses were in a heightened mode and there was no chance of anything in his vicinity going unnoticed. Even Maddie, the 'Goddess of

Observance', would've bowed in awe at him. The skilled soldier that had lain dormant within Ben for the last three years had never forgotten what it had been taught so well to do. No sir—Tío Sam didn't train his elites to forget so easily.

"Ben? Ben is that you?" Tommy asked, still half hiding behind a tree.

Ben turned around and walked over to where Tommy was taking cover.

"Hello, Tommy."

"Damn. You done went and grow'd up. You look good. Real good, Ben. Except for that eye I guess. Does it ever hurt? What happened to it?"

Ben completely ignored the absolutely stupid questions and decided to ask one of his own.

"How's it been hanging, Tommy?"

Ben's voice had zero emotion. It was monotone and as cold as...as cold as the day in that damned audio-book he couldn't get out of his freaking head.

Goddamn Baron.

"Oh, I been doin' good. Got a steady job with the city, believe it or not. Been sober now for two years."

Tommy reached into his front pocket and showed Ben his 'Addicts Anonymous' two year chip.

"I took Raina's death pretty hard. I guess ya never knew. She and I, we fell in...well, doesn't matter I suppose. I figured that if ya weren't dead then if Angie's passin' didn't bring ya back then nothing would. So I've been waiting and watching out for ya. I ah...I'm glad you did show. I actually missed ya, Ben. I know I was an asshole to ya. And I never did anything to help ya when p-p-p...pop. Well, I just wanted the chance to tell ya I'm sorry is all. I really am, Benji."

Fuck! Benji. Haven't heard that since the last time he said it. Fuck!

Tommy's show of affection was a curve ball that Ben hadn't expected. He actually felt sorry for the sad man standing before him. He'd held on to hate for so long that he'd only realized at that moment just how much it had blurred the lines. Tommy had been just a kid, too. Sure, he was older than Ben, but a kid just the same. And he'd also experienced his fair share of abuse at the hands of Jessup. Ben then thought that maybe the Rabid Dog turned his aggressions more towards Tommy after he ran away—after his primary punching bag was gone. Ben could also see that Tommy suffered, just like so many other people who'd been caught in the wake of the Rabid Dog and Wade. And so Ben extended his hand to Tommy, which was something he'd never imagined doing in a hundred lifetimes. Tommy took Ben's hand and followed it in with a strong hug. Ben patted him on his back as Tommy sobbed on Ben's shoulder.

Oh for fuck's sake! Ben, don't you dare cry. Do NOT cry. I will kick your ass, I shit you not! Fuck, I'm going to cry.

Ben gently broke free from Tommy's embrace and looked at the man whom he'd always remembered as an asshole jock-strap-linebacker. He wasn't even a shadow of that high school boy anymore. The man Ben now saw was a frail, defeated shell of something that could've been but never had, which was the same goddamned conclusion he'd had about his mom. The rage started to build in Ben at the thought of how many lives the Rabid Dog had fucked up, Tommy's included. Ben actually had to take a deep breath to steady his anger. He closed his eyes to reset his mood and then took the cassette tape from his front pocket and handed it to Tommy. Tommy looked down at the cassette and immediately recognized the handwriting that he knew so well and then started sobbing again when he read the words: 'To: T From: R'.

- 42 -

10W-30

GILMER, TEXAS – JUNE 1995

TOMMY HAD BEEN SITTING in his car for hours, trying to work up the courage to listen to the cassette. The last glimpse of daylight had just snuck away and he just stared at the tape that he'd only half-way inserted into the player. He was afraid of what was on the recording—afraid of the wounds it would open. So he continued to sit and stare out at the landscape without really registering it until he finally worked up the nerve to push the cassette in all the way. When he heard Raina's voice play through the speakers, his heart melted all over again. By the time her beautiful, sultry voice had finished the song, Tommy had already started heaving in heavy sobs as he'd done so many times in the last few years. The heat from his sadness had fogged up the windows and snot was flowing down his face and onto his clothes, but he didn't care. He was lost all over again in Raina. And he went through every extreme range of emotions as he beat the steering wheel with his palms and then grabbed the wheel and used it as an anchor. Then his rage started building to the point where he had to get out of the car. He slammed the door and paced in a circle like a madman. Out of nowhere a right-hand hook smashed the driver's side window. Tommy looked down at his bloody fist and could only think of making the pain go away—not the pain from his hand, but the pain in his heart. And there was only one way he knew that would work for sure.

MT. PLEASANT, TEXAS

BEN DIDN'T WANT TO TAKE ANY CHANCES of being spotted by Jessup or Wade, so as planned, he checked into a motel in Mt. Pleasant, steering clear of Gilmer for the night. It just so happened that the motor inn that he checked into was the same one Octavio had stayed at after being released from prison. Coincidentally, Ben was given the same exact room and if he'd known to look, he would've found a gash in the wall made by the desk that Octavio had thrown across the room. The fine establishment never did repair the damage. In fact, once Octavio had died a hero, the motel owner had intended to hang a memorial plaque next to the destroyed drywall, hoping that by putting the Octavio Muñoz damage on display, it would bring in droves of curious guests.

Ben used the bedside phone to call Maddie's cellphone but she didn't answer. He tried their home number but no answer. Finally he tried her work number, but again no luck. He sat in bed unable to sleep and he could feel the onset of a severe migraine. The additional stress of worrying about Maddie was something he certainly didn't need—plenty of rest, however, was something that he did need for the following day's mission.

For fuck's sake, Maddie! Answer the goddamn phone! A phone. Any phone. Goddammit!

"It's on me and I know it. You should've called as soon as you landed, Ben. You dumbass. She's so pissed off at you that she's not even answering."

No, she wouldn't do that. She'd answer just to chew my ass out. What the hell?

He dialed her cellphone one last time and left a message.

"Maddie, it's Ben. I'm sorry I didn't call as soon as I landed. No excuse other than my head is not in the best place. But where in the hell are you? I've tried calling a million times. I'm using the hotel phone because I lost my damn cell. Call me at..."

At the end of the voicemail, Ben left her the motel's contact information along with his room number. He then dialed Carl's number.

"Hello," Carl answered.

"Carl, it's Ben. Have you heard from Maddie?"

"No, why? You can't reach her?"

"No, and I'm getting worried."

"Alright, let me get dressed and I'll go track her down."

"Thanks, man. I really appreciate it. Please call me as soon as you know something."

"Will do. Don't worry. I'm sure she's fine."

"Just call me as soon as you can. Thanks."

I hope Carl is right. Maybe she fell asleep. Or maybe she's in bed reading a book listening to her country music with those damned headphones on.

Ben never did understand how she could read her books while listening to music at the same time. He was dumb enough to bring the subject up to her once and her response to his inquisition had been, "It's simple. I can do it and you can't because I have more brains than you." He'd smartly decided that there was no rebuttal to argue the fact and henceforth had perpetually left the subject alone.

Ben was exhausted from the long day along with all of its emotional activities. He knew he needed his rest, but there was no way in hell he would be able to sleep without knowing that Maddie was okay. And then his cellphone rang.

"Carl, did you find her?"

"Carl? This is your wife, *asshole*. And let me just say it again—you are an *ass...hole*."

"Maddie! Oh thank God! I was so worried about you!"

"Yeah, I totally get that. Again. Asshole."

"I'm so sorry, beautiful. I know I should've called. I lost my damn phone and—"

"I listened to your voicemail already. No need to repeat."

"Jesus, you are fuming mad at me."

"You have no idea."

"Where have you been? Where are you?"

"I'm in Salt Lake City."

"What? Utah? What the hell?"

"I'm on my way to you, asshole. I have a layover and won't get to your room until really late tonight. Sounds like a real classy place, by the way. You know when an establishment has the words 'Motor Inn' in its name, then you're in for a lavish treat."

"Why are you coming here, Maddie?" Ben asked, so taken aback by his wife's initiative that he completely ignored her snarky wit.

"That has got to be the stupidest question I've ever heard you ask."

"Don't come here. Catch a flight back to Seattle the first chance you get. Repeat, do NOT come here."

Maddie laughed. It was not at all a funny sort of laugh, either.

"Fuck 'Y'-'O'-'U'. I'm coming and you can't stop me. Something's going on and I know it. You will just have to deal with me. Goodbye, asshole."

"Goddammit, Maddie!"

Click.

"Fuck!"

GILMER, TEXAS

THE FINAL LEG of Maddie's flight didn't touch down at DFW until 10:32PM. After picking up a rental car and figuring out how to navigate her way out of the DFW area, she finally made it to the

Gilmer city limits at 1:19AM. Maddie had to pee so bad it hurt, and didn't think she could make it all the way to Mt. Pleasant, so she pulled into the first 24-Hour gas station she came to. She was racing in such a hurry to get to the restroom that she accidentally bumped into an older man and knocked a pouch of Red Man chewing tobacco right out of his hand. She quickly apologized and made her way to the ladies room. Five minutes later she came back out, grabbed a bottled-water from a beverage cooler and headed to the counter.

WADE PRETENDED TO LOOK at the motor oil on a shelf as he waited for the pretty young woman to come back out of the restroom. When she grabbed a bottle of water and took it to the counter, he picked up a quart of 10W-30 and walked up behind her. She dropped her keys on the store's floor and before bending over to pick them up, she laid her lady-wallet out on the counter, splaying it wide open in the process. Wade used his hawk-eye vision to first scan in the view of the young lady's fine ass He then casually glanced at her wallet's inside flap, focusing in on a photograph. It was a good pose of her with her man and it just so happened that Wade recognized the young feller as none other than little Benny Boy.

Well, ain't that intrastin'.

On the other flap of the fine woman's wallet he read her Washington State driver's license.

Madeline Lewis River. Yup, that's def'nutly intrastin'.

Wade decided he didn't need oil after all and set the quart on the counter before leaving. On his way out, he checked his camo vest's breast pocket to make sure the small bottle of chloroform was there.

Yup.

TOMMY COULD ONLY DIG UP eighty bucks and he smoked through that in just three hours. Two hours later he was coming down off of his high and knew he needed more. He considered robbing a convenience store or breaking into a neighbor's house, but then a better idea came to him. He quickly twitched his head back and forth before starting his car and heading south on the Octavio Muñoz Highway.

- 43 -

CROWN ROYAL

TOMMY PARKED AROUND THE CORNER of Jessup's house and camped out for the rest of the night in his car, but he never did sleep. He wouldn't have even if the drugs had allowed him to. He was too busy thinking about Raina and what he was going to do next, so sleep was not an option. Not long after the sun finally rose, he watched as his Pop's blue Nova pulled out of the drive and disappeared in the opposite direction. He got out of his car and walked to the house he'd grown up in. He wasted no time with reminiscing on anything nor did he stop to chug the milk from the fridge like he always used to do. Instead he headed straight for his pop's bedroom closet. Tommy knew that was where all of the guns were kept.

Too many fucking guns, anyway. Time to collect early on a portion of my inheritance. I'll start by hocking that old antique pump action 20-guage and then maybe even some of Angie's cheap-ass jewelry. Good Lord knows she don't need it no more.

Tommy leaned into the closet to grab the shotgun when he got lightheaded from his fleeting high and stumbled forward. He caught himself on the inside closet wall, causing one of the wood wall planks to give under his weight.

What the fuck?

He reached up and tugged on the closet light's pull-string. The bulb woke up and provided miserable illumination, but it was enough. Tommy looked at the top of the plank and saw that it had a concealed piano hinge. He pulled the plank out, lifted it up, and let it rest on his shoulder. He saw the shadow of something inside the wall but couldn't make it out. He reached in and pulled out an old purple and yellow Crown Royal velvet pouch. He turned the bag upside down and all kinds of different jewelry poured out into his hand.

Jackpot!

One of the pieces caused him to do a double-take. Using his other hand, he picked up the piece that caught his attention and held it to the light. His heart sank as he saw what looked like the necklace and heart locket that he'd given to Raina eleven years ago. He dropped all of the other jewelry, closed his eyes and held his breath as he unlocked the heart to reveal what was inside. He opened his eyes and right away saw the *T+R=4EVR* inscription. Tommy Boone let out a heart-wrenching yelp and fell to his knees as he experienced the worst agony yet in his young, hurtful life.

JESSUP PULLED INTO THE DRIVEWAY while singing along with Bocephus on the radio station. He felt better than he had in a long, long time.

Should've got rid of that bitch years ago.

He walked in through the back door holding a large cup of coffee in one hand and a box of donuts in the other. He saw Tommy sitting at the kitchen table with his shotgun leaned against the nearby wall.

"Mornin', fucker. Just so ya know, if you think you're goin' huntin' with my gun, you're thinkin' wrong. Go buy your own. Oh wait, that would require you to actually work for a change," Jessup said.

"Look who's talkin'," Tommy replied.

"What the fuck did you just say to me, boy?"

"You know, I should've figured it out a long time ago."

"Figure what out, you pathetic little pussy?"

"I loved her you rotten piece of shit. But you wouldn't know what that means. You're too much of a fucking demon to know."

Jessup saw Raina's necklace sitting on the table in front of Tommy and he quickly caught on to what had crawled up Tommy's ass. He knew his boy better than anyone and therefore knew he had about four seconds to go for that shotgun, five seconds tops. Jessup dropped the donuts and coffee and made his move, but Tommy was waiting for it. With a sweeping motion, Tommy grabbed the shotgun, which already had a shell pumped into its chamber, and used his feet to push back on the floor. The push caused his chair to slide across the dilapidated linoleum, finally coming to a ruckus halt at a wall. With his back was up against the wall, Tommy waited

371

until Jessup got right up on him, and then he pulled the trigger and sent a full charge of buckshot into the Rabid Dog's face, blowing it clean off in the process. Those dirty old kitchen walls would shake three times that day. The first time was from the shotgun when Tommy killed his pop and the second time was when Jessup's dead-weight body fell to the cheap floor.

Tommy looked down at his pop lying lifeless—lifeless and faceless. He turned his head and puked into the kitchen trash can, but he hadn't planned the aim, it was just blind luck that the waste bin happened to be there to catch his vomit. Tommy then unconsciously switched his stare to the dirty bare kitchen wall. He didn't know it, but it was the same kind of stare his little step-brother knew all too well. Thirty minutes after staring into nothingness, Tommy pumped the 20-gauge, braced the stock on the floor, leaned forward and quickly put his chin over the barrel. Before he could hear Raina say, "No, don't you do that!" Tommy reached down with his thumb and pushed hard on the antique shotgun's trigger, causing the Rabid Dog's kitchen walls to tremble their third and final time that day.

BEN UNINTENTIONALLY FELL ASLEEP waiting on Maddie to arrive and didn't wake up until after seven in the morning. He frantically called her cell. No answer. Then he checked his room phone for messages. There were none. He called the front desk. No messages there either. His heart sank deeper than it ever had in his life. He knew something was wrong. Very wrong. He again dialed Maddie's cellphone number. Wade picked up on the first ring.

"Benny-Boy. Long time."

"Wade? You motherf—"

"Now-now, boy. Settle down. She's fine, f'ur now."

"You fucking hurt her and I'm going to—"

"There ya go 'gain. Reckon I should jus' let ya git it out of y'ur system."

"What do you want, you motherf... What do you want!"

"Now we're gettin' somewhere. How about you meet me at y'ur step-daddy's? I'll bring Maddie with me. We'll have us a fam'ly reeeeeeunion."

"When?"

"Now's a good a time as any I s'pose."

"On my way."

"Oh Benny-Boy, before you hang up. If you do anythin' stupid before I get there, jus' keep in mind that I've got y'ur lovely wife with me. Now go on. Get to it."

Click.

Fuck! Motherfucking son-of-a-bitch! Maddie! Jesus Christ! God, why? I fucking hate you! God, are you listening? I fucking hate you!

WADE LOOKED OVER AT MADDIE who was already bound and gagged and crying her heart out.

Jus' like they all do.

Wade dialed Jessup's number. He knew his old buddy would be up by then and well over his hangover—it never did take Jessup long to shake one off the morning after getting shit-faced. Wade let the phone ring over a dozen times and finally hung up.

"Well now purdy girl, looks like you can't come to the party after all. Don't worry, I'll bring the shindig back here to you."

- 44 -

HALO

BEN PARKED THREE BLOCKS AWAY from the Rabid Dog's house. He was praying to God, whom he still hated, that he had beaten Wade there. He reached behind the passenger seat and grabbed the package he'd picked up from the local postal center in Mt. Pleasant where he'd had it shipped to. He stared at the box for a moment before opening it, and then he pulled out the WWII Colt M1911A1 that Dr. Reeves had gifted him five years ago for graduating from the good doctor's alma mater. He took one of the clips from the box, double-checked that it was stocked, pushed it into the gun's handle, and pulled back on the slide to load the first bullet into the chamber. He got out of the car and slid the extra clip into his back pocket and then, with the gun still in his hand, quickly started towards the house.

Ben's adrenaline was pumping harder than it had since the last, fateful Red Devils training mission. Just like then, he let the years of military training take over his movements and he hardened his senses for the mission he was about to execute on. He approached the Rabid Dog's house in a crouched run and quickly cut across to the side—then he slowed, hugging the external wall and followed it to the backyard. With trained stealth, he opened the back door and entered the kitchen. The very first thing he saw was Jessup lying dead on the floor and the very first reaction he had was jealous-anger. Then his eyes scanned in Tommy. The macabre sight of his headless step-brother made Ben cough out a cry and fall to one knee.

WADE'S NONDESCRIPT CAPRICE pulled in behind Angie's dirty van just in time for him to catch a glimpse of Ben easing around the back of the house. Wade quickly got out of the old car and for the first time since the day the Asian girl went into labor, he forwent his usual routine of spending a few moments with the old steel dinosaur in the overgrown front yard. Instead, he took the same path Ben had taken alongside the house and made-up the distance by sprinting faster than most men half his age could. Wade's agile movements painted a stark contrast from his outward hillbilly appearance that would've made anyone watching do a double-take. Once he got to the back door, he pulled out his own gun and slowly crept in until he saw Ben on one knee with his back to the door.

"Tommy. Fuck," he heard Ben say.

Consequently, Ben had let his guard down for a split-second, and that was all Wade needed. It was an error that all of Ben's military training had made a point of *not* letting happen. But it wasn't a goddamn Army mission and it sure wasn't a black-and-white objective, either. What Ben was doing was as personal as any one thing ever could be, and with that, all training flew out the door faster than a Red Devil on a 'HALO' jump. *Hoo-fucking-ah!*

Wade wasted no time taking advantage of Ben's mistake. He quickly snuck up on the little shit that was busy having a pity party for Tommy, and then pistol whipped him in the back of the head. The blow knocked Ben unconscious but as an added security measure, Wade covered Ben's face with the infamous chloroform. He then picked up the Colt .45 from Ben's hand and nonchalantly studied the gun's wood-inlaid stock and cast-iron body with General Patton's name engraved in the side. He stuffed the gun down the back of his pants and then mumbled.

"Hmm, I be damned."

He noticed the extra clip in Ben's back pocket and took that as well.

Looks like you was intendin' on doin' some shootin' there Benny Boy.

Wade then looked up at the cranberry chunks of skull and scalp shrapneled into the kitchen ceiling. Only after appreciating the overhead work of art did he take in the entire kill scene. His eyes finally tracked in on Raina's necklace that was still on the table. He walked over and carefully picked up Tommy's love-gift and became amused at discovering that it had miraculously escaped any blood or flesh drippings. He then navigated around Tommy's slumped body to head down the hall to Jessup's bedroom where he knew more kill-trophies were in need of disposal.

- 45 -

BLUE EYES

WITH EACH TUG, the straps dug deeper into the skin of her ankles, but Maddie kept kicking anyway. She was tied to the same bed that dozens of other women had been bound to over the years. The very same bed on which they'd all lived for a short while, endured unspeakable acts, and then eventually died. And just like all the others before her, Maddie's mouth was stuffed with the mandatory red-and-black ball-gag that made any vocal communication impossible. Of course, Wade would take it off later so he could listen to her screams of anger turn to screams of agony, which was one of his absolute favorite things in the world to hear. But Maddie had no idea about any of that. All she knew was that both she and Ben were bound and gagged. She could see him catty-corner through the doorway in another room and since spotting him there, she had been trying to make as much noise as she could to wake him up. Unfortunately, there was little noise to be made in her position.

Ben was tied to a chair in Wade's bedroom, positioned diagonally just inside the doorway so that he directly faced the torture room with a perfect view of Maddie. Ben finally started stirring in pain and eventually woke up to a throbbing headache. He opened his eye and blinked hard for a couple minutes before he could finally focus. His first sight was of Maddie kicking her legs while being tied down to that same goddamn death-bed. Ben immediately knew where he was. He'd had nightmares about the place ever since that horrible night so many years ago. It was all too familiar, all the way down to the fucking lump that he felt throbbing on the back of his head.

Motherfucker!

Ben's eye bulged in anger and then in terror as he thought about what Wade was going to do with his pregnant love. He screamed but only a grunting noise came out. He desperately tried to free himself but after several minutes of struggling, he knew that it was hopeless. Not only had Wade done a much better job tying him up this time around, he'd also bolted (to the floor) the steel framed chair that Ben was bound to. Ben had pulled with adrenaline-fueled strength, but the numerous winds of climbing rope that constricted his hands and legs just tightened all-the-more with each pound of force he applied.

Fuck! Please God! Please! God! No!

Tears started streaming down the left side of his red-hot face to his vein-bulged neck as he helplessly looked at his beautiful wife.

He'd been slowly realizing that there was nothing he could do to save the woman he'd die a million times over for. Maddie saw the defeated look come over her husband's expression as he finally looked away from her eyes and then down to the floor in front of him. Maddie's own tears began their journey towards the demonic cradle that over the years had become accustomed—even addicted—to the saline substance.

Wade walked down the hall and glanced to his right to see that Ben was awake. He stood in the doorway and just stared for a few moments like an evil grinning statue. He was relishing in his big catch and was feeding on the crushed resolution that he saw on Ben's countenance.

"Guess this is pro'lly a daaay-jaahhh-voooo moment for you, ain't it Benny Boy? Don't worry, I'll take that gag out soon 'nough, but there's a few things I'd like to get off my chest first. That is if you don't mind."

Wade gave a short chuckle and continued.

"Where to begin. How 'bout we work our way back'ards. Startin' with y'ur wife o'er there. I guess she was coming to y'ur rescue. Little Benny Boy always needin' someone to come to his rescue. Always too little too late. Well, she and I made our 'quaintance last night at a gas station."

If you lay one hand on her, you son-of-a-bitch! Ben shook violently as he emitted the muffled scream.

"Don't worry, I ain't spoiled her yet. And I almost didn't notice that little bump on her stomach. Wudd'nt 'til I was tyin' you up and she started carryin' on like a banshee did I notice it. I'm thinkin' hard about keepin' her until she has that baby. You, too. Will be just like old times, huh little Ben?"

I'm going to kill you, you mother-fucker!

"Ya know, I felt y'ur presence here that night—felt ya watchin'. I almost turned and walked in on you, but I wanted to see what you'd do, in case my gut was right and you were there. You may not b'lieve that, but it's true. God's honest truth."

You're proof that there is no God!

"I knew'd as soon as I saw that baby gone from the john that my instinct was dead on. You'd been standin' right there watchin' the whole time. And I didn't let your step-daddy know neither. Ole Jessup was too hot headed. Didn't want him a-runnin' off to kill ya. So I let ya go. Don't worry, you'll have plenty of time to thank me later."

I'm going to kill you later. Goddammit! Fuck!

"You know, I'd be lyin' if I didn't admit that you s'prised me boy. Didn't think you had gumption before that. Made me a little proud, as proud as a man like me can get, if ya catch my drift. But I'm gettin' ahead of ma'self.

Please God, make him stop!

"Seems the sand niggers took care of ole Octaveeeeo for me. Shame, too. I looked forward to makin' that boy suffer. He wudd'nt been no damn hero once I got a hold of 'em, gaaaaroooooteeed."

Guaranteed he would've kicked your ass, you fuck!

"Who's nex' up? Hmmmm. Oh that's right. Let's talk 'bout old man Morgan River. Say, did you ever fig'r out that Jessup and I paid 'em a'visit? I'll give that a second to sink in."

Wade paused a few moments and began humming the tune from the *Jeopardy* game-show before continuing.

"Yup. By those fresh tears, I guess it means you never figured it out. Don't worry, you'd be grateful to know that he didn't suffer none. Wudd'nt no time f'ur that. Otherwise, who knows."

No, no...no! Oh my God! Why? You mother...fucker...I'm gonna...!

"And then there was y'ur nigger friend and that fat boy. You can thank y'ur step-daddy f'ur that one. We had to clean up his mess. Jessup wudd'nt the sharpest tool in the shed. Dudd'nt matter no way, I guess. They had to go just the same."

Jesus, please!

"'Course then there was that purdy nigger girl. Boy, I still have sweet dreams 'bout that night. She was one of my all time fav'rits."

Raina! Her name was Raina you fu...

"But don't worry, I have high hopes for Mad'lin o'er there.

No! You better not touch her you...

"Guess we're back down to that slant-eyed girl you saw have the baby. I was disappointed to lose her. Another one of my fav'rits. 'Course there's been so many more since then, as I'm sure you can 'magine. And even more goin' back a long ways. I'll never forget the first one though. Not that it was my best. Not by a long shot. But you never forget y'ur first."

Please just shut up!

"She was the only one I never killed. Couldn't tell you why I never did. S'ppose it was beginner jitters maybe. It was before I'd figured things out, ya see."

I don't care, you egotistical piece of shit!

"Last time I'd let one live though. It was the last for a lot of things. The last time I wore a silly mask to hide my face. You just can't enjoy y'urself properly while wearin' one, is what I discovered. Oh yeah, and it was also the last time I did it alone. Your step-daddy joined me ev'ry time after that first one. Yes, indee-dee."

I've got to get out of this chair. Think Ben, think!

"Funny thing though. That first whore, she resurfaced a few years later and old Jessup took a like'n to her. And even though she had a little boy, he still took 'er in. Maybe it was so his own boy could have a little brother. Hell, who knows."

What?!

"Never could really figure out why. She was a lousy lay. God's truth. And wouldn't nobody else a'tall have her. She was rurnt, believe me. But she was still a little purdy, I s'pose. Boy howdy, I guess by the way y'ur lookin' up at me, you've figured it all out."

You're fucking lying!

"Do these blue eyes look familiar to you now, little Ben?"

No!

Wade chuckled. It was the kind of chuckle with no energy or effort, just a dull growl of laughter, straight from the devil himself.

You're a fucking liar! Not possible. No!

"Truth is I got a little out-a-order. But it was for eeeefect. You see, the last one I killed just so happened to be the one I let get away the first time. That's right Benny Boy, y'ur real daddy killed y'ur no-good whore of a momma."

Son of a fuck!

"Jessup pract'lly begged me to. 'Bout goddamm time, too. I swear if I had to hear that man bitch one more time 'bout her I was gonna have to shut *him* up f'ur good. But it looked like good ole Tommy boy did a damn fine job of that now didn't he? I will miss ole Jessup though. Made me laugh."

Ben was sobbing uncontrollably. He was heaving and choking on the goddamn ball-gag. His eye burned from crying so much. He just wanted to wake up. It couldn't be real. It just couldn't.

383

"Boy howdy, all this talkin' has made me thirsty somethin' awful. I'm usually not the talkin' type you see. Gettin' a lil' dryyyyyy. So, I'm gonna go have me a beer and let you think on things for a while. When I come back, you're dear ole daddy will show you how it's done right."

No goddammit, no. Don't you dare you mother fu —

"I doubt you'll enjoy it as much as me, but you never know. My blood runs through those veins of y'urs so anythin' is possible I s'ppose."

You're a liar. We're nothing alike...you're nothing.

But Ben knew it was true. He knew the moment that Wade went there. Maybe he'd known it deep down for a long time. Maybe that was what ate him alive for the last thirteen years. Didn't matter though. All that mattered now was Maddie and the baby. Ben knew he needed to calm down. His anger and tension were making matters worse, so he slowed his breathing and started taking deep breaths. Ben then closed his eyes and tried his best to clear his mind. It was the hardest thing he'd ever had to do, and it made his Ranger training seem like a cake walk in comparison.

Ben finally managed to compose himself and let a sense of tranquility come over him. He did this the only way he knew how and that was by thinking of the day he spent with Maddie at the airport. He kept playing it over and over in his mind. He thought of nothing else. Soon the blood in his veins slowed and along with it his vascularity diminished. The blood in his body started to regulate normally and transfer more equally throughout his system. As a result, his hands got a little smaller. Not much, but it would have to be enough. Ben slowly and slightly moved his right hand over his left thumb and started pushing back to engage his double joint. His left thumb bent all the way back, but it wasn't enough to free his hand.

Fuck! Give me a break, God! Please! A little fucking help for chrissakes!

Calm down, Ben. Don't get worked up again. Breathe. Okay. You're going to have to just break it. Break it off if you have to. You'd die for her, so rip your fucking fingers off if you have to.

Ben got a strong grip on his left thumb, took a deep breath, and on exhale he jerked as hard and as fast as he could. The pain was excruciating and would've made most men pass out, but Ben pushed through and kept pulling well after he heard bones snap and ligaments tear. He felt blood starting to run where a small bone had compounded out, but he still didn't stop, not until he felt the rings of rope slide over his ruined thumb. Once the binding started to give, he pushed harder until his left hand freed completely from the snare. The pain made him want to vomit, but he had no time. He worked his right hand free and took just a quick second to grab his left hand and pull his left thumb back in place. He screamed out in pain and truth be told, he'd been screaming the entire time while breaking his thumb. The old ball-gag had muted his agony and in doing so, the bondage device turned out to be a friend after all. He untied his feet as fast as he could, which to him seemed as if he was neck deep in mud, moving in slow motion.

MADDIE'S EYES WIDENED as she witnessed her husband doing the impossible, but she thought it was just a dream—like watching a scary movie where you're rooting for the good guy to get away from the boogie-man but you know he won't. He just won't. The boogie-man isn't human and doesn't play by the same rules as humans do. It's omnipotent and all-knowing. And so it knows what the good guy is up to at all times. It's right around the corner waiting until its victim makes a run for it and then the boogie-man will appear with its evil smile and end it all.

Maddie had never imagined that being so wrong about something could feel so good. She finally realized it wasn't an illusion when her husband freed his legs and then jumped to his feet. She watched with hope as Ben pulled the ball-gag out of his mouth and glanced over at her with a look she'll never forget. He then mouthed the words, 'I LOVE YOU' and disappeared down the hall.

Wait! Where are you going? Come back! What are you doing? Untie me! You asshole! Fucker! What in the hell do you think you are you doing? Fuck!

- 46 -

FOR THE TIME BEING

HAWKEYE HAD JUST STUCK the end of a water hose into Colonel Potter's horse's ass to give it an enema. B.J. started to climb a water tower's ladder with the other end of the hose. He looked up at the tower and sheepishly said, "It's pretty high."

Hawkeye looked over at B.J. on the ladder and with a smartass tone asked, "You want the other end?"

B.J. looked at Hawkeye who was busy feeding the hose into the horse's rear. He shook his head and surrendered, "It's not so high."

Wade started laughing at the episode of *M.A.S.H.* and took a sip of his beer. Ben had already crept up and was directly behind the motherfucker. He noticed a framed photo on the end table next to where Wade was sitting. It was the photograph of Ben and Morgan that Wade had taken from the pawnshop that final day of Morgan's life. The stolen photograph even further stoked the fire that was burning inside Ben. It was now beyond personal and all of his Ranger skills were primed and ready.

Ben grabbed a handful of Wade's hair with one hand and cupped the underside of Wade's neck with the other hand. Ben ignored the excruciating pain from his thumb and yanked as hard as he could. Wade came straight back out of the recliner to surprisingly find himself being dragged backwards by a really pissed off ex-future Army Ranger. Wade grasped at his hair and neck frantically until he felt himself being lifted up and off of the ground. Ben commenced opening the biggest can of whup-ass that even Wade himself had ever given to anyone in his scrappy life, by tenfold. That was damn impressive considering that the evil son-of-a-bitch had been in a lot of scrapes over the years. Ben beat Wade to a pulp until he could no longer throw his fists in violence. His legs felt fine though, so he started front-kicking the shit out of Wade. Ben pivoted to switch legs as Wade slumped down and fell over limp.

"Not good enough fucker—I can still see you breathing," Ben said.

Ben's break for communication turned out to be a grave mistake. Wade was playing possum and took advantage of Ben's hesitation. When Ben reached down to pick Wade up, Wade pulled out his Bowie knife and with lightning speed sliced Ben across the mid-section. Ben's blood flew across the room and landed on a beige-colored partition in an arc pattern that looked like someone had just pissed red urine on the wall. Ben staggered back almost tripping before the kitchen bar stopped his posterior fall. Wade wasted no time and started charging forward. Not in a run, but in an eerie press just like the damned boogie-man.

Ben felt his jeans getting wet from a steady flow of blood and he could also feel his body go weak as the life-force drained from him.

You fucking snap out of it, soldier! Man-up motherfucker!

Ben swung his head back and forth quickly to shake it off and in the process his peripherals caught the butcher-block knife-set on the counter next to him. He pulled out three of the six steak knives from their hardwood sheath and set them down flat on the counter. Wade stopped coming forward when he saw what Ben had just done.

"Mine's bigger, boy. And somehow, I always knew it would be." Wade said as he chuckled.

Ben was so tired of the shit spewing from that man's mouth and was so ready to put an end to it. With a blinding flick of his right wrist, just like Gramps had taught him, he hurled one of the steak knives and it hit its mark dead-center. Wade's smiling expression straightened into a look of confusion as he lifted his hand to his face and traced the wetness of his blood up to the knife's handle that was protruding from his left eye socket. He fell to one knee in shock and then swallowed hard.

"How does that feel, motherfucker?" Ben taunted.

Ben's words made Wade's blood boil. He reached up and pulled the knife out of his eye, stood and took one step towards Ben. Before he could take another, Ben flung the second knife into Wade's right rectus-femoris, but with much more force this time around. Wade looked down with his one good eye at the steak-knife handle in his thigh. His eye teared-up with pain as the foreign steel woke up all of his nerves, having penetrated deep into his femur's marrow.

"You still haven't gone through anything I haven't, fucker. Dry up those tears, you pussy."

Again, the words made the blood boil until Wade made his full transition into the boogie-man. It pulled the blade out of its thigh and moved forward again. Ben allowed two more steps. He wanted the monster to be a little bit closer for the third round. After the boogie-man's third step, Ben hurled the final knife into its Adam's apple. Ben had thrown the knife with such velocity that only the very tip of the knife's handle was visible. It was exactly the same way Gramps had pierced the Kraut to save the good doctor's life, only from the front-side.

The boogie-man fell to its knees and desperately pulled on the tip of the handle, but there wasn't enough surface area to pinch, much less pull out. It grabbed the blade from the back of its neck and pushed it enough so that there was a nub to grab from the front. It began pulling the knife out of its neck, making a meaty wet wispy sound in the process. Ben walked up to the monster, grabbed the knife's handle and twisted it so that the serrated edge of the blade pointed upward. Then Ben slightly bent his knees and thrust his entire body up towards the ceiling as if he were doing a basketball layup. His feet left the floor and the jagged edge of the steak utensil cut through the monster's upper neck and at the same time dissected its brainstem.

Only when Ben saw a lake of blood on the beautiful natural stone tile floor did he stop twisting and lifting. The red pool was half Ben's and half the monster's, but Ben didn't care. The boogie-man was no more and that's all that mattered. Ben let go of the knife and the evil shell fell forward until its skull landed on the hard surface and came to its final rest with an eerie crack sound.

Ben grabbed one more steak knife from the butcher block and with slow steps, walked down the hallway, using the wall to help keep himself upright. He'd lost a lot of blood and was now pushing through again like RAP had taught him how to. He made his way to Maddie, fell forward on top of her, and then passed out. She began wiggling under his weight and screaming behind the ball-gag. The vibrations from her movements snapped him back to consciousness and he began to slowly cut her bindings loose.

Once her hands were free she pulled off the ball-gag and started yelling, "You asshole! Why did you leave—"

And then Ben shut his beautiful wife up the only way he knew how, by leaning in and kissing her with all the love he knew how to give, which turned out to be just enough—for the time being.

EPILOGUE

GILMER, TEXAS – JUNE 1995

FOR ONCE IN HIS LIFE, Ben finally woke up in a strange place without wondering where the hell he was. When he opened his eyes, the first thing he saw was the face of his beautiful wife, and that's when he knew he was right where he was supposed to be. Once Maddie noticed that Ben had come to, she leaned over from her chair to kiss his hand and then tears of relief fell from her face onto his swollen, bruised knuckles. She gently crawled into the hospital bed next to him and pressed her strawberry lips against his and subsequently made things stir in her man. In return, he caressed her soft face, looked into her chestnut eyes and likewise made things stir in his woman.

The police, of course, had made several visits to interview both

Ben and Maddie throughout the remainder of their stay in the great state of Texas. One fellow in particular that Ben actually liked was Texas Ranger Maynard Jameson. He'd been very respectful with his questions, as well as being thorough in how he handled the matter, even to the point of impressing Maddie. When the man first introduced himself as a Texas Ranger, Ben's adrenaline spiked through the roof of his child-like heart. For a fleeting moment, he'd thought that maybe he'd missed his calling—instead of being an *Army* Ranger, perhaps he was supposed to be a *Texas* Ranger. He'd looked over at Maddie at that moment and had imagined what she'd say to the idea, which is precisely why it had been merely a fleeting thought, squashed by just the hypothetical ridicule that would've surely come from the all-powerful Madeline Lewis River, had he actually been stupid enough to mention the crazy notion.

Almost stupid enough.

Texas Ranger Jameson had revealed to them that he was actually on to Jessup and Wade from complaints his office had received regarding them poaching trees from the same acreage where Raina was murdered. So, it would've been a matter of time before they pieced it all together to make a case and arrest them both. In the same breath, Ranger Jameson had admitted that he was honestly glad it turned out the way it had. Saved him a lot of headache and saved the state of Texas a heck of a lot of money. Ben thought how he couldn't agree more, sans Tommy's death and his own ruined thumb, and of course Maddie's trauma. But Octavio had been right all along—the Rabid Dog and Wade may have done quite well inside prison walls and maybe even would've enjoyed it.

Nope, they're right where they belong—roasting in hell. Orda-lay.

The tall tale that they had concocted for the authorities was that an army buddy of Ben's who was killed in action, Octavio Muñoz, had confided in him the identity of the persons responsible for the murder of Raina Snow. The story continued to explain that Ben and Maddie had traveled to Texas to privately investigate the soldier's accusations in order to prove or disprove them. It was their intention to then take any evidence straight to the police without any provocation, but unfortunately, things didn't go as planned. That's what they said at least, and of course the tall-tale was completely Maddie's idea. Ben had no pride issue with that as he clearly understood that he was the brawn and that she was the brains of their partnership. His only contribution to the story was that he claimed to have made a promise to Octavio to make sure justice had been served. Maddie had thought that it was a little over the top, but allowed it just the same. Besides, it had actually only been half a lie, as he and Octavio had in fact talked about avenging the deaths of Raina and the other Black Machetes.

EIGHT DAYS AFTER being admitted into the hospital, and after all the visits from the authorities, Ben had *finally* healed enough to go home.

"Maybe", the doctor had said.

"Hopefully", Maddie had replied.

Definitely, Ben had thought.

LATER THAT MORNING, Maddie stood in the hospital room's doorway and when Ben noticed her, locking his eye on hers, she asked, "Do you feel up for a visitor?"

"Visitor?" Ben responded and then Gabe Snow poked his head into the room from behind the door. "Mr. Snow! Come on in! It's so good to see you, sir."

"Good to see you too, Ben. And don't worry, me and the misses are the only ones in town who've figured out who you really are and we're not telling a soul. I just wanted to see you before you went back home."

"I'm glad you did, sir. I've wanted to thank you for so many years now. For that night, sir."

"You wanted to thank me?"

"Yes, sir. When you got out of the car to help me. That was the first time any adult had ever stood up for me as a kid. I never got to say thank you for that."

Gabe's eyes watered up, he lowered his head and turned away for a moment to regain his composure before finally facing Ben again.

"No, son. I should apologize to you for that night. Everything that happened after that is on me."

"That's not true, sir."

"I didn't stop those men. I could've stopped them. I should've stopped them. If I had only—"

"No sir. You saved your fam..."

Ben stopped, knowing he was about to say something that would probably hurt more than it helped, and it was probably too late to stop that from happening, but he tried to recover as best he could.

"I'm sorry, sir. I'm sorry for everything."

Tears escaped from the sides of Ben's eyes and Gabe reached over and squeezed his shoulder, just like Gramps used to do.

"I'm thankful to God above that you're alive and well, son. I've been praying for you all these years. I didn't think I could ever be happy again, but it seems that you and the Good Lord may just prove me wrong, yet. So, thank you."

Ben's doctor walked into the room and said, "Okay, Ben. Let's take a look at those stitches and see if you can make like geese and get the flock out of here."

Gabe turned and said, "I best be getting back anyway. Ben, promise me that you'll call from time to time or at the very least write this old man a letter or two?"

"Of course sir, but only if you reciprocate."

Gabe nodded with a kind smile and left the room. The doctor leaned over and took a look at the stitches on Ben's mid-section. The room door opened again and a young teenage girl poked her head in and said, "I'm sorry, please excuse me for intruding. Umm...Daddy, Jen is here, so I'm leaving now." The doctor waived her on over.

"Ben, Maddie, this is my daughter Aileen," the doctor said.

"It's a pleasure to meet you," Aileen asserted.

Ben offered his hand and said, "Likewise, pleasure."

When she leaned in to take his hand, Ben noticed the boomerang shaped birthmark on the left side of her forehead. She caught him staring at it and then made the handshake a quick one. Aileen covered the blemish with her hair as Ben continued to stare at her blushing face and at her azure blue eyes that had a slight Asian shape to them. Aileen turned towards her dad and hugged him and they held the embrace for several moments. She then said goodbye to Ben and Maddie and then one more time to her dad before leaving.

After the door closed behind the girl, Ben waited for the doctor to turn back around from watching his daughter exit.

"It's a good thing she got her mom's looks," Ben said.

"Funny guy. Truth is, my wife and I adopted her when she was a baby. As hard as it is to believe, someone had abandoned that beautiful angel at the front of this very hospital's emergency room doors. The horrible things that people do in this world. Well, you know all about that don't you?"

"Yes, I do." Ben said as he choked down tears that were starting to swell.

"Aileen is a special person though, an authentic child prodigy. She just completed high school this year and at the top of her class. She's the youngest student to ever graduate in the state of Texas. And what makes me even more proud, she wants to go to med school and work in the field of research. I wouldn't be surprised if she finds a comprehensive cure for cancer. Listen to me...proud father. Well, I suppose I am a tad biased."

"She sounds brilliant, doc. It also sounds like she's lucky to have you for a dad."

The doctor smiled and said, "Thank you, Ben. I appreciate that."

"Good. So now can I go home?"

"Yes, I suppose you can."

GILMER, TEXAS – DECEMBER 1995

IT HAD BEEN six months since Ben damn near ripped his thumb

off to free himself and Maddie, and he still couldn't grab anything normally with his left hand. He'd gone to an orthopedic surgeon who told him that his thumb would probably never function correctly without reconstructive surgery, and of course Ben had just shrugged it off with a positive attitude and classic cheesiness that only he could get away with.

"Don't worry, doc. It'll heal fine on its own and if it doesn't, hey that's okay, too. I'm used to having *'missing parts'*."

The doctor had laughed out of respect for his attempt at humor and of course Maddie had just rolled her eyes. She had also shaken her head and made eye contact with the doctor as if to say, "He *will* have the surgical procedure done, mark my words." But until then, Ben was going to have to figure out something so that he could get back to writing software. He'd come up with the idea to hire a ghost-writer to type the code for him as he dictated it, given he couldn't use a keyboard properly. He'd shared the idea with Maddie and as expected, she called him a big dork.

And now, almost six months to the day since Ben and Maddie narrowly escaped the snare of the boogie-man, both of them were back in Texas for a quick visit. First, Ben wanted some alone time at the cemetery in Gilmer, and then he had promised Maddie that he would take her to Hope and show her where he spent the *good* years of his childhood with Gramps. She also mentioned that she would like to maybe drop by the Hope Public Library to meet Evelyn Rogers, the lady who helped her solve the mysterious 'BWR' case. Maddie thought that she owed the kind woman more than a cup of tea, and genuinely looked forward to the possibility of hearing more of the librarian's slow, Southern drawl.

Maddie waited in the rental car as Ben made his way down the cemetery's hill. He was wearing his old Army rucksack on his back and in his right hand he had a dozen red roses. With his left hand, he pressed the stems of a dozen yellow roses against his side to improvise for not being able to use his thumb.

Ben visited Angie's grave first and sat the red roses down in front of the large pink granite headstone. His mom's new memorial towered over all of the others in her row and he hoped that it would somehow, somewhere make her happy. Ben knelt down and stared at her name that was fancily chiseled into the stone. After a few moments of silence, he finally spoke to her.

"I'm sorry I left you, Mom. I'm sorry I never came back for you. I'm sorry I never understood. I'm sorry about everything."

Ben wiped his tears away and looked at the epitaph he came up with as a tribute to the woman he'd wished he'd known under different circumstances. The words didn't come easy, but he'd thought that they were appropriate:

'BEAUTIFUL BIRD, SPREAD YOUR WINGS AND FLY AT LAST'

He stood up and looked out over the hundreds of headstones and wondered about all of the tragic stories that they could tell. He hoped that there were more good than bad, even though he personally had more of the latter—but then he smiled knowing that life, for him, had started tipping the scales the other way into the good side of peace and happiness.

The worm is turning.

He walked to a different section of the cemetery until he finally found Raina's grave. He placed the yellow roses at her memorial and dimple-grinned at the memory of her.

"Hi Raina. I sure do miss your smile. I listened to that tape you asked me to give to Tommy—many times in fact. I hope you don't mind. And I hope I hear your beautiful voice again someday."

Ben noticed Demarcus's memorial marker just to the right of Raina's. He knew Demarcus's body wasn't buried there because the authorities had never found it, and since both Wade and Jessup were dead, they had no idea where to look. Nevertheless, Ben thought that Demarcus's spirit was there at the memorial resting aside his beautiful sister's. As such, he took off the rucksack and from inside, he pulled out a brand new black-handled machete that had 'DEMARCUS' handsomely painted on the blade in white and gold paint. He then placed the symbol of their friendship on the stone tablet and nodded.

"Sometimes I wonder how far you would've went, my friend. I heard how well you had been doing at M.I.T. It didn't surprise me one bit. Sometimes I dream that we write software together. I miss you always, Demarcus. I don't think I could've made it back then without your friendship. I love you, man."

Small flakes of snow started to fall onto the wooded cemetery. Ben looked up at the gray sky and at then over at the old oaks in the distance. He buttoned up his coat and pulled out his hoodie to cover his head and started walking to the next site. It was getting dark and he still had three more machetes that needed to be delivered. Ben had decided to induct Tommy into the Black Machetes Hall of Fame, and he smiled at the thought as he continued along.

BEN FINALLY MADE HIS WAY BACK to Maddie in the rental car.

He climbed in behind the steering wheel, but before doing anything else, he used his index finger to softly trace the outline of her forehead and then her cheek and finally her chin. He lovingly leaned in and kissed her perfect lips, looked into her warm chestnut eyes, and told her he loved her. Maddie smiled as Ben gently caressed her stomach, and then his final act of affection before starting the car to head towards Hope was lifting Maddie's shirt, leaning down close to her small precious belly and whispering the words, "Daddy loves you too, Raina."

– THE END –

Dear Valued Reader,

Thank you so much for taking the time to read my book—I sincerely hope you enjoyed it. If so, please let your family and friends know about Black Machetes.

As a new independent author, I rely heavily on my readers to help me publicize my stories. As such, I'd really appreciate you leaving me a positive online review and also you using your online social media platform of choice to spread the word about the book.

Until next time,

Ryan K. Howard

P.S. To learn more about me and my current projects, please visit my website:

http://www.ryankhoward.com

I can also be found on Facebook:

https://www.facebook.com/ryankhoward

And on Twitter:

https://twitter.com/RyanKHoward